I0819416

A Murder in Marylebone

Books by Emily Sullivan

A DEATH ON CORFU

A MURDER IN MARYLEBONE

Published by Kensington Publishing Corp.

A Murder in Marylebone

Emily Sullivan

kensingtonbooks.com

KENSINGTON BOOKS are published by

Kensington Publishing Corp.
900 Third Ave.
New York, NY 10022

All Kensington titles, imprints, and distributed lines are available at special quantity discounts for bulk purchases for sales promotion, premiums, fund-raising, educational, or institutional use. Special book excerpts or customized printings can also be created to fit specific needs. For details, write or phone the office of the Kensington Special Sales Manager: Attn. Special Sales Department. Kensington Publishing Corp., 900 Third Ave., New York, NY 10022. Phone: 1-800-221-2647.

Library of Congress Control Number: On file

ISBN: 978-1-4967-5144-7
First Kensington Hardcover Edition: May 2026

ISBN: 978-1-4967-5146-1 (ebook)

10 9 8 7 6 5 4 3 2 1

Printed in the United States of America

The authorized representative in the EU for product safety and compliance
is eucomply OU, Parnu mnt 139b-14, Apt 123
Tallinn, Berlin 11317, hello@eucompliancepartner.com

To all the meddlesome bluestockings.

Author's Note

Thank you so much for picking up *A Murder in Marylebone*, the sequel to *A Death on Corfu*. Like the first book in the series, this is a murder mystery, but it also touches on some heavier topics. If you would like to avoid spoilers, skip the following paragraph. If you would like to see some content warnings, please continue.

In addition to a murder and Minnie's ongoing journey with grief, this book includes topics that may be difficult for some readers, including miscarriage, an aging parent with memory issues, some discussion of blood, physical violence, and gun violence. Take care.

Chapter 1

October 1898
London, England

It is often said, and usually with great sorrow, that one can never go home again. But then that presumes one would want to do such a thing. The admittedly unkind thought came to me as I stood before my parents' pristine, white stucco town house in Portman Square.

"Mama, why have you stopped?"

I tore my gaze away from the imposing black front door and looked down at Tommy, my eight-year-old son, and forced a smile. "Sorry, darling. I was just thinking of something."

More specifically, the last time I had been here. And, in truth, it was harder to remember than I'd like to admit. Had I really forgotten so much of my own life?

"Well, come along," he said, mimicking the stringent tone I used when he was running late. "Grandmama and Grandpapa are waiting for us."

I pursed my lips. Tommy, certainly. But I doubted my presence was much anticipated. For I was the errant daughter finally returning home after a scandalously long absence.

And though my parents' letters had been perfectly polite over the years while I was living in Greece, I truly wasn't sure how I would be received.

However, I kept such thoughts to myself and allowed Tommy to lead me up the steps, his free arm swinging with purpose, and wished for a bit of his enthusiasm. We had been in London for nearly a month now, having moved here from the island of Corfu so that my daughter, Cleo, could attend school in Hampstead. My aunt Agatha had graciously offered the use of her home, as she was off galivanting around the Italian Riviera until Christmastime. But between helping Cleo adjust to her new school and settling into our temporary residence, I simply didn't have the chance to arrange a proper visit.

Nor the desire.

But I had put it off for as long as possible. Tonight we were having dinner at my parents' house, and the rest of my family would be in attendance. Or, rather, the family that lived in England. My brother Samuel, the sibling I was closest to by far, lived in Bombay. How I longed for his company this evening. Our eldest brother, Jack, was an ass of the highest order, and our sister Delia, the youngest, was an unknown quantity, given that she had been little more than a child the last time I saw her.

I had left England immediately after marrying my late husband, Oliver, and we had spent our entire married life abroad, first in Athens, where he worked for the British embassy, and then on Corfu. Oliver had died suddenly about five years ago, and I decided to remain on the island until Cleo confessed a desire to return to England for school. And because she had aspirations to attend Girton College at Cambridge, just as I had, it was in her best interest to leave the small English school in the town of Corfu for a more academically rigorous institution.

It was Aunt Agatha who had suggested the school in

Hampstead run by Lady Artemis D'Arcy, a well-respected champion of female education with a flair for the dramatic. Understandably, Cleo was quite determined to make a go of things at her school, and new students were strongly discouraged from leaving the campus during their first term. But I wasn't yet sure how long Tommy and I would remain in London. We were allowed to visit on Saturday afternoons, which had made the situation more bearable, at least for me, but I still couldn't imagine going all the way back to Corfu without my daughter. And, in truth, my impression of the island had changed since last spring.

The front door opened just as we reached the top step, and we were greeted by my parents' dour-faced butler, who looked even more ancient than I remembered.

"Hello, Morris."

"Mrs. Harper," he replied flatly before shifting his dark gaze lower. "And this is young Mr. Harper, I presume?"

"Hello," my son said cheerily. "I'm Tommy."

I gripped his shoulder and shot Morris an apologetic smile. Our life on Corfu had been much less formal than what was expected in London, and Tommy was still learning the different rules of etiquette here. That children should be seen and not heard was a particular sticking point. As was the treatment of the servant class.

Our housekeeper, Mrs. Kouris, was like a member of our family. But here in London, maintaining the hierarchy between servants and employers was of particular importance, especially to a man like Morris, whose entire existence was built around following the most archaic rules.

He arched a brow. "Yes. Quite." Then he stepped back from the doorway so that we could enter. There was a distinct trace of disapproval in his gaze as I passed by, but Tommy seemed entirely unconcerned by his faux pas.

While a young footman silently collected our coats and hats, Tommy wandered ahead into the grand, marble-floored entryway, and his mouth actually dropped open as he stared up at the massive crystal chandelier. Behind us, Morris loudly cleared his throat. "The family is in the drawing room, madam. Please follow me."

I turned around and shot him a bright smile. "No need, Morris. I remember the way."

The look of disapproval deepened ever so slightly. "Of course," he said with a stiff bow, then disappeared.

I took Tommy's hand. "Come along. Everyone is waiting."

"Mama, did you really grow up here?" Tommy whispered as we crossed the entryway.

"Of course, darling," I replied. "Why do you ask? And why are you whispering?"

Tommy craned his neck, taking in the various gilt-framed paintings and assorted objets d'art that covered every available surface. "It's like a museum," he marveled.

"Yes," I agreed on a sigh as my gaze traveled over the cold, elegant space. "It certainly felt that way."

Then, just as we reached the hallway, the elusive memory suddenly came to me, and I nearly tripped on the Aubusson carpet.

Oliver.

Of course. The last time I had been home was for my engagement. After we were introduced by my brother Samuel, Oliver and I corresponded for over a year, as he was working for the British embassy in Athens at the time. But he returned to London for the Christmas holiday, and after gaining my father's permission, he proposed to me. In the very room we were about to enter, in fact.

Will you make me the happiest man alive, Min, and consent to be my wife?

I had been in the middle of pouring the tea and overfilled his cup, as I was too busy staring at him in shock.

Our letters, while detailed and frequent, had never crossed over into love missives, though I had often imagined what I would write to him and what I wished to read in return. No, I truly thought Oliver only saw me as a friend. As Samuel's peculiar younger sister. And that he had called on me that afternoon out of politeness. But Oliver strenuously assured me otherwise and claimed that he had fallen in love with me from nearly the first moment of our acquaintance, but didn't think I would want to live abroad. I quickly rid him of this notion and gave him my enthusiastic acceptance. I don't think my parents had ever been so proud of me as when we announced our engagement.

I had nearly been as nervous that afternoon as I was now. Oliver came from an old, aristocratic family, though he was only the second son and in the civil service. Still, it was a far better match than they had hoped for, given that I was considered an odd, mousy bluestocking by everyone else we knew. They fully expected us to marry immediately, but I had a term left at Girton, and Oliver supported my decision to finish. I could still recall the shock on my father's face when Oliver explained this to him shortly after announcing my acceptance. His large, warm hand had tightened over mine, and I had never felt so sure of anything or anyone in that moment.

Mrs. Minnie Harper.

But, in truth, a small part of me never stopped wondering if he had married me out of a sense of duty. Because our parents moved in the same circles. Because I had a healthy dowry. Because many of our acquaintances had begun to marry one another, and we were of an age. It was easy to come up with practical reasons. Even after Oliver died, I still maintained that I had been unbelievably lucky that he had chosen *me* to be his wife. But lately, I had begun to see things differently. That perhaps I had been too dismissive of my younger self and a little too generous towards my late husband. As genuinely wonderful as he was, I could now accept that he hadn't married me for any reason other than simple desire. Why it had taken me well over a decade to realize this was another matter.

I flexed my free hand now, searching in vain for a whisper of Oliver's calming touch. But only the drafty air of the hallway slipped through my fingers. As we drew closer to the drawing room, I could hear the soft murmur of voices on the other side, and my heart began to race.

I gave Tommy a tight smile. "Are you sure you wouldn't rather go to that sweets shop we passed on the way here?"

But he only laughed, thinking it was a joke. "Come on, Mama."

"Very well," I muttered. Then I let out a resigned sigh and pushed the door open to face my family for the first time in over fifteen years.

The room fell silent as we crossed the threshold, and for one perilous moment, I worried we had come at the wrong time. But Morris would *never* have let us make such an error. The room itself was remarkably unchanged, and even the air still smelled of the rose-petal potpourri my mother loved, though it was dark in here—much darker than I remembered it ever being before. The curtains were drawn shut, and aside from a gas lamp in one corner of the room, the only other light source was the blazing fire in the hearth. Or perhaps I had simply grown used to our light and airy house on Corfu.

Regardless, I had to squint a little in the gloom and wait for my eyes to adjust.

My father was seated on the dark green brocade sofa, my mother next to him, while Dolly, my sister-in-law, was in a high-backed armchair.

I cleared my throat as I gripped Tommy's shoulders. "Hello, there."

My mother was the first to speak. "It's Minerva. Hello," she said in the cool, controlled voice that had echoed in my head all these years. Then she rose with that perfect smoothness I remembered so clearly from childhood and beckoned to Tommy. "Come over here, Thomas. Good heavens, you're big."

Tommy pulled out of my grip and rushed over. "I'm so pleased to meet you, Grandmama and Grandpapa." He said this with a charming little bow, and my mother actually *beamed* at him.

"Aren't you the dearest thing," Dolly cooed.

"Yes, very polite," my mother added, smiling her approval.

I will admit to feeling a twinge of jealousy just then, as I could barely remember my mother smiling at me in such a way. But then, Tommy was a remarkably charming child.

"Well, don't hover in the doorway, Minerva," she scolded, in the tone I was much more familiar with. "Come here and join us. Your sister is upstairs, but she will be down shortly."

I did as she bade, and as I approached, I could feel my mother's sharp blue eyes skimming over me in assessment. She was widely considered one of the most beautiful women of her generation and had never failed to point out all the ways in which I failed to measure up. Even now, with her hair far more white than blond, she was still stunning.

"Agatha mentioned you were looking well," she said, sounding a touch reluctant, after I gave her a kiss on both cheeks. Then her eyes narrowed. "Though you have too much color. Don't you wear hats in Greece?"

"Yes, Mother. But the sun is quite strong there."

She made a hum of uncertainty, as if she wasn't sure I knew of what I spoke.

"Well, I think you look simply marvelous," Dolly said as we embraced. She still had the same cherubic face I remembered, though her brown hair was now streaked with silver at her temples.

Dolly and I had never been close, as she was about six

years older than me. When she married my brother Jack, the age difference had made them seem positively ancient. But as I returned her easy smile, I hoped we could be friends now that I was in London.

"Thank you. How is my brother?" Who was noticeably absent.

"Oh, you know. Busy as usual," Dolly said with a sigh. "He so wished he could be here tonight, but something came up. We'll have to have you over soon so you can have a proper catch-up."

Jack was the MP for Kensington, though there was no limit to his political aspirations. I gave her an understanding smile. "I'd like that."

Then I turned to my father, who had yet to speak or even look at me, and noticed the black, lacquered cane by his side. "Hello, Father."

As I bent down to kiss his cheek, I could make out the deep grooves lining his forehead and bracketing his mouth. While my mother had been a great beauty, my father had a keen financial mind. I never knew exactly what he did, only that he made already wealthy people even more money. In my memories, he was a tall, imposing man who rarely smiled. And though I didn't expect any of them to look the same, it was still a shock to see how frail he had grown during my absence.

His eyes finally met mine as I pulled back, but they remained strangely blank.

I cleared my throat, which had grown thick with emotion. "How are you?"

He blinked slowly, and a spark of recognition finally ignited in his gaze. "Minnie?" His voice was a paper-thin version of what it had once been.

I smiled, unable to contain the rush of joy that swept through me. "Yes, it's me."

Then he frowned. "What are you doing here?" He sounded much closer to his old self now, and thus this resembled more of a demand than a question.

"I— "

"You aren't supposed to *be* here," he insisted, and I drew back, feeling rather hurt.

"Hush now, Bertie," my mother cut in. "I told you Minerva was back from Corfu. You've just forgotten."

But my father ignored her. Instead, he kept staring at me with a look of agitation until I had to turn away.

"Is he all right?" I asked my mother.

She balked, as if this was a ridiculous question. "Your father is fine. He's just a bit forgetful these days. Perfectly normal at his age."

I very much wanted to point out that this reaction seemed far more than a *bit forgetful*, but my mother had never responded well to being challenged.

"Thomas, some of your cousins are upstairs in the nursery," she continued. "Would you like to join them?"

Tommy nodded enthusiastically, and my mother tugged the bellpull by the hearth.

"I'm afraid my eldest boys are all away at school, but John is still at home," Dolly said. "He's five now. And there's Franny, of course. She's eight, just like you, Tommy."

"A boy his age really should be at school, you know," my mother cut in. "Perhaps Jack can get him in at Harrow. The term has already started, of course, but I'm sure he could easily catch up." Then she addressed my son directly. "Isn't that right? A bright boy like you?"

Tommy looked perplexed by the question.

"Mother . . ." I began. But then Morris entered the room and saved me from having to defend my educational choices to a woman who thought it completely normal to send her boys away to school at six.

"Madame, supper is served."

"Excellent. And show Thomas to the nursery," my mother said, with a wave of her hand.

Tommy shot me a nervous look, and I gave him a smile. "It's all right," I said softly. "I will see you afterwards."

He nodded and walked over to Morris. "Follow me, Master Thomas," the butler intoned, then turned on his heel and exited the room, with Tommy trailing behind.

As my mother helped my father to his feet, I approached Dolly. "How long has Father been . . . forgetful?" I asked under my breath.

"Hard to say," Dolly said, as she frowned in recollection. "It's been little things here and there over the years. I don't think anyone really noticed the full extent until more recently."

"I see." I would need to harangue my brother about this whenever he deigned to meet with me. "And the cane?"

"Since the fall, certainly," Dolly said with a dismissive wave of her hand.

"*What* fall?"

She raised her eyebrows in surprise, but before she could respond, my mother called to us from the doorway. "Come along, girls. I won't wait any longer for Delia."

We exchanged a look and followed my parents to the dining room. I could admit that my father, now on his feet, moved well enough, but it was still shocking to see how much slower he had become. In all of my mother's letters, she had never mentioned anything about my father's declining health. But she didn't seem to see it very clearly herself, or want to—or perhaps I simply hadn't prepared myself for the inevitable. Time certainly hadn't stopped while I was away. Life moved on, quite quickly in fact. And I needed to catch up.

Chapter 2

Like the drawing room, the dining room also appeared to be frozen in time, from the heavy crimson curtains and massive silver candelabras down to the gold-embroidered table linen that had been a wedding gift from the queen. My grandmother had been one of the queen's favorites at the time, and my mother greatly benefited from the association. Grandmother eventually fell out with Queen Victoria over her gambling debts, but my mother never failed to mention her association with royalty.

Our family had enough aristocratic roots to maintain good social standing, but my mother had only been born an honorable, while my father was descended from the second son of an earl. Lucky for him, the second son was good with numbers and unencumbered by a crumbling estate in Yorkshire, so he made a fortune speculating in railroads that only grew thanks to my father's lucrative banking career. The Everlys of Portman Square might not boast any titles, but we did have a good bit of money, especially compared to our more blue-blooded relations.

And yet my mother began plotting Delia's marriage to a

title while she was still in the cradle. But, to everyone's surprise, Delia had eschewed a second London season in favor of attending the Slade School in Kensington. Since then, I had heard little talk of her marriage prospects.

As my mother deposited my father in his usual spot at the head of the table, I instantly moved to the second chair to his left—and nearly bumped into Dolly.

"Pardon me," I blurted out.

"Entirely my fault," Dolly said, though that was not at all the case. "Do you want to sit here?"

Before I could reply, my mother cut in: "Come beside me, Minerva," she instructed as she moved to her seat.

I gave Dolly an apologetic look and hurried to the other end of the table, while my cheeks flushed with embarrassment.

Luckily, my mother excelled at ignoring faux pas and immediately instructed the footman to begin serving the soup.

I settled into the high-backed chair as the same footman who had taken my coat earlier now ladled a helping into my bowl. I murmured my thanks out of habit, and he hesitated in surprise for just a moment, but it was enough to draw my mother's attention. As I caught her sharp look, I could hear her reprimand echoing in my head.

One does not thank the help for performing their duties.

I immediately turned my attention to the steaming consommé and picked up my spoon. This promised to be a very long meal.

A dull silence fell over the room as we began to eat. No one even attempted conversation. I cast a glance at Dolly, but she seemed perfectly content to sip her soup. Had meals always been like this? Surely not when Jack and Samuel were present, although they had often bickered in each other's company, so perhaps this was preferable.

I decided to enjoy the silence, which was a rare commodity in my home, and had nearly finished my soup when the dining room door burst open behind me.

"Did you *really* start without me?"

My mother, who never put a foot wrong, no matter the situation, actually rolled her eyes in response. "Of course, we did, Delia," she huffed.

That was nearly as shocking as my sister's equally indignant response.

"But I told Morris I'd only be a moment," she said as she marched fully into the room. "You could have waited."

Delia hadn't bothered to change for dinner and wore a plain grey muslin gown that bore several noticeable streaks of paint on the sleeves. I had forgotten how much she favored our mother, with dark blond hair that gleamed like polished brass in the gaslight. She was breathtaking.

My mother let out a weary sigh that sounded identical to the one I often made in response to my own headstrong daughter. And, for the first time in my life, I felt a bit of sympathy for her. "As I have explained many, *many* times, this household does not revolve around you."

Delia looked primed to say quite a bit more in response to that, but then her blue eyes fell on me, and they widened with excitement. "Oh, Minnie! I'm very sorry I wasn't here when you arrived. It's so easy to lose track of time when I'm in the studio." Then she rushed over to my side. I barely had time to react before she wrapped me in a hug.

"I understand, Delia," I said against her shoulder. She pulled back and gave me a long look.

"Aunt Agatha was right. You truly have blossomed."

My cheeks heated again at the unexpected compliment, and I couldn't help but look away from her assessing gaze.

"For God's sake, Delia," Father suddenly barked from the other end of the table with startling clarity. "Sit down. You're interrupting the flow of the courses."

Indeed, the footman hovered nervously by Delia's empty seat, still holding the soup tureen.

Delia rolled her eyes and looked so much like our mother in that moment, that a laugh bubbled out of me. I quickly slapped a hand over my mouth, but we exchanged a knowing look.

"We'll have a proper catch-up later," she whispered. Then she marched around the table with her head held high, as regal as a queen.

"Don't worry about that, Cartwright," she said with a grand wave of her hand. "Bring out the next course." The footman gave a little bow of relief and scurried out of the room.

"Sorry, Father," Delia said as she smoothly took her seat.

He grumbled in response, but the presence of my sister had lightened the atmosphere considerably. The rest of the meal passed in a flash, as Delia asked about our journey and how the children were settling in. She even offered a few suggestions for things Tommy might like to see while we were visiting. Dolly chimed in every now and then as well, but my parents remained noticeably silent for the remainder of the meal.

When dessert was finally brought out, I was delighted to see that it was apple charlotte.

"My favorite! I didn't think you remembered," I said to my mother.

She gave me a blank look. "I didn't. Cook planned the menu. She must have done it since you were coming."

Delia let out an indelicate snort into her water glass. "Leave it to Cook to know Minnie better than you."

"Please send my regards to the kitchen," I said brightly to the footman, hoping to dispel another confrontation between my mother and sister, who were now staring daggers at one another.

The footman bobbed his head and rushed out of the room

as soon as the charlotte was served. For a fleeting moment, I very much wished I could have joined him, but consoled myself with a bite of cake. It was just as good as I remembered.

Luckily, the dessert captured everyone's attention, and for a few blessed minutes, silence prevailed once more until we finished.

"Shall we all move to the parlor," my mother began, before fixing her eyes on Delia. "Or do you have some scandalous party you can't bear to miss?"

Delia calmly dabbed the corner of her mouth with her napkin. "Not tonight, Mother. I want to visit with my sister. But don't worry. There is something on for tomorrow."

Mother made a hum of disapproval in response and rose from her chair. From across the table, Delia caught my eye and winked. She really was quite cheeky. And while I could certainly sympathize with our mother to an extent, I found myself smiling back at her.

As we entered the parlor, I braced myself for another long stretch of silence, but to my surprise—and, frankly, relief—the children were waiting for us. Tommy was seated on the carpet by the hearth, playing a game of checkers with a girl about his own age, who must be Dolly's daughter, Franny, and right beside him was John. I couldn't help smiling as Tommy patiently explained the rules to his cousins.

"Thank God they're here," Delia murmured beside me.

I gave my sister a sympathetic smile, but before I could respond, the children took notice of us, and Tommy scrambled to his feet. "Mama! I have cousins!" he exclaimed in delight as he ran over to me.

"Yes, darling, I know. And this is your aunt Delia, my sister."

He stared at her in fascination. "Are you older or younger?"

"Tommy!" I chastised, just as Delia burst out laughing.

"Younger. *Much* younger," she added.

But Tommy remained quite serious. "Was my mother a good older sister?"

The question took me by surprise.

"Yes," Delia answered immediately. "The very best."

Tommy bowed his head. "My sister, Cleo, says I'm annoying."

"Well, do you perhaps do things to annoy her on purpose?" Delia asked.

The corner of his mouth lifted in an impish smile. "Sometimes," he admitted.

She gave him a knowing look. "Then you can't really blame her, can you?"

"I suppose not," Tommy said, with a shrug. Then he turned back to Franny and John.

"Come and meet my mother," he beckoned.

The children had been watching us closely but hadn't moved from their place on the hearth. They seemed far more reserved than my son. But at Tommy's invitation, they joined us.

"Hello. I'm Frances, and this is my youngest brother, John," Franny said with surprising formality.

"It's very nice to meet you," I replied.

"My father says you live in Greece," she continued.

"Yes. We're here for a visit."

"He also said you went to Cambridge."

"I did. To Girton."

"Father thinks sending girls to university is a waste of time," Franny said. "That it fills their heads with nothing but nonsense when they should be thinking about finding a husband and—"

"That is quite enough, my dear," Dolly said as she rushed over and shot me a nervous smile.

"Well, your father is wrong, Franny," Delia replied. "And despite what he says, that is a frequent occurrence for him."

Franny's eyes went wide.

"Oh, look! The tea cart is here," Dolly cut in. "Let's see if they have those shortbreads you like." She then quickly ushered her children away.

"May I have a shortbread?" Tommy asked me.

"Of course."

"In case you were wondering," Delia began, once Tommy had bounded over to the tea cart, "Jack has become even more tiresome over the years."

"Yes, I expected as much. Samuel mentioned they nearly came to blows the last time he was here."

"Oh, Sam," Delia said, with a wistful look. "I wish he would come home too."

Like my husband, Oliver, Samuel had joined the Foreign Service after Cambridge. For many years, he had worked as an attaché in Istanbul, so we saw him fairly often in Greece. But not long after Oliver's death, he had taken a post in Bombay. I hadn't seen him in person since then. We kept in touch over frequent letters, but it wasn't the same, and I missed him terribly. He was the sibling I had always felt closest to growing up, not just in age but in temperament and scruples. Which often put us diametrically opposed to Jack.

"It's been hard being here without either of you," Delia continued.

I was genuinely shocked to hear this. "Has it?"

She turned to me then. "You can't be that surprised. I thought the two of you hung the moon."

I confess, that was not how I remembered my sister. She was much younger than me, and my last memories of her were of a frivolous young girl fixated on nothing but ball gowns and beaus. In short, all the things my mother had wanted me to be interested in. Time and experience had softened my impression of Delia, but I suppose I had never truly considered her impression of me.

"I had no idea," I admitted.

Her face fell in disappointment. "I suppose it wasn't really until after you left and I had my season. It was awful. And *so* boring. Then I . . . I understood why you chose Girton instead."

I huffed a laugh. "I wish it had been that easy."

The truth was that I had fought my parents for years. And, even then, it was only because Aunt Agatha was the only person who could bully my father that they eventually relented and I was allowed to enroll. But I had never forgotten how dismissive they were about my educational aspirations, and it had driven a wedge between us that still remained to this day. And why it had been so easy for me to leave after I married Oliver.

Delia looked chagrined. "Right. Well, I'm glad you were able to go, in any case. If not for you, I don't think I would have gone to Slade."

I gave her a smile. "You would have gotten there, Delia, with or without me. I've no doubt of that. And I'd love to see your work."

Her eyes lit up, and she gripped my arm. "You should come with me tomorrow!"

I tilted my head. "To what?"

"A gallery opening. One of my paintings will be there. It will be great fun!"

"I couldn't possibly . . ."

"You absolutely *could*. And Mama will be so pleased that I have a proper chaperone for once," she added with a laugh.

"But I have Tommy," I explained, even as I wondered exactly who had been chaperoning Delia—if anyone.

My sister furrowed her brow in confusion. "Don't you have a nanny?"

I laughed. "No, Delia. I do not."

My aunt's housekeeper didn't mind keeping an eye on him if I needed to run an errand or two, but I couldn't ask the woman to stay the night so I could traipse around London until all hours.

"Well, perhaps he could stay with Dolly for the evening and play with his cousins."

Before I could object to this, Delia marched over to our sister-in-law, who was still by the tea cart. "Dolly! What do you think about having Tommy stay with you tomorrow evening so Minnie can accompany me to a gallery opening?"

"That's fine with me," she said, then she shifted her gaze to me. "That is, if it's all right with you, Minnie."

"That is a marvelous idea," my mother suddenly chimed in from her seat on the sofa.

"I really don't think—"

"Let the boy spend some time with his cousins," she interrupted as her blue eyes narrowed on me.

I very much did not appreciate being badgered into leaving my child for the night in the home of people he had only just met—family or not—and was just about to say so when I felt a tug on my skirt. I looked down and found Tommy looking up at me with a pleading expression on his sweet face.

"Please, Mama."

"Are you sure?" I murmured, but he nodded eagerly in response.

"It will be great fun, I think."

John and Franny joined us then, both with equally eager expressions.

"Yes, please, Auntie Minnie," John said. "I can show him our collection of fossils."

Oh, goodness. I had forgotten all about my brother Jack's penchant for fossils. He had been properly obsessed as a boy and must have cabinets full of them by now.

Tommy began to tug on my skirt with more urgency, and I knew the matter was settled. He missed his friends and even his sister, as adversarial as their relationship could be, and I would not let my own worries get in the way of his joy.

"All right," I replied.

The children then let out a cheer, which was, admittedly, rather adorable, and scampered off to make plans while Dolly came over to hand me a cup of tea.

"Don't worry about a thing," she said, with an encouraging smile. "I'm used to managing a house full of rowdy children. Enjoy yourself."

I accepted the cup and managed to return her smile. "I'll try."

Tommy spending the night away from me was one thing. Going out on the town with Delia, however, was another matter altogether . . .

"Don't worry," my sister said with an easy grin. "I'll make sure you have a marvelous time. Now, I'm off to finish my work. Shall we meet here at eight o'clock?"

I held back my grimace at the hour and nodded. "Yes, that's fine."

I preferred to be in bed, and ideally asleep, no later than nine o'clock most evenings, likely when the London social scene was just warming up.

"Until tomorrow, then," Delia said as she gave me a tight hug and kissed my cheek. "Good night, all," she added with a grand wave to the room before disappearing through the doorway.

Dolly took in the dazed expression on my face and smiled. "You'll have fun."

"I've never experienced London nightlife before," I admitted.

Dolly tilted her head in surprise. "Truly?"

"Well, I went to Girton once I came of age. And then Oliver and I left for Athens as soon as we were married."

"I'd forgotten all that," she said softly. "We were so disappointed not to have the chance to celebrate with you."

The regret on her face took me by surprise, but before I could respond, my mother cut in.

"Come here, Minerva."

The hairs on the back of my neck tingled, and for one brief moment, I felt like a girl again, being calling into my mother's sitting room to be admonished for some way in which I had unintentionally embarrassed her: I hadn't made enough conversation at tea with the ladies, or I wore the wrong dress to church, or I didn't respond the right way when questioned about my plans for the summer.

I had been henpecked for nearly every choice I made until the day I left for good. Only now, after being removed from this treatment for well over a decade, could I truly understand how damaging it had been. And perhaps worst of all, it was futile to discuss any of it with my mother, who believed she had done everything right by me. Everything a woman of her class and status was supposed to do. My few successes were only because of her guidance, and the many ways in which I had failed could only be because of my own stubbornness. It had been a frequent enough refrain for years, including one of the very last things she had ever said to me in person:

You are lucky a man like Oliver Harper is willing to overlook so very much in order to marry you.

I swallowed hard and forced my feelings aside as I moved to sit beside her. "Yes, Mother?"

She patted my arm, and for a moment, I was struck both by the gesture and by how frail her hand looked. "I'm glad you are spending time with Delia. You can be a good influence on her."

I nearly choked on my sip of tea and had to clear my throat several times before I could respond. "Oh?"

My mother didn't seem to notice my surprise. "I'm sure you can see that Delia has become rather . . . *willful* since you left. Perhaps I indulged her too much as a girl, but that doesn't really account for some of her behavior," she added, lowering her voice.

I glanced over at the children, who were in another corner of the room with Dolly.

"What kind of behavior?" But even as I asked the question, I had a fair idea.

"I don't care so much about the painting," my mother insisted. "Lots of ladies paint. It's just that some of the people she has surrounded herself with are not quite—"

"A bunch of bloody bohemians," my father suddenly interjected.

I managed to hold back my laugh, as he clearly wasn't trying to make a joke. There was a sharpness in his gaze now that had been missing for most of the evening. "Well, that can't be terribly surprising for an artist."

My mother scowled. "Things have changed while you were away. I don't know what to make of this younger generation. The women refuse to marry, they live on their own, they *work*. And these are girls like your sister! Girls from good families who should know better."

"I see," I said slowly, though my reaction was far different than my parents. It appeared my sister had bucked even more conventions than I had. Frankly, I was thrilled for her.

"Try to talk some sense into her, will you?" my mother pleaded.

"I'm not really sure what you want me to say."

She huffed in exasperation. "Tell her about the joys of having a family. Of being a wife. A mother. Perhaps if she spends more time with you and Tommy, she will see what she is missing out on."

I very much wanted to point out that, technically, I was no longer a wife, given that my beloved husband had died quite suddenly and that I would wish that pain on no one, but I could see her point. "Perhaps she just needs to meet the right person," I offered gently.

"That is not the issue," my mother insisted. "She was the most popular girl of her season. She had half a dozen marriage proposals from the most eligible men in London and turned every single one of them down."

"She was very young then," I pointed out. As I recalled, Delia had been only seventeen for her coming out.

"And now she is even older than you when you married," my mother countered.

I pursed my lips. She had made up her mind, and there was no arguing my way out of this. "Fine," I relented. "I will speak with her about her future. But I can't promise anything."

Nevertheless, my mother looked relieved. "She will listen to you. Delia rather idolizes you now," she added with a laugh.

It was her emphasis on the last word, and the carelessness with which she said it, that dug under my skin. But I only responded with a weak smile. "I will do my best."

"She's been spending an awful lot of time lately with a man called Charles Pearson," my mother continued. "At first, Delia claimed they were only friends, but I don't think that is—"

"No man is friends with a *woman*," my father scoffed. "Ridiculous idea."

My mother subtly rolled her eyes, but did not bother to respond to his comment. "His family is respectable enough, but I don't know what his intentions are. And she shouldn't spend so much time with him if it isn't going to lead somewhere. You understand?"

"Yes. Perfectly."

"I have no desire to act as my daughter's jailer," my mother said, looking visibly uncomfortable. "But if she gets herself into trouble, I may not have a choice."

I balked at this rather draconian statement. "Mother, I really don't think—"

"Just make sure you keep a close eye on her tomorrow night," she said. Her eyes were as hard as steel now, and I knew from much experience there was no point in trying to reason with her.

"Of course. Even if it means enduring an evening with a group of bohemian artists," I added, attempting to lighten the mood.

But my mother arched an elegant brow. "I can't imagine it will be that difficult. Agatha mentioned some writer you knew on Corfu."

My mouth went dry. I had barely said a word to my aunt about that situation. Why on earth would she think—*Cleo.* No doubt my daughter had told Aunt Agatha all manner of nonsense.

"Mr. Dorian only hired me as his typist temporarily," I explained. "We didn't—we didn't socialize."

No, we just investigated a murder and traveled together before he rescued me from certain death.

Then, just as I began to think that more was possible, he made a shocking claim against my late husband, insinuating that he had been stealing Grecian artifacts and selling them on the black market. We argued, and he left Corfu shortly afterwards. I hadn't heard a word from him since. Unless one counted an admittedly vague dedication in his latest book—which I did *not.*

But I would rather face death once again than discuss any of that with my mother.

As she held my gaze, I could feel my cheeks heating, but I would say nothing more about it.

"I see. Agatha must have misunderstood. As usual," she added under her breath.

The instinct to defend my aunt began to well inside me, but it was swiftly overruled by the desire to move on from the subject. "Not to worry," I said with a tight smile, before casting a glance at the clock on the mantel. "I had no idea it was so late. We really must be going."

It could have been two in the afternoon and I would have said the exact same thing. This reunion had gone on long enough.

My mother made no objection, so I moved to collect Tommy from the corner. We then said our good-byes, and I promised Dolly I would send him to her home tomorrow in time for tea.

"That was nice, Mama," Tommy said once we retrieved our coats.

I cast a wary glance at the footman who, like any well-trained servant, was pretending to ignore us. "Yes. Very nice. Now let's go home."

Chapter 3

My aunt's London residence was not far from my parents' home, just across the way from Hyde Park. As a young woman, she had essentially been married off to a much older associate of my grandfather's. But, in her own words, her late husband had been "reasonably kind, blessedly inattentive, and was gracious enough to die not long after the wedding." This left her with a good deal of money, which she turned into a great deal thanks to some canny investments. He also left her the stately town house we currently inhabited while my aunt wintered in Italy. The walls were painted in a shade of pale yellow she claimed matched the interior of a villa she had stayed at once on Lake Como, while the rest of the house was filled with treasures she had collected during her various trips over the years. But unlike my parents' residence, my aunt's home felt distinctly cozy, and we had settled in quite easily.

It also helped that my aunt kept her staff very small, which I preferred. In addition to her housekeeper, there was a maid of all work, a coachman who also functioned as both a handyman and gardener, and a cook who came a few times a week, while other staff were hired as needed. On Corfu, Mrs. Kouris assisted me with the cooking and cleaning, but that was all. As my aunt did not employ a butler, her housekeeper, Mrs. Ford, essentially occupied both roles. And from what I could tell, the woman was so efficient, she could have run a British warship all by herself.

As Tommy and I entered the foyer, she came to greet us.

"Hello, Mrs. Harper. How was your dinner?"

"Long," I answered, just as Tommy said, "Splendid!"

Then I barely got his coat off before he scampered away to his room.

She gave me a sympathetic smile and took his coat from me. As my aunt's most trusted and longstanding employee, Mrs. Ford was well aware of the mutual disdain between Agatha and my mother. "Shall I make you some tea and warm some milk for Tommy?" she asked as she hung up Tommy's coat.

"That would be lovely," I replied as I shrugged out of my coat. Yet I still felt as if a great weight hung around my shoulders. The evening had been even more exhausting than I had expected, and it must have shown on my face.

"Why don't you get to bed?" Mrs. Ford said gently. "And I'll make sure Tommy does the same."

"I would be so very grateful."

"It is no trouble at all," she insisted as she took my coat. "Get some rest. I'll be in with your tea shortly."

"Thank you."

I proceeded down the hall, stopping to give Tommy a good-night kiss, then entered my bedroom. As the door clicked shut behind me, I slumped against it with a sigh.

Agatha mentioned some writer you knew on Corfu.

My lips twitched, and I pushed away from the door, furiously unbuttoning my dress as I went. But it was of no use. I could not rid myself of those memories. And heaven knew I had tried *very* hard these last months. Yet it seemed that as soon as I had set sail for England, I was forced to acknowledge the continued existence of Stephen Dorian: famous mystery author, scandalous divorcé, and, yes, a writer I knew on Corfu.

Upon returning to London, I had expected that his popular Inspector Dumond series would line the shelves of bookstores. But I was entirely unprepared for how often I would encounter them casually strewn on side tables, taking up dusty corners of charity shops, or even left behind on the chairs of the neighborhood tearoom. Why, even Aunt Agatha had his first few novels crammed into an overflowing bookcase in the parlor.

And then there were the newspapers.

I had never paid much attention to the gossip columns, but Cleo lived for them, and as we crossed the Continent and grew closer to England, her access to the very latest news increased exponentially. She had excitedly shared every single line written about Mr. Dorian, and given that we were trapped together on both boats and train cars for days, there wasn't much I could do to avoid it without admitting to feelings I did not care to discuss with anyone. So instead, I had to listen. To all of it.

While Mr. Dorian had largely kept to himself on Corfu, it seemed that now he was a regular man about town, attending various plays, soirees, lectures, and restaurant openings nearly every night—and always with a different woman. Begrudgingly, I acknowledged that at least he was rather egalitarian in the company he kept, as a variety of aristocrats, actresses, artists, and even fellow writers were named. The man might be a cad, but at least he wasn't a snob.

I could not fault Cleo entirely for her interest. After all, this was someone we knew. Someone who had come to the house on Corfu for dinner, even. But I still felt a twinge in my chest every time she told me the whereabouts of a man I very much wished to forget.

However, now that Cleo was boarding at her new school in Hampstead, I was blessedly ignorant of Mr. Dorian's latest movements these last few weeks. And I intended to remain so for as long as possible.

I had just finished changing into my nightclothes when there was a soft knock on the door and Mrs. Ford entered with the tea tray.

"Here we are," she said, setting the tray down on the small table before the hearth. "I also brought the hot-water bottle. There's a chill in the air tonight."

"Thank you, Mrs. Ford," I replied, with palpable relief. "I really did underestimate how ill prepared I was for a chilly English fall."

The housekeeper gave me an indulgent smile as she poured out the tea. "Not to worry. Your aunt sleeps with one all winter. And she hasn't spent over a decade in Greece."

I sat down in the high-backed chair by the table and tucked the wool-wrapped bottle against my torso. A contented little sigh escaped my lips while Mrs. Ford handed me a cup of tea.

"Much better," I murmured as I accepted the cup. "And Tommy?"

"Already asleep," she assured me. "He was chattering away about his cousins, then dropped right off."

We both chuckled. "He had great fun with them this evening. So much that he's going to spend the night there tomorrow," I said, then took a sip.

"That will be nice. And you will have a little time to yourself."

I shook my head. "No, I'm afraid I've agreed to accompany my sister, Delia, to a gallery opening."

Mrs. Ford raised an eyebrow. "You don't sound very excited about it."

I hesitated a moment as I gathered my thoughts. "Apprehensive would be more accurate. My sister and I were never that close growing up. Then I married and moved abroad while she was still young. We don't really know each other, frankly, and our lives are very different now."

Mrs. Ford gave me a thoughtful nod. "Is that such a bad thing?"

"No," I said quickly. "It's not. But my mother seems to think that I can exert some sort of influence over her, and she is likely to be disappointed. Both because I don't think that is necessary, and I doubt Delia would even listen to me if I tried," I said on a laugh. "She's an artist, you see. Not married and doesn't seem to have much interest in changing that." Unless Mother was right and her connection to this Charles Pearson was more than a friendship. I ran my finger along the rim of the teacup. "But I might not be the best person to recommend the institution anyway," I murmured.

The housekeeper cocked her head in surprise. "Truly? You regret your marriage?"

I turned my gaze to the softly glowing hearth. "I love my children more than anything on this earth, and I was very happily married while my husband was alive. But widowhood has been another matter entirely," I admitted. "I suppose . . . I suppose I find it hard to recommend marriage when it can only ever end in death. In sadness."

We were both quiet after that, and the silence went on for so long that I jerked in surprise when Mrs. Ford grasped my hand. She stared at me with her dark eyes full of sympathy.

"You were made a widow very young, with two young children. That is a difficult cross for anyone to bear, and it is no surprise that you feel that way. When I lost my Alan ten years ago, we were both older and our children grown. But do try to remember all the joy you experienced when your husband was alive. If you could go back and make different choices, would you really give it all up?"

My throat tightened, and I shook my head, for I knew no other answer would do. She squeezed my hand and gave me a satisfied smile. "Get some sleep. Things always seem hopeless this close to midnight."

"I will."

Then she left the room, and I turned back to the firelight. There was more that I hadn't shared, of course. Things Mr. Dorian had told me about my husband that threatened to destroy the man I had thought him to be. Things I still hadn't been able to confirm nor deny. Because I hadn't decided which was worse: learning that my husband had actually been involved in a black-market antiquities scheme or doubting him enough in the first place to seek the answer. Either path would mean a betrayal of some kind. So for now I did nothing except sit with these thoughts. But, deep down, I knew that would not satisfy me for much longer. Eventually I would seek the truth, and I could only hope that the answers I found would not destroy me further.

At some point, I drifted off to sleep in the chair and awoke much later to find the fire nearly out, the water bottle cool to the touch, and the room dreadfully chilly. I forced my stiff body to rise and shuffled off to bed, where I managed to garner a few more hours of precious sleep in fortification for the long night that awaited me. But while my doze in the chair had been blessedly free of dreams, this time I was not so lucky. It was disjointed memories of my argument with Mr. Dorian about Oliver that flooded my unconsciousness this time. Memories I had managed to repress for all these months, including the last words I had ever spoken to him:

I think you hoped to discover something unsavory about him so that I could be as full of resentment and bitterness as you.

I awoke with a start, as though the very memory had driven me from sleep. I pressed a hand to my chest and found my heart racing, while a wave of regret washed over me. I had spoken those words out of anger. And fear. Yet it was so obvious to me now that Mr. Dorian had only been acting out of a sense of duty. Of, perhaps, friendly concern. And I had thrown it all back in his face. Behaved as though he were trying to come between me and my late husband. As if he were some jealous beau. My jaw tightened. He must have thought me absolutely delusional. I had been so careful not to allow thoughts of him to slip through the cracks. But perhaps it was time for me to face my error head on and deal with the consequences. In any case, I was certain of one thing: I would never allow myself to entertain such ridiculous thoughts about him *ever* again.

I flung back the covers and sprang out of bed, as if I could outrun the voice in my head, then headed for the en suite bathroom. My aunt had renovated her home to include all the latest amenities, and I would miss them very much once I returned to Corfu. Our little villa, known as the Lemon Grove House, was quite charming in its own way and just steps from the Ionian Sea, but it was still admittedly rustic in comparison to the homes I had visited here in London.

Once I had washed and dressed, I returned to the bedroom and pulled back the curtains. The skyline was a dull grey that seemed to reflect my mood. I let out a sigh. London may have hot water on demand, but it could never match Corfu's glorious weather. I headed for the wardrobe and chose a dark blue dress made of heavy wool. As I changed, I could hear Tommy chattering away downstairs with Mrs. Ford. I smiled at the muffled sound of his voice. No doubt he would be bursting with excitement over spending the night with his cousins. I decided then that a trip to Hyde Park was in order, as we could both do with some fresh air and exercise. With another glance towards the grey skyline, I donned my heaviest petticoat and hoped it would be warm enough.

The rest of the day passed by in a haze of activity. Tommy and I spent hours wandering around the park until our cheeks and noses were red with cold. If it were up to Tommy, we would have stayed even longer, but I drew the line once I lost feeling in my toes. Then we returned to the house, where Mrs. Ford had prepared a hearty lunch of vegetable soup and cheese-and-pickle sandwiches. After which I directed Tommy to pack his bag and then helped him pack it again with items he would actually need. By the time we were done, I hustled us outside and into the waiting carriage.

My brother lived on the other side of Hyde Park, not far from Kensington Palace, in a home that was a wedding gift from Dolly's parents. Yet this was an inconsequential detail to Jack, as his self-importance seemed to increase along with his proximity to the palace. While it was true that my parents had both descended from lesser branches of aristocratic families, their social standing was largely thanks my father's personal fortune. But once Jack got into politics, he used every opportunity to present himself as the perfect aristocratic ally firmly in favor of maintaining the old guard. This, in my opinion, also made him an insufferable snob.

Even Oliver, who had gotten along with everyone, found my brother frustrating. We had made a little game of signing our letters as the "Honorable Mr. and Mrs. Oliver Harper," merely to needle Jack, who was quietly jealous of my husband's inherited title, something he never bothered to use elsewhere.

"Mama, what are you laughing at?"

I turned to Tommy just as the carriage rocked to a stop. I had indeed let out a laugh at the memory. "I was just thinking of your father. He could be very amusing," I added, with a fond smile.

Tommy's gaze grew solemn. "I wish I remembered him better," he said softly, and any mirth I felt vanished entirely. Tommy had been barely four years old when Oliver died suddenly from a hemorrhage in the brain. "Cleo remembers so much more than me," he added with a frustrated sigh.

I grabbed Tommy's hand and gave it a squeeze. "Only because she is older," I reminded him. "But you can always ask me about him. Anything you'd like."

His mouth tilted up in a hopeful little smile. "Really? Anything?"

"Yes," I said, with a nod, despite the warning note ringing in my head. I had learned over the years that Tommy's mind worked very differently from my own, and there was no telling what questions he would come up with.

"All right," he replied with a thoughtful look.

We then exited the carriage, and the front door of the house promptly swung open, thanks to an attentive footman. Dolly greeted us as soon as we crossed the threshold.

"Hello there! Come in, come in. The children are very excited to see you, Tommy. They're waiting upstairs in the nursery."

"Splendid!" Tommy said and began to eagerly take off his coat.

"Is Jack in?" I asked Dolly, bracing myself for my brother to come round the corner any minute and start barking questions at me.

Thankfully, she shook her head. "No, he couldn't get away. Still at his club, I imagine. But he sends his regards and hopes to see you soon."

I managed to plaster a smile on my face. "Yes, I hope so too." Then I turned to give Tommy a hug. "Good night, darling. I—"

"Bye, Mama!" he cried out, as he shoved his coat into my waiting arms and headed down the hallway. "I will see you in the morning."

"Yes," I said weakly, giving him a little wave.

I could hear Dolly sigh beside me. "It was like that with my older boys around his age. One day, they were wrapping themselves in my apron strings, and the next, I was only getting in the way."

My gaze followed Tommy as he bounded up the staircase. He hadn't even turned back to look at me. Just as it began to feel like someone was taking a grapefruit spoon to my heart, I turned to Dolly. "Oh, I don't think he's reached that stage," I said, though the assurance in my voice sounded hollow to my ears.

Dolly shrugged. "Perhaps not yet. But most boys his age have been away at school for years by now. Or have you forgotten how things are done here?" she added with a teasing smile.

"Not at all. That's largely why we left in the first place," I said, with more confidence than I felt. But when Dolly's smile fell, I realized my error.

We.

She reached out with solemn eyes and patted my arm. "It must be hard to be back here without your dear Oliver."

"Yes," I murmured. In truth, I associated Greece with Oliver far more than London, but it was not something I cared to explain.

"Would you like to have some tea?" Dolly asked gently. "We can sit in the parlor for a bit and talk."

"Some other time," I said with a tight smile. "I was hoping to have a nap before I have to meet Delia."

I also did not wish to play the part of the grieving widow this afternoon.

"Ah, a good plan," she replied, with a knowing smile.

We then parted ways, and I returned to the flat alone in the carriage. But even as I grew farther and farther away from South Kensington, Dolly's ominous words stayed with me all the way to Hyde Park Street: *And the next I was only getting in the way.*

Perhaps raising Tommy on Corfu had put off the inevitable for a bit longer, but one day he would grow up. And if nothing else, this afternoon had taught me that I needed to do a much better job of preparing myself for that. If such a thing were even possible. Cleo was only a few miles away, and yet sometimes it felt like she might as well be on the moon. Of course, I was happy that she was taking her education so seriously, but it was a cold comfort at times. The carriage then rocked to a stop, and I headed up the front steps to my aunt's home. Perhaps I could take up traveling or become a paid companion once the children were gone.

There's always the typing. Perhaps you could ask Mr. Dorian for a reference.

I let out a loud snort as I entered the house, but luckily Mrs. Ford wasn't around to hear me. As I tore off my coat and hat, I could think of absolutely no circumstance in which I would willingly contact that man. After all, he had made his indifference towards me quite obvious when he left Corfu without a word. While I may have mistaken his intensions previously, *that* message had been received loud and clear.

Once I hung up my things, I stomped up the stairs and paused on the landing. My heart was racing, but I knew it could not be blamed on the exercise. It was that lingering resentment I felt towards Mr. Dorian. I let it upset me far too much. Forcing those thoughts aside, I took a deep breath and continued on. Besides, I had far more important things to think about than a grumpy mystery writer with unintelligible handwriting. Tonight I was going out in London. And I needed to decide what to wear.

Chapter 4

"Good heavens, Minnie," Delia said. "Don't tell me you're wearing *that*?"

I had just entered the foyer of my parents' home and automatically looked down at my sapphire dress, though I very well knew what I had on. "What's wrong with it? Aunt Agatha ordered it for me in Paris." And at an eye-watering expense. But she had insisted I needed at least one serviceable evening gown for London, and this could be worn to a number of different events.

But perhaps that was the issue, given that my sister wore a much more eye-catching mint-green gown trimmed in pink organza.

"There's nothing *wrong* with it," Delia began, in a slightly more amicable tone. "It just isn't right for tonight. Maybe if we were attending the opera or some such. But not this."

I let out an exasperated sigh. "Well, I'm not going home to change."

"No, no. Of course not. You can wear something of mine. We're nearly the same size, I think."

I shot her a dubious look. We were about the same height,

but Delia had a slim waist and narrow hips, whereas I had given birth to two children and possessed neither.

Delia seemed to read my thoughts, but she remained undaunted. "I have just the thing. Come with me."

I reluctantly followed her upstairs to her room. Though it was only a little after eight, the house was as silent as a tomb. "Are Mother and Father out tonight?"

Delia gave me a quick, confused glance. "Certainly not. They're abed. I hardly ever see them after six these days, unless we have company. Otherwise, we all eat separately."

"Oh, I had no idea."

Delia shrugged, unconcerned. "How could you?"

"Is it because of Father's fall?"

I still hadn't had the chance to inquire about the state of his health.

"I suppose it started then. He hasn't really been the same since," Delia said softly. "Though I will say that his memory has grown worse these last few months, especially if he is tired or hasn't slept well. On those days, it's as if he's traveled back in time."

"I see." I frowned, recalling his surprise at seeing me yesterday in the parlor, along with the strange words that followed:

You aren't supposed to be *here.*

"Mother performs her little circuit of afternoon calls and ladies' guild luncheons to keep up appearances, but she is rarely away in the evenings now. There is a nurse who comes by most days to help, but she's little more than a glorified nanny. I've caught her napping in the afternoon more than once."

My mouth dropped open. "I had no idea he needed so much care."

"Did you think he would go on forever?" Her tone was light enough, but the question still stopped me in my tracks. I certainly didn't think he would live forever, but I hadn't really accounted for how much he had aged while I was gone. Delia, who was a few steps ahead, glanced back at me.

"Oh, Min," she said as her face fell. "I'm sorry. I forget this is all new for you."

I cleared my throat and shook my head as I moved towards her. "It's fine. I suppose I just have some catching up to do."

She gave me a sympathetic look and patted my hand. "You will."

As if I had a choice.

We then entered her bedroom and Delia marched over to the wardrobe, where she pulled out a stunning black-and-white-striped gown with puffed, elbow-length sleeves.

"Goodness," I breathed as I ran my fingers down the intricate black-lace bodice. Even though it boasted a high collar, the lace made it seem much more daring. "It looks very fashionable." And far different from the sort of things I usually wore. Delia seemed to be drawn to things that helped her stand out, while I had to work just to fit in.

"It should be. The modiste assured me it was the latest style in Paris, and it cost enough," she added with a careless laugh, then held it up to my front with an assessing eye. "Yes, I think this complements your coloring beautifully. More so than mine, anyway."

"I really don't— " I began to demure, but Delia would have none of it.

"Off you go," she insisted as she shooed me behind the dressing screen,

I had forgotten how domineering she could be. Only now, instead of a little girl, she was a full-grown woman, and I could not evade her so easily. I dutifully took the gown and moved behind the screen.

"So, who will be at the gallery opening?" I asked as I began to change.

"Oh, the usual crowd," Delia drawled. "A few friends from Slade and other acquaintances."

"Do you always attend these kinds of events alone?" I failed to hide the scandalized note in my voice.

But Delia only laughed. "No. Mother is not quite that permissive. Mrs. Braithwaite usually plays chaperone for me. But I told her she had the night off since you were coming."

"Mrs. Braithwaite? I don't think I know her."

Delia laughed again. "Certainly not. She was my classmate at Slade. But she married a man who is a cousin of Earl Drummond, so Mother considers her a suitable companion."

From Delia's wry tone, I suspected that this Mrs. Braithwaite was not, in fact, *that* suitable when it came to actually chaperoning. I stepped into the gown and was relieved to find that it slid easily over my hips and waist. Then I pulled my arms through the sleeves, draped my discarded dress over the back of a chair, and stepped out from behind the screen.

Delia let out a theatrical gasp. "Oh, Minnie! You look dazzling!"

I ducked my chin at her praise and turned around. "Can you button me up?"

"Of course."

She made quick work of the buttons and then ushered me over to the floor-length mirror in the corner. "See? *Dazzling*."

I smiled at my reflection and ran my palms down my sides, where the gown nipped in at my waist to flattering effect before flaring out around my hips, while the skirt featured several artfully placed pleats. It accentuated my figure far more than what I was used to wearing, but I couldn't deny that it was a flattering silhouette.

I met Delia's eyes in the mirror and found her frowning at my hair, which I had worn in a tidy but simple chignon. "A pity we don't have time for your hair."

"It's fine, Delia."

"I have a comb you can borrow," she said, then scurried away before I could dissuade her. She returned with a large ebony comb trimmed with pearls. "Don't worry. It's all paste," she said as my eyes widened.

"That's a relief," I said honestly. The last thing I needed was to be worried about losing her pearls this evening.

Delia chuckled as she gently placed the comb on the side of my head. "There. Just a little something to elevate the look."

"Thank you. It's lovely."

"You don't wear much jewelry, do you?" she said as we made our way back downstairs.

"No, not really. It isn't very practical on Corfu, where I spend most of my time in the garden or doing chores."

Now it was Delia's turn to look shocked. "Don't you have a maid?"

"I have a housekeeper, but there is too much work for only one person. And besides, I like feeling useful."

I did not add that, since Oliver's death, money had grown tighter with each year. My work with Mr. Dorian over the spring had provided a much-needed surplus of funds, but it was only a temporary solution. I could always approach my parents for a loan, but I intended to avoid that scenario for as long as possible.

Delia looked dazed. "How wonderfully rustic your life sounds. I must come to Corfu one of these days."

"Yes, you should."

"Do you miss it?"

"I do," I said. "But a change of scenery has been nice too." After my near-death experience last spring, coupled with my tumultuous parting from Mr. Dorian, a strange kind of restlessness had come over me. When my aunt had come to visit over the summer and offered to pay for Cleo's school, it seemed like the perfect opportunity to escape for a bit. Though

I was sad to leave our home, I had easily found a tenant for the fall and winter. Our housekeeper, Mrs. Kouris, offered to stay on, so I knew the place would be well cared for until our return. When exactly we would return remained to be seen. As much as I didn't like the idea of Cleo being at school so far away, I couldn't very well stay in London indefinitely. Tommy loved our life on Corfu even more than I did, and it didn't feel right to keep him here.

We then reached the entrance, where Morris was waiting. "The carriage is ready for you, ladies."

"Thank you kindly, Morris. And don't wait up!"

The usually dour-faced butler looked faintly amused and gave her a nod. "Yes, Miss Delia."

"My goodness. Don't tell me you can charm Morris," I teased as we walked down the front steps.

Delia turned to me in surprise. "What do you mean? He is an absolute angel."

"Not that I remember," I said with a laugh. "We used to be terrified of the man as children."

"Well, you and the boys were rather a handful," Delia pointed out with a teasing smile.

"Perhaps," I acknowledged. "I suppose it's different when you're the youngest."

"*And* a delight. Don't forget that," she said with a wink, before letting the coachman help her into the carriage.

I threw back my head and laughed. "As if I ever could," I replied and followed right behind her.

I don't know what I expected a gallery opening to be like, but it certainly wasn't an absolute crush. Yet that was what greeted us when we entered the Elysium Gallery, located at the edge of Soho. My first instinct was to turn back, yet Delia sailed through the crowd, completely unperturbed, and I nearly lost sight of her in the swell of bodies until she grasped my hand.

"Come along, Min," she said and tugged me behind her while she called out "Excuse me" and "Pardon" every few steps. Eventually we made our way towards the back of the gallery, where it was much less crowded.

Delia brushed a stray golden curl off her face and led me to the cloakroom. "I'm absolutely parched," she said, once we checked our coats. "Did you see any trays of champagne going around?"

I shook my head. "Are gallery openings always like this?"

My sister looked around in confusion. "What do you mean?" Then she turned back to scan the room. "I suppose it's crowded. Though everything in London is like this on opening night. Everything exciting, anyway. Oh! There's Charlie," she said and began to wave at someone behind me. "Come."

Before I could respond, she took my hand again, and we headed back into the fray. I held back a sigh and straightened my shoulders. Perhaps I was simply out of practice with the social whirl. My life on Corfu had been quiet, mostly. And even when Oliver and I had lived in the more bustling Athens, we didn't attend these kinds of events. Our social life had revolved around dinners with friends from the British embassy or excursions with the children.

Delia led me over to sandy-haired man of average height in a sleek evening suit with the kind of boyish handsomeness I never quite trusted. He smiled widely at my sister and greeted her with a kiss on the cheek.

"Darling, you look lovely as usual," he said before turning to me. "And who is your enchanting friend?"

"This is my sister, Minnie Harper," Delia replied. "The one I was telling you about."

His eyes lit up in recognition and I could see that he possessed a kind of magnetism that was hard to miss. "Oh yes! The one who's been living in Greece. Wonderful to put a face to a name. I'm Charles Pearson," he said, then took my hand and kissed the back of my fingers.

"Well," I replied, suddenly feeling bashful at his attention. "It's nice to meet you."

He grinned at my awkwardness and released my hand. "You ladies look in need of some libations."

"Yes. Greatly," Delia replied.

"I'll be right back," Charles said before disappearing into the crowd.

"He seems . . . charming," I offered.

Delia, who had kept her gaze on his retreating form, snapped to attention. "Charlie is the most wonderful man I've ever met."

I raised an eyebrow at her sudden intensity, and my father's words surfaced: *No man is friends with a* woman.

While I didn't agree with the sentiment, it seemed fairly obvious that whatever was between Charles and my sister, it was not limited merely to friendship. He then returned with two glasses of champagne, which saved me from having to respond to my sister's comment. I took a sip and winced, as it was both flat and tepid. Then again, it was highly unlikely I would find anything better at the moment. So I took another.

"Where is your painting?" I asked.

Charles had been whispering something in Delia's ear, and they broke apart at my question, like a pair of naughty children caught red-handed. "Oh! It's in the next room, I think," Delia replied, her cheeks flushed with something that could not be blamed on the untouched glass in her hand.

"Let's go," Charles said, pointedly avoiding my questioning gaze as he led us towards a connecting room.

This one was much less crowded than the main reception room and seemed to house most of the work on display. My eye was immediately drawn to a large, vibrant painting prominently displayed in the center of the wall. A small circle of people were admiring it, and I joined them. It featured the silhouette of a woman wearing only a strip of cloth unraveling all around her against a backdrop of luminous colors that called to mind a particularly eye-catching sunset.

"Extraordinary," I murmured.

As a couple moved on, I stepped closer to read the exhibition label:

A Woman Unbound

Oil on canvas. D. Everly.

I straightened in shock and turned around. Delia stood just behind me.

"Do you like it?" she asked with a surprisingly shy smile.

"I . . . I had no idea," I began, struggling to find the right words. "You're so talented."

Delia glanced away, her smile fading a little. "Thank you."

Now I understood why my parents had let her go to art school. And why they looked the other way at her antics. They must have seen her potential or, at the very least, been told about it by someone they respected.

"Henshaw says it has already generated an immense amount of interest. He's the gallery owner," Charles explained to me before addressing Delia. "He expects it to sell before the end of the evening. Congratulations, my dear."

"That is wonderful news," I added and happily raised my glass in a toast.

She dipped her head in a rare display of bashfulness. "Thank you. And thank you for coming tonight," she added, glancing up at me.

"Thank you for inviting me. I'm having a nice time," I admitted.

"Then you won't object if we go somewhere else?" Delia asked cautiously.

"I have a friend who throws the most wonderful themed parties. Tonight's is based in the supernatural on account of the season," Charles added with an eyebrow waggle.

I very much did not like the idea of going to a second location, and my instinct was to play the part of the disapproving older sister. But as Delia looked at me with such an eager, hopeful expression, I couldn't find the will to deny her. At least, not this soon after our reunion. And besides, I strongly suspected she intended to go to this party with or without me.

With my decision made, I swallowed the rest of the champagne and handed my empty glass to Charles. "Sounds amusing. Let's go."

He broke out into a wide, approving grin. "Excellent. Follow me, ladies."

Chapter 5

Once Charles had retrieved our coats and expertly maneuvered us outside, I looked around for our parents' coach. But it was not among the long line waiting in front of the gallery.

"Over here, Minnie!" Delia called out. I turned around and spotted her and Charles at the corner, where a hansom cab waited. I clutched my coat tighter as a burst of wind whipped around me, and hurried over to them.

Delia climbed inside first, and Charles helped me in after her.

"Where is our coach?" I asked as I settled into the seat beside her.

"I sent Warwick home," she replied blithely. "No use having him wait for us all evening."

I gave her skeptical look. "That is his job."

But Delia only waved a hand. "It's nice to have a little privacy, don't you think? Besides, I wouldn't want him reporting anything back to Mother."

"Reporting *what* back?"

She tilted her head, as if I was being willfully obtuse. "Well, you can't imagine she would approve of our going to this party. A gallery opening in Soho is nearly too scandalous for her."

I thought of the conversation I had had with our mother just yesterday. "I'm not sure you are being as discreet as you think, as she seems to have a fair idea of what you get up to anyway."

"Not everything," she replied, with an eyebrow waggle.

But before I could form a response to this, Charles joined us. I kept the rest of my thoughts to myself and let the two of them carry the conversation as the cab took us not far away to a tony street in Mayfair.

Once we stopped, Charles got out first and helped Delia and then myself down. I stepped onto the pavement and took in the elegant, Georgian-style mansion looming up ahead. Every window in the entire place was lit up, and the silhouettes of dozens of people moving within could be seen from the street, while more still were ascending the front steps.

"Quite the place, isn't it?" Charles said.

"It looks even more crowded than the gallery," I admitted a little warily as we approached.

He chuckled. "Not to worry. Lord Linden is an impeccable host. I'd wager it's just a hair short of a crush inside."

This wasn't exactly reassuring, but I kept the thought to myself as Delia slipped her arm through mine. "Come. I haven't met Lord Linden before, and I confess, I'm terribly curious."

"He's a first-rate scoundrel," Charles drawled, but his mouth tightened ever so slightly, and I suspected he was a bit jealous of my sister's undisguised interest.

"That is a large part of the appeal," she said with a laugh. "I've heard he always invites the most eclectic crowd, too," she continued on, tugging me up the front steps. "Everyone from writers to inventors and actors. Even Ellen Terry has been rumored to attend!"

I feigned a hum of interest as she began to rattle off a list of other names, but, in truth, I had not kept up with the latest theater news since I had left England.

The door was manned by a bald-headed butler so large and intimidating that he made Morris look as gentle as a kitten.

"A pleasure to see you again, Mr. Pearson," he said in a dour tone that seemed to indicate the exact opposite, though he immediately stepped aside.

"Thank you, Thompkins," Charles replied cheerily as we crossed the threshold.

"You must be a frequent guest here," I began, "for the butler to recognize you on sight."

"Yes," he replied idly. "But not just from these little parties. I've known Linden for years."

I glanced back and caught the butler watching him with a sharp gaze, until he noticed me and looked away.

We then left our coats with a footman and crossed the spacious, marble-floored entryway. I looked up at the vaulted ceiling high above our heads, where a paned glass dome let in slivers of moonlight. Gold stars danced along the rest of the ceiling in a surprising touch of whimsy.

"Our host is a lord, you said?" I asked as my gaze wandered over the heavily decorated walls boasting the usual accoutrements of the aristocracy: a lavish coat of arms, a few portraits of stern, disapproving relatives, and a landscape that looked to be a genuine Constable.

"A baron, to be exact," Charlie explained. " As I recall, the family fell out of favor during the reign of George IV and lived in a kind of genteel poverty for many years until his grandfather invested in an ammunitions factory and made an awful lot of money during the Crimean War."

My lips pursed in disapproval. So, this house was built on blood. I kept that thought to myself and nodded in reply. "It's a stunning property," I admitted.

"It was designed by Robert Hooke," a deep voice said from behind me.

I turned around and found myself face-to-face with a striking man. His chestnut hair nearly brushed his shoulders, while his green eyes were fixed upon me quite intently. "Truly?"

In addition to being Christopher Wren's assistant, Robert Hooke was a polymath who was credited with a number of scientific discoveries.

The man raised one auburn brow. "You're familiar with him?"

The skepticism in his voice needled me, and I lifted my chin a little. "Of course. I had a professor at school who claimed he was as brilliant as da Vinci."

This seemed to intrigue the man, and he took a step closer, which I thought rather impertinent. "And what school would that be?"

Though I was growing uncomfortable with his attention, I refused to show it. "Girton."

The corner of his mouth lifted in a slow smile, though his eyes never left mine. "You brought a bluestocking to my party, Pearson?"

When Charles laughed, I blinked. I had completely forgotten about him and Delia. "Ladies, allow me to introduce our host: Lord Linden. This is Miss Delia Everly and her sister, Mrs. Minerva Harper."

His lordship stared at me for another moment before he turned to my sister. "Miss Everly, a pleasure. I've heard great things about your work."

Delia dipped a curtsy. "Thank you, my lord."

Then he turned back to me, and his eyes glinted with a distinct air of mischief. "And I suppose that makes you Mrs. Minerva Harper."

Given what Charles had said about the man, I had no doubt that he was used to women finding his insouciant manner supremely charming, but I would not give him the satisfaction. "I suppose it does," I replied dryly.

He held my gaze for longer than was polite before addressing my companions. "There's a buffet in the dining room, dancing in the ballroom, and Madame Fontaine will tell your fortune in the drawing room. Enjoy yourselves," he said and cast me another look before strolling off down the hall.

Delia grasped my arm excitedly. "Let's see Madame Fontaine. She's very popular."

I rolled my eyes. "Really, Delia. That's all such nonsense."

"Come on. It will be *fun*," she said, already pulling me down the hallway. "And we can ask if you have a future as a baroness," Delia added with a teasing look.

"Oh please," I scoffed.

"Don't try to deny anything," Delia insisted. "I saw him flirting with you with my own two eyes."

"Might I remind you that Charles described him as a known scoundrel?" I pointed out. "That is how scoundrels act."

Delia immediately turned to Charles for support, but he just shrugged. "It's true. That's not to say the baron *wouldn't* flirt with you out of genuine interest," he added quickly.

"Thank you," I said on a laugh. "Rest assured, I have reached the age where I am quite immune to shallow flattery from rogues."

Charles looked relieved to see I hadn't taken offense, but Delia still frowned. "I don't see why it's so difficult for you to believe he would be interested in you."

I let out a sigh, but was saved from having to respond further as we entered the drawing room. Delia immediately came to a halt. "There she is," she murmured as she gestured across the room, where presumably Madame Fontaine sat behind a small table draped in black cloth. The woman also wore black, which created a striking contrast with her ghostly pale face and dark brown hair.

"Well, she certainly fits the image of a fortune teller," I said. "Although she's missing a crystal ball."

"She doesn't need one," Delia replied defensively. "She simply holds your hands. Isn't that right?" she asked Charles.

He gave her an indulgent smile. "That is what I've heard. But you go on ahead. I believe I spotted a business associate in the hall just now and should speak to him. I'll join you in a bit."

"All right." Delia nodded, unconcerned, and pulled me across the room. Madame Fontaine immediately took notice of us and tracked our approach with her dark eyes.

"What kind of business does Mr. Pearson do?" I asked.

Delia glanced back at me and shrugged. "Something in antiques. But it's really more of a lark for him. I don't think he makes much money off it."

I very much wanted to ask how exactly he *did* make money then, but we had reached the table. Delia released my hand and sat down on the open seat.

"Good evening. I'd like a reading, please."

Madame Fontaine stared at her for a moment, then lifted her gaze to meet mine. "I'd prefer to read your sister first, if you don't mind," she said softly, in a low voice with an indecipherable accent that seemed to waver between French and Russian pronunciations.

Delia gasped, and I will admit that I was equally shocked, though I managed to hide it behind a smile. "I'm not interested in a reading," I said politely.

The woman arched one dark brow. "No? Not even after you came all this way?"

I frowned at her intentionally vague response, but Delia was enthralled. She turned around in her chair and grasped my hand. "You *must*."

"Very well," I relented. "But only for fun," I added, shooting Madame Fontaine a stern look while Delia practically leapt to her feet.

"Of course," she said with a sage nod and gestured to the now-empty chair. "Please, sit."

As I sat down, I used the opportunity to inspect Madame Fontaine more closely. Her dark eyes were lined with kohl, and her lips were painted a deep red. Her face was heavily powdered, and she had a small beauty mark on her lower left cheek just above her mouth, but I couldn't tell if it was real or fake. Either way, I had to commend the woman on a truly excellent costume.

Unaware of my internal critique, Madame Fontaine laid her ungloved hands on the table with her palms facing upward. "Remove your gloves and give me your hands please."

I peeled off my evening gloves and placed them on my lap before reaching for her. She took my hands in a firm grip, her hands cool and dry, and closed her eyes. A sense of calm slowly drifted over me, and she was quiet for so long that I was tempted to close my eyes as well.

"As I said," she suddenly began in a low voice, "you have traveled a great distance. Over land and sea—"

"That's right!" Delia chimed in over my shoulder.

I shot her a scolding look, just as Madame Fontaine cracked one eye open. "No talking, please. I must concentrate."

"Terribly sorry."

The fortune teller nodded at Delia's apology and closed her eyes once more. "You experienced a great loss and have carried this pain with you for many years," she continued. My grip tightened inadvertently, and I silently cursed myself for reacting. After all, what person my age hadn't experienced a loss of some kind?

"You are also worried about someone," she went on. "A child perhaps. But there is no need. I see a brilliant future ahead for them."

I didn't need to have my fortune read to know that about either of my children, but just as my mouth began to curve in a smile, Delia leaned over my shoulder. "And what about romance? What about a *man*?"

"Delia," I hissed, but Madame Fontaine seemed unperturbed by the interruption this time.

"Ah, yes. I do see a man in your future. He is very handsome. And tall."

Without warning, I immediately conjured a memory of Mr. Dorian, in his dressing gown, glowering at me, while his dark hair flopped over his brow in an appealing, rakish sort of manner. I cleared my throat and soundly forced the image from my mind.

"Ooh, go on," Delia urged.

Madame Fontaine frowned, as if she was actually concentrating on something and not just spinning a yarn for our entertainment. "He is a stranger to you, I think. But won't remain so for long."

"I like the sound of that," my sister teased.

"Delia," I snapped, but I was far more irritated with myself and the disappointment that had swelled inside me. For Mr. Dorian was anything but a stranger.

The fortune teller suddenly opened her eyes and held my gaze with an imploring look. "Tread carefully, madame," she said. "I cannot say for certain whether this man is to be trusted or not."

"Oh," I croaked, taken aback by her grave tone. She stared at me for another moment. "I will," I added, and she looked visibly relieved that I had taken her warning to heart. Then she gave me a small smile before releasing my hands.

The din of the room seemed to grow louder all of a sudden, as if we had been tucked away in a little cocoon. But that was impossible, wasn't it? I gave my head a dazed shake as I came to my feet.

Charles had rejoined us by then and offered me his arm as Delia took my seat. "You look like you could use a drink."

"Yes," I said, as Madame Fontaine gave me a slight nod

before turning her attention to my sister. "I rather feel that way."

"Then let us go in search of libations," he said cheerily as he whisked me from the room. But I sensed that Madame Fontaine's warning would not be left behind quite so easily.

Charles ushered me into the next room, which contained a number of guests, some in costume, and a long, marble-topped bar filled with various libations.

He turned to me. "What will you have, Mrs. Harper? Another glass of champagne, perhaps?"

"Please."

"I'd wager the baron is serving much better stuff than that swill Henshaw was serving us at the gallery," Charles said as he gestured to the man working behind the table.

"I don't think it was *that* bad," I demurred, as he ordered my champagne and a glass of whisky for himself. Hadn't Delia said Charles was a friend of his?

Indeed, he seemed to read my thoughts. "I admire your tactfulness," he said with a grin, as he handed me my glass. "But it is misplaced. Henshaw is a terrible cheapskate, and we all tease him mercilessly for it."

"I see," I said with a laugh.

Charles then raised his glass to mine. "To Delia and the sale of *A Woman Unbound*."

That was certainly something I could toast. As we clinked our glasses, I couldn't help smiling with approval. I didn't agree with my father that a man couldn't be friends with a woman, but my mother had been right to suspect there was more than just friendship between my sister and Charles. And while he was certainly a charming young man, it was his support of Delia's painting that elevated him in my estimation. As I took a sip, the cool, crisp bubbles fizzed in a burst of flavor.

"Goodness," I said with surprise. "I really was drinking swill."

Charles laughed. "I told you. Good champagne is *entirely* worth the expense, in my opinion."

I considered this comment as I took another sip. It was possible he was simply making a joke, but it seemed more likely that Charles Pearson enjoyed the finer things. At issue was whether or not he possessed the necessary funds to support such a lifestyle. Delia would have a good dowry when she married, even larger than mine, since Father's wealth had grown exponentially since my own marriage. But that meant she needed to be mindful that she didn't fall prey to a fortune hunter. Privately, I resolved to uncover as much as I could about him before I allowed myself to be further swayed by his charms.

"I didn't know bluestockings allowed themselves to indulge in vices like champagne," a familiar voice drawled by my shoulder.

I turned around to face the baron. "They do when it is as good as this," I parried back.

The corner of his mouth lifted as I took another sip. Why on earth I cared about impressing this man was beyond me, but I couldn't ignore the little glimmer of pride in my chest. Or perhaps I was just dangerously close to overindulging. Indeed, a kind of lightness began to wash over me. I no longer felt tired or out of place, and as the evening stretched before me, I was filled with a sense of anticipation. Of excitement. I hadn't felt that way in a long time. At least, not since—

"And how was your reading with Madame Fontaine?" the baron asked, thankfully distracting me.

"Vague enough to sound insightful," I replied. "She puts on an excellent performance, though. I will give her that."

"Then you aren't a believer in the supernatural, Mrs. Harper?"

"No, I am not," I said primly. "I believe in things that can be proven. Things I can see."

The baron took a step closer. "And what about the things you can only feel?"

This comment caught me by surprise, and I will admit that, for a moment, I simply stared back at him, a little dumbfounded. "In my experience," I began in a measured tone, "feelings can often prove to be false upon further inspection."

He held my gaze as he considered this, then nodded. "Very true."

I cleared my throat and glanced away, but I could feel the baron's eyes still upon me. "Excuse me. I need to find my sister."

The baron immediately stepped aside to let me pass, and I hurried from the room. It had been a harmless comment, but it struck me far more deeply than I had liked. I returned to the drawing room and saw Delia still seated at Madame Fontaine's table. My sister's back was to me, but I could see that the medium seemed to be speaking to her with some urgency. Delia then shook her head and shot out of the chair so quickly that I thought it would fall back. As my sister turned around to steady it with her hand, her face was contorted in anguish. I rushed over to her, but as soon as she noticed my approach, she smoothed her expression.

"What's wrong?"

"Nothing," she said much too quickly. "I'm fine."

"What did she say to you?" I asked, as I looked past Delia to Madame Fontaine, but someone else had slid into the vacated chair as soon as it was open, and she was occupied with speaking to them.

"It doesn't matter. It's just for fun, like you said."

I frowned in concern, but before I could press Delia further, Charles joined us.

"Here you are." He handed Delia a glass of champagne. "I

trust Madame Fontaine had nothing but good things to say about your future?"

"Yes," Delia said as she accepted the glass with a strained smile, but Charles didn't notice as he was too busy looking around the room.

Someone behind me then caught his attention. "Good God, Dorian," he suddenly called out with a smile. "You tore yourself away from your typewriter long enough to come down here?"

As I had still been focusing on Delia, I was certain my ears were only playing tricks on me and I had misheard. But then he spoke:

"I made an exception this evening, as I heard Linden always invites the most beautiful women," he said with a low laugh.

My throat went dry as my face went up in flames, and my haze of good cheer vanished entirely. I knew that voice. I would recognize it anywhere, as it had been haunting me for months.

Charles continued speaking, but I didn't hear a word. My ears had begun to ring, and I felt frozen in place. My gaze was fixed firmly on my sister, who now smiled expectantly at the man just behind me. The man I was now certain could only be Stephen Dorian. There was no escape. The doorway was to my back, and even if I did make a run for it, he would clearly see that it was me.

Vaguely, I heard Mr. Pearson introducing Delia. And then . . .

". . . and this is her sister, Mrs. Harper."

I swallowed my heart, which had momentarily lodged in my throat, and turned around.

"Mr. Dorian," I said, with as much grace as I could manage. "What an unexpected pleasure."

Chapter 6

I will admit that I had imagined this exact scenario more than once. After all, Mr. Dorian lived in London, and it was not entirely outside the realm of possibility that our paths would cross at some point. What I had not imagined was the very beautiful woman with silky, dark hair and warm, olive skin clutching his arm. He stared back at me in absolute shock for a long, tense moment, and when it became clear that he would not be making introductions, I turned to his companion.

"Hello, I'm Mrs. Harper," I said with a beatific smile.

The woman cast a quick, confused glance at her silent partner before smiling back at me. "I'm Mrs. Langham. Pleasure to meet you."

Her cordial greeting seemed to shock Mr. Dorian to attention, and he cleared his throat. "Mrs. Harper and I met on Corfu last spring," he rasped.

The woman's eyes lit up. "Oh! He was just telling me about that. How he was having such a wretched time there, and then on top of that, he was forced to hire some poor local woman to type for him," she said on a laugh.

Based on her rather theatrical manner, enviable appearance, and what I had gleaned from the gossip sheets, I wondered if Mrs. Langham was an actress—not that I was casting judgement. I supported any profession that allowed a woman to make a safe, comfortable living for herself.

My smile tightened. "Yes, that was me. The poor local woman." Then I turned to Mr. Dorian. "Though I didn't realize you were having such a wretched time," I said with mock sympathy.

He narrowed his eyes in an unamused look so achingly familiar that my breath caught. "I don't think I used the word 'wretched,' Mrs. Langham," he replied while holding my gaze.

"Oh, no. Of course not," she said quickly. "I'm afraid I tend to exaggerate for dramatic effect," she added with a laugh before addressing me. "He did say how lovely the island was."

I gave her a gracious nod. "Yes, it is."

"So then," he prompted in a brusque tone, "what has finally compelled you to return to England's shores?"

I was obliged to turn back to him, which I did with obvious reluctance. "My daughter has enrolled in school, and I came to see her settled."

"How old is your daughter?" Mrs. Langham asked. Though she was clearly trying to make up for her earlier faux pas, I was grateful for her interest as it allowed me to ignore Mr. Dorian.

"Fourteen."

"A wonderful age!" Mrs. Langham exclaimed, making it clear that she had no fourteen-year-olds of her own or must not remember her own youth particularly well. These last years with Cleo had been challenging. An endless mixture of highs and lows, often occurring within moments of each other. Though I missed living with her very much, my nerves were grateful for the reprieve.

As the woman continued to wax on about the glories of being fourteen, I could still see, out the corner of my eye, Mr. Dorian watching me. However, I would not engage with him any longer. When Mrs. Langham paused to take a breath, I wasted no time cutting in.

"I'm so sorry, but I'm afraid I must be going. This is a terribly late night for me," I added with a strained laugh. My head was beginning to throb from the champagne, and I could not keep up this pretense much longer.

The woman looked genuinely sorry. "Of course." Then she turned to Mr. Dorian. "You must let her use your carriage. You'll never find a hansom here at this hour," she explained to me. "And we parked just round the corner."

"I couldn't possibly— "

"It's not a problem," Mr. Dorian insisted curtly.

I let out a weary sigh as I turned to him and nearly reared back at the trace of concern in his dark eyes. How dare he act as though he cared. "Fine," I said more sharply than I intended. "Do you mind?" I asked Delia.

She had been watching this entire exchange with undisguised interest and quickly shook her head. "Not at all. Thank you, Mr. Dorian. We're just over in Portman Square and will send the carriage right back for you."

"No need to rush," Mrs. Langham said cheerily. "This one never leaves a party early."

A dry laugh escaped my lips then, which I tried to cover with a cough, but Mr. Dorian wasn't fooled. He narrowed his eyes at me, and I lifted my chin in response.

"Come along, then," he muttered. The three of us followed in his wake, while Mrs. Langham stayed behind.

As Charles moved to walk alongside Mr. Dorian, Delia

slid her arm through mine. "You have an awful lot to explain when we get home," she murmured.

I sighed again. "Must I?"

Delia merely shot me a look in response.

I should have felt vindicated. After all, my worst suspicions about Mr. Dorian and his character had now proved to be true. He was a feckless womanizer. A libertine. And yet I could not deny the heaviness that settled over my shoulders as we made our way towards the exit. My gaze strayed to his tall form just ahead, and my traitorous heart lurched in my chest.

The crowd had grown far more raucous in the time since we arrived, so our progress towards the exit was slow. The baron caught sight of us just as we were retrieving our coats and sauntered over.

"Leaving already?" he said to me.

"I'm afraid so. It is well past this bluestocking's bedtime."

He tilted his head and gave me a considering look. "But I haven't had the chance to engage you in some frivolous debate yet."

I laughed a little louder than I normally would have, just in case Mr. Dorian was watching. "Another time, perhaps."

The baron smiled. "I look forward to it," he murmured before addressing the rest of our party.

When I glanced over, I did indeed see Mr. Dorian glowering in my direction. I raised a questioning eyebrow, and he immediately looked away. I couldn't help feeling a keen little sense of satisfaction, but guilt quickly followed. For what was I trying to prove to him anyway? That I could garner the fleeting attentions of another man for a few brief moments? That was petty, even for me.

With our good-byes said, we stepped out into the night, and the biting October air sent a shiver through me. I hugged myself and tucked my chin to my chest, but it made little difference.

"Here," a gruff voice barked, and before I could look up, Mr. Dorian draped his dinner jacket over my shoulders. Just as his all-too-familiar scent began to envelope me, I shrugged the jacket away.

"I'm fine."

He shot me an irritated look, but relented. "The carriage is just ahead anyway."

I resisted the instinct to thank him for the gesture and looked ahead to where a black-lacquered coach stood waiting.

"Thanks again, Dorian," Charles chimed in.

"It's no trouble," he said flatly, then moved ahead to speak with the coachman.

"How do you know him?" Delia asked Charles, while we huddled together on the pavement.

"We've met out in London many times. I'm a great fan of his books," he added, then turned to me. "You must tell me *all* about his writing process."

"I don't know much about that. I only did some typing for him."

He had come to Corfu exhausted and barely able to work properly, thanks to the endless swirl of gossip surrounding his recent divorce. Though we got off on the wrong foot, I soon felt a kind of sympathy for him. And then, something more. But the man I had met then bore little resemblance to the one before me now, who apparently swanned about London until all hours and in all sorts of company.

Just as Charles began to respond, Mr. Dorian called over to us: "You said you're in Portman Square?"

"Yes," Delia replied before giving the house number.

The coachman nodded and climbed up onto his seat, while Mr. Dorian opened the door for us. Charles helped Delia inside, and when it was my turn, Mr. Dorian stuck his hand out. I stared at his gloved palm for a moment, then looked up. He was watching me closely, with a look of challenge I recognized all too well.

I narrowed my eyes and put my hand in his. "Thank you," I said primly as he helped me inside.

"Oh, but the pleasure is *all* mine, Mrs. Harper," he replied in a mocking tone.

I rolled my eyes as I took the seat beside Delia. Mr. Dorian was clearly in one of his moods. Hopefully, his companion was prepared. Charles then exchanged a few words with Mr. Dorian before climbing in after me.

"Thank you again, Mr. Dorian," Delia said a little breathlessly. "You must come and visit us very soon."

Somehow I resisted the urge to nudge her with my elbow—not that the man would take her up on the offer, of course. But then Mr. Dorian caught my gaze as he answered her: "Yes. I think I will." Then he shut the door just as I began to scowl.

Charles and Delia chatted away as the carriage took us back to Portman Square, but I confess I barely heard a word. I was far too distracted by my thoughts. Thoughts that, I will admit, mostly revolved around Mr. Dorian.

He couldn't possibly mean to come visit us. No, he had only said that to needle me, which he found endlessly amusing for some reason. When the carriage turned onto my parents' street, the full weight of the evening descended upon me, and my eyes grew heavy. I really *was* quite tired. That had not been a lie to avoid Mr. Dorian's company.

"Here we are," Delia said as the carriage came to a stop. "Thank you for a lovely evening, Charlie."

"An evening spent in your company can be nothing but lovely," he replied with an earnest look before turning to me. "It was very nice to meet you, Minnie. I hope we can all have a night out again while you are here."

"I am not sure I have the stamina for another late night," I said with a smile. "But yes, I hope we will meet again soon."

Charles then climbed out of the carriage and handed me

down. As I waited on the pavement, I noticed he and Delia exchange a few quiet words before she joined me. My sister's cheeks were flushed, though I couldn't say whether that was from the cold or something she had said. I shot her a questioning look, but she only gave me a bright smile.

"Good night, ladies," Charles called to us with a wave. "Sleep well!" Then he climbed back into the carriage, and we ascended the front steps of the town house. The footman opened the door, and as he took our coats, the grandfather clock in the entryway chimed the hour. It was one o'clock in the morning. I pressed the back of my hand to my mouth and failed to stifle a yawn.

"Come on. To bed with you," Delia said, as she looped her arm through mine and led me up the staircase. "Mother had your old room made up."

"Did she?" I was much too tired to properly ruminate on this, as I had assumed I would stay in one of the guest rooms kept perpetually at the ready for such a purpose.

"You needn't sound so shocked. You must know how thrilled she is that you've finally come home."

Normally, I was able to contain my sarcasm, but a hearty snort slipped out. "*Our* mother thrilled? I think not."

Delia turned to me with a weary smile. "You would be surprised. Here we are," she added as we reached my door. She pushed it open and entered, while I lingered in the doorway for a moment. A small fire glowed in the hearth, and the coverlet on my old canopy bed was turned down, ready and waiting for me. The familiar scent of dried rose petals tickled my nose, and I inhaled. It smelled like home. Like childhood. I blinked rapidly and stepped into the room. Delia helped me unbutton the dress and loosened the corset.

"Shall I do the same for you?" I asked as I stepped out of the gown, but she shook her head.

"No need. I manage quite well on my own. Here," she said

briskly as she picked up a nightgown that had been laid out on the bed. "Get some sleep. I will see you in the morning."

She was acting a bit odd, but the need to sleep was pressing down on me so heavily that it was difficult to think clearly. "All right," I relented and took the nightgown.

Delia moved to the door as I finished unlacing the corset. Then she paused and looked back. "Mother isn't the only one who is thrilled you've returned," she said quietly.

I tilted my head and smiled. "I'm glad to hear that."

Delia smiled back, then slipped from the room. Finally alone, I let out a sigh and finished preparing for bed. Then I climbed onto the mattress and pulled the covers over me. My head had barely touched the pillow before I fell into a deep, dreamless sleep.

It felt as though I had only just closed my eyes when someone began shaking my shoulder. Hard.

"Minnie."

I tried to turn over and escape this bothersome person, but they were very persistent.

"Minnie, *wake up.*"

It was the note of distress that finally pulled me fully from sleep. I blinked and looked up to find a shadow hovering over me. It was my sister.

"Delia? What's going on?" Then I sat up as alarm bolted through me. "Is it Tommy?"

Her face looked ghostly pale in the low light, but she shook her head. "No. He's fine," she croaked. "It's Charlie. I think—I think he is dead."

I reared back a little, confused. "What? But he was just here," I said groggily, vaguely aware that I wasn't making much sense.

Delia fell against me then. "I found him in his flat," she sobbed. "There was blood and—oh, it was *so* awful!"

I began to rub her back and made a soothing sound, while my muddled mind slowly whirred to life. "What did the police say?"

Delia stilled in my arms. "The police?"

"Yes. When they arrived."

"I didn't—that is, I haven't—I came straight here. To you."

I pulled back and frowned. "You mean you just left him there?"

Delia's eyes were wide with fright, and she nodded. "Yes," she whispered. "I was scared. I didn't know what to do. Then I thought I heard something, and I left."

"But, Delia, what if he *isn't* dead?"

"He is," she said quickly. "I'm certain. No one could survive . . . that."

I turned away and pressed my hands to my eyes as my thoughts swirled. "We must go back there," I said, once I was able to better focus. "Now. You might have left the scene of a murder."

She looked bewildered. "Murder?"

"You said there was blood. And that you heard something," I pressed, nearly shouting now. "Is there any chance it could have been an accident?"

Delia shook her head. "I . . . I don't know."

"My God," I muttered as another thought occurred to me. "What time is it?"

"A little after two, I think?"

Then she must have left immediately after I went to bed. I threw back the covers. "We need to go to the flat and alert the authorities."

Delia gripped my hand. "I can't," she begged. "I can't go back there."

"You must," I insisted as I placed my other hand on top of hers. "It is the right thing to do. Besides, someone might have seen you there already," I pointed out. "And then you will have much more to worry about."

She swallowed hard as understanding dawned and released me. "Right. I see."

"They will need to establish the timeline," I explained as I began to dress. Unfortunately, the only gown readily available was the one I had just worn. "That will help to prove your innocence. You have an alibi in me and the footman. I suppose no one else saw you leave?" She shook her head, and I tugged the gown over my head, not bothering with a corset. The shape wasn't as nice as before, but that was of no concern at the moment. "Did you walk?"

"Yes. His flat is just a few blocks away in Marylebone. It doesn't take more than ten minutes."

I gave her my back, and she began to button me up. "Why did you go there?" I asked softly, though the answer was perfectly obvious. Young ladies did not visit the homes of bachelor gentlemen in the dark of night for purely innocent reasons.

Her hands stilled on the last button. "I know what you must be thinking, but it wasn't like that."

I glanced back. "Then enlighten me. Please."

Delia let out a sigh. "I love him. I won't deny it. And tonight wasn't the first time I've been to his flat." Then she paused as she finished the last button. "But we are—that is, we were to be married," she said thickly.

I took a moment to choose my words as I turned to face her. "You were engaged?"

Delia's cheeks turned red, and she looked away. "Not yet. Not properly, anyway. But we talked about it, quite often."

"I see."

Delia wiped her cheeks and let out a strangled laugh. "You could at least *try* to sound like you believe me."

I huffed. "Well, if it wasn't like *that*, then why were you really there?"

She was quiet for a moment. "It started with my reading with Madame Fontaine."

I recalled the look on Delia's face back at the baron's mansion. She had been so distraught before she hid it all behind a smile. "She said something to you about Charles?"

She nodded. "That he couldn't marry me because he was already married. I went there to confront him. And instead I found him like . . . like that."

Delia looked absolutely wretched, and my heart tugged in my chest. But we couldn't waste any more time. "I'm truly sorry, my dear. I can't imagine how awful it was, but right now we need to alert the police and return to the flat."

"All right," she said, then paused as she appeared to remember something. "Charlie has a telephone."

"He does?" This was surprising and seemed the height of excess to me. I certainly didn't know anyone who had a telephone in their home.

Delia nodded. "He said he used it for work."

I frowned at this explanation, given that earlier she had described his work as little more than a lark, but the sooner we made the call, the better it would be for Delia.

My hair was a fright, but I fixed it in a semblance of a Psyche knot, then took her hand and led her from the room. No one would be awake now, and it was easy enough to retrieve my coat and slip out the back entrance. Delia led the way through Portman Square. It was as silent as a graveyard at this hour, and I pulled my coat closer to me. We slunk through Portman Close as Delia led us to George Street in Marylebone.

"His flat is over there. On the third floor," she said and pointed to an elegant brick building. "There's a servant's entrance around the back. He made sure it was unlocked so I could . . ."

I hid my disapproval behind a short nod. "Fine. Let's go."

Delia lowered her eyes and we crossed the street. The servant's entrance was still unlocked, and she led the way up the darkened staircase to the third floor. The hall was empty, the only sound the low hiss of gas from the wall sconces. Delia stopped in front of the door closest to the servants' stairwell, marked with the number eight, and looked at me over her shoulder.

"This is it," she rasped, clearly hesitant to enter.

"It's all right," I murmured with a hand on her shoulder. "I'm here."

She took a breath and opened the door. The gaslight was still on, and as we entered, I was immediately struck by how handsomely decorated the entryway was. The walls were lined with framed pictures of all shapes and sizes, while a cabinet displayed a variety of artifacts. Under any other circumstances, I would have loved to pore over everything. But, of course, now was not the time.

"The telephone is just over there," she said, pointing to a contraption on top of a small table.

It reminded me of a candlestick standing on a wooden base. I gingerly removed the black conical piece, which I supposed one spoke into, then hesitated. "Do you know how to use it?"

Delia took it from me. She held up the cone to her ear and pressed a button at the top of the candlestick, waited a moment, and began to speak into it. "Scotland Yard, please. Thank you."

Well, I had gotten that *all* wrong.

Delia then held out the contraption to me with a pleading look. "Can you speak to them?" she asked, pressing the earpiece into my hand before I could respond. "Just hold it like this," she explained, drawing my hand up to my ear. "And speak here."

I gingerly pressed the earpiece to my ear, but all I could here was a dull crackling sound. "It will take a moment," she added when she saw my look of confusion.

Then I heard a tinny voice that sounded like someone whispering down the end of a long hallway. "Scotland Yard. What is the purpose of your call?"

"Hello, yes," I began. "I need to report a murder. Well, a body," I added with a wince. "I'm not sure if they were murdered or not."

The voice on the other end then asked something. I could barely understand them, but I assumed they wanted to know the location.

"I'm at The Carleton on George Street in Marylebone," I replied, nearly shouting now. "Flat number eight on the third floor."

A muffled response came, and then the line went dead. I frowned in confusion at the earpiece and then handed the blasted thing back to Delia. "They are on their way, I think."

She nodded and put the telephone back in its place. "Now what?"

"We wait," I said. Then hesitated. "Where is he?"

Delia looked past me down the hall. "The study. But I . . . I can't."

"Understood," I replied. "I'll just be a moment."

I didn't exactly relish the thought of seeing a dead body once again and was suddenly flooded with memories of Daphne Costas, the maid I found murdered on Corfu. I forced my gaze ahead and crept down the hallway. The first room on my right was a cozy little parlor with a Persian-style rug on the floor and two wingback chairs before the hearth. Like the entryway, the walls and shelves were lined with treasures of one sort or another. The door on my left was closed, possibly a bedroom. But up ahead, the door to the study stood open, and warm lamplight spilled out onto the hallway. As I grew closer, I could make out shelves of books and another fine rug. I held my breath as I reached the doorway and had to take a moment to settle my rattled nerves before I peered inside.

A massive oak desk took up a corner. And there, right in front of it, was the body of Charles Pearson in a puddle of blood. Delia was right. No one could have survived that, as it seemed someone had bashed his head in quite thoroughly.

Chapter 7

I forced myself to enter the room and bent down beside the body, taking care not to disturb the scene. The metallic scent of freshly spilled blood hung in the air, so I took shallow breaths. Charles Pearson's head was turned towards me, and his blue eyes were frozen open, as if in surprise.

"Poor chap," I murmured and rose.

I glanced around the study, but there didn't appear to be any sign of the weapon used to bludgeon him. In fact, the space looked remarkably undisturbed, apart from the body on the floor. I backed out of the room with a frown and rejoined Delia in the entryway.

"He is dead, then?"

I glanced up, distracted by my thoughts. "Yes," I said softly. "I'm so sorry, Delia."

Her eyes welled with tears. "I had hoped that I was mistaken," she choked out. "That it had all been some horrible dream." Then she brought a hand to her mouth.

I understood that impulse all too well and pulled her into my arms. "There now," I hushed, as she cried against my shoulder, and wished for all the world that I could bring her some comfort. But, unfortunately, this was a road she would have to tread mostly on her own.

After she had quite thoroughly soaked my shoulder, I pulled back. "Why don't we wait in the parlor," I suggested, taking her by the arm. "I've no idea how long it will take the police to arrive."

Delia nodded and wordlessly allowed me to lead her into the room. I was more convinced than ever that she could not have been involved in Charles Pearson's death—and that it was not an accident. No, this had been caused by a horrific act of violence, and I would do whatever I could to keep my sister safe.

As I sat her down on a dark green velvet sofa, her long coat parted, revealing the front of her dress along with a smear of rust-colored blood. Based on the placement, she must have knelt by his body when she found him—an understandable impulse. I swallowed and turned away to set about building up the fire in the hearth. From what I could tell, it had been banked for hours. I used the poker to dig through the coals just in case someone had burned any potential evidence, but there was no sign of that. While I rustled the coals back to life, the image of the body burned in my mind. It seemed most likely that Charles Pearson had gone straight to his study—and hadn't left. But what was he doing in there? Had his killer been lying in wait, or did Charles welcome him inside?

With the fire now giving off a good bit of heat, I turned back to Delia. She was staring blankly off into the distance. I sat down beside her and took her hand in mine. It felt far too cold.

"I know it is difficult, but I think you should tell me everything you can remember. Even the smallest detail may prove to be important."

She gave a slow nod. "All right. I left the house as soon as you went to bed and walked over here."

"Did you see anyone on the way?"

"I passed a few people. Strangers. But I kept to the shadows and wore my veiled hat." Then she shot me an arch look. "I know enough to be discreet."

"Good. Then what?"

"Like I said, I came up the servants' staircase. And I didn't see anyone there either," she added before I could ask. "The hallway was empty too, which isn't unusual. This building is full of bachelors, and they keep late hours."

I pursed my lips at this description. "I see."

Delia's mouth curved in the barest hint of a smile at my obvious disapproval. "I didn't make it a habit of coming here, you know. It was only a few times. And I never saw anyone else."

"That's a relief," I said dryly.

Delia let out a mournful little sigh. "Anyway, I opened the door and—"

"It was unlocked?"

"Yes. Charlie always left the door unlocked if he knew I was coming. That way I could slip in as quickly as possible."

"And avoid being seen," I added. Delia glanced away with a sheepish nod. It also would have made things exceptionally easier for the killer. "Sorry. I don't mean to sound so judgemental. Only I . . . I'm worried for you."

"I understand," she said after a moment, then met my eyes. "I've been a bit reckless lately. And I know Mother is upset with me. I'm sure she gave you an earful last night."

"She did," I admitted. Had that only been last night? It seemed like an age ago. "But given what's now happened, I can't say I blame her." Delia grimaced in response. "What did you do after you entered?"

"I don't know. It all happened so quickly."

"Give it a think," I said gently.

Delia sighed and shut her eyes for a moment. "I called out to him while I took off my coat and hat. I assumed he was in his study. That's where he spent most of his time. I noticed the light on, so I walked towards the room. And then . . ."

"You found him," I finished. Delia choked back a sob and nodded.

"I knelt down beside him. I tried to help, but the blood—"

"I know. It's all right," I soothed. "There was nothing anyone could have done for him, Delia. You must believe me." Her glistening eyes were full of pain, and she managed a nod. "Back at home, you told me you were frightened," I continued. "That you may have heard something."

She cleared her throat. "Yes. It sounded like someone was in the flat moving around, but I was in such a panic, I could have misheard."

"Or not. The killer may have still been here when you entered, then left while you were in the study."

Which meant that, if she had been just a few minutes earlier, Delia would have interrupted the murder—and possibly become a victim herself.

Delia seemed to share my thoughts and shuddered. "My God."

Suddenly, there was a loud knock on the door, and we both jumped.

"That must be the police," I said, trying to sound calm, even while my heart pounded in my chest. "You wait here. Let me do the talking." Delia made no argument as I headed for the entryway.

I opened the door and was surprised to find a single, rather bored-looking constable. "Hello."

"Good evening, ma'am," he said with a tip of his hat. "We received a call about a body."

"Yes, that was me. Do come in."

The constable entered the flat, but seemed far more interested in the treasures on display.

"It is our friend," I said. "He's just back there in the study."

The constable looked dubious. "You're sure he's dead? You know, ma'am, sometimes a fellow has too much to drink and just needs a bit of sleep."

"Yes. I'm quite certain," I gritted out. Of all the possible scenarios, I had never imagined the police would actually question the very existence of a dead body.

Yet, the constable did not appear convinced, but proceeded down the hall while I waited. After a few moments, I heard a low whistle, which I assume meant he had seen Charles for himself. Then he returned clicking his tongue.

"Terrible business," he muttered. "And you say you found him like that?"

"Yes," I said tersely.

"All right. I'll have to contact the Yard and have them send the detective over," he replied, as if this was a great inconvenience and not his *job*. "Do you mind if I use your telephone?"

"Not at all. I will wait in the parlor with my sister."

He waved me off, entirely unconcerned to learn of the presence of another person in the flat. Once again, I was struck by the lackadaisical manner of a law enforcement officer. It was what had spurred me to involve myself in the death of Daphne Costas, and clearly I would need to do the same here in England. I rolled my eyes as I entered the parlor. Delia was still huddled on the sofa and looked up at me with an anxious expression.

"He's calling for reinforcements," I explained. "Apparently, he needed to confirm first that someone was *actually* dead."

But Delia didn't share my annoyance. She only looked more worried. "Are you sure about this?"

"Absolutely," I replied, with as much confidence as I could muster. I had decided that cooperating with the police was better than attempting to hide her from the crime, but only time would tell if this gamble would pay off.

* * *

While we waited for the detective to arrive, the constable introduced himself as Officer Byrne and took down our names and information.

"Shall we tell you what happened?" I asked, but the constable shook his head.

"Better save it all for the detective inspector, ma'am," he said. "He will want to have the story fresh from you. I've learned that the hard way," he added with a chuckle that did nothing to quell my uncertainty. "This chap was a collector then?" he asked me, but I turned to Delia.

"Yes," she answered quietly. "He bought and sold art and antiques."

The constable hummed in response and began inspecting the shelves. "Quite the little museum he has here, ain't it?"

Delia shrugged, either uninterested or unable to keep up the conversation. He continued to peruse the contents of a large cabinet in the corner, but had the irritating habit of whistling while he did so.

"Would it be all right if I made us some tea?" I asked after a moment.

The constable paused to think. "I don't see why not," he answered. "Let me make sure nothing is amiss in there first." That at least spared us a few blissful moments of peace while he left the room.

Once he was out of earshot, I turned to Delia. "How long was Charles in the business of selling things?"

"I'm not sure," she replied. "A good while, though, I think. He had an inheritance from his father, but I believe most of his income came from his sales."

"I see," I said, casting a look around the room and wondering about the true nature of his finances. He seemed successful enough, what with the flat in this neighborhood and the undoubtably expensive telephone, but he would hardly be the first person to hide money troubles behind a veneer of wealth.

"Do you think his murder was connected to his business?"

"I don't think anything yet," I said carefully. "But it is certainly a possibility. We cannot assume. Only theorize." As soon as the words were out, I realized what I had done.

Delia raised a questioning brow. "Now *you* sound like a detective."

Inspector Dumond, in fact. Mr. Dorian's most famous creation.

I let out a huff, as I was exceedingly cross with myself, just as the constable returned. "I think it's fine for you to put the kettle on, ma'am."

"Excellent," I said, practically leaping to my feet. It was good to stay busy at a time like this. If nothing else, it would help keep my mind off thoughts of arrogant inspectors, dead bodies, and, most of all, irritating mystery writers.

I had just finished pouring our cups of tea when there was a loud pounding at the door.

Officer Byrne let out a weary sigh as he set down his cup and moved to answer it. "Prepare yourselves, ladies," he said ominously.

Delia and I exchanged a look. There was the low murmur of voices in the entryway and the shuffle of feet. The detective had not arrived alone. Officer Byrne returned to the parlor, while three other men walked past down the hall.

He gave us a smile. "They're taking a look around first. Then the detective will come speak with you."

"Anything we can do to help," I said genially, then took a sip.

The murmur of voices and the sound of footsteps continued as the men moved methodically around the flat.

Eventually, a young man with dark hair and a strangely familiar stern expression entered the parlor.

"Good evening," he said, radiating a kind of smooth, self-satisfied air that caused me to dislike him immediately. "I am Detective Inspector Dorian."

Out the corner of my eye, I could see Delia glance over at me, but I could not meet her gaze. I was simply too stunned to look away from the detective.

Mr. Dorian had mentioned his younger brother once during our investigation on Corfu. It had taken us to the island of Paxos and, after the man we had hired to ferry us there had gotten extremely drunk, we were forced to spend the night. It was over dinner that Mr. Dorian revealed that he had a younger brother who followed in their late father's footsteps by joining Scotland Yard. I also recalled that this man did not think very highly of Mr. Dorian's literary pursuits.

"Please give me your names," Detective Inspector Dorian prompted before turning to me.

"I am Mrs. Minerva Harper," I began. "And this is my sister, Delia Everly."

With a frown, he turned to her. "Is that true?"

Delia nodded sheepishly. "Yes."

He looked between us for a moment, considering something. Then the front door opened once more, and a large man with a shock of red hair and a beard to match entered the parlor. "Inspector Donnelly. Excellent timing. You will take Miss Everly into the kitchen for questioning." Then his dark gaze narrowed on me. "While Mrs. Harper will remain here with me."

Delia inhaled sharply, and I reached for her hand. "Might we not stay together, Detective Inspector?" I asked in a cloying tone of voice I only used when trying to charm a man, which, frankly, did not happen very often. But my attempt to appeal to the man's emotions utterly failed.

"No, you may not," he said flatly.

"It will be all right," I murmured to Delia. She shot me a dubious look, but squeezed my hand and stood.

Inspector Donnelly held out his arm. "Right this way, Miss Everly."

He seemed genial enough, which was a relief. Better that I was to be questioned by Inspector Dorian than my sister. She cast me one last look before exiting the room. After a moment, I heard the door to the kitchen shut soundly behind her.

Detective Inspector Dorian then walked to the armchair the constable had set in front of the sofa for our tea and took a seat. "Alone at last," he said as he steepled his hands. "Now then, Mrs. Harper. Would you be so good as to tell me about your evening and how you came to find Mr. Pearson's body?"

A part of me whispered caution. That I shouldn't tell this man a thing. But this was also an opportunity to guide his investigation. It was clear to me that, at the very least, Delia and I were both now suspects. And that this might be my only chance to plant the seeds of doubt in his mind.

I shifted in my chair and cleared my throat. "Certainly. I agreed to attend an opening at the Elysium Gallery in Soho with Delia. She is an artist and had a painting on display. I met her at our parents' house in Portman Square at approximately eight o' clock, and we left for the gallery around nine. There we met Mr. Pearson, who is a friend of Delia's. We stayed at the gallery for about an hour, I suppose, before we headed to the home of Lord Linden, who was hosting a gathering."

The inspector had been taking notes, but at the mention of the baron, he raised an eyebrow and glanced up at me. I surmised that the baron's parties were well-known enough to reach the ears of Scotland Yard. Interesting, though perhaps not surprising.

"I see. Go on," the inspector prompted.

"We stayed there for another hour or so before we left at my request—"

"Why?"

The sharp question startled me. "Because I was *tired*," I shot back.

The inspector sat back in his chair and gave me another one of those considering looks. "By my estimation, it was just after midnight. That is considered quite early for a guest to depart from a society function."

"Well, I am not most guests, Inspector Dorian," I said crossly. I was being rather impertinent and expected to be chastised, but to my surprise, the man only smiled a bit and took up his pen once more.

"All right. Please, continue."

"As my sister, Mr. Pearson, and I were making to leave, another guest offered the use of his carriage to take us home, which we accepted."

"His name?" he asked, without looking up from his scribblings.

Admittedly, I am not proud of how I behaved in this moment. But given the series of events I had endured over the course of the evening, coupled with a lack of sleep, I could not help but engage in a bit of pettiness. I paused until the inspector glanced up at me in question. Then I pretended to think, as if the name had escaped me. "Stephen Dorian," I finally said. "The author."

An outright scowl clouded his expression. "And you did not think to mention this sooner?"

I widened my eyes. "Oh! Is he a relation of yours?"

He scoffed, clearly not believing my reaction. "He is my brother."

"Well, I would never assume," I explained.

He narrowed his eyes at me. "And was tonight the first time you met?"

I hesitated. I had underestimated his interest in his brother. For a very brief moment, I considered lying, but that could only lead to more complications. "I don't see how that is relevant to this matter, but no, it was not," I replied with as much disinterest as I could muster, as if the subject bored me.

But instead of responding, the inspector began to study the paper before him. "Minerva Harper," he drawled. I felt an uneasy prickling at the base of my neck, as though this man knew far more about me than he was letting on. Then he shot me a challenging look, as if he had heard my thoughts. "And I suppose it's only a coincidence that your initials happen to match the dedication in his latest book?"

Somehow I managed to keep my composure and simply tilted my head in question. "You've read it?"

The inspector's look of surprise was most gratifying. He had not meant to admit that. He began to say something, then seemed to think better of it and shook his head. "Never mind. As you said, it bears no relevance to this case." Then he straightened his spine and resumed his questioning. "What time did you arrive at your parents' house?"

"One in the morning," I replied, somewhat relieved that we had moved on from discussing Stephen Dorian. "I remember because the grandfather clock chimed just after we entered. Then Delia and I went upstairs and talked for a bit before we went to bed. I fell asleep, and she woke me up a short while later in great distress as she had found Mr. Pearson's body. We then returned here and called the police."

He raised an eyebrow. "So your sister first came to the flat alone, encountered the body and left, and then you both returned here."

"That is correct."

"And how did you enter?"

"The servant's staircase."

"Ah. Naturally."

I lifted my chin at his sarcastic tone. "I will not pretend that I was not scandalized by her actions, Inspector," I began. "But my sister had an understanding with Mr. Pearson and only came here to discuss a related matter. I would thank *you* not to insinuate anything that would damage her reputation," I added.

"I am not at all concerned with the reputation of young ladies, Mrs. Harper," he said hotly. "A man was murdered in his own home. Violently, I might add."

The image of Charles Pearson's lifeless body lying in a dark, glistening pool of his own blood flashed through my mind.

"I know," I murmured as my throat went dry. "I did . . . I did see him."

He softened ever so slightly. "Right. I am sorry for that."

"I realize how all this must sound to you. But you must admit that we could just as easily have not informed Scotland Yard."

He looked incredulous. "And do you expect me to thank you for that?"

"No. I expect you to conduct a thorough investigation. And it seems perfectly obvious to me that my sister does not possess the strength needed to bash a man's head in."

His eyes glittered with purpose. "It is my job not to make assumptions about anyone, Mrs. Harper. And let me assure you that I only seek the truth. If your sister is innocent—and *you*, for that matter—I will prove it."

Though I knew perfectly well that I was innocent, I felt a shiver race down my spine nonetheless. Clearly, this was not a man to be trifled with. I tried to find some comfort in that knowledge, but couldn't shake the feeling of uncertainty. This situation had become far more complicated than I expected. But I couldn't lose my nerve. Not now. Not when my sister's life, and possibly my own, was at stake.

"We arrived home just before one," I began in a measured tone. "And it was only a little past two when Delia returned and woke me. We then placed the call to Scotland Yard here. I'm sure there is a record of it for you to confirm."

"And I will. But if you are suggesting that it clears the two of you of suspicion, then—"

The detective was cut off by a loud bang from the entryway as someone slammed the door open.

"All right! That's enough," cried a highly irritated voice I hadn't heard in years—and not a moment too soon.

"Oh God," I muttered before glowering at the detective. "Who called *him*?"

Inspector Dorian frowned in confusion at my question, but I was already getting to my feet.

I swung open the sitting room door and found my brother Jack in the middle of haranguing Officer Byrne.

"I am John Francis Everly, the MP for Kensington," he said, with the kind of inherent self-importance I had only found in men who had accomplished the dizzying feat of being born into wealth and privilege. "And you cannot detain people without charge. This is my solicitor," he continued, gesturing to a tall, thin man in spectacles who stood just behind him. "And he excels in investigating police corruption. Or shall I form a committee and drag you down to parliament and make you answer for your crimes?"

Oh, but he was in a full-on bluster now. Officer Byrne shot me a panicked look over his shoulder.

"Jack, that is quite enough," I said as calmly as I could manage. "We are not being detained against our will."

My brother paused and turned toward me. The look of surprise on his face was almost worth having to deal with him in this state. "Minnie? What the devil are *you* doing here?"

I crossed my arms. "Funny, I was going to ask you the same."

He frowned in confusion just as our sister stepped into the hallway wearing a sheepish expression. "I rang him while you were in the study earlier," she admitted to me.

"Oh," I replied, feeling rather betrayed. "Why didn't you tell me?"

Delia shook her head, wide-eyed. "I suppose I just panicked and—"

Jack cut her off with an impatient huff. "Might we first deal with the more pressing issue before delving into a squabble?" Then he turned to the inspector. "You won't get another word out of either of them without my solicitor present."

"Jack," I began on a sigh. "We are cooperating—"

"That's all right, sir," the inspector cut in with a self-satisfied smile of his own. "They are free to go. Your sister has been *very* helpful. Though I strongly suggest they both remain in London, should we need anything more from them."

I did not appreciate being discussed as if I wasn't even in the room, and as the two men stared each other down, I couldn't decide who was being more insufferable.

"Come along," I said to Delia. "I have no interest in watching a battle of egos. We will wait for you in the carriage, Jack."

Then I turned on my heel and headed for the exit, with my sister following in my wake.

Chapter 8

We had nearly reached the pavement outside when Jack caught up to us.

"All right," he prompted, once we had all piled into the coach. "Care to explain yourselves?"

Before I could respond, Delia blurted out our entire evening.

When she got to the bit about the party, Jack shot me an accusing look. "You let her go to Lord Linden's house? The man is a notorious scoundrel!"

"Well, how was I to know? It's not as though his reputation has reached Corfu," I said.

Jack grumbled something under his breath and bade Delia to continue. When she had finally finished, Jack muttered a curse, then fixed his dark gaze on me.

"And I suppose it was your idea to call the police?"

I balked at his derision. "What else was I supposed to do?"

"Anything, Minnie," he insisted. "*Anything else.*"

"Right. And when the police came to call after realizing that Delia and I were among the last people to see Charles Pearson alive, you expected the two of us to simply lie?"

"It never would have come to that," he said with his typical high-handedness. "And now we have a much bigger problem: keeping your connection to a murder out of the papers."

"Really, Jack," I scoffed. "That is what you are worried about?"

"Well, perhaps not so much you," he said with a sardonic lift of his brow. "But Delia is a young, unmarried woman with her whole life ahead of her. There is no need for her future to be ruined over this."

Delia inhaled sharply beside me, and I shot him an irritated look. "You are being needlessly dramatic."

"Am I?" he challenged as he leaned forward in his seat. "You haven't lived here in well over a decade. You have no idea what the papers are like. Especially for a man in my position—"

"Come off it, Jack," I said, rolling my eyes.

"I am up for re-election next year," he snapped. "And my challenger would love nothing more than to exploit a piece of gossip about anyone connected to me."

"Of course," I said. "Everything always comes back to your precious political career."

Jack leaned forward, his eyes glittering with anger. "Now listen here—"

"Stop it, both of you!" Delia suddenly cried out. "Neither of you seem to care about the fact that the man I love was just brutally murdered."

My brother and I exchanged a chastened look.

"Sorry, Delia," Jack grumbled.

"We do care, darling," I soothed, but she shook her head.

"I don't give a damn about my reputation," she said in a quavering voice. "I want to know who did it."

"Of course," I replied. "And we will find out."

"Not *we*," Jack cut in. "The police."

I pursed my lips. Now was not the time to argue with him

about that. As Jack pulled a hand down his face, he suddenly looked quite haggard. "That detective gave me his word that he would keep your identities hidden for as long as possible. And I've a contact at the *Illustrated Police News* who owes me a favor. That should help your names stay out of the papers until the killer is apprehended."

"Fine. Thank you," I added softly.

Delia gave a slow nod, but her gaze was unfocused.

"In the meantime, you should stay home as much as possible. Well, Delia should," he amended. "I know you've never had much of a taste for society anyway."

I narrowed my eyes at the derision in his voice, though he was quite right about that. We then lapsed into an awkward silence as the coach grew closer to Portman Square.

"God. Mother will have a fit," Delia breathed.

"You aren't to say a word," Jack cautioned. "I will speak to her later today. Understand?"

I bristled. "I think we are quite able to explain ourselves."

He arched a brow. "Yes, but do you really want to explain this?" I cleared my throat as the image of Mother's disapproving gaze flashed through my mind. "I thought so," Jack added at my silence.

I turned to Delia, but she was gazing listlessly out the window. I hated to see her in such a state. Only hours ago, she had been bursting with a zest for life that was infectious. I didn't want this incident to snuff out the light inside her nor impact her promising future as a painter.

I took her hand in mine and gave it a comforting squeeze. She glanced back at me and managed a weak smile that was a mere shadow of her usual expression. As we grew closer to Portman Square, Jack directed the coachman to take us to the mews behind the house. No use in announcing to the neighborhood that we were returning home at close to five in the morning.

Jack got out first to help Delia down. He murmured

something to her, and she nodded before entering through the back door. Then he turned to me and held out his hand.

"I told her I wanted a moment to speak with you alone," he said, no doubt reading the curious expression on my face.

"Oh," I said as he handed me down.

"It's about Father. I'm sure you've noticed his . . . condition."

"I did. I understand he had a fall some time ago," I said pointedly.

Jack pursed his lips. "Yes. About four years or so. He missed the last few steps coming down the staircase and broke his ankle. It was slow to heal and hasn't been the same since. Then he started having trouble with his memory. More than the spottiness that comes with age. Sometimes he's just like his old self. As sharp as a knife. But other times it's as if he's lost in the past. And it's only been getting worse," he added.

"Well, what do the doctors say? What can be done?"

Jack's gaze turned sympathetic. "Nothing, Minnie."

"But Aunt Agatha is older, and she is as sharp as ever," I said, as if this was an argument I could win.

"Yes, because Aunt Agatha has had nothing to worry about other than which spa town to visit for the last forty years," he snapped.

I crossed my arms and huffed, though it was a fair point. "I just don't understand why no one bothered to tell me any of this. Not even when Aunt Agatha came to Corfu."

"I can't explain Agatha, but you know what she's like," Jack said. "She swans in for a fifteen-minute visit every few months so she and Mother can snipe at each other. If she came on one of Father's better days, she may not have even noticed anything amiss. And it isn't as though Mother would have willingly told her."

I had to admit that did sound entirely possible. "Fine. But what about the fall?"

Jack sighed and looked off towards the end of the mews.

"It wasn't long after Oliver passed, and Mother didn't want to worry you further. She thought we would just tell you when you returned home, but then . . ." He trailed off.

I swallowed and lowered my head. After Oliver died, nearly everyone I knew assumed I would pack up and leave Corfu as soon as possible. For over a year, every letter from my family asked about our travel plans, but I kept putting it off. There was too much to deal with on Corfu: Oliver's export business had to be closed down; then I didn't want to disrupt the children's school, or take them away from their friends. Eventually, I ran out of excuses, and people stopped asking.

"Yes. I'm sorry about that," I murmured. "I suppose I was . . . afraid. For a long time."

Jack turned back to me, confused. "Afraid of what?"

You must promise me, Min. Promise me you won't go back there.

Oliver's ominous warning echoed in my head, but I couldn't get into all that. Not now, anyway. "I don't know. Everything?" I said this with a hapless little shrug that seemed to be answer enough for Jack.

"Well, I'm glad you're here now," he said as he reached out and patted my shoulder.

"Me too," I replied, surprised by how much I meant it. "Is it all right if I come for Tommy later this afternoon once I've had a bit of sleep? He spent the night at your house," I added at his questioning look.

"Did he? I didn't realize . . ."

I reared back a little. "You mean you haven't been home yet?"

"No," he said, a touch defensive. "I had a committee meeting and then drinks at Bedivere's. My club. And I occasionally stay there for the night, depending on the hour, so I don't disturb the household. Everyone knows to try there first if it's late."

"Really," I said, unable to hide the skepticism in my tone, to which he responded with a scowl, effectively ending this little interlude of brotherly affection.

"I have no need to explain myself to you," he replied tightly, as he tugged on his gloves and turned back towards the coach. "Now get some sleep," he called over his shoulder just before he climbed in.

I let out a sigh and watched as the coach rumbled down the cobblestoned mews.

That was how things had always been with Jack. We seemed to be forever seesawing between undisguised contempt and fleeting moments of understanding. I knew I should try harder to at least be cordial with him. We weren't children any longer, and I could now accept that our strained relationship wasn't entirely his fault. But I had a few more pressing things to deal with first. And time was of the essence. So, for now, Jack would have to wait.

I hurried into the house through the back entrance, but Delia was nowhere in sight. I heard the faint sound of feet shuffling and pans clattering in the direction of the kitchen, indicating that the staff was already up and about. I ducked down the hall and headed for the back staircase, as the very last thing I needed was to run into Mrs. Reynolds, the housekeeper, or heaven help me, Morris, and try to explain what I was doing awake and in evening dress.

Luckily, I made it back to my bedroom without spotting another soul. As I shut the door behind me, I was struck full on by the weight of exhaustion. I stumbled through dressing for bed and managed to climb under the covers. Then I slipped into a deep, dreamless sleep the moment my head hit the pillow.

I awoke, feeling bleary-eyed and disoriented, some hours later and glanced at the small bedside clock and groaned. It was half-past noon already. I fought the urge to continue sleeping, as I would surely pay for it later that evening. Slowly, I sat up while the events of the previous night and morning filtered through my woolly brain. And yet, despite all that had occurred—all that I had witnessed—it was one memory in particular that brought an immediate frown to my face.

I had seen Mr. Dorian, of all people. I did take some comfort in the fact that I had been wearing a very fine gown, then immediately chastised myself for caring in the first place. After all, this was a man who had not even seen fit to say good-bye to me before leaving Corfu and made no attempt to contact me afterwards.

And I suppose it's only a coincidence that your initials happen to match the dedication in his latest book?

I grimaced as I recalled the inspector's insinuation. Regrettably, I had also made the same inference at first. But even if that was the case, that blasted book dedication was probably Mr. Dorian's idea of a joke. Or maybe he had simply run out of people to dedicate books to, so why not include the silly little widow who typed up the blasted thing? Just as I felt my cheeks heat, I gave myself a shake. No. I refused to dedicate any more time or emotion to that man. I certainly had not known he would be at that party, and would have avoided the place if I had.

Would you?

I ignored the sly voice in my head as I threw back the coverlet. However, the room was shockingly cold, and I immediately retreated back to the bed. Goodness, was this room always so frigid? But then I looked towards the hearth and found the fire had entirely gone out. Well, that explained it. I tugged on the bellpull and then headed for the wardrobe. There must be something I could throw on. As I recalled, I hadn't taken very much with me when I left for Greece on account of the vast difference in climate and had to purchase a whole new wardrobe when we arrived in Athens.

I tugged open the heavy wooden door of the wardrobe, which always had a habit of sticking, and was hit anew with the scent of dried rose petals. It was mostly empty now, as I'm sure Delia had raided the best bits long ago. A sad-looking pair of shoes remained, along with a few plain skirts and shirts that I couldn't blame her for not taking. But there on a hook hung a heavy wool cardigan that would do quite nicely. I grabbed it and pulled it on, then found a pair of thick cotton socks to match. Now that I had on an extra layer, I shuffled over to the washstand to wipe my face and clean my teeth. I had just finished when there was a scratch at the door, and it opened.

A young, brown-haired maid bustled in with a tray. "I'm so sorry, ma'am. We forgot you were in here, and no one tended the fire this morning," she said in a great rush.

"Entirely understandable," I said, as she set down the tray on a table, then set about lighting the fire.

"Mrs. Reynolds gave us all a good dressing-down just now," she said with a sheepish glance over her shoulder. "It won't happen again."

The corner of my mouth lifted. As I recalled, the housekeeper could be rather terrifying when she was in a lather over something. "I will speak with her. It's really no trouble. And I will not be staying another night," I insisted, mostly for my own benefit.

The maid flashed me a grateful smile, then turned back to the hearth. I approached the table and looked over the tray. She had brought me a pot of tea and some rolls with jam and butter. A bit spartan, but then I had missed breakfast, and no doubt they were right in the middle of serving luncheon downstairs.

"What's your name?" I asked as I poured a cup of tea.

"Deirdre, ma'am," the maid replied.

"How long have you worked here?"

"A little over a year."

I hummed in response as I took a sip, savoring the strong brew. I didn't like to admit it, but no one could make a pot of tea like the English. It simply tasted better here. I very much wanted to interrogate Deirdre about what she knew about my family, but the girl had endured enough this morning on my account. So I settled for a more innocuous question.

"Is my sister awake?"

"No, ma'am. But your mother wishes to speak with you. When you are ready, of course," she hastened to add.

My lips flattened. I had expected as much, but was surprised that Jack had already been back here to talk with her. Did that man ever sleep? "I see. And I take it she is downstairs having luncheon?"

"Yes, I believe so. With Mr. Everly."

Delia had mentioned that our parents usually had supper alone in their rooms, so I was glad to learn luncheon was a more communal affair.

The fire was beginning to catch, so Deirdre rose. "Do you need anything else, ma'am?"

"No. Thank you, Deirdre."

With that, she bobbed a quick curtsy and scurried from the room, leaving me alone once again. As I was not in a great rush to face my mother and attempt to explain anything about the previous evening, I enjoyed a leisurely breakfast in front of the now roaring fire. Then I returned to my wardrobe and pulled out some of my old clothes. The pickings were very slim indeed, but I did not want to wake Delia simply to retrieve my discarded dress. She needed lots of rest to fortify herself for what lay ahead. My shoulders tightened instinctively at the thought of mourning a lost love, but I could still recognize how far I had come since Oliver's death. Especially since the spring.

I brushed aside some very inconvenient thoughts and mindlessly pulled out a skirt and blouse. They fit more tightly than my usual clothing, but nothing I couldn't manage for a few hours. I also found some old underthings and stockings in the chest of drawers. When I was done dressing, I looked over my reflection in the bronze-edged, full-length mirror.

A smile touched my lips. In my navy wool skirt and white shirtwaist with the frill at the collar, I rather looked like a university student—that is, if one didn't get close enough to notice the faint lines around my eyes. I chuckled at the thought, then sat at my old vanity table and began to pick apart the worst of the snarls in my hair with an ivory comb. Once that was accomplished, I brushed out my hair, then tied it back into a simple chignon at the back of my neck. I still looked a touch too pale, and there were distinctive shadows beneath my eyes, but there was no use in fussing any longer. I had never managed to satisfy my mother anyway, no matter how much effort I put into my appearance.

She always seemed to find something to criticize. Whether it was as small as a loose lock of hair or as inherent as the curve of my smile, I was always lacking in some specific way. I had learned many years ago that it was better not to seek her approval, for then I would not be quite so disappointed by her inevitable criticism. Absently, I rubbed my palms on the front of my skirt and stilled my hands.

"No more dithering," I murmured to myself.

Besides, the sooner I spoke with her, the sooner I could leave and get Tommy. The thought filled me with a rush of love that brought me to my feet. I clung to that feeling as I headed for the door. These last hours had been so terribly dark and filled with such sadness and worry. I was struck anew by how very grateful I was for my two children and the joy they had brought me over the years. Without them, I was certain I could not have gone on after Oliver's death.

I had just reached out to turn the knob when there was a knock at the door, and it opened, not a moment later, to reveal my mother standing in the doorway. "Hello," I chirped at her sudden, unexpected appearance. But she was too busy looking me over to notice my surprise.

"Are you wearing your old school clothes?"

I rather thought the incredulous tone of her voice was a bit much. I didn't look *that* ridiculous.

"My other clothing is in Delia's room," I replied. "So I picked something out of the wardrobe."

Her sharp gaze fell on the furniture in question. "I didn't even know anything was still in there. I thought we gave it all to the maids or the charity shop."

I cleared my throat. Then Delia hadn't raided my old wardrobe after all. "Well, I'm glad you didn't so I wasn't forced to wander the halls in my nightgown."

This little quip was met with an unamused tilt of her head, and I wondered for a moment if my mother thought anything was funny. I certainly had never seen her utter more than a light, ladylike chuckle, and even then, it had been more out of politeness rather than a genuine response. It was just another thing about her that would forever remain a mystery.

She swept farther into the room and looked back at me over her shoulder. "I hope you slept well?"

I nodded, as I knew from long experience she wasn't really interested in the answer. It was merely a precursor to what she truly wanted to discuss. She stopped by the hearth and turned to face me. Then I noticed her hands were locked tightly at her front. She opened her mouth to speak, then hesitated. Then it dawned on me: she was nervous. My mother. I moved towards her, as if drawn by some unseen force to see this up close.

"You spoke with Jack," I began, when it became clear she would not broach the subject first.

"Yes. He came here just after breakfast."

"Then I don't need to go over the details of what occurred."

My mother let out a breath. "No, you do not." Her face had taken on an ashen color, and for a brief moment, I worried she might swoon. But then she gave herself a shake and met my eyes. "I am sorry."

I blinked, certain I misheard her. For my mother had never apologized to me before. About anything. "Pardon?"

"I encouraged you to spend time with Delia. But I never thought she would involve you in anything like *this*."

"Mother, it's all right," I said. "I wanted to go out with Delia last night."

She stepped quickly towards me then and grasped my arm. Her hands were cold and clammy. "But Jack says you are now both suspects. That you could go to prison for being her accomplice! What will happen to your children? They've already lost their father. If you are then sent away, they—"

"Mother. Stop," I stressed. "We aren't suspects. They would have taken us to Scotland Yard if they truly thought so." She let out a little gasp, but I pressed on. "I am not Delia's accomplice, and she is innocent. Believe me. I saw the body, and there is no way she could have killed him."

"You must prove it," she blurted out.

I reared back a little. "Me?"

My mother nodded furiously. "Yes. I don't trust the police on this, Minnie. They won't be able to find the real killer and will blame the two of you instead."

"Mother, I really don't think that is the case here—"

"I know what you did on Corfu. Agatha told me," she added. "The local police didn't care about finding the real murderer of that girl, so you stepped in."

I was tempted to point out that I very nearly was murdered myself in the process, but that would hardly help calm her down. "Yes, but this isn't Corfu. And the detective I met seemed very capable." That at least was true.

My mother scoffed. "The papers go mad for murderesses. Can you imagine what they will do over a pair of sisters?"

"But we *aren't*," I felt the need to state. "What I told the police was the truth. And I believe Delia. There is no reason to think we will be charged with murder. Perhaps we will be questioned again, but I'm sure they found loads of evidence in that flat and will find even more once the investigation is underway."

I thought that all sounded very sensible, but my mother didn't seem to hear a word. She had begun to pace and was biting her thumbnail, of all things. I would have been less surprised if she'd burst into a merry little jig.

"Besides," I continued, "Jack thinks we should stay home, and I agree."

"No," my mother said decisively, "Delia should, but not you." Then she stopped and pointed her finger at me. "You must find out everything you can. So we can be prepared."

I had never seen her in such a state. Then a thought occurred to me. "Is something else going on?"

She shot me a haughty glare. "You mean something other than my two daughters being connected to a murder?"

I held up my hands in supplication. "Sorry. I know this must be very upsetting—"

"It's *shocking*, Minnie!"

"Right. Yes," I agreed, then gestured to the chair by the hearth. "Why don't you sit?"

"I can't sit," she snapped, flashing me a desperate look. "There are too many *feelings* running through me."

I gave her a sympathetic smile. No doubt this was a new experience for her. Like everything else in her life, my mother was used to controlling her emotions with an iron fist. "Please," I said, taking her by the arm.

She eyed me for a moment, then let out a reluctant huff and sat down. Since there was only one chair, I made do with the footstool.

"Now," I began, "I have not agreed to investigate, but I do think you are right about being prepared."

My mother's mouth curved in the faintest hint of a smug smile. "Good."

"What do you know about Charles Pearson and his family?"

She considered this for a moment. "His parents are both dead. The father had a position in the government, though I don't know exactly what he did."

"Does he have any siblings?"

My mother frowned in thought. "A sister, I believe. But I don't think she lives in London, though she'll probably come down for the funeral."

Funeral.

I would have to attend, of course. Funerals could be very informative in these kinds of situations. The murderer might even be in attendance themselves, if only to make sure they were not under suspicion.

"Do you know about his work?" I asked, trying to distract myself from the shiver running through me. "Delia said he dealt in art and antiques."

My mother let out a scoff. "Lots of gentlemen dabble in such things. I can't imagine he made much money off of it. And I'm sure he knew *all* about Delia's dowry," she added with a glower.

Barely two days ago, she had considered Charles Pearson to be a perfectly fine match for Delia, but I decided to hold my tongue. Besides, if he really was married, Delia's dowry was of little consequence to him. Unless the man intended to commit bigamy. And I was still stuck on the telephone in his flat. It seemed like an unnecessary expense for a man who was merely dabbling in art and antiques.

"What are you thinking about?" My mother's voice cut through my thoughts.

"Nothing," I answered automatically. "I'm just trying to

form a picture of Charles Pearson in order to decide whom I should speak to next."

Apprehension flashed in her face. "Perhaps you shouldn't be involved in this, after all. I didn't think—"

"Mother," I said gently, "I'll be fine."

She gave me a long look. "You must take care."

"I will. Of course." I gave her my most reassuring smile, but she didn't return it, only sighed in response. "I should go and get Tommy," I said as I rose. "But I'll come see Delia tomorrow."

"Good," she said with a distracted nod as she also stood.

We then exited the room and headed for the staircase, only to find Morris waiting on the landing.

"Madame, Mrs. Harper," he began with a little bow. "There is a gentleman downstairs—"

"I told you we aren't receiving callers today," my mother said with a huff.

"Yes, madame," Morris continued smoothly, ever the professional. "I told the man, but he was very insistent. He said it concerned Mrs. Harper and Miss Delia."

My mother froze beside me, but my heart lifted. Perhaps it was the inspector calling because he had caught the perpetrator. Then this could all be over.

"Who is it, Morris?"

The butler turned to me with a barely veiled look of interest. "Mr. Dorian, madame. And he asked specifically for you."

Chapter 9

I blinked at Morris, certain I had misheard and he meant the inspector. "You mean the detective?"

The butler shook his head. "No, madame. Stephen Dorian. He is an author of some renown. Mysteries, in fact. I've read a few myself. Very diverting," he added, with the barest hint of a smile, and I was so shocked to learn that Morris liked Mr. Dorian's books that for a moment I forgot all about my distress over his unexpected arrival.

However, my mother did not look the least bit impressed. "Well, you must tell him to go away. We don't want some *writer* here snooping about looking for ideas for his next book."

"No," I sighed. "It's nothing like that. We saw him last night," I murmured by my mother's ear.

Understanding dawned. "I see."

Then I turned to Morris. "I will speak to him."

"Very good. Shall I show him into the drawing room and call for refreshments?"

"That's fine," I said with a distracted wave, and Morris descended back down the stairs.

My mother placed a hand on my arm. “Shall I come with you?”

“No,” I said quickly. The only thing that could make this more awkward would be if my mother was in attendance. “I’ll be fine. He . . . he is the writer I knew on Corfu.”

Her eyes widened as understanding dawned. “I see.” My mother then waited for me to continue, clearly expecting me to say more, but that would inevitably lead to more questions I did not want to answer.

“I should go find your father anyway. It’s nearly time for his nap, and I am supposed to call on Lady Addison in an hour,” she said after a moment. “Good luck, Minnie. And thank you for helping your sister.”

“Of course,” I murmured.

She gave me a weak smile, then headed down the hallway to their suite. When she disappeared around the corner, I moved towards the stairs and paused at the landing, but couldn’t hear anything coming from the entryway. Morris must have already shown Mr. Dorian in. That was just as well, as I very much needed a moment to gather my thoughts. I continued down the stairs and stopped by a gilt-framed mirror in the hall to fix my hair. Then I gave a quick look around to make sure I was alone before giving my cheeks a pinch. There. I still looked tired, but not quite as ghastly pale as before.

Then I took a deep breath and charged into the drawing room.

I found Mr. Dorian, with his back to me, stooped over a dark walnut sideboard that was covered with a small collection of framed photographs. He held one in his hand and appeared to be studying it so intently that he did not notice my entrance at first. My eyes lingered ever so briefly on the broad set of his shoulders. His hair was also a bit longer than it had been on Corfu. I hadn’t noticed last night, probably because I had been trying to look at him as little as possible.

"Hello," I said, attempting for a casual, breezy air and failing miserably.

He immediately replaced the frame and whirled around. "Hello."

I glanced away from his inquiring gaze and walked towards an open chair, but I could feel his eyes upon me with every step. As I couldn't begin to know how to converse with him, I decided to stick with the strict rules that dictated social calls. "The tea cart should be here shortly," I said as I sat down.

"Ah. Thank you, but I won't stay long," he said, then strolled over and dropped into the chair opposite me.

My hands tightened on my lap, and my spine stiffened in response. Why on earth did I feel disappointed? I smothered the feeling and forced my mouth into a polite smile. "Very well. What brings you here?"

He tilted his head and gave me a wry look. As if we were something like friends. "Surely you have already deduced that."

I pursed my lips and cleared my throat. "Yes. Fine. The murder." If he wasn't going to bother with the standards of polite society, then I wouldn't either. "That still doesn't explain why you are *here*," I said pointedly.

His eyes narrowed. "Have you already forgotten that it was my coachman that brought Mr. Pearson home?"

"No," I said slowly.

"That makes him one of the last people to see the victim alive, apart from you and your sister."

"Yes, I am aware," I snapped.

He sat forward in his chair. "Then you are also *aware* that my brother is the detective on the case."

I shrugged, now assuming his earlier nonchalance. "Of course. I met him last night. He seems like an intelligent fellow. I suppose that is how you learned of the murder?"

Mr. Dorian's jaw tightened. "He woke me up at six this morning."

"Well, that must have been very difficult since you like to keep such late hours," I drawled.

His dark eyes flashed with irritation. "I haven't seen him in nearly a year. Not since the— "

But just then there was a scratch at the door, and a maid came in with the tea tray.

The divorce.

I was certain that was what he had been about to say. He had once mentioned that he and his brother were not close, and that the young inspector took issue with Mr. Dorian's line of work. Now I avoided his gaze and rose to meet the maid, grateful for an excuse to remove myself from Mr. Dorian's eyeline.

"Thank you," I said to the blond girl, who looked about the same age as Deirdre.

She gave me a shy nod. "Yes, ma'am." Then she cast a blatant look of interest in Mr. Dorian's direction.

I raised an eyebrow, which she noticed, and then quickly hurried out of the room. I rolled my eyes as she shut the door behind her, and began pouring myself a cup of tea.

"Are you sure you can't stay?" I called to Mr. Dorian over my shoulder. I had little interest in resuming our topic of conversation and hoped he would follow suit. "Visitors always rave about our Madeira cake."

"Not today," he replied. Only once I turned back to face him did he continue: "I'm working on a book, and the deadline is fast approaching."

I did my best to suppress any reaction, but I must not have been successful since his mouth curved just a bit. "Oh?" I said once I sat down. "Another Inspector Dumond novel?"

"No. It's something different," he replied as he crossed his legs, assuming that irritatingly casual air once more. "I don't want to talk about it much yet. Not until it's finished, anyway."

"Well, then I suppose you had better get back to it."

He watched me for a moment, no doubt trying to assess my interest, but I kept it carefully hidden beneath a stiff mask of politeness. "Yes, I suppose I should. But first I want to make sure you aren't planning on doing anything foolish, like involving yourself in this murder."

I had just taken a sip of tea and choked a little.

The absolute nerve of this man.

Once I recovered, I set down the teacup and shot him a glare. "I don't see how that is any of your concern."

"It isn't," he said, matching my expression. "But my brother seems quite certain you will meddle."

I huffed. "Did you say something to him about me?"

"Oh no," Mr. Dorian chuckled. "He came up with that all on his own."

Was the man actually amused by this?

"And your response?"

His amusement slowly faded. "I told him you should not be underestimated, but that you are an honest woman. Exceedingly so," he added, and I couldn't shake the feeling that there was more behind those words.

But I certainly wouldn't show my interest nor ask, so instead I simply lifted my chin. "I will take that as a compliment."

He chuckled again. "I certainly didn't mean it as an insult. How are the children?"

The sudden question took me by surprise. "They're well."

"I take it Cleo is here attending that school she was interested in back on Corfu?"

"Yes. In Hampstead," I answered, unable to hide my shock that he remembered.

Mr. Dorian nodded. "And Tommy is with you?"

"He is. We're staying at my aunt's home while she is on holiday," I replied, though it certainly wasn't necessary to tell him that little detail.

But Mr. Dorian only gave a thoughtful hum. "Have you taken him to the Natural History Museum yet?"

"No," I said, feeling a touch defensive. "But I plan to."

He smiled. "Good. He'll enjoy it." Mr. Dorian then pulled out his pocket watch and frowned. "I should go."

Before I could even respond, the man was already on his feet, heading for the door.

"All right," I managed to rasp, feeling a bit dazed.

Mr. Dorian paused with his hand on the doorknob and looked back at me.

"I meant what I said before, Minnie," he murmured, his gaze as stern as ever. "About the murder. This isn't Corfu. You must let Miles do his job."

Then, without another word, he opened the door and left the room.

I remained frozen in place, until I was certain that if I left the room there was no chance of us meeting again. And also because I needed time to regain my bearings.

I meant what I said before, Minnie.

I couldn't decide if I was annoyed by his outrageous presumption both in issuing such a warning to begin with *and* in using my first name, or touched that he cared enough to even bother making the trip.

Then again, I had no idea where he lived. For all I knew, he had simply strolled one street over. Perhaps Morris knew—*No.*

A warning note sounded in my head.

It didn't matter. None of it mattered. Not why he had come here nor where he had come from. I didn't want to know. Besides, I had mistaken his concern for more once. Much more. In fact, I had been on the verge of embarrassing both of us with some kind of impromptu declaration I could barely remember now when I learned that Mr. Dorian had packed up and abruptly left Corfu without bothering to say good-bye.

In the end, I was glad he had gone, of course. It was nothing more than a moment of temporary madness, no doubt brought on by the stress of our last investigation. Even still, as I waited there in my parents' drawing room, doubts began to creep in until I was forced to reassure myself that I really hadn't said anything to him. And that there was absolutely no way he could know what I had intended that day last spring.

Now you're being delusional in addition to absurd.

I gave myself a shake. I had lingered here long enough, and there was much to do. For despite Mr. Dorian's overbearing presumption, I would not simply stand aside and wait for the authorities to do their job. It did not matter that this was London and not Corfu. In my experience, incompetence could happen anywhere. And while I certainly had no intention of meddling, I did intend to do everything in my power to protect my sister.

But just as I made to leave, my gaze caught on the sideboard with the photographs. Curiosity suddenly burned through me as I approached and wondered what on earth had so interested Mr. Dorian. I stopped and glanced over the familiar pictures. Most of these were formal photographs of me and my siblings as children, along with Jack and Dolly's wedding portrait. But there was a new picture among them. I let out a surprised gasp as my hand shot forward to pick up the frame. It was my wedding portrait. I had stuck my copy away in a drawer somewhere when I couldn't bear to look at it after Oliver's death. I hadn't seen it in years and was struck anew by Oliver's handsome face and friendly smile—not to mention how very young we both looked. So full of hope and excitement.

We had posed for it shortly after the ceremony at a chapel in Cambridge. None of our family were in attendance, as everything had happened rather quickly because Oliver was due back in Athens. At the time, it had felt adventurous and exciting, but now I understood that there was an edge of callousness there as well. Back then, I had been utterly convinced that my family wanted to be rid of me and ignored anything to the contrary. But now I held that very evidence in my hand—framed in gold, no less. Slowly, I put the picture back down in its place as a wave of regret washed over me. Then I frowned and tilted my head as I studied the rest of the photographs. I looked over them three times just to make sure, but they were all framed in varying shades of silver. Which meant that the photograph Mr. Dorian had been studying so intently when I entered the room could only have been my wedding portrait.

I charged out of the drawing room, determined to outrun the strange swirl of emotions this realization had unearthed, and gathered my things. Morris then appeared out of the shadows to helpfully inform me that my mother had given me permission to use the family coach, so I took it to Jack and Dolly's house in South Kensington. I spent the entire ride chastising myself for daring to think for even a moment that Mr. Dorian's actions could indicate anything other than perfectly normal curiosity. And by the time I arrived, I was certain I had embellished the entire scene to the point of absurdity. I was promptly ushered inside by a footman who took my coat just as Dolly appeared in the entryway.

"Hello, my dear," she said warmly as she slipped her arm through mine and led me down the hall. "The children and I are in the parlor, while Jack is in his study, as usual." Then, once we were safely out of earshot, she lowered her voice, and her gaze filled with sympathy. "Your brother told me everything. What an awful business."

"Yes, it is."

I will admit I was a little surprised to hear that Jack had confided in Dolly. I rather expected him to keep his wife in the dark on most things, given how little time he seemed to spend in her company, but the nature of their relationship continued to mystify me.

"How is Delia?"

We paused just outside the parlor door, and I could hear the muffled sounds of the children chattering away inside.

"I'm not sure," I said on a sigh. "Last night was a horrible shock, of course. And I haven't seen her yet today."

Dolly made a hum of agreement. "Jack is quite worried about her. Poor thing. And your mother too."

We entered the room to find the children were playing some kind of card game by the hearth.

Tommy was not as thrilled to see me as I was to see him, but I suppose that was to be expected. And he certainly didn't know about the night I had.

"I know that look," Dolly said when Tommy immediately returned to the card game after giving me a halfhearted greeting. "Don't take it too much to heart. They have all been having such fun together."

I let out a little sigh as I sat down on the sofa beside her. "I am glad of that. Truly. It's only . . ."

Dolly gave me an understanding smile. "He's your little boy. And he's growing up."

The pang in my chest was sharp and swift. "Yes," I murmured, watching Tommy from across the room. "He is."

I startled a little as I felt a warm hand pressing against my arm. I met Dolly's sympathetic gaze, and for a moment I could see myself the way she must: a sad little widow on the cusp of middle age with her two children swiftly approaching adulthood, after which she would be alone forever.

"If you ever need anyone to talk to . . . ," she began, but there was no need to finish the rest, and I was grateful that she seemed to sense that.

"Thank you," I replied with a brittle smile.

Perhaps I wasn't being fair to Dolly. Or myself, for that

matter. For I was filled with a strange kind of certainty. An understanding that I didn't *want* to be that person. Didn't want that version of my future. I knew all too well that there was so very much I couldn't control about the world around me and the people I loved. But I could still forge a different kind of life. Find a new purpose now that my children were growing older.

"And you know," Dolly went on as she leaned towards me conspiratorially. "I was about your age when I had Franny. Then John came along as well. Our happy little accident," she added with a chuckle.

This was quite different from the scenario I had begun to imagine for myself, but Dolly mistook my surprise for encouragement and continued: "It is the perfect opportunity to find someone now that you are back here. Why, I can't imagine there are very many eligible men on Corfu. And I can think of several gentleman who would happily take on a widow, even one with children—"

"Thank you, Dolly," I said with a tight smile. "That is very kind of you, but I am not interested in being courted at the moment."

That was putting it mildly. In truth, I had absolutely no desire to be *taken on* by anyone. Least of all a man who thought he was doing me a great favor by marrying me. No, that didn't interest me at all.

Dolly nodded. "Of course. But do let me know when you are."

"I will," I said graciously, while thinking to myself *never*.

We chatted amiably about other more mundane topics while the children finished their game. "Are you sure you can't stay for tea?" Dolly asked.

"Not today, I'm afraid. Besides, I think I've imposed on you enough," I said with a glance at Tommy.

"Oh, heavens. Don't worry about that. He is welcome here anytime," Dolly replied.

"I appreciate that," I said, and meant every word.

Then I gathered my reluctant son and we said our goodbyes, while Franny and John extracted several promises from me that we would visit again very soon.

Tommy and I then left the room, and as we headed towards the front door, he told me every little detail about his visit. It was soothing, listening to him chatter away about inconsequential details. So much so that I didn't notice Jack descending the main staircase just as we were passing by.

"There you are, Minnie," he said. "Glad I caught you."

He made it sound as if I were trying to sneak off, never mind the fact that I had been here for nearly three-quarters of an hour. "Give us a moment, will you, Thomas?"

I prickled a little at that. Firstly, because no one called him Thomas, and secondly, because Jack hadn't bothered to ask if *I* wanted to speak with *him*. But Tommy looked entirely unbothered and loped off down the hall, likely returning to the parlor.

I let out a sigh, knowing that our exit would be delayed even more, and turned to Jack. "What is it?"

But he was still watching Tommy. "Does Harold know you're in town?"

"No," I said pointedly.

That was Oliver's older brother, the viscount. Tommy was currently his heir, though I still held out hope that Harold Harper, Viscount Mandeville, would have a boy after fathering four girls. After Oliver's death, the viscount took issue with my decision to stay on Corfu—or rather, my decision to keep Tommy on Corfu—and tried to bully me into sending him back to England for schooling. Things had taken an ugly turn, and I had to involve a lawyer. But Oliver's will was very clear, and the viscount had no legal standing. Eventually, I allowed him to write to Tommy, but there had been no communication between us since. And I had every intention of keeping it that way.

Jack frowned. "If he finds out you're here and didn't tell him, he'll be very cross."

"Well, I can't imagine why he would, unless someone goes out of their way to inform him," I snapped.

"Minnie," Jack warned, "you can't keep them apart forever. And there are things the boy should know about for when he inherits—"

"I don't want to talk about this," I said stubbornly. "And you know it isn't certain anyway."

Jack let out a dry laugh. "Given that Harold is nearly fifty and his wife is not much younger, I'd say it is all but guaranteed that Thomas will become the next viscount." Then his gaze softened ever so slightly. "Is that really such a bad thing?"

I glanced away. "Oliver thought so."

Jack sighed. "They had a difficult relationship. But that doesn't mean you need to as well."

I whipped my head back, outraged. "He tried to take my son from me," I growled.

"Only so he could go to school here. And be around his peers."

I closed my eyes and inhaled slowly. It was useless trying to argue with Jack about this. We simply had very different ideas of how the world should work. I didn't want Tommy surrounded by lazy, overprivileged boys. Oliver had been adamant about that. We wanted our children to have a different upbringing than our own. That was why we had moved to Corfu in the first place. And why Oliver made me promise to stay there, or so I had thought.

I opened my eyes and found Jack staring at me in concern. "I'm not trying to upset you, Minnie."

"I'm not upset," I said quickly. "I just don't want to discuss this. I've made my decision. Now then, I trust that wasn't what you wanted to talk about."

Jack looked reluctant to move on, but relented. "No. I

wanted to tell you that I have instructed my solicitor to look into Detective Inspector Dorian."

"Why?" That was not at all what I expected.

My brother huffed in exasperation. "Because if he doesn't do his job and tries to pin this murder on Delia, we need to be prepared."

I shook my head slowly. "Are you suggesting you're gathering evidence to use against him?

Jack's mouth tightened. "Only if necessary."

I may not have complete faith in the authorities, but I still found this rather appalling.

"That's—"

"How things are done here," he said sternly.

I scoffed at this rather convenient justification, then another thought occurred to me. "Are you having someone look into the murder as well?" My brother shrugged in answer. "I can't believe you!" I hissed. "And after all that rot you said about not wanting me to be involved!"

"Well, I *don't*," he insisted. "Because it isn't safe. But that doesn't mean I'm going to sit back and twiddle my thumbs while some upstart detective from Hackney tries to blame a murder on my sister."

The Dorians were from Hackney? I couldn't ignore my interest in this bit of information Then I shook my head. Now was not the time. "That isn't remotely the case."

"Not yet," he corrected. "And as I said, we will only act if necessary. Though I expect we will find something worth ensuring his cooperation, especially if he's anything like his brother," he added.

I pressed my lips together. Mr. Dorian's divorce last year had been the subject of intense speculation and gossip. That scrutiny had been a large part of why he had fled to Corfu in the first place. Luckily, Jack didn't seem to know of our connection. At least for now.

"Well, I do not support this at all," I said primly.

"I think you will if things take a turn. But what I said this morning still stands. You aren't to involve yourself. Besides, Delia needs you."

On that we agreed, at least.

"I know," I said softly. "I will visit her tomorrow."

Jack gave a distracted nod. For once, I didn't want to know at all what he was thinking about. "Good. I will keep you informed of any developments. And I made sure Scotland Yard knows to go through my solicitor first if they want anything from you."

"Thank you." It was, admittedly, a relief to know I couldn't be brought in for additional questioning without any notice. That would be a very difficult scenario to explain to Tommy.

"Of course." Jack then gave me a short nod in good-bye and headed down the hall. For a brief moment, I rather envied the cozy scene that awaited him: the children and Dolly all gathered around the warm hearth with a full staff waiting at the ready to supply their every desire. Then I turned away sharply. "Tommy?" I called out. "It is time for us to go."

Chapter 10

Despite my exhaustion, my sleep that night was not as restful as I would have liked. I awoke several times, spurred by disjointed memories of both the previous night and my meeting with Mr. Dorian. As such, I woke much later than usual. When I was finally dressed and ready to face the day, I found Tommy cataloguing to our housekeeper all the various insects he had found on Corfu over the years.

Mrs. Ford was doing a decent job of feigning enthusiasm until Tommy mentioned earwigs. Then she shot me a panicked look.

"Good morning!" I trilled.

"Good morning, Mrs. Harper," she said with a grateful smile. "Tommy has just finished a plate of creamed eggs, toast, and some fruit."

"I ate all of my breakfast, Mama," Tommy crowed as I sat down beside him.

"Yes, he did," Mrs. Ford said. "And what can I get for you?"

"The same would be lovely. And a pot of tea. Thank you, Mrs. Ford."

"Oh no. Thank *you*," she murmured with a wink and slipped out of the room.

I then turned to Tommy, prepared to listen to the all-too-familiar litany of creatures, but instead he surprised me: "May we go to the Natural History Museum today, Mama?"

I blinked, immediately recalling Mr. Dorian's suggestion from yesterday. "What on earth made you think of that?" I braced myself for the answer—though, of course, there was no way he could have seen Mr. Dorian.

"My cousins were talking about it. They go all the time. Franny says there is a skeleton of an entire *whale*."

"Ah," I said with relief. "Well, I'm afraid we can't go today since I have to visit Aunt Delia. But perhaps tomorrow?"

Tommy pouted a little, but then gave a nod. "All right. May we go to the park instead?"

"Yes. For a bit. But I must have my breakfast first, darling."

Tommy granted this request and loped off somewhere. Hopefully, he wasn't planning to accost Mrs. Ford with more descriptions of insects. As I waited for my food, I turned my gaze to the picture window that overlooked the back garden. Another grey London sky today. And likely a chill to match. A little sigh escaped me, as I thought longingly of our terrace on Corfu, where we ate many of our meals. I had grown quite spoiled with the weather in Greece. But now I resolved to appreciate the abundant sunshine and warm dry air with wild abandon when we returned, whenever that would be. This elicited yet another sigh. When I first left, I had imagined returning before the worst of winter came to England, but the likelihood of that grew dimmer by the day. Now, with this murder business, we might well and truly be stuck here for some time. And if that was the case, there were things I needed to attend to, including buying Tommy and myself some more warm clothing.

Mrs. Ford returned with my breakfast a short while later. "Here you are, Mrs. Harper."

"Thank you. This looks lovely."

I hadn't realized just how ravenous I was until she placed the tray before me, and I wasted no time tucking in. I had eaten several bites of egg and toast before I noticed she was still standing by the door, waiting. I tilted my head in inquiry.

"I was just wanting to make sure you are all right, Mrs. Harper."

After I put Tommy to bed last night, I had told her a little about the murder, and she was, of course, horrified.

"Yes, thank you for asking," I replied. "I'm well, all things considered."

She watched me for another moment and seemed satisfied by whatever she saw. "Your aunt did say you were made of sterner stuff than most ladies."

A surprised laugh escaped me. "Did she?"

Mrs. Ford nodded. "Oh yes. And she is an excellent judge of character."

I responded to this with a smile. I loved Aunt Agatha dearly and appreciated everything she had done for me over the years, but she was often overbearing and quick to judge. Frankly, I was lucky she had taken such a liking to me when I was a child. For she had never warmed to Delia in the same manner, and there had been a stark difference in the way we were treated, though I wasn't sure my sister was old enough at the time to notice.

"And should you need any more help with Tommy," the housekeeper continued, "I am happy to oblige. Just as long as he doesn't mention those foul bugs again," she added warily.

"Thank you. That is very generous," I said. "I do need to visit my sister this afternoon, if you don't mind. And I will absolutely make sure Tommy does not discuss that with you anymore."

"Yes, that is no trouble at all," Mrs. Ford said before turning apprehensive. "Those ear . . . things he mentioned. Are those real?"

"Earwigs, and yes. I'm afraid so."

"Good heavens," she muttered under her breath. "I don't know how you could ever live in such a place."

"Well, it helps that they aren't found inside. Usually," I amended, but that was little comfort to the housekeeper. She left the room with a stricken look on her face, and I ate the rest of my breakfast alone.

Afterwards, I accompanied Tommy to the park, where we explored for nearly two hours until I had to practically force him back to the flat for luncheon. I was chilled to the bone, and our noses and cheeks were as red as apples, but Tommy only seemed exhilarated by the bracing fresh air. We enjoyed sandwiches and steaming bowls of soup before it was time for me to leave. Tommy seemed unconcerned, and when I left, he was tucked up on the sofa in the parlor with an old world atlas that must have belonged to my late uncle and thus was likely very out of date.

On the way to Portman Square, I stopped in a nearby flower shop and bought a small bouquet of hothouse flowers for Delia, then took a hansom cab the rest of the way. By the time I arrived, the bouquet had wilted a little from the cold, and I couldn't shake the feeling that it was an omen for what was to come.

So now, in addition to delusional, you've become superstitious as well?

I silenced the snide little voice in my head as I paid the driver and ascended the stairs to my parents' home. I had grown so accustomed to entering the house over the last few days that I no longer felt that awkward hesitation. Cartwright, the same footman who usually manned the door when Morris was busy elsewhere, ushered me inside.

"Are my parents in?" I asked as he took my coat.

"Mrs. Everly is out at the moment, ma'am."

"And my father?" I prompted after a moment.

"He is . . ." Cartwright hesitated, as if searching for the right word. "Indisposed."

I frowned at that description. "Is he ill?"

"Not that I am aware," the footman said as panic flashed in his eyes.

I gathered that people didn't come to call on only my father very often anymore. Though it was probably for the best, given his current state, the thought still made me very sad.

"I understand. Thank you."

He gave a quick nod and disappeared with my coat, no doubt eager to leave before I could ask him any more bewildering questions.

I took my bouquet upstairs and knocked softly at my sister's closed bedroom door. Her muffled voice responded after a moment, and I entered.

Delia was tucked up in bed with a book open on her lap, but her gaze was listless and unfocused, and I surmised she hadn't read a word.

"Hello, darling," I said as I shut the door behind me.

A look of surprise flickered across her face for just a moment. "Oh, hello there."

I sat down at the edge of the bed and handed her the bouquet. "For you."

Delia managed a faint smile as she took them from me and brought them to her nose. "Beautiful. Thank you."

"How are you feeling?"

Delia avoided my gaze as she placed the bouquet on the bedside table. "How did you do it?" she whispered.

I tilted my head, confused. "The flowers?"

She looked at me then, her eyes suddenly bright with desperation. "Go on. After Oliver."

I was silent for a moment as my mind flooded with a haze of disjointed memories of those awful weeks after his death. There were times when I could barely bring myself to get out of bed, which no doubt was how Delia felt now. And, if I was very honest with myself, I'm not sure I would have bothered if it hadn't been for the children. But I couldn't tell her that. Shutting herself away would not make this any easier. That was something I had learned.

"I took things as they came," I answered. "And sometimes I could only manage for an hour at a time. Then, eventually, I could get through the entire day."

Delia nodded in understanding. "I'm so sorry," she rasped.

"Whatever for?" I asked, genuinely bewildered.

"For not being more understanding about how difficult it must have been for you. And why you were so determined not to leave Corfu." Then she hesitated. "I'm afraid we all were rather too hard on you back then. Making demands you couldn't possibly accommodate."

"Oh." I wilted a little, not unlike the bouquet I had brought. There had been times when I felt that my family hadn't really understood the impact Oliver's death had on me and disapproved of my decision to stay on Corfu rather than return to England. No one had ever mentioned anything outright, of course. But it was one thing to wonder and another to have it confirmed.

Delia reached out and took my hand in hers. She felt far too cold. "Forgive me."

I grasped her chilled fingers. "Of course. And you were so young. How could you have possibly known?"

Her mouth flattened into a line. "I resented you for leaving. And when Oliver died, a part of me thought it was a kind of punishment. It was so awful of me. I suppose now this is my punishment," she added quietly and hung her head.

Perhaps if I had been younger, I would have found her admission appalling. But motherhood had given me insight into the viciousness of love. Delia felt abandoned by me, and in a way, she was right. I had been rather dismissive of her and our relationship.

"Don't," I urged. "Don't ever think that. You did nothing to deserve this. No matter what you may have thought about me. I should have been more understanding of your feelings as well. And I am sorry for that. But this . . . Delia, I know you loved Charles, and what happened to him is awful. But it doesn't need to color the rest of your life. Especially if he really was married to someone else and lying to you about it. Not that he deserved to die, of course," I added hastily, but Delia didn't seem to be listening.

She looked up at me then, her face ashen. "I think I'm with child."

My ears rang as the meaning of her words slowly sunk in.

"But—but I thought you said you were careful," I sputtered, feeling a bit thick.

Delia glanced away. "I meant we were careful not to be seen alone together. Not that we hadn't . . ."

I let out an exasperated sigh. Well, this certainly complicated matters. "Did he know?"

"No. That was another thing I meant to tell him. It's only been a little over a week since I missed my courses." I sighed again, as any other response I could manage at the moment would not be helpful. Delia suddenly looked fearful. "You won't tell Mother, will you?"

I let out a harsh laugh. "If you really are pregnant, I'm afraid she will catch on eventually."

"I know. But maybe by then I will have found a solution."

"Delia, the only solution would have been to marry as

soon as possible," I snapped. And now that option was gone. Charles already being married was far less of an obstacle than death.

My sister's eyes filled with tears, and I felt horribly guilty. "I've been such a fool," she said as she buried her head in her hands.

"No, I'm sorry. I shouldn't have spoken so harshly," I said as I rubbed her back. "We will figure something out. I promise."

Delia wrapped her arms around me in a tight embrace. "Thank you," she said through her tears.

I was glad she had such faith in me, but I couldn't ignore the pit in my stomach.

For it was now more imperative than ever that I determine who the murderer was. And there wasn't a moment to waste.

I sat with Delia a while longer, and when she admitted she hadn't had anything to eat since breakfast, I rang the bell to request tea and soup.

"You must keep up your strength," I said while we waited. "Especially now."

She gave me a faint smile. "Thank you. It's nice to be doted on. You're very good at it."

I paused in the act of fluffing her pillow. "Am I?"

Delia rolled her eyes good-naturedly, and it was nice to see some of her old spark return. "You know you are."

Like most women of her class, our mother had been distant, both emotionally and physically. Nanny had provided the affection we craved as children, but it hadn't entirely made up for being kept at arm's length from one's own parents. Raising my children away from London society had emboldened me to treat them with the loving care I longed to have from my own mother.

"It's nice to see you with Tommy as well," she added with a thoughtful look. "To know that there is another way to be a parent."

"There are many, many ways to be a parent," I said. "But thank you. I try my best and have failed more often than I would like to admit."

Delia smiled at that. "I appreciate your honesty."

I laughed. "Glad to hear it. Because you will be hearing quite a bit more from me."

A maid arrived then with the tray of food, and I helped Delia settle back against the pillows.

"Now then," I began once we were alone again, "I have no intention of leaving until you finish your soup."

"Very well," Delia said as she dutifully picked up her spoon. But after a few sips, she turned pensive. "Do you think the police will find the killer?"

"I think Detective Inspector Dorian seems very capable."

"He's the brother of Mr. Dorian, isn't he?" I was surprised that she had picked up on that little detail while in the midst of a great personal tragedy. "They look alike," she explained, noting my surprise. "Especially when they're frowning at you."

A surprised laugh erupted from me, and Delia smiled in return. "You never did mention what happened between you on Corfu," she said after another few sips.

I narrowed my eyes, not at all fooled by her casual tone. "I told you I was his typist."

"I think it must have been a good deal more than that."

I bristled at the suggestion in her voice. "What on earth does that mean?"

She set down the spoon and tilted her head. "Did you really not notice the way he looked at you?"

I crossed my arms. "Like he was just as surprised and annoyed to see me as I was to see him?"

Delia choked out a laugh that nearly upset the tray. Then

she sobered. "My God, you're serious. Minnie, you can't possibly think— "

But I was saved from whatever rubbish she was about to say when there was a scratch at the door and the same maid from earlier entered. "I'm so sorry, Mrs. Harper, Miss Delia," she said in an anxious rush. "But there is a gentleman downstairs. He's come to call on the both of you. Mr. Morris asked me to see if you are at home."

Delia and I exchanged matching looks of surprise. It was outside normal calling hours, and I couldn't think of anyone in London who would call on me, especially here. Well, anyone except Mr. Dorian.

"Here is his card," the maid continued, holding it out.

As I took it, I immediately noticed the fine quality of the cardstock. And a glance at the name revealed why.

"It's Lord Linden," I said as I handed Delia the card. This was surprising indeed.

"I suppose he has heard the news," she replied cryptically. Then she lifted her eyes to mine. "Perhaps you should speak to him."

It seemed unlikely that his lordship would have already spoken to the police. And I would not miss this chance to ask him some questions. "All right." Then I turned to the maid. "Tell Morris I will see him."

The girl gave a little curtsy. "Yes, ma'am." And hurried from the room.

"How well did Charles know the baron?" I asked my sister.

"Quite well, I think. I believe they had known each other since school. Or at least since Cambridge."

"Hmm. I wonder if either of them knew Oliver." He had also attended Cambridge, and likely around the same time.

But Delia shook her head. "Charlie certainly didn't. I told him about Oliver, and he would have mentioned knowing him. There was no reason to lie about it."

I gave a bland smile in response. "Of course." While I certainly didn't think Charles was necessarily lying about knowing Oliver, it was possible that the man did possess a capacity to lie about very important things. And I should probably approach the baron with a healthy dose of skepticism as well. I rose from the bed. "I'll come check on you after he leaves. And to make sure you've finished your soup," I added archly.

Delia picked up the spoon with a heavy sigh. "Yes, yes. There won't be a drop left."

"Good," I said, then kissed her forehead and left the room with a newfound determination thrumming in my veins.

It was time for the investigation to begin.

Chapter 11

Morris had ushered the baron into the drawing room, and as I walked down the hall, I was struck by a sense of déjà vu. Not a full day had passed, and here I was engaging with yet another male visitor—alone. But, of course, neither visit was anything close to romantic in nature. Mr. Dorian had stopped by merely to issue his warning, and the baron was likely here to pay his respects. I forced my brow to relax, as it seemed to automatically frown whenever I thought of Mr. Dorian, and stepped into the room.

Unlike that irritating man, I found Lord Linden reclining on the sofa looking a bit bored and not at all interested in his surroundings. Someone, possibly Morris, had had the good sense to open the curtains in this room, and the baron's hair looked several shades lighter than it had the night of his party. It was more auburn than chestnut. He noticed my entrance and immediately rose and bowed over my hand, every bit the perfect gentleman—also very different behavior from Mr. Dorian.

Stop thinking about him.

"Mrs. Harper," the baron said, entirely unaware of my

thoughts, "thank you for seeing me. I'm so terribly sorry about Mr. Pearson. I came to offer my condolences."

"That is very kind, my lord," I said, with a polite smile. "Please, sit."

He returned to his place on the sofa, while I took the chair across from him. "How is your sister? I'm sure she must be devastated," he continued, his eyes full of what seemed like genuine sympathy.

"It has been a difficult time, yes. I will tell her you called. And may I also offer you my condolences? I understand Mr. Pearson was an old friend of yours."

"We had known each other for many years, yes. He will be missed, indeed. The funeral will be held at St. Mark's at the end of this week," he continued. "I've taken the liberty of planning it since Charles's sister does not live in town."

"That is kind of you," I said.

"It is the very least I can do for an old friend," he replied with a solemn nod. "It is a private affair, but I can make sure that you and your sister are on the guest list."

"Thank you. I'm not sure Delia will be well enough to attend, but I will." It could also be an excellent opportunity to see who made up Charles Pearson's circle. The murderer could be among them.

"Consider it done," the baron said.

I briefly considered asking him if Mrs. Pearson would be in attendance, but decided it was better to claim ignorance on that front. If the police learned that Delia had gone to Charles Pearson's flat that night specifically to discuss his marital state, they might consider it a motive for murder, and the investigation would be further diverted away from finding the true killer. Besides, there was someone else I could speak to if I wanted to learn more about this supposed spouse.

"Could you allow me another imposition on your kindness, my lord?"

He leaned forward a little in interest. "Certainly."

"I was hoping to contact the medium at your party."

"Madame Fontaine?" He sat back in surprise.

"Yes, do you know where I might find her?"

The corner of his mouth lifted in amusement. "Why? Are you thinking of hiring her for a soiree?"

"No, nothing like that. Just something she had said during my reading that I wanted clarification on. It's silly, I know." I lowered my head, pretending to be bashful and hoped it worked.

The baron chuckled as he pulled out a card case from his jacket pocket. "Say no more, Mrs. Harper." He flipped through a handful of cards, then stopped. "Ah. Here we are." He held up a card and read the front while waggling his eyebrow: "Madame Fontaine: Acclaimed Medium and Spirit Guide to the Other Realm," he read with dramatic flair before handing it to me. "She is in Soho."

"Thank you very much," I replied, as I took the card from him.

"I must say, I'm a bit surprised," he added, giving me an assessing look.

I tilted my head, genuinely curious. "Why?"

He shrugged. "You didn't strike me as the superstitious sort."

I wasn't, in fact. And yet I couldn't help feeling rather offended by his judgement. "Sorry to disappoint," I said a bit icily.

"I never said I was disappointed," he murmured, while holding my gaze. "Merely intrigued by what she told you."

Something about the way he looked at me caused my cheeks to heat, and my mind scrambled for a reply. This conversation had spun away from me rather quickly. "It . . . it was to do with my late husband."

"Oh." This had the intended effect, as the baron sat back

in his chair, while the gleam in his eyes dimmed. "I'm sorry for your loss."

"Thank you," I said with a gracious nod as another opportunity presented itself. "Perhaps you knew him. Oliver Harper? He was a student at King's College."

The baron furrowed his brow. "Was he a relation of the Viscount Mandeville?"

"The viscount is his older brother."

"Ah, well then. I'm afraid I didn't know your husband, but I was friendly with Harry. Good chap. Haven't seen him in years. How is he?"

"Fine," I replied, forcing my mouth into a smile and hoping he didn't notice my clipped tone.

The baron waited a moment, and when it was clear I wouldn't offer any further update on my brother-in-law, he returned my bland smile. "Well, I don't want to keep you. I just came to pay my respects and tell you about the funeral."

"It is very much appreciated," I said, as we both stood.

"Good afternoon, Mrs. Harper," he said with a short nod, then headed for the door. Just as he reached it, the baron paused and looked back at me. "And do let me know how your visit with Madame Fontaine goes," he added. "I find myself rather curious if her talents extend beyond entertaining my guests at parties."

Then he disappeared into the hall before I could reply. Alone once more, I sat back down on the sofa and turned over the card in my hand.

Though the baron seemed like the type of man who set out to charm every woman he met, I couldn't help feeling a little flattered by his attentions, as shallow as they might be. I was not used to being in the company of such a man, and it was a good reminder that things were different in London. Especially now that I was no longer an unmarried young lady. I would be treated much differently as a widow and had heard tales of women who reveled in unparalleled levels of freedom granted by their new status. While I wasn't interested in engaging in anything close to wild, reckless debauchery, I could admit it was intriguing to think of having new experiences. In many ways, my life on Corfu had been small and simple. That had also been by design, of course. And in the years after Oliver's death, I needed the pace of my life to be slow and predicable. But now, for the first time since I had arrived, I pictured all that the great metropolis of London had to offer and felt a little rush of excitement. An eagerness to see what lay in store. I looked down again at the card in my hand and my fingers curling around the edges. It seemed my first stop would be a visit to Soho.

I looked in on Delia before I left and was relieved to find her fast asleep. Then I dashed off a quick note, explaining how the baron had stopped by to pay his respects and that I would come visit her again tomorrow. I decided not to mention the funeral, at least not yet. She was certainly in no state to attend, and in her condition, it could be much too overtaxing.

Rather than take the family coach and risk someone gossiping about my destination, I decided to hail a hansom cab. The journey from our genteel little corner in Portman Square down to Soho was quite different in the daylight than it had been the other evening. As we drew closer to the location of Madame Fontaine's salon, the streets grew more crowded, the shopfronts shabbier, and the pavement littered with all kinds of discarded refuse.

When the cab finally stopped in front of a dingy building, I peered out of the window. There, just above the doorway, was a sign that read: MADAME FONTAINE'S SPIRITUAL SALON in bold, if slightly weathered lettering. I hesitated for a moment, then paid the driver and climbed down.

As I gazed up at the front of the four-story building, a voice echoed in my head: *You wanted an adventure, didn't you?*

I pursed my lips, straightened my shoulders, and marched towards the entrance. The door opened onto a little stairwell, and I looked over the directory. The building was home to an eclectic assortment of professions. In addition to Madame Fontaine, who occupied the top floor, there was also a dentist, a bookkeeper, and a wigmaker. As I ascended the stairs, I amused myself by imagining a person who patronized each of these businesses in the course of a single day. But as I passed each floor, they were all eerily quiet, save for the dull sound of the dentist's drill, and I picked up my skirts to move a little faster. When I finally reached the top floor, I was breathing hard and had to stop to catch my breath before I entered the salon. A frosted door was embossed with the same title as the sign outside, but as this one had not been exposed to the elements, the lettering was as bold and crisp as the day it had been painted. I approached the door, then paused, unsure of the etiquette. Did one knock or simply enter a spiritual salon? I decided to try both and gently rapped on the door as I turned the knob. It opened easily, and I stepped into what appeared to be a waiting area.

I let out a breath, relieved that I hadn't interrupted anyone's reading or walked into the middle of a séance, and moved around the small space. It was surprisingly cozy and far nicer than the outside of the building had led me to expect, decorated with a thick burgundy carpet and emerald drapes, while a sofa in matching emerald fabric took up one wall. A red-beaded curtain hung in a doorway, and the air was perfumed with a heady mix of musk and roses.

Framed photographs lined the walls, and as I examined one, it took me a moment to understand what I was looking at. It was a spirit photograph. They all were. I had read of such things, but never seen any in person. This one depicted a woman in widow's weeds, and just above her head was a cloudy mass. I leaned in closer and squinted, but then the features of a child's face came into focus, and I drew back with a start.

"Goodness," I murmured under my breath and turned away from the unsettling image. While some people found comfort in such things, I was not among them. I moved towards a small, black-lacquered desk set before the hearth with a bell and a placard that read RING FOR SERVICE. I glanced around, then picked up the bell and shook it. A clear, high-pitched trill rang out through the empty room, and I put the bell back in its place. After only a few moments, I heard the tread of footsteps, and a figure appeared on the other side of the beaded curtain. Black-gloved hands parted the curtain with a dramatic flair as Madame Fontaine practically glided into the room. She was dressed in another modest black gown, and while her face was not quite as pale as before, her lips were painted a similar shade of deep red.

"Welcome to my house of spirits," she said in the same heavily accented voice from the party. "I am Madame Fontaine and"—she stopped short as her dark eyes widened—"it's you."

"Hello," I said with a bright smile, noting that her accent had gone from vaguely Eastern European to distinctly East London. "I guess you remember me, then."

Madame Fontaine crossed her arms and lifted her chin. "I have nothing more to say."

I tilted my head, curious at her reaction. She was acting awfully defensive, and I hadn't even asked her anything yet. "Have the police been here?"

She looked aghast. "Certainly not!"

"But someone else has," I said, narrowing my eyes. "I came here to ask you about the baron's party, though I take it I am not the first?"

Madame Fontaine glanced away from my admittedly prying gaze. "No," she said slowly.

I waited for her to continue, but apparently she was not in

a chatty mood. I let out a huff. "You told my sister something about Charles Pearson."

Indeed, she gave me a mulish look. "Then why don't you ask her?"

My jaw tightened with irritation, and I reminded myself I needed this woman to help me. "You said he was married. Is it true?"

"I charge five shillings for readings," she said flatly.

"Fine."

She held out her gloved palm. "And I take payment first."

"Very well," I muttered as I pulled out my reticule. "There," I said, after I gave her the money.

She flashed me a wide smile. "Follow me," she said as she turned around and glided back through the beaded curtain.

"I don't need the theatrics," I called out. "Just the information."

But her only response was the swish of the beads. I let out a grunt and followed in her wake. This room was smaller and darker, lit only by a pink-shaded lamp. The musky scent was much stronger too. Madame Fontaine had taken a seat behind a small round table covered in a damask cloth and gestured to a chair before her.

"Please, sit."

"Now will you tell me?" I asked as I slid into the chair.

"I wanted to be somewhere safe," she said, lowering her voice, "in case anyone was listening."

I reared back a little. "Like who?" As far as I could tell, we were the only people on this entire floor.

The woman looked incredulous. "Charles Pearson was killed, wasn't he?"

"Well, yes. But—"

"Can't be too careful when there is a murderer afoot," she said with a sage nod.

"I really don't think—"

"So," she continued, "you want to know what I know about Charlie."

"If you don't mind," I replied with exaggerated politeness.

"I met him years ago when I was just a chorus girl," she began, looking a bit wistful. "Well before I became Madame Fontaine."

I frowned. "What is your real name?"

But she smiled and shook her head. "It will cost you quite a bit more for that information."

"Go on, then."

"I didn't know him very well on a personal level," she continued. "But he came by the theater regularly to see Miss Adeline Brooks, the leading lady of that particular production. It sent all of us chorus girls into a frenzy. He was so dashing, we thought he was like a prince. They married in secret once the show closed."

"If it was in secret, then how do you know?"

"Theater people are the worst gossips in the world. If you want to spread a rumor, tell an actor you have a secret in the morning, and it will have reached every corner of London by noon." When I did not join in her laughter, she continued. "Anyway, the story went that once his father heard about the marriage, he demanded an annulment. But it was too late for that, if you follow my meaning, so dear old Charlie paid Adeline to keep quiet about their marriage. Promised her he'd make a formal announcement once his inheritance was secured."

From what I understood, his parents were both long dead. "And did he?"

Madame Fontaine shrugged. "Last I heard, Adeline took his money and went to Italy. I don't think she's been back in England since."

My shock must have been clear on my face because Madame Fontaine sobered. "Listen, love. I saw Charlie sniffing around your sister, and when she asked me about her future with him, I told her the truth: that as long as he was still married, they didn't have any to speak of. At least, not in the legal sense. And she didn't seem the type to be content as a mistress."

I pinched the bridge of my nose. "Not at all. She expected him to propose."

Madame Fontaine's gaze turned sympathetic. "Well, I could be wrong. Perhaps Charlie and Adeline had reached some kind of agreement so he could marry again. I haven't a clue."

I frowned. "Even if he had, that doesn't excuse him lying to her about his marital state in the first place."

"No. It doesn't," Madame Fontaine agreed. "But what I do know—what I believe deep down to the very marrow of my bones—is that men like Charlie are always looking for the next new shiny thing. And that sister of yours looked pretty new and shiny to me. I'm sorry she's been hurt, but if you ask me, things would have been far worse for her in the end if she had been able to marry him."

As callous as the sentiment was, I couldn't say I disagreed with it. I sat back in my chair as I mulled everything over. "Do you think Adeline had a reason to kill him after all this time?"

She let out a barking laugh. "I think a lot of people had a reason to kill Charles Pearson."

I narrowed my eyes. "What do you mean?"

Madame Fontaine waved a hand. "I overhear a fair amount in my line of work. And I know you can't be a man about town like he was without running up a few debts and double-crossing someone. Charlie probably got himself into a situation he couldn't charm himself out of. I've seen it more times than I can count," she added, with a mournful shake of her head. "Those fellows think they're invincible right up to the very end. They can't seem to help themselves."

"A terrible shame, death by hubris," I said dryly.

She let out a surprised laugh. "I must say, you're quite different than the usual toffs at the baron's parties."

"Well, don't be fooled," I replied drolly. "I'm just as spoiled as the rest of them."

She watched me for a long moment. "You're here, though. Asking about him."

I shifted a little, uncomfortable under her inspection. "My reasons are purely mercenary, I assure you."

Her mouth curved in a slow smile. "I don't believe that for a minute."

I cleared my throat. Time to change the subject. "So this," I began, gesturing to the room, "is all an act then."

She tilted her head. "I prefer to call it a performance."

"What about my fortune? You said I had come from a great distance. That I had suffered a loss. And that there was a man in my future I needed to be careful of."

I tried to control my voice, but the desperation seeped through. The subtext was clear: *How did you know?*

Madame Fontaine lifted a shoulder in an elegant shrug. "A reasonable guess, given that crowd. And it's never a bad idea for a woman to be cautious about the men in her life."

A fair point. "And the photographs?" The question was out before I could stop myself, along with the distinct note of disappointment.

Her eyes softened. "People believe what they need to," she said gently.

I blinked as if I had been in a daze. What was the matter with me? Of course, none of this was *real*. Yet I was determined to argue with this woman over the veracity of her own lies. I gave her a stiff nod, but her gaze remained sympathetic.

"I know not everyone approves of what I do," she went on. "That there are those who claim I am preying on the grieving. But I do try to help my clients find some solace. If they think their loved ones are at peace, then they are better able to let go. To move on in some small way. Often, that's the best they can hope for."

I glanced away from her knowing look. Her ability to communicate with the dead may have been a sham, but the woman seemed uncommonly perceptive to me. "I understand."

"Then perhaps you can tell that to your friend," she said, with sudden acidity.

I snapped my gaze back to her. "Friend? What friend?"

"That writer. Mr. Dorian." She practically spat out the name. "He threatened to ruin me."

I shook my head, confused. "He was here?"

Madame Fontaine's eyes widened as she appeared to realize something. "Yes. But never mind. I've said too much."

"I think not," I said archly.

But the woman was already out of her seat and hurrying to the curtain. "I have an appointment. It is time for you to leave." She extended her arm towards the doorway.

I eyed her for a moment before deciding that attempting to cajole more information out of her was a waste of time and that I would have better luck with my *friend*.

"Very well," I said, as I rose with all the dignity I could muster. "Thank you for your time."

She gave a little nod of acknowledgment. "Have a good day." But just as I passed by, she grasped my arm. "Do remember what I said, though. About the man."

I cannot say for certain whether this man is to be trusted or not.

I raised my eyebrows in question as I recalled her words. "I thought it was only general advice."

Her dark eyes held mine. "Then call this intuition. Anyone can possess that, Mrs. Harper," she added, as I began to respond. "It is no trick."

I gave a little nod and left. My thoughts swirled as I descended the staircase, mulling over all I had learned. Mr. Dorian had been here. But why? Was he investigating the murder as well? That bothered me a great deal, especially after he had made such a show of warning me away. Of not interfering in his brother's investigation. I let out an irritated huff as I reached the street. I had just successfully hailed a passing hansom cab and was about to climb inside when something else occurred to me:

I had never told Madame Fontaine my name. Yet she knew it all the same. And there was only one person who could have told her. The reason escaped me, but it would not for long. I frowned as I gave the driver my aunt's address. Then I took my seat and shut the door with more force than necessary.

Mr. Dorian had a great deal of explaining to do.

Chapter 12

Upon returning to my aunt's flat, I found Mrs. Ford in the kitchen preparing our evening meal and Tommy playing with some toy soldiers in his room. He was so occupied by the scenario he had created that he barely acknowledged my greeting, which was just as well because I had work to do. I disappeared into my room, pulled out a notebook, and began to record my encounter with Madame Fontaine.

I had started this practice during my last investigation, and it proved particularly helpful in keeping track of details. After nearly an hour, I had dutifully recorded our exchange as well as everything I could remember from the night of Charles Pearson's murder. I had been remiss in not writing down those details earlier and promised myself I would not be so careless in the future. By that point, the sky had darkened considerably, and I could smell something delicious coming from the kitchen.

The rest of the evening passed quickly. Over a delectable supper of roast chicken and vegetables, Tommy told me about how he had spent his day while I was out. And I was grateful that he had not yet reached the age where he was particularly curious about how I had spent my time away from him. For instance, if Cleo had been here, she would not have been satisfied by my brief explanation that I had visited my sister. In fact, I was certain she would have already learned about my reunion with Mr. Dorian, if not the murder itself. As much as I was relieved that I had been able to keep that information to myself, my chest still twinged at the thought of my absent daughter and her insatiable, insistent curiosity. Though she was only a carriage ride away in Hampstead, it often felt like a much greater distance. Or perhaps it was the knowledge that she was on the cusp of womanhood now, and soon enough she would have a life of her own entirely independent from mine.

"Mama? May we?" Tommy's voice cut through my maudlin thoughts, and from his tone, I knew this was not the first time he had asked.

"Sorry, darling," I said. "May we what?"

"May we go to the Museum of Natural History tomorrow? You promised we would," he added with a knowing little look that reminded me more of an adult than an eight-year-old boy.

I couldn't help my smile. "You're right. I did promise. And yes."

His eyes lit with excitement. "First thing?"

"First thing," I agreed.

Naturally, this was all Tommy wanted to talk about as we finished our supper and I put him to bed. Rather than reading another chapter from *Treasure Island*, he insisted on the entry for the museum in the Baedeker guidebook, and I'm certain he must have fallen asleep to images of animal skeletons and ammonites.

The next morning, Tommy was up with the sunrise, even though, as we had learned last night, the museum didn't open until ten. He passed the time by reading the guide again, then searched my aunt's shelves for any book remotely connected to the subject of natural history. While he made a mess of her shelves, a thought occurred to me: I didn't know where Mr. Dorian lived, but perhaps I could send a message through his publisher, Mr. Howard.

He owned the villa next to ours on Corfu and had given his star client the run of the property last spring. I didn't know Mr. Howard very well, as he rarely spent time in Corfu, but I felt certain that he would pass on a message to Mr. Dorian for me. What I would relate in said message was another matter I still needed to think on. At least, it should be something more substantial than the accusations currently swirling around my mind.

At half-past nine, Tommy practically pushed me out the door, and we descended down the front steps. He wanted to be there right when the doors opened. That seemed rather unnecessary to me, but as Tommy was a ball of excitement, it was better to get him out of the house.

"I think we should start with the Mammalian Collection first," he began. "Then the Geological and Paleontological Collection. That's the fossils, Mama."

"Oh, yes. Good idea," I replied rather absently.

He continued to happily dictate our itinerary while my thoughts wandered, which was why I failed to take notice of the man walking towards us until I felt Tommy stop short at my side.

"Mr. Dorian?"

I frowned down at my son, entirely confused for a moment. Had I somehow spoken my thoughts aloud? But before I could question him, his face lit with joy, and he broke into a run.

"Tommy!" I called after him as he raced down the pavement towards someone.

Only then did I realize that it was, in fact, Mr. Dorian. He grinned as Tommy approached, and I could barely make out their muffled greetings. After a few moments, they both looked back at me, and I realized I hadn't moved from my spot. It was as if I was frozen in place.

"Mama, look! It's *Mr. Dorian*," Tommy said, as if I was very dense and hadn't recognized him.

I blinked and gave a stiff nod as I willed my legs to move. "Yes. Yes, of course. Hello," I said, once I joined them.

"Mrs. Harper," Mr. Dorian said, returning my nod before addressing Tommy. "I heard you were in London and came to pay the two of you a visit."

"Is that so?" I said flatly at the lie. "I'm amazed to see you conscious at this hour," I added in a low voice.

Unfortunately, my barb did not have the desired effect, given that the corner of the man's mouth curved up. "I hoped to catch you before you started your day."

"We are going to the Natural History Museum," Tommy chimed in.

"Are you, now?" Mr. Dorian replied before shooting me a smug smile. "A wonderful place."

"You should come with us then," Tommy said eagerly.

"Tommy," I began, "I'm sure Mr. Dorian is very busy—"

"Not really," he interrupted. "I'd be happy to join you. If you'll have me, that is," he added with an innocent little look that did not fool me at all.

I narrowed my eyes at him. The odious man very well knew he had put me in an impossible position. "Fine."

"We can take my carriage," he said. "It's just round the corner."

Tommy let out a whoop of delight and took each of us by the hand. "Let's go!"

I could feel Mr. Dorian's gaze on me as we were tugged towards the direction of the carriage, but I refused to look at him. The cool morning air had a bite to it, and I instinctively curled inward. Tommy, of course, seemed completely unaffected and practically skipped down the pavement.

Suddenly, I felt a heavy hand at the small of my back and nearly jumped from the unexpected sensation. "Come, Mrs. Harper," Mr. Dorian murmured by my ear. "The coach is warm."

"Thank you," I rasped, then stepped quickly ahead until his hand fell away from me. The place where he had touched me still prickled from the sensation.

If Mr. Dorian noticed this rejection, he did not comment on it. "Here we are," he said once we reached his coach. The driver had climbed down from his perch and opened the door for us. Tommy moved to climb in, but Mr. Dorian placed a hand on his shoulder.

"Ah, ah. Ladies first, Tommy," he said, and my son immediately fell back.

I raised an eyebrow at Mr. Dorian, reluctantly impressed. "Thank you," I said, as I picked up my skirt and allowed the driver to hand me in.

Mr. Dorian was right. His coach was warm and cozy. Far more so than I had noticed on the night of the murder. As I settled into the plush seat, Tommy clambered onto the bench across from me. Mr. Dorian was right behind him, and I was surprised when he slid next to me. Then he pulled out a soft cashmere blanket that had been tucked in a corner by the door and wordlessly spread it over my lap. It was only when he tilted his head and gave me a questioning look that I realized I had been staring at him in openmouthed surprise.

"Thank you," I muttered, then quickly turned away as the coach rocked to a start.

But since Tommy was eagerly staring out the window, he could not provide the distraction I sought. Luckily, the trip should not be terribly long, so I settled for staring out the window as well.

"Aren't you going to ask why I came to see you?" Mr. Dorian murmured once we had been traveling for some minutes.

I kept my gaze fixed firmly on the passing street outside. "No."

He hummed, as if giving my short answer great consideration. "Because you don't care or because you have already deduced the reason?"

I pursed my lips and resisted the urge to roll my eyes, lest Tommy see such an obvious display of contempt. "A little of both."

Mr. Dorian let out a soft chuckle. "Indulge me then, Mrs. Harper."

That elicited a scoff from me, and I whipped my head to face him. Of course, unlike me with my stiff posture, the man was practically lounging beside me, one arm slung across the back of the seat, his hand dangerously close to my person. "I assume you came to scold me," I whispered as I darted a glance to Tommy, who seemed blissfully unaware of our exchange. "Which is neither your place nor your concern."

Mr. Dorian said nothing for a long moment as he stared back at me intently with that dark gaze of his. This silence was nearly as maddening as his presumption, and I was on the verge of saying so when he finally spoke: "You are wrong," he said smoothly. "On both accounts."

I frowned and sat back. "You overreach, sir."

Anger sparked in his eyes then, and he leaned towards me, just a little. "Well, someone needs to protect you from yourself," he hissed.

A strange combination of anger and embarrassment began to spread through my chest at his words, and I turned away. There was nothing more I could say to this man in front of my son. But though I could not see Mr. Dorian, his presence was like a lodestone around my neck. Heavy, stifling, and impossible to ignore. I stared out the window, seeing nothing, while his words echoed in my head. As the minutes ticked by, the coach seemed to become smaller and the air stuffier until I thought I would burst if I could not get out.

Then, all at once, the coach came to a stop.

"Here we are," Mr. Dorian drawled, as if the last quarter hour had been nothing more than an amusing little diversion rather than a particular kind of torture.

"Mama, look!" Tommy gestured out the window.

I blinked. It felt as if I had just woken from a dream and noticed that we had arrived. I had forgotten how much the museum looked like a cathedral.

"Isn't it marvelous?" Mr. Dorian said, as if he had read my thoughts. But he did not wait for my response and instead opened the door. Tommy practically leaped after him, and together they stood on the pavement waiting for me.

I forced a smile as I climbed out of the carriage. There was already a group of people out front waiting for the doors to open.

"Have you been here before?" Mr. Dorian asked as we ascended the steps that led to the grand entrance, where two towers flanked the arched doorway.

"Once. Not long after it first opened," I said. "My brothers were a lot like Tommy as a boy. Jack, the MP, loved fossils, but Samuel was absolutely mad about all sorts of animals. Sea creatures in particular."

I inadvertently smiled at the memory and Mr. Dorian returned it before his gaze followed Tommy racing just ahead of us. "What does he do now?"

"Samuel works for the Foreign Office. He joined at the same time as—as my husband. Only he was stationed at the embassy in Istanbul. But now he is in Bombay."

I hoped Mr. Dorian hadn't noticed my slight hesitation when speaking of Oliver. It remained something of a sore point between us, given the accusations he had made against my late husband.

Somewhere above our heads, a bell rang out the hour, and the doors to the museum were opened. We slowly moved through the entrance alongside the other visitors.

"Tommy," I called out. "Stay with us, please."

He reluctantly returned to my side, and together we made our way into the Great Hall. I only had a vague memory of my last visit here of a cavernous space full of sunlight and oddities. But as we entered the room, I saw that my memories were not so very far off. The Great Hall was massive, with a ceiling that stretched towards the heavens and really did resemble a cathedral. Only instead of an altar and religious relics, this was a monument to earthly creations. A massive skeleton was displayed in the center, while glass cases containing all manner of flora and fauna surrounded it.

"There it is!" Tommy cried out, pointing to the skeleton. "*Physeter macrocephalus!*"

I cocked my head. "What?"

"It's a sperm whale," Tommy explained in a rush before he ran towards it.

"No running!" I called, after which he slowed down only marginally.

"So then," Mr. Dorian continued as we trailed in Tommy's wake. "You and Samuel have both lived abroad this whole time?"

His question caught me off guard. "Well, yes. We have. But that is not so uncommon," I added, unable to keep the defensive note out of my voice.

"It isn't," he agreed. "I'm just surprised, is all. You seem to be very close with your sister."

I shot him an incredulous look. "How could you possibly know that?" The man had seen us together for all of ten minutes, at most.

"I don't," he replied, meeting my eyes. "It was merely an assumption. Then I take it you're not?"

I pointedly turned away and kept my gaze on the massive skeleton before us. I didn't want to answer his question. Didn't want to talk about myself with him at all. The man had seen me at my most vulnerable back on Corfu and then proceeded to suggest my husband had been both a liar and a traitor.

"I am close to a decade older than her and have been out of the country for even longer," I said, by way of explanation.

He was silent for a moment as he considered this. "But you are here now. And determined to protect her."

"Yes," I agreed softly. "I am."

"No matter the cost to yourself? Or your children?" He stopped short and turned his whole body towards me.

I stopped as well and let out a harsh sigh. "No, Mr. Dorian. I learned my lesson on that front quite thoroughly last time and am taking better care. You should be able to find comfort in that."

He narrowed his eyes at my flippant remark. "I will not apologize for being concerned for your welfare."

"Concern is not the same as control," I shot back, and unfortunately, the words rang out in the large space. A few heads turned in our direction, and I made sure to lower my voice when I spoke again: "You cannot truly expect me to just sit at home while my sister is in distress and simply hope the authorities do their job. Meanwhile, how many people have you interviewed?"

"That is not the issue—"

"No, that is the *entire* issue," I hissed. "You don't have any more confidence in the police than I do, or else you wouldn't be making your own inquiries."

"Mrs. Harper—"

"She is my sister," I said, pressing a hand to my chest. "I know she is innocent. But I also know how this case must look to a man like your brother. And perhaps he really will conduct a thorough investigation, all in the name of justice. But I am not willing to bet her freedom—her *life*—on it. And I will not apologize for that."

Then I turned on my heel and marched towards my son,

who had reached the head of the great beast and was staring up at it like the marvel it was. I tamped down my anger as much as I could and focused my tattered attention on Tommy. "Wherever did they find this?"

He didn't even tear his eyes away. "It washed ashore in Thurso, Scotland, in 1863," he replied.

I raised an eyebrow. "I take it that was in the Baedeker as well?"

"No," he said, finally looking at me. "I read about it in one of Aunt Agatha's books."

"Oh." I could feel Mr. Dorian behind me, but I refused to look back at him.

"Was it the one about Sir Richard Owen?" he asked.

Tommy's eyes lit up as he turned to him. "Yes! That's it. He was a natural scientist, Mama, and it was his idea to open this museum. He even came up with the name for dinosaurs."

"Fascinating," I replied, though I was still distracted by my exchange with Mr. Dorian.

"I think I would like to be a natural scientist someday," Tommy said quietly, his eyes on the skeleton once more. Well, that certainly got my full attention.

"An excellent idea," Mr. Dorian said. "Lots of schooling ahead of you, though."

Tommy nodded solemnly. "Do you remember our neighbor on Corfu? Mr. Papadopoulos?"

"I do," Mr. Dorian said, and I could have sworn his shoulders stiffened at the mention of the man. He had never particularly taken to Mr. Papadopoulos, though I didn't understand why.

"He said I should go to Cambridge if I want to be a scientist," Tommy explained. "Because that is where Mr. Darwin went."

"Did he now?" I said archly, for this was the first I had heard of this. Though my son had a seemingly insatiable interest in the animals and plants on Corfu, he had never discussed making a career out of it. And yet he had apparently come up with an entire educational plan with Mr. Papadopoulos.

Tommy frowned in thought. "But if I want to go to Cambridge, I would need to go to a school like Cleo is doing so she can go to Girton." Then he turned to me. "Right, Mama?"

My heart vaulted to my throat, and I was unable to do more than a single short nod in response.

"Why don't we move on?" Mr. Dorian stepped in. "I believe there is a mammoth skull around here somewhere."

That immediately garnered Tommy's attention, and he took Mr. Dorian's offered hand. I followed a few steps behind them as my mind whirled.

Chapter 13

I spent the rest of our visit in a kind of dull haze, moving from display to display, but barely able to focus. Mr. Dorian, however, was in fine form and provided an excellent audience for Tommy's boundless enthusiasm. When we had finally finished, he suggested we visit a tearoom nearby.

We found a table tucked away in a corner, and as we took our seats, Tommy went up to the counter to view the cakes and pastries on display.

"Thank you for today," I said. "You were very patient with him."

He flashed me a crooked smile. "It's no trouble, Mrs. Harper. I enjoy the boy's company." Then his gaze softened to concern. "I take it this was the first time he mentioned wanting to attend school in England."

I gave him my profile. "I don't want to talk about that."

He let out a sigh. "Then would you at least like to hear about the latest developments in the case?"

I whipped my head back. "You would tell me?"

"I hadn't planned on it," he remarked sardonically. "But

since you are so determined to involve yourself, you should at least be informed."

I leaned forward in my seat, unable to hide my excitement. "Well? What do you know?"

"They have ruled out a burglary gone wrong, as nothing of value appears to have been taken, even though the place is stuffed to the rafters with treasures."

My stomach twisted a little. Though I hadn't ever really thought a burglar had bashed Charles Pearson's head in, it was another possibility that would have taken the suspicion firmly away from Delia. "So, they think it's personal," I said.

Mr. Dorian nodded. "They are looking into his background as we speak. And of course, that means . . ."

"Delia is still a possible suspect."

"I'm afraid so."

I swallowed hard. "What of Madame Fontaine? You spoke to her, didn't you?"

But before he could respond, a young woman in an apron approached our table, followed swiftly by Tommy.

"Good afternoon," she said with a sunny smile. "What can I get for you?"

"A large pot of tea for the lady and a coffee for myself," Mr. Dorian said before addressing Tommy. "What have you decided on?"

"The Victoria sponge looked very good, Mama," Tommy said, with pleading eyes.

I couldn't help smiling at him. "All right. We will take a slice of that," I told the girl.

"That one is my favorite too," she told Tommy with a wink, and he ducked his head shyly as she walked away.

As his cheeks turned pink, I felt a bittersweet pang in my chest. He was growing up so quickly now, and all I could do was watch. But I did not have much time to ruminate as the girl swiftly returned with our drinks as well as the cake, which was as delicious as it looked.

"Did you really only visit the museum once before?" Tommy asked between comically large bites of cake.

"Yes, I'm afraid I was more partial to the South Kensington Museum as a girl," I replied, as I poured us both a steaming cup of tea.

Mr. Dorian gave me a considering look over the rim of his coffee cup. "That one is mostly art, correct?"

Tommy made a face. "Sounds dull."

I laughed. "Not to me. My favorite was the room with all the casts of masterpieces like Michelangelo's *David*. It's an important museum," I said, now warming up to the subject. "Not everyone can travel to places like Rome or Athens to see such things in person, but why should that stop them from experiencing great works of art?"

Mr. Dorian was watching me with one of those inscrutable looks I couldn't begin to interpret. "Well said," he murmured, while Tommy shrugged and took another forkful of cake.

"I suppose," he conceded. "But I still like the Natural History Museum better. Because that one has skeletons."

"To each their own," I said with a smile.

Once we finished, Mr. Dorian insisted on paying, despite my protests.

"May we walk home through the park?" Tommy asked once we were back on the pavement.

"Certainly." By then, the day had warmed considerably, and there was even a bit of sun poking through the clouds. I was just about to bid Mr. Dorian good-bye when Tommy asked him to accompany us.

"If that is all right with your mother," he replied, turning to me.

I managed to mimic our server's sunny smile. "Of course."

Together, we headed to Hyde Park, which was just a short walk away from the tearoom, and once we were past the gate, Tommy raced ahead.

"I truly do not know where he finds the energy," I marveled.

Mr. Dorian chuckled. "It's because he doesn't have to worry about anything or work for his supper."

"Yes, that's true." I hadn't thought about that. But then, from what he had shared back on Corfu, Mr. Dorian's childhood hadn't been very idyllic.

"You asked about Madame Fontaine," he said, as if he had heard my thoughts and was deliberately steering the conversation away from himself.

I nodded. "What made you visit her?"

"Mrs. Langham suggested it," he said, and my jaw tightened. But, of course, he would have discussed this with his . . . his . . . whatever Mrs. Langham was to him. "They know each other from the theater scene, and apparently she knows a great deal about the baron's set on account of her . . . work." His mouth twisted a little as he said the word, and I recalled his threat to expose Madame Fontaine.

"You don't approve of her," I replied, and he turned to me, surprised.

"Of course not. She's a charlatan. It's one thing to provide entertainment for people like Lord Linden, but she makes the bulk of her coin preying on those who can barely afford it. Surely you can agree."

I tilted my head in consideration. "I might have thought so before I met her. But I can see how she provides a kind of comfort for the grieving. And anyone who is so desperate as to try to commune with the dead needs all the solace they can find. Even if it's made up." Mr. Dorian scoffed, and I raised an eyebrow in challenge. "Is that really so different from speaking with a priest?"

He stared back at me in wonder. "Are you telling me you are a nonbeliever, Mrs. Harper?"

I looked ahead. "I'm merely saying that both provide a service that is based on faith. On a belief in something that cannot be seen." Mr. Dorian hummed in response. I turned back to him. "So what did she tell you, then?"

"That Charles Pearson was a bit of a cad—and married to boot. Madame Fontaine seemed to think he owed people money."

"She said the same to me." Then I pursed my lips. "I need to know more about his business with antiques. The man had a telephone in his flat, you know."

That seemed to take Mr. Dorian by surprise. "Did he, now?" Then he frowned in thought. "I assumed he inherited much of his wealth and the antiques were more of a hobby."

"No, I don't think so. One doesn't install a telephone over a hobby."

"Quite right."

"Perhaps he double-crossed someone, and they killed him," I suggested. "I know your brother doesn't think anything was taken from the flat, but how would he even know? From what I saw the man had a number of valuables in his possession."

"That is one possibility," Mr. Dorian allowed. "But I am afraid you are overlooking the most likely suspect: the wife."

"But Madame Fontaine said she lives abroad."

"She could have returned, though," he pointed out. "And she will likely inherit everything. The spouse is always the prime suspect for that reason."

I mulled over this for a moment. "All right. Say she did return to kill him. Why now?"

Mr. Dorian shrugged. "Maybe she needed money."

"Or," I began as an idea formed, "she knew Charles wanted

to marry again and that she would no longer be his beneficiary. Even if he was in debt, I'm sure that collection of his is worth a pretty penny."

He raised an eyebrow. "That is certainly a motive."

I leaned forward. "Have you discussed any of this with your brother? Does he think Mrs. Pearson is a suspect?"

Mr. Dorian rolled his shoulders. "I haven't spoken to him about this case since the morning after the murder."

"But then how did you know about the development—"

"Because I paid for that information," he said grimly. "Don't look so shocked."

"I'm not shocked," I lied. "I'm confused. Why can't you just ask him?"

His jaw tightened. "My brother would never willingly share information about a case he is working on with me. And he would only do that under great duress. He does not approve of my profession, Mrs. Harper."

I shook my head. "I thought he read your books."

He let out a humorless laugh. "My brother doesn't read my books."

"But he mentioned—" Then I stopped short, as I very much did *not* want to finish that sentence.

"Mentioned what?" he prompted.

"Just . . . something he said made me think he had read your last book," I replied, hoping that would satisfy him.

Mr. Dorian narrowed his eyes. "What did he say?" He spoke slowly, emphasizing each word.

I swallowed and looked for Tommy. He was up ahead near the Serpentine, but too far to save me from this conversation. "He seemed to think the dedication was connected to me," I said in a great rush as my cheeks heated.

It sounded utterly ridiculous now that I spoke it aloud, and to him of all people. The deafening silence that followed was all the confirmation I needed from Mr. Dorian.

"I see," he finally replied.

I managed a nod in response, as I couldn't look at him just yet. At least I could blame this assumption on his brother and found comfort in the knowledge that he would never know that I too had made the same inference once.

I cleared my throat, desperate to move on. "You told Madame Fontaine about me, then?" I cast a quick glance at him.

"I merely asked to be informed if you came to call on her." Then he shot me a look. "It seemed a good way to know if you really were conducting your own investigation."

Given the woman's reaction to my appearance, I suspected he did more than simply ask. "And did you say that to anyone else?"

"No. But then I haven't gotten around to speaking with anyone else," he admitted. "Have you?"

"I'm not telling you," I said, like a petulant child.

He gave me a rather smug smile. "That's a no, then."

I rolled my eyes, but was secretly glad we were back on safer ground. It was far better to be annoying each other than attempting to broach the past. At least now I could lay that last delusion to rest and put it all behind me.

"I was thinking of speaking to Mrs. Pearson," he said after a moment. "If she is in town, of course."

"And how exactly do you intend to find her?"

"Well, I expect she will make an appearance at her own husband's funeral," he said easily.

I arched a brow. "You're going?"

He mirrored my expression. "Aren't you?"

I turned away with a scowl. It felt as though the man had a copy of my diary. "Yes," I said with a reluctant nod. "But that isn't until the end of the week."

"I'm open to your suggestions in the meantime," he said, spreading his arms. I snorted in response. "You may as well tell me what you're planning, Mrs. Harper. I'll find out anyway."

I bristled at his confidence. This man really did think he had me all figured out. "I haven't decided yet," I said loftily.

He watched me for a moment. "Very well. But do let me know who you land on."

I did not respond to this and instead moved ahead. Tommy was now on the bank of the river, poking at something with a stick, and I needed to intervene.

"You can't do this alone," he called out.

I did not look back and simply raised my hand. I did not agree, of course, and Mr. Dorian would never think such a thing about himself. I felt more determined than ever to seek out the truth, now with the added benefit of proving him wrong.

Once I shepherded my son away from the water, we did not speak of the murder again. Instead, I let Tommy lead the discussion, which naturally revolved around all the creatures we had seen at the museum. Mr. Dorian walked us all the way to Hyde Park Street, but just as I was about to bid him good-bye, Tommy spoke up.

"You must call on us again next week, Mr. Dorian," he said eagerly.

"Only if your mother allows it," the fiend replied, shooting me a questioning look.

I bit back a sigh. "Of course. If you can find the time, that is. I know you are very busy," I added.

Mr. Dorian smiled. "I am. But I can always make time for the Harpers."

It took everything in me not to narrow my eyes at this pronouncement, while Tommy cheered in delight. We then mercifully parted ways.

"Did you not tell Mr. Dorian we were coming to London?" Tommy asked as we headed back to my aunt's flat.

"No, I did not," I admitted and held my breath, as I truly did not want to explain that Mr. Dorian and I hadn't been on speaking terms these last few months, or the events that had precipitated that. But luckily, this answer seemed to satisfy Tommy, and I let out a breath of relief. If Cleo had been with us, for example, she would have been relentless in her pursuit of the truth.

We arrived back at the flat around three in the afternoon, and I decided to pay a visit to Delia and see how she was faring. I asked Tommy if he wanted to come with me, but he was more interested in reading through more of my late uncle's reference books. After Mrs. Ford assured me she didn't mind keeping an eye on Tommy, I set out for Portman Square.

I was ushered inside by Cartwright, the footman. "Hello. I've come to see my sister."

He nodded as he took my coat. "I believe she is in the parlor with a visitor."

Well, this was encouraging news. Not only was Delia up, she was receiving guests.

"Good. And is my mother in?"

"No, Mrs. Harper. She has gone out."

I was just about to reply to this when a young woman came down the hall. She wore a long, dark blue coat that matched her eyes and a hat I recognized as being a few years out of fashion, as mine was quite similar. Her light brown hair was tucked neatly, if plainly, under her hat.

"Hello there," I said as the footman took my coat. "I'm Mrs. Harper. Delia's sister."

Her eyes lit with recognition. "Yes, of course. I'm Mrs. Braithwaite. I came to call on your sister."

This was the woman who had acted as a chaperone during Delia's outings with Charles—though given my sister's current state, I assumed she hadn't taken her role very seriously. But perhaps that was unfair of me. Even a diligent chaperone couldn't watch their charge all the time. In any case, this was someone I very much wished to speak to. And better still, someone Mr. Dorian had no idea existed.

"That is very good of you. I came to do the same."

"She's just gone upstairs for a lie-down," Mrs. Braithwaite said, then leaned in towards me. "Poor dear. I think the grief is taking a toll on her," she murmured.

I gave a sober nod even while I was relieved that the woman must not know of the pregnancy, as that was the more likely explanation for Delia's late-afternoon nap.

"Do you have a moment?" I asked, flicking a glance towards Cartwright, who was still manning his post by the door.

Mrs. Braithwaite followed the movement and gave a hesitant nod. "Certainly."

"I will be in the parlor with Mrs. Braithwaite," I said to the footman before ushering the woman down the hall.

She and Delia must have only recently vacated the room because a healthy fire still roared in the hearth and the tea service still remained.

"Shall I ring for more?" I asked, gesturing to the teapot.

"Only if you wish," she said. "I'm very well."

As I moved to tug on the bellpull, I took a moment to look over Mrs. Braithwaite. Admittedly, I had assumed she was older than Delia, given her marital status, but with her round, angelic face and nervous expression, she seemed younger. I took the seat across from her and noted that the cuffs of her coat were worn and several buttons on the front had been replaced by ones that did not exactly match. Delia had mentioned that her husband was a relation of Earl Drummond, but I knew very well that being related to an aristocrat was no guarantee of wealth.

"My sister said you met at Slade," I began after I asked for a fresh pot of tea from the maid who answered my ring.

"Yes," she said with a quick nod. "We were in all the same classes, Delia and I. She sat next to me on our very first day and introduced herself. She was so friendly. Some of the other girls were not as welcoming." She hesitated. "I was there on scholarship, you see. But Delia never made me feel like I didn't belong because of it. We've been friends ever since."

I smiled. "I'm glad to hear that. And have you been married long?" I couldn't help wondering how a scholarship student crossed paths with the relation of an earl.

"No. Just under a year," she said, dipping her chin shyly. "We met at the Royal Exhibition, actually."

"How lovely."

"My husband is a barrister, but he always wanted to be an artist," she explained with an indulgent smile. "He's been so supportive of me. I feel like the luckiest woman in the world." Then her expression clouded. "What an awful thing to say with poor Delia upstairs. I was so sorry to hear about Mr. Pearson, and even sorrier that she found him. I can't imagine . . ."

I let the silence stretch for a moment before I continued my questioning.

"I understand you were the one who introduced them."

She gave a solemn nod. "Charlie—that is, Mr. Pearson—was a friend of my husband's. Back in the spring Delia, myself, and a few other girls we knew from Slade put on a little art show and Charlie came by one night with my husband."

I narrowed my eyes. "And that is when they began courting?"

Mrs. Braithwaite's cheeks flushed prettily, and she looked away. "More or less, I believe."

The woman might be married, but Delia seemed far more worldly than this shy creature.

"She said you often acted as their chaperone."

Mrs. Braithwaite cleared her throat and kept her gaze on the rug. "I did. Yes."

"I'm not here to chastise you. I know that my sister and

Mr. Pearson were not exactly following all the rules of courtship."

She glanced up in surprise. "You do?"

I nearly laughed at her expression. "Yes. Though I trust that you will keep any indiscretions on their part to yourself."

"Of course," she said with a fierce nod. "Yes. Delia is my very best friend, and I would never do anything that could hurt her."

God help me, I believed her. "Then you must understand the gravity of the situation and how important it is that we find the murderer."

She cocked her head in confusion. "Is . . . is Delia in trouble?"

I leaned forward. "You must tell me everything you know about Charles Pearson. For Delia's sake."

Mrs. Braithwaite reared back a little and blinked rapidly. "I . . . I don't know much. At least, not anything that would be helpful."

"You would be surprised," I said with a gentle smile. "Do you know anything about his work involving antiques?"

"Only that he was mad about them," she said. "But I don't know if he did anything I would classify as work. He was a gentleman." Then she paused, as if remembering something and flushed again.

"What is it?" I coaxed.

She shot me a hesitant look. "Benjamin, that's my husband, complained about him once, even though they really were great friends," she added hastily. I nodded for her to continue. "He had come back from a night out and was grumbling because Charlie never paid for anyone else's drinks even though he inherited a fortune from his father."

I raised an eyebrow. "When was this?"

Mrs. Braithwaite shook her head. "I'm not sure. Months ago. The summer, at least."

"Did your husband think he was having money troubles?"

She snorted a laugh. "Not at all. He thought he was tight-fisted. But I really don't know." Then she paused again. "Charlie was very keen on ancient artifacts, though. Especially these peculiar little marble statues from Greece. Very crude-looking things. Large heads with no defining features to speak of. Smooth bodies. I don't know what he saw in them."

The hairs on the back of my neck stood. I knew the statues she spoke of. They were called Cycladic figurines. While Oliver had still been working at the embassy in Athens, the pieces were quite popular with collectors abroad and were often smuggled out of the country. "Are you sure?"

"Oh yes. He loved to talk about his collection and was always adding new pieces. Perhaps you saw some of them in his flat?"

"I'm afraid I didn't look very closely," I admitted.

"Right. Of course. I think he might have sold pieces to people as well, but I'm not sure."

I narrowed my eyes. "Mrs. Braithwaite, these pieces are illegally sold on the black market."

Her eyes widened. "What?"

"I lived in the country for many years, and it was an ongoing problem. Dealers would claim they were duplicates or worthless in value in order to circumvent the current law."

She shook her head. "I had no idea."

"I'm sure that is true, but a collector like Mr. Pearson would absolutely have known." And likely priced such items accordingly. Now I very much regretted I hadn't taken the chance to look around more carefully while I had been in his flat.

"How awful," Mrs. Braithwaite said. Then her gaze shot to mine. "You don't think his murder had something to do with it?"

I shrugged. "People have certainly killed for less."

My flippant answer seemed to horrify the young woman, but before I could attempt to mollify her, a maid entered the room with the fresh pot of tea.

Once we were alone again, I began to pour myself a cup. "My apologies if I've upset you. But, unfortunately, this is not the first time I have encountered a murder."

She gave a slow nod, though her face remained pale. "It's just a shocking thing."

"Can you think of anyone I could speak to who might know more about his collection?"

Mrs. Braithwaite thought for a moment. "I suppose Mr. Henshaw might know something. He runs the Elysium Gallery."

I took a bracing sip and set down my cup. "Excellent. Thank you."

She looked confused. "But aren't the police conducting an investigation?"

"They are," I admitted. "However, in my experience, it is still a good idea for one to pursue all possible avenues of inquiry."

"You mean . . . you don't trust them," she said meekly.

For a brief moment, I regretted that I was about to shatter her illusion. "No, Mrs. Braithwaite," I said gently. "I'm afraid I don't. And I must do everything I can to protect my sister."

She sucked in a sharp breath as understanding dawned. "Oh, dear lord. They think she might have done it?"

"I believe she is a suspect, yes. But she did not kill Charles. I am absolutely certain of that."

"No. No, of course, she didn't," Mrs. Braithwaite said,

then her face fell. "But, oh. She could go to prison—she could *hang*!"

"Calm yourself, Mrs. Braithwaite. We are a ways off from that, at least at the moment. That is why you must tell me anything that may be of use."

She nodded. "I will. I promise. And I'll ask Benjamin anything too."

"That would be very helpful," I said with genuine gratitude.

Chapter 14

Mrs. Braithwaite left a short time later, as she needed to be home to greet her husband. But she promised to ask him everything he knew about Charles and write when she had more information.

I then remained in the parlor alone, mulling over all I had learned. I was determined to speak to Mr. Henshaw next and felt confident he would know more about Charles Pearson's dealings. But it was the mention of the figurines that spurred another memory long forgotten. While working at the embassy, Oliver had often lamented the Greek government's poor laws on the antiquities trade, which allowed for the export of artifacts if they were labeled as duplicates or considered superfluous. Unsurprisingly, these labels were often applied with abandon and with the full knowledge of the superintendent of antiquities. Oliver's attitude seemed at odds with Mr. Dorian's accusations about him trading on the black market. But perhaps it had all been some kind of misunderstanding and my husband had actually been rescuing these artifacts? I let out a sigh and pressed my hands to my face. Was I just being hopelessly naïve again or was this something I could actually prove?

As I didn't have time at the moment to embark on yet another investigation, I decided to focus on a task I could actually complete. I had just resolved to go upstairs and check on Delia when the door to the parlor swung open and my mother entered.

"Morris told me you were in here," she said by way of greeting.

I rose as she approached. "Hello, Mother." Then I bussed her cheek, and we both sat down.

"Did you speak with that Mrs. Braithwaite?" she asked.

"Yes. She was very helpful."

My mother tsked. "I should hope so, given that she is the reason your sister is in this mess in the first place."

"That is quite a leap, Mother. The woman merely introduced her to Charles. She isn't responsible for Delia's actions afterwards."

She waved a hand in frustration. "I know all that," she said crossly. "Still, she should have known better."

It was on the tip of my tongue to ask *who* should have known better, but it felt fruitless. We weren't going to agree on this, so I decided to change the subject. "You were out making calls today?"

She perked up a little. "Yes. I've just come from Lady Asquith's. I thought it best to pay my calls as usual, so as not to create any suspicion," she added.

I raised an eyebrow. "I can't imagine any of that set know of Delia's connection to Mr. Pearson."

My mother wrinkled her nose. "Of course not. People spoke of the murder, of course. But no one said anything about Delia and we must do everything in our power to keep it that way." I relaxed a little. Her reputation was still safe, for now. "I did meet an old school friend of yours while I was there. Mrs. Wentworth. She is Lady Asquith's niece. You probably remember her as Miss Cecelia Morton."

I perked up. "Yes, we were at Girton together."

We hadn't kept in touch after I left England, but I had always liked Cecelia.

My mother nodded. "A very amiable young woman. Her husband works at the Home Office, and she has two boys and a girl."

I couldn't help bristling at the approval in her voice. "How nice."

"I believe her husband was also friends with Oliver at Cambridge."

The name didn't sound familiar to me, so I shrugged. "I wouldn't know."

My mother narrowed her eyes, and only then did I recall her intense dislike of shrugging.

Use your words, was her frequent refrain. *You aren't a common bricklayer.*

I almost smiled at the memory, but doubted she would find that quite so amusing.

"She was very keen for you to call on her," my mother continued. "I believe she is at home on Wednesday afternoons, which is convenient. I told her you would be there tomorrow."

"I'm a bit occupied at the moment, Mother," I gritted out, irritated by her high-handedness.

She actually had the gall to look confused. "With what?"

"I am trying to solve a murder," I said, making no attempt to hide my exasperation.

"But surely you can do both," she insisted. "And besides. It is more important than ever for us to keep up appearances right now."

That sounded just like something Jack would say. I bit back a sigh. "I won't have time this week. I'll have to go next Wednesday."

My mother clearly didn't like this, but I would not be moved. "Then at least send her a note. Her card is in the hall."

"I will." That was something I could manage.

"Good," she said with a nod. Then her eyes widened. "Oh! I nearly forgot." She pulled something out of her pocket and handed it to me. "This came for you. From Lord Linden."

I ignored the knowing look she shot me as I took the envelope. "It's about Mr. Pearson's funeral, I'm sure," I said as I opened it.

My mother balked. "You can't go to that. Think of how it will look." Then she leaned forward and lowered her voice, even though we were very much alone. "There are rumors going around that he was married to an *actress*."

I pursed my lips. "Mother, if you were so concerned with Delia's friendship with Mr. Pearson, whyever did you let her associate with him in the first place?

"I didn't know about *that*," she insisted. "Otherwise, I never would have let her go near him!"

"Surely it can't be that scandalous for a gentleman to be connected to an actress," I said drolly. "He's hardly the first."

My mother did not look amused by my cavalier tone. "Associating is one thing," she said crisply. "Marrying is another."

"Well, regardless, I am going to this funeral." Especially now that I knew Mr. Dorian would be there. I couldn't let him find out anything before I did.

My mother sighed, as though I was being quite tedious. "Fine. Just don't tell Delia. When is it anyway?"

I scanned the note. "Friday at eleven at St. Mark's."

She nodded. "I'll make sure she has something to keep her occupied."

"Surely that isn't necessary."

"Let me take care of your sister, Minnie," she said with a frown. "And I will leave you to this murder business."

Fair enough.

I decided then that it was time for me to leave as this conversation had left *me* in need of a nap.

"Tell Delia I stopped by. When I arrived, she had already gone upstairs to have a lie-down."

My mother frowned again. This time in concern. "She's been napping every afternoon. That's not like her."

"She probably isn't sleeping well at night," I said, praying that was enough to convince my mother.

She slowly nodded. "Yes. You're probably right."

"I will come to see Delia tomorrow," I said, hoping to further distract her.

"As you wish."

We then said our good-byes, as stiff and formal as they were, and I left.

I set out for the Elysium Gallery the next afternoon, after spending most of the morning helping Tommy research whales, which he had become particularly fascinated by. Unfortunately, most of my late uncle's books on the subject were several decades out of date, so I promised to take him to the British Museum's reading room as soon as possible in order to leave the house.

Much like my last visit to this area, the gallery looked a bit shabbier in the daytime, especially now that it was not filled to the brim with glamorous guests. As I entered, a young man immediately greeted me, and I asked if I could speak with the owner.

His expression dimmed a little as it became clear he would not make a sale with me today. "Mr. Henshaw is in his office, but indisposed at the moment. May I ask what this refers to?"

I hesitated, not wanting to mention Charles Pearson to this fellow, but I had the feeling I wouldn't be able to speak with Mr. Henshaw today if I didn't make my intentions clear. "Tell him Mrs. Harper is here to discuss Mr. Pearson. He will know what it is about," I added in the lofty tone I had often witnessed my aunt and mother use on everyone, from store clerks to particularly strident butlers, with great success.

The young man's eyes flashed, and he nodded. "Of course. I'll be right back."

I smiled at his retreating back and took a turn around the empty gallery while I waited. Most of the same paintings that were on display the night of the opening were still here. I then moved towards the back room, where Delia's painting had been, but the place where it had once hung was now empty. Disappointment sank through me. I was glad the painting had been sold, for my sister's sake, but I would have loved to see it one last time. As I stared at the blank spot, I became aware of the tread of heavy footsteps behind me.

"The painting was delivered yesterday," a smooth voice said over my shoulder, and I whirled around. A man I assumed was Mr. Henshaw stood a few feet away. He looked about my age, perhaps a little older, and was of average height and build. He wore his auburn hair in a severe side part that only drew more attention to his receding hairline.

"The buyer was very eager to have it in their possession. Not that I blame them," he added with a coy smile as he moved closer and cast an assessing glance over me.

I already didn't like him. There was a slickness to the way he spoke and moved that got my hackles up, but, of course, I couldn't betray that. I needed information from this man, so I gave him a smile of my own. "It is a beautiful painting. I'm Miss Everly's sister, actually."

His dark eyes gleamed with interest, and I fought against

the urge to step back and put more distance between us. "Ah. I had wondered who this mysterious Mrs. Harper was demanding my attention."

I forced out a light laugh. "I don't think I demanded your attention, sir. But I do have some questions about our mutual acquaintance, Mr. Pearson."

The man had the decency to look upset. "Poor Charles. I heard about his death. A terrible tragedy." He paused for a moment and gave me an assessing look. "I suppose you know that he and your sister were particularly . . . close?"

I cleared my throat. "I know that there was an understanding between them."

"An understanding," he repeated, dark eyes gleaming once more. "Yes."

"I don't like what you are implying, Mr. Henshaw," I said crossly. Though I may need information from him, that didn't mean I had to put up with his vile behavior.

He chuckled, as if I had made some great joke. "I think I like you, Mrs. Harper. Why don't we go to my office, away from prying ears."

I looked back towards the doorway and noticed the young man I spoke with earlier hovering nearby. "Fine."

Mr. Henshaw extended his arm towards another doorway to my right and placed his hand on the small of my back. "Come this way."

I moved quickly towards the doorway to avoid his touch.

"Just up there," Mr. Henshaw said as we stepped into a short hallway with a single open door at the end.

I entered the room and then stopped with a halt, surprised by the vibrant display before me.

While the gallery itself was rather sparse, the walls of Mr. Henshaw's office were lined with all kinds of artwork. "My goodness," I breathed, as my gaze wandered over the array of images in all manner of styles, shapes, and sizes.

A desk in dark walnut took up most of the space, and behind it was an eye-catching painting of what appeared to be a lush meadow in spring. A sense of calm washed over me as I stared at the shades of green and blue. It was so vivid that I could almost feel the sun on my face. A lone figure stood in the center, just out of focus.

"Isn't it marvelous?" Mr. Henshaw said beside me. "Painted by a Frenchman named Renoir. One of the Impressionists. Have you heard of them?"

"Only a little," I said as I turned to him. "The brushwork is one of the defining features, correct?"

He looked surprised. "Yes, it is. Among others." Then he gave me another one of those oily smiles. "Are you sure your sister isn't the only artist in the family?"

I couldn't help the snort that erupted from me. "I can barely draw a house, Mr. Henshaw. I am quite certain."

"A pity," he said as he gestured for me to take a seat in front of his desk. "Female artists are becoming rather popular with collectors these days. In fact, next month, I'm holding a show called The Hidden Genius of the Feminine, featuring only female artists."

Hidden Genius. My goodness, what drivel. I had met a number of extremely intelligent women at Girton, both lecturers and students, and absolutely none of them were hiding anything. Rather, they were deliberately overlooked, their work outright stolen, or they were dismissed by men threatened by their obvious talents. But I could tell Mr. Henshaw thought himself very clever for coming up with that title, so I managed a smile. "A splendid idea," I replied as he came around the desk and took his seat.

"I hope your sister will be able to participate," he said. "The painting I sold inspired quite a fierce little bidding war, in fact."

"Did it indeed? Well, I'm very pleased to hear that," I said. "Who was the winner?"

"Ah, my apologies, Mrs. Harper," he began with what

looked like genuine remorse. "But the buyer was adamant they remain anonymous."

I frowned. "Is that normal?"

"For works by popular artists, yes. Collectors don't necessarily want the public to know which valuables are in their possession."

"But my sister isn't well known."

"No, not yet. But I will say that the person who bought her painting has a keen eye for talent. No doubt they expect her work to become incredibly valuable someday." I wondered if that day would come in her lifetime. It seemed that often the most talented among us were not recognized until decades after their death. I hoped the same would not prove true for Delia. "But I know you did not come here to discuss the variables of the art market with me," he continued, giving me a knowing little smile as if we shared some secret.

I resisted the urge to shudder and stiffened my spine. "I did not. I came here to find out what you know about Charles Pearson's antiques business."

Mr. Henshaw stared at me for a moment, then let out a bark of laugher. "My goodness, you do get straight to the point, Mrs. Harper."

"I apologize for my bluntness, but I am particularly interested in the circumstances surrounding his death. I'm sure you can understand why," I added, with a knowing look of my own.

Mr. Henshaw leaned back in his chair and gave me an assessing look. "I heard that he was killed in a botched burglary attempt. Which would make sense, given the treasures he was fool enough to keep in his flat." I made no attempt to confirm or deny this and instead let the silence stretch between us, which seemed to make Mr. Henshaw uncomfortable. He shifted uneasily in his chair. "I told him he should have locked some of his pieces up in a vault. That soon enough someone would get word that he had valuables on hand and try to break in, especially the way he carried on."

I cocked my head. "What do you mean, the way he carried on?"

Mr. Henshaw suddenly threw up his hands in exasperation. "The same way he went about everything! Charles was careless. He was careless with money, with people, and with things. He never took his business as seriously as he should have. I wouldn't be surprised if he was crowing about acquiring some priceless artifact in the pub one night and was targeted by a rough fellow who happened to be within earshot." He then narrowed his eyes. "Why are you so interested, anyway?"

It was time to show my hand. "Because as I understand it, Charles Pearson was not killed in a burglary attempt at all, and I am trying to deduce if he was murdered."

Mr. Henshaw stared at me in shock. "You—you're doing *what?*"

"I'm trying to find his murderer," I said, unable to hide my growing frustration. "And I believe it may have had something to do with his antiques business. Possibly a disgruntled client or professional rival."

However, my explanation didn't appear to relieve Mr. Henshaw's confusion. "But . . . but you're not a detective. Why aren't you leaving it to Scotland Yard?" He was as incredulous as Mrs. Braithwaite had been, and I found myself warming to him just a little for his naïvety.

"Because I don't trust them," I said plainly. "I lived on Corfu before this, and when a local maid was murdered, the police there came very close to pinning the crime on the wrong person simply because they didn't approve of the victim's reputation."

He frowned at me. "Well, what can you expect? It's Greece. They haven't had a properly working government since the Age of Enlightenment."

I pursed my lips. "Corfu was a British Protectorate until the 1860s, and the police there largely follow English procedures."

"Even still," he said mulishly, "you can't compare the two."

"I'm worried that Delia will be found guilty," I began quietly. "She discovered the body, and if another potential suspect isn't found soon, it is entirely possible that she will be charged. You may be able to trust that the authorities will find the culprit, but I will not gamble my sister's entire future on a handful of officers at Scotland Yard."

It wasn't until Mr. Henshaw leaned away from me with a distressed look on his face that I realized my voice had risen. "Of course," he murmured, his eyes still wide. "Entirely understandable. Then he slowly reached for a piece of paper and a pen, as if I were a jungle cat who might lunge at him any moment. "I don't know much about who his clients were, but Charles did make sure to attend a private auction on the second Monday of every month. It is run by Sir Armstrong-Hughes and held at this address. He might be able to tell you more."

"Thank you," I said sincerely as I took the paper. "That is very helpful, Mr. Henshaw."

He gave me a short nod, but didn't meet my eyes. I could tell he was extremely uncomfortable, but I resisted the urge to set him at ease. There was power to be had in frightening a man, just a little, and I will admit here that I rather liked it. I rose from my chair and bid him good day, to which he mumbled a reply. I could tell he was glad to see me go, and I felt his anxious gaze on my back all the way down the hall.

Chapter 15

I couldn't help smiling to myself as I left the gallery, certain that this Sir Armstrong-Hughes held the key to this case. But as I stepped out onto the pavement, my smile died.

"Hello, Mrs. Harper," Mr. Dorian said with a grin, as he leaned against a brick wall just by the entrance of the gallery. "Isn't this a nice surprise."

Surprise my foot.

"What are you doing here?" I hissed, though I already knew the answer.

As the infernal man pushed away from the wall and walked towards me, I reluctantly acknowledged that, in comparison to Mr. Henshaw, his smile appeared refreshingly genuine. However, that did not dispel my annoyance.

I lifted my chin, still feeling rather bold from my exchange with Mr. Henshaw. "I don't need you chasing me around like a nursemaid. You should have made yourself known."

He had the audacity to look surprised. "You think I've been following you?"

I frowned at his feigned incredulousness. Perhaps I had

given him too much credit, thinking him genuine. "Then what, pray, are you doing here?"

"I was visiting a friend across the way and happened to see you entering this building. So I decided to wait." Then he looked past me and squinted at the gallery's sign. "Are you purchasing some art?"

I ignored this. "Who were you visiting?"

He gave me an indulgent smile. "Answer my question first, and I'll tell you."

I held his gaze as I pretended to consider the offer, and it was then that I noticed the slight strain in his face. The man may be acting friendly, but if I had to guess, he was actually very cross with me and only kept up appearances because we were in public.

I let out a short sigh. "The gallery owner was a friend of Charles Pearson's, and I came to see if he knew anything about his business."

Mr. Dorian nodded. "And were you successful?"

I narrowed my eyes. "Tell me what you are doing here first."

He huffed a laugh. "I was meeting Mrs. Langham."

I did my best to keep my expression neutral, even at the inconvenient flare of jealousy in my chest. "Oh?" I asked, managing to sound bored.

"She had some information for me. About the case."

Without thinking, I stepped closer, unable to hide my interest. "Really? What did she say?"

But Mr. Dorian clicked his tongue. "You know the rules. What did this gallery owner know?"

I cast a wary glance behind me, thinking of that nosy clerk. "Perhaps we should discuss this somewhere more private."

"Come," he said as he offered me his arm. "I know just the place."

I hesitated at first, then took it before the moment could turn awkward.

Just as I feared, being this close to Mr. Dorian took me back to Corfu. To the last time he had touched me. And all I could remember was how safe I had felt in his arms, though I had been on the brink of death. And the anguish in his voice as I had slipped from consciousness.

No. Not yet.

"Are you all right?" He was giving me a look of concern.

I must have shivered involuntarily at the memory. "Yes. Of course," I lied. "Let's go."

He watched me for another moment, then led me down the street. "It's around the corner. A tearoom I like."

I couldn't help smiling. "Do you make it a habit of visiting every tearoom in London?"

He shot me a mock frown. "Certainly not. Only the good ones. Why do you look so amused?"

"It's just very . . . quaint," I said. "I never would have thought a man like you would be so found of tearooms."

"A man like me? What does that mean?" Then he arched a brow. "You expect I spend all my free time in gambling dens and bordellos?"

I tripped at that last word, and Mr. Dorian was forced to grip me more tightly. "No," I said, once I recovered, but his hold didn't loosen. He gave me an expectant look, and I scoffed. "I do not think you spend all your free time at such establishments."

The corner of his mouth lifted. "You can't say the word, can you?"

"Well, of course I can *say* it," I shot back. "I just choose not to. It isn't proper," I added, then immediately regretted it.

Rightly, Mr. Dorian laughed. "Since when are you concerned with what is proper?"

"Never mind," I grumbled.

Luckily, I spotted the lace-trimmed windows of the tearoom up ahead. This one was called Polly's.

Mr. Dorian paused at the door and shot me a look. "And just to be perfectly clear," he began, "I don't spend *any* time at such establishments."

My cheeks heated and I gave a nod. "Understood."

He then held the door open for me, but I couldn't meet his eyes as I entered the tearoom. I sat down at the first empty table I spotted, and Mr. Dorian joined me.

"The scones are particularly good here," he said conversationally, as if we hadn't just been speaking of houses of ill repute.

I cleared my throat. If he was going to act unbothered, then so would I. "You do seem to like them," I commented. He had ordered scones at the last tearoom as well.

Mr. Dorian looked affronted. "What kind of Englishman would I be if I couldn't appreciate a good scone?"

The corner of my mouth lifted. "Quite right. I suppose I will have to try them then."

A girl came over to our table, and Mr. Dorian ordered scones for us both along with a pot of strong black tea. Once we were alone again, Mr. Dorian took off his gloves and folded his hands on top of the table.

"All right," he prompted. "What did this gallery owner tell you?"

I let out a sigh as I stripped off my own gloves. "He claimed not to know much about Charles Pearson's business, but did say that there was a private auction he always attended each month."

Mr. Dorian looked up, distracted. "Where is it?"

I had the strangest suspicion that he had been watching me remove my gloves. But no. That was ridiculous. "He gave me the address," I began, as I searched through my reticule for the slip of paper. "It's run by a man called Sir Armstrong-Hughes. Do you know him?"

He shook his head. "Never heard of him. But then, I don't spend my leisure time at private auctions."

My fingers tightened as I recalled how Mr. Dorian did spend his leisure time: at various shows, salons, and restaurants, always with a different lady. "Here it is," I said as I pulled out the slip and handed it to him.

"This is an address in Belgravia," he commented as he scanned the paper.

"Then I suppose Sir Armstrong-Hughes really is a knight."

Mr. Dorian rolled his eyes. "They will give anyone a knighthood these days."

"It could be a completely legitimate organization," I pointed out.

But he didn't look convinced. "If it's a private auction held in someone's home, there is a fair chance at least a portion of the items are stolen from somewhere. But there is a larger issue."

"What?"

"There will be a guest list," he said with a frown. "They won't just let anyone waltz in and start asking questions."

I sat back in my chair, feeling defeated. "I see."

Mr. Dorian gave me a sympathetic look. "Give me some time. I'll ask around and see if I can find a way to gain entry."

I narrowed my eyes. "Don't think you are going alone."

He let out a laugh. "You can't be serious. Mrs. Harper—"

But he stopped himself from saying more as the girl returned with our tea and scones.

"Here we are," she said with a cheery smile, as she doled out our food and tea.

"Thank you," I replied. The scones smelled heavenly, and my mouth began to water from the buttery aroma.

"Can I get you anything else?"

"No, we are very well," Mr. Dorian said as he eyed the scones with a hungry gleam.

She gave a nod and turned on her heel, leaving us alone once more. Mr. Dorian offered me the plate of scones first, and I took one. It was still warm. Then he tore into his own and spread on it a thick layer of cream and jam. We were both silent for a long while as we ate.

"You can't come with me," he finally announced once his plate was nothing but crumbs.

I placed my half-finished scone down and daintily wiped my mouth with my napkin. "Why not? And don't say because it's too dangerous," I added just as he began to speak. "It's an auction in Belgravia."

Mr. Dorian gave me a sour look. "And yet a man is dead possibly *because* of this auction in Belgravia," he countered. "If the murderer is connected and they learn that we are there looking for them, it certainly could become very dangerous indeed."

I was unmoved by this explanation. "So then you've decided that Mrs. Pearson is no longer a suspect."

"Don't change the subject," he scolded. "And no, I haven't. But I agree that this is another angle that should be pursued."

I preened a little. "Then I must insist that we pursue it together. We can use false names and go in disguises. Then no one will know who we are."

Mr. Dorian scoffed. "No disguises."

"Why not? Surely your friend Mrs. Langham can help with that," I said innocently, unable to keep from baiting him.

A muscle in his jaw ticked as he held my gaze. "Perhaps she can," he said.

It felt like a challenge. One I had no choice but to meet. "Excellent. Then it's settled."

He raised an eyebrow. "For now. And only if I can find a way in."

"I'm sure you will," I replied and took a bite of my scone. I should have felt victorious, but it was difficult not to sulk.

"Don't you want to know what Mrs. Langham told me?" he asked after a moment.

No. I don't ever want to hear that woman's name again, I thought. But somehow I managed to restrain myself and gave him a sunny smile. "Of course."

He was giving me one of those inscrutable looks again. "Adeline Brooks, the rumored Mrs. Pearson, is in London. And allegedly has been for over a week, in fact."

My jaw dropped open. "So she was here before the murder took place." Mr. Dorian nodded. He was obviously relishing in my reaction, but I didn't care. If this was true, then she was another potential suspect—and the most likely culprit, according to Mr. Dorian. For the first time since the night of the murder, I felt something close to relief. Delia wouldn't be the prime suspect anymore. "Does your brother know this?" I asked.

"I don't know. Possibly. And if he doesn't, he will very soon."

"Do you mean . . . you're going to tell him?" He had surprised me again.

Mr. Dorian took a sip of tea and nodded. "No sense in keeping this from him."

"Thank you," I murmured. Given their strained relationship, Inspector Dorian would likely not appreciate learning that his brother had been poking around his case, no matter what information he had uncovered. And I suspected this would lead to a quarrel.

"We all want justice to be served," Mr. Dorian said with a shrug. He then reached for the last scone, but I batted his hand away. He gave me an incredulous look. "What on earth was that for?" I gestured to the window, where a young girl in very worn clothing stood on the pavement staring wistfully up at the tearoom's sign. Mr. Dorian let out a mock sigh. "Fine. But you know it will do little good."

"Perhaps. But it's better than doing nothing."

"Shall I pay the bill, then?" he added, already getting up.

I watched as he walked over to the counter and began to chat up the girl who had served us. He said something to make her laugh, and she blushed fiercely. Yet, I couldn't bring myself to feel annoyed. Not when he was about to risk invoking his brother's ire on my account, or rather my sister's. The thought brought a smile to my lips, and even when he glanced back, I didn't try to hide it. The moment seemed to stretch between us as we stared at one another until the girl handed him some change. Then it was over. Mr. Dorian turned back to her, though he seemed reluctant to do so, and I began to gather my things. It was time to get back to work.

Once we exited the tearoom, I gave the girl the scone along with all the coins I had in my change purse. Her face lit up as if I had presented her with the crown jewels, and my heart ached all the more, as she couldn't have been much older than Tommy.

"Oh, thank you," she said profusely. "Thank you, ma'am."

"Do you have any parents?" I asked.

"Only my Mam, but she is ill and missed work, so her pay was short this week." The girl hesitated. "I've been giving most of my food to my two younger brothers. It's harder for them to feel hungry."

"I'm very sorry to hear that," I said. "You sound like a good older sister."

Her dark eyes brightened, and she stood a little straighter. "Thank you."

Then I turned to Mr. Dorian, who scowled but dug into his pockets. "Here," he barked, shoving what looked like several bank notes at the girl.

Her eyebrows rose, and she took the money in a daze. "Thank you, sir."

Then he took my elbow. "Come along," he said gruffly

and pulled me away. "Christ, that was like something out of Dickens."

I was incredulous. "You think she was lying?"

"I wouldn't have given her money if I did," he replied archly, but I could tell that he was as rattled by the girl's story as I had been. He just hid it behind a veneer of sarcasm.

"I know poverty touches so many people in this city," I began. "But it is harder to ignore the children."

Mr. Dorian was quiet as he ushered me towards his carriage. "I am very familiar with the plight of the wretched, Mrs. Harper," he finally said.

There was a certainty in his words. A kind of knowingness that I felt sure could only come from firsthand experience. I stared at his profile as curiosity warred with concern. Mr. Dorian had shared little about his background. I knew he had lost his mother at a young age, and though his father had once been named chief detective inspector, he had succumbed to drink. How old had Mr. Dorian been when this happened? What sacrifices had he been forced to make to support his brother?

"I—"

But he cut me off as we reached his carriage. "Here," he said brusquely, "let me take you home."

Though a part of me wanted the opportunity to pursue this line of inquiry, I was heading to Portman Square, and the very last thing I needed was for someone to spot us together.

"That is kind of you, but I'd prefer to take a cab."

He raised his brows in surprise, as no one could possibly prefer a cab to his carriage, but he hailed one anyway without pressing me further. Perhaps he knew I was curious and did not want to spend the ride avoiding my questions.

"Well, it's been a pleasure as always, Mrs. Harper," he said drolly as he handed me into the conveyance. "I will see you at the funeral on Friday."

Then he shut the door before I could respond, and flashed me a devious little grin as the cab pulled into traffic. I let out a huff of irritation, but as I was alone, it did not have quite the desired effect.

As the cab made the slow trek through Soho, I recalled everything I had learned. While I agreed with Mr. Dorian that it was worth tracking down the mysterious Mrs. Pearson, I still thought this private auction, or perhaps Sir Armstrong-Hughes himself, was the key to solving this case. I just had to hope that Inspector Dorian could be swayed by his brother.

By the time the cab arrived at my parents' house, I had begun to feel the full weight of the day and was sorely tempted to return to my aunt's flat. But no. I needed to see Delia, if only to give her some reassurance. I paid the driver and hid a yawn behind the back of my hand as I ascended the steps. Once more, the footman ushered me inside.

"Is my sister in?" I asked as he took my coat.

"I believe she is in the parlor with your brother, Mrs. Harper."

"Thank you," I replied, not even bothering to hide my disappointment. Jack was the last person I wanted to see right now. But like any good servant, Cartwright pretended not to notice my disdain and simply nodded before he disappeared with my coat and hat.

I let out a sigh and straightened my shoulders as I headed down the hall. Idly, I wondered if Mother had told Jack that I was conducting my own investigation, then decided against it. No doubt he would have disapproved, but only because he liked to be the one in control of things and would see my actions as undermining his own.

I paused just outside the parlor door, but no sound came from within. Perhaps Cartwright was mistaken and Jack had already left through the mews. It was on this thought that I entered the room and was immediately disappointed. First, because Jack was there, and second, he was alone.

He glanced up from his chair, a newspaper in hand, and shot me a frown. "What are you doing here?"

I fought back the urge to roll my eyes and moved farther into the room. "Good afternoon. I came to see Delia."

He tossed the paper on the table in exasperation. "Well, she's asleep. I came here to speak to her as well and have been waiting for over a quarter hour." Jack considered it a personal insult if he was made to wait any longer than five minutes, so this was a grievous offense on Delia's part. "What's the matter with her anyway? Mother said she's taken to sleeping every afternoon."

"She did just suffer a loss," I pointed out as I took the seat across from him.

"Come off it," he scoffed. "It isn't as though they were married."

I raised an cyebrow, and he seemed to realize that he sounded like an absolute ass. "Sorry," he grumbled and pulled a hand down his face. For a moment, he looked far older than his forty-one years. I tried to keep in mind that even though his pompousness was incredibly frustrating, he did have a great number of responsibilities. And this murder certainly wasn't helping. "It's just that I've heard from my solicitor."

My heartbeat quickened. "What did he say? Is Delia still a suspect?"

He let out a sigh. "Yes, at the moment. But he believes it is only a matter of time before they focus on someone else. Apparently, they found the murder weapon in the bushes outside the building, and it is unlikely that a woman of Delia's size could have wielded it with the force needed to cause the blows that killed Charles Pearson."

"Goodness. What on earth was used?"

"Some kind of marble orb," Jack said with a grimace. "They think Charles Pearson was using it as a doorstop."

I couldn't help imagining the scene: Charles coming back from our evening out, entirely unaware that his murderer was lying in wait for him. After all I had learned about him, I was hardly a fan of the man, but I hoped, for his sake, that death had come quickly.

"Well," I began, clearing my throat, "that's good news, isn't it?"

Jack gave a halfhearted shrug. "The longer this case drags on, the harder it will be to keep Delia's name out of the papers. And yours, for that matter."

I ignored his look of disapproval. "A bit of scandal is much preferable to being wrongly hanged for murder," I said pointedly.

But Jack shook his head and mumbled something about headstrong sisters under his breath. Then he glanced at the clock on the mantel. "I can't wait any longer. Some of us have work to do in the afternoons," he added unnecessarily.

"I will speak to Delia," I said.

"Just make sure she continues to keep close to home," he said as he stood. Then he shot me a look. "You as well."

My jaw tightened, and I narrowed my eyes. Even after all this time, no one could get under my skin as quickly and easily as my brother. "I'm fine, thank you."

Jack didn't bother to respond to this. But just as he reached the door, he looked back. "You should know I saw the viscount yesterday."

I instinctively gripped the arms of my chair. "And?"

He had the nerve to look disappointed. "I didn't tell him anything about you, Minnie."

I let out a sigh of relief. "Thank you."

But Jack frowned. "That doesn't mean he won't hear about

it from someone else, though. If I were you, I would contact him first. If only for a show of good faith. That would go a long way towards repairing things between you."

"*He* is the one who damaged things when he tried to take Tommy from me," I said hotly.

"He only wanted Thomas to attend Eton, like Oliver. And the rest of the Harper men."

How dare he invoke Oliver in an attempt to guilt me. I shot up from my chair as that old anger blazed through me. "Are you truly taking his side in this?"

"No," Jack said quickly. "And I don't approve of how he went about it." I let out a snort, but he continued. "I just mean that the boy is growing up. And you can't keep him beside you forever."

"Yes, thank you very much for that invaluable piece of information," I snapped. "I never could have come to that conclusion without the input of my male relatives."

Jack raked a hand through his hair, mussing the perfect strands. "Christ, Minnie. I'm only trying to help."

I lifted my chin. "Well, you've done quite enough."

"Fine," he growled, then hauled open the door and stomped out of the room.

I let out a frustrated groan and threw up my hands. I hadn't felt so angry since . . . since . . .

Since Corfu.

Since Mr. Dorian had made his accusations against Oliver. The anger all but fled from my body at that realization, and I slumped back into my chair. I turned to the hearth, where the fire still crackled, and stared at the flames while my mind thrummed.

I had been fighting so hard not to see the connection, but I couldn't keep ignoring it. This investigation was no longer just about finding Charlie's killer. It was also about Oliver. And determining once and for all if Mr. Dorian had been right about him. A soft rain began to fall outside, and the light patter on the windows drew my attention away from the hearth. Then I noticed that the sky had darkened, and I sat up. Nearly half an hour had passed since Jack stormed out. I needed to return home, but not without looking in on Delia first. I rose from my chair and exited the room.

Chapter 16

As I ascended the stairs to my sister's room, the rain began to fall harder, and I couldn't help noticing the house's eerie silence. It had never been like this when I lived here. One of us was always shouting about something or running on the stairs or down the hall. Or, on very rare occasions when no one was looking, sliding down the banister. A smile touched my lips as I remembered the afternoon Jack showed me what to do and how proud he was when I mastered it. For a moment, my heart ached for those lost years, even though I had often felt hopelessly misunderstood by my own family. But I could see now that it hadn't been as bad as all that. We had all tried to love each other in our own misguided ways, and no matter how much we had clashed, it had certainly been better than this. No wonder Delia had felt abandoned. The house was like a tomb.

I stopped in front of her bedroom door. No light shone underneath, yet I knocked anyway.

"Delia? It's me," I said softly as I tried the knob. The door creaked open, and I poked my head into the room. Her bed was empty. I frowned and opened the door all the way. She wasn't here. I turned around and shut the door behind me. Where on earth was she? I continued down the corridor and checked the other bedrooms, but they were empty as well. Then I remembered. I moved faster down the hall to the back staircase that led to the top floor. At dinner last week, Mother had said her studio was up there. I opened the door to the staircase and could see a faint glimmer of light from the very top. By the time I reached the top, I was panting for breath. Some of the servants' bedrooms were in this part of the house, but at the other end of the hall, I could see light peeking out from under a shut door. I hurried towards it and knocked.

"Delia? Are you in there?"

There was a beat of silence, and I heard some rustling.

"The door's open," she finally said, though her voice was heavily muffled.

I opened the door and found her standing with her back to me in front of a large canvas.

"Hello, darling. I've come to check on you."

She didn't answer at first and instead began swiping the canvas with long, bold strokes. "Mother said you were here yesterday," she replied without turning around.

"Yes, but you were asleep." I moved slowly, as if I were approaching a wild animal.

She hummed in response, a flat, joyless sound, and continued her work. I craned my neck to peer at the canvas and came to a halt. Like *A Woman Unbound*, this piece immediately caught my attention, but the emotions it evoked could not have been more different. It depicted the shadowy figure of a woman painted against a background of muted shades of brown, green, and grey, like the sky before a terrible storm. The woman's hair was loose and wild, as if a great wind was whipping all around her. And right in the center of her chest was a gaping black hole. I felt that sorrow like a lance through my chest.

I must have let out a gasp, because Delia glanced back at me. "What do you think?"

"I . . . I don't know," I answered honestly—and yet I couldn't look away. It felt like a painfully accurate depiction of grief.

Delia's mouth curved up in a mirthless smile, and she turned back to the canvas. "Is Jack still here?" she asked after a moment.

I had to blink and give myself a shake. "No. He just left."

Her shoulders relaxed a little. "Good. I can't face him right now."

"That is understandable," I said on a sigh. "He saw his solicitor earlier. It's good news. Well, good enough for now," I amended.

Delia stopped for a moment, as if considering something, then set down her brush and palette. Then she wiped her hands on her apron and faced me. "What is it?"

I frowned in concern. Her eyes were red, as if she had been crying, and the dark smudges under them indicated she had not been sleeping well, despite her afternoon naps. "Darling . . ." I began gently, but Delia shook off my concern.

"Just tell me, Minnie."

"The solicitor thinks that you won't end up being charged based on the evidence at hand. Apparently, whoever killed Charles needed a great deal of strength based on the murder weapon."

Delia was silent as she absorbed my words then let out a tsk of disbelief. "So they think it was a man, then?"

"Nothing has been decided just yet, but it seems likely, yes."

Her eyes turned glassy, and she sat down hard on a stool beside her. "I really thought they would accuse me," she murmured.

"I know," I said as my throat tightened with emotion. "But I think you are safe."

She let out a breath, then met my gaze, her eyes full of sorrow. "Then who did it, Minnie? I've been racking my brain for the last few days, and I truly can't think of who would do such a horrible thing."

I think a lot of people had a reason to kill Charles Pearson.

As Madame Fontaine's ominous words echoed in my head, I wondered how well my sister had really known this man. Or had she simply ignored the parts she didn't wish to see?

"Try not to upset yourself," I said as I rubbed her shoulder, knowing full well my words were cold comfort. "I am looking into it, and based on what I've learned so far, I don't think it was anyone you would have known."

She frowned in confusion. "What does that mean?"

"Do you know anything about an antiques auction in Belgravia that Charles attended?"

Delia considered the question and shook her head. "I know he attended auctions on occasion, but I don't know about anything specific. Why?"

"I think his murder is somehow connected to his antiques business."

Delia screwed up her face. "But . . . that was just a little hobby for him. It wasn't anything that someone would *kill* him over."

I wondered if that was her own observation of his work or the way Charles had explained it to her. It was certainly in his interest to portray it as more of a lark, so he wouldn't look like a fortune hunter. "I'm not sure. As I understand it, he was quite serious about it."

Delia chewed her lip, then let out a harsh breath and pressed her palms against her eyes. "God, I feel like such a fool. I didn't know him at all, did I?"

I wrapped my arms around her in a fierce hug. "He showed you the parts of him he wanted you to see. How could you know what he was willfully hiding?"

As I said the words, I realized I wasn't only speaking of her and Charles, but of myself and Oliver. He had been hiding *something* from me on Corfu. I could accept that now. And while I still held out a sliver of hope that his intentions had been noble, I was deeply hurt that he had kept anything from me in the first place. Now I was forced to question the motivations of the man I had loved for so long. It felt like trying to put together the pieces of a puzzle I couldn't quite see and was afraid to complete.

Delia sniffled against my shoulder. "I suppose you're right," she said glumly.

"I am," I insisted, possibly for my benefit as much as her own. "Now, let's go downstairs."

She nodded and allowed me to lead her towards the door. But just before we left, I cast one last look at the painting. How strange that one could feel such sustained grief over the loss of another, even after learning of their deception. It was not just the loss of a person, though, but of an idea. An image you both had a hand in creating. Perhaps that was why it hurt so much, and was so difficult to leave behind.

I tucked Delia into bed and promised to have a tray sent up for her. I briefly considered searching for my mother, but decided against it, as my nerves already felt frayed and I had no wish to fall into a quarrel with her. So, instead, I slipped away from the house. But before I could head home, I needed to stop off at one of those ghastly shops that catered to mourning clothing. I couldn't borrow anything from Delia without revealing my intention to attend the funeral, and as the black gowns I did own had been made for the Grecian climate, I hadn't bothered to pack any. So off I went to Regent Street, where I purchased a ready-made black cashmere gown, as it was warm and I absolutely abhorred crepe. The saleswoman then tried to sell me an extravagant hat decorated with black silk roses and a long black veil, but I opted for a simple but elegant black velvet toque. I didn't really need another hat, but the crowd tomorrow would be well-heeled, and this would help me blend in. That the hat also happened to be very flattering was merely a happy coincidence. With my purchases in hand, I returned to the flat just as Mrs. Ford was setting the table for our supper.

I spent the rest of the evening in Tommy's entertaining company and let him lead the conversation. He had found another book on the natural sciences in my late uncle's collection, though he insisted a trip to the reading room was still necessary, and he regaled me with a number of facts about reptiles, both interesting and horrifying. After we finished Mrs. Ford's delicious bread pudding, I helped Tommy wash and dress for bed before reading three chapters from *Treasure Island*. By the time I reached the part where Long John Silver confronts Captain Smollett over who should get the buried treasure on Skeleton Island, I could barely hide my yawns.

"Mama," Tommy said, "perhaps you should go to bed."

"Yes. Thank you, my dear. It has been a long day."

Tommy's eyes were heavy-lidded as well, and he nodded in agreement. "You're always away," he murmured sleepily as he sank down onto the pillow.

I pressed a hand to his cheek as guilt bloomed in my chest. "I'm sorry. Something's come up. But it will be over soon."

He sighed a little and closed his eyes. "It's Mr. Dorian again, isn't it?"

I reared back in surprise. I had never said a word to Tommy about what had happened on Corfu, but perhaps it was woefully naïve of me to think he hadn't noticed anything all on his own. "It's . . . it's nothing you need to worry about," I said weakly, knowing that would do little to quell his interest.

But Tommy didn't reply. He was already fast asleep.

The morning of the funeral, I escorted Tommy to my brother's home so he could visit with his Everly cousins.

Dolly met us in the entryway. "Go on upstairs, Tommy. The children are waiting for you in the nursery," she said with a smile.

"Have a good time," I called after his swiftly retreating form. "Thank you for doing this," I said to Dolly once we were alone.

"He is welcome here anytime," she replied. "How is Delia? Jack said she hasn't been feeling well."

I longed to confide in Dolly, but it wouldn't be right to share Delia's news without her consent. I decided to ask if we could share her condition with our sister-in-law, for soon enough the time would come when decisions would need to be made.

"No," I said. "She's taken everything very hard."

Dolly frowned in sympathy. "The poor dear. But Jack did mention that the police no longer consider her the primary suspect. That's a bit of good news."

"It is," I agreed. "But, frankly, I'll feel better when they make an arrest."

"Understandable." Then she turned her sympathetic gaze on me. "And what about you? Are you sure you're able to attend the funeral? It won't bring back any bad memories?" she added hesitantly.

"Sadly, this is not the first funeral I have attended since Oliver's. But thank you for your concern," I said with a grateful smile.

"Of course. And please, don't worry about Tommy. He is a dear boy, and we're happy to have him here."

"Thank you. I appreciate that."

I'm not sure what my brother did to convince Dolly to marry him, but he was a lucky, lucky man. I left shortly afterward, as I still needed to dress for the funeral. I hadn't wanted Tommy to see me in my black dress, as that would only lead to questions I didn't want to answer. Back at my aunt's flat, Mrs. Ford pressed my dress and then helped me fix my hair. When she finished, she stepped back with an admiring look.

"That dress fits you very well, if you don't mind me saying so, Mrs. Harper."

As I looked at my reflection in the floor-length mirror, I was tempted to agree, though it wasn't really appropriate for the occasion. "Thank you. If only I was going to a dinner party and not a funeral."

But Mrs. Ford looked unconvinced. "I've known more than a few ladies who met their husbands at funerals. There's something about realizing how fleeting life is that gets the blood running," she said with a sage nod.

"Goodness," I marveled. "I never considered that." Then I turned back to my reflection. "I do wish I had brought one of my brooches from home. I hardly ever wear them as it is. They spend most of the time tucked away in a drawer."

Mrs. Ford's eyes suddenly lit. "I know just the thing." She then moved to the dressing table and pulled open a drawer. "Your aunt took all her best jewelry with her, of course. But she has a few lovely pieces in here. And you'd never know they were paste."

I had a vague memory of hearing about Aunt Agatha's penchant for jewelry growing up, but could only recall her spectacular moonstone engagement ring from her visits to Corfu. Mrs. Ford pulled out a red-leather jewelry case, set it on the dressing table, and opened it. The baubles glittered in the morning sunlight, and as I leaned down for a closer inspection, I saw that she was quite right. They really did look genuine.

"The pearl and gold one would look best, I think," she said, pointing to a brooch designed to mimic a flower. "Understated, but lovely."

"I agree." The rest of the pieces were quite ornate: a pair of ruby earrings, a large sapphire necklace, and a thick diamond bracelet. If these were my aunt's paste jewelry, I could only imagine what she had taken with her. Mrs. Ford then pinned the brooch to my dress and stepped back.

"That looks marvelous."

I touched it daintily. "I'll be very careful," I said solemnly.

But the housekeeper just waved me off. "Do as you like. It's all to be yours someday anyway." I shot her a confused look, and she tilted her head. "Surely she told you."

"That she's giving me her jewelry?" I said on a laugh.

Mrs. Ford continued to stare in surprise. "She's giving you everything. Said it before she left."

"Oh." I truly couldn't form more of a response. Aunt Agatha had always been incredibly generous to me, and even more so since Oliver died, but had never said a word about an inheritance. "Why—why wouldn't she tell me?"

Mrs. Ford shrugged off my distress. "Who else would she be putting in her will? She has no children. And you must know how fond she is of you and the children."

"I do." But now I worried we hadn't done nearly enough to earn such a gift. My aunt was a wealthy woman, and while I sincerely hoped she would live for at least another decade, even a small sliver of her estate could be life-changing.

Mrs. Ford seemed to intuit my worry. "You can talk all about it with her when she comes back. But it's nearly time for you to leave," she said, glancing at the clock on the mantel.

I followed her gaze and let out a groan. "Heavens, yes."

I retrieved my reticle with the funeral invitation already tucked inside while Mrs. Ford fetched my coat. The service was being held nearby at St. Mark's in Mayfair, and as it was a fairly nice morning, I decided to walk. There was a line of carriages in front of the towering neoclassical building, and as I neared the entrance, I wondered if this church had been chosen to reflect the deceased's interest in antiquity. Vaguely, I noticed the figure of a well-dressed man just up ahead, pacing rather idly, as if he was waiting for someone. As I grew closer, the man took notice of me and stopped. It was Mr. Dorian.

"Hello, Mrs. Harper," he said as I approached. "You look nice. Is that a new hat?"

I lifted my chin, determined not to blush at his compliment. "Yes. What are you doing out here?"

"Waiting for you, of course."

I glanced past him at the steady stream of people entering the church and frowned. More than a few had already shot curious looks in our direction. "We can't be seen entering together."

"Why not?"

I huffed at his innocent expression. Was the man being purposefully dense? "Because it might cause *talk*."

I did not wish to be identified in the gossip columns as yet another one of his female companions. But of course I couldn't say that, for then he would know that I had been reading about him. Luckily, Mr. Dorian seemed to accept this answer and extended his arm towards the church entrance. "Then you go on ahead, and I will enter after a few moments. Unless we cannot even be in the same vicinity without creating a scandal?" he added wryly, arching a dark brow.

For a moment, I was tempted to agree to this ridiculous notion simply to see that smug look wiped from his face. But the triumph would be fleeting indeed. And, though I would never admit it, I was feeling rather apprehensive. "I think it is perfectly acceptable for us to acknowledge one another once we are both inside," I said in measured tones.

Mr. Dorian nodded, but the wry look remained as I walked past him and into the church. The last time I had attended a funeral had been on Corfu, and in the company of the very same man. However, that was where the similarities ended. For that funeral had taken place in a humble Greek

Orthodox chapel, while St. Mark's was one of the finest churches in Mayfair, with its imposing columned entrance, towering Gothic ceiling, and trio of stained-glass windows. A church organ bleated out the notes of "Nearer My God to Thee," as some guests mulled around the vestibule waiting for the service to begin, while others had taken their seats. The crowd was larger than I had expected, especially for a private funeral. As I scanned the sea of unfamiliar faces, I noticed Lord Linden just up ahead, greeting people as they entered the nave. He stood next to a woman in full mourning who I assumed was Charles Pearson's sister. Beside her stood a thin man with a large, drooping mustache who must have been her husband.

"Is it safe for us to acknowledge one another now?" whispered a familiar voice by my ear, completely interrupting my thoughts.

I shot a frown at Mr. Dorian. "Yes," I hissed, then turned my attention back to the baron and company.

"Hmm," Mr. Dorian said, following my gaze. "I didn't realize Linden was so close with Pearson's sister."

I bristled at his skeptical tone. "She doesn't live in London, so he has helped her arrange the funeral. I'm sure at his own expense," I added in an offhand way.

"What makes you say that?"

I cast a look around, but there was no one behind us at the moment. "I have come to suspect that Charles Pearson was rather short of funds," I murmured. "And I'm sure a funeral like this does not come cheaply."

"Well, you are right on that point, at least," Mr. Dorian replied dismissively as he gazed up at our surroundings. "Time will tell about your other assumptions."

I frowned at his profile, but before I could respond, it was our turn to greet the family. Lord Linden gave me a warm smile. "Mrs. Harper. How good of you to come. And Mr. Dorian." His gaze turned curious, and I could tell he was trying to determine our relationship. "This is Mrs. Pembrooke, the sister of our dear departed friend," he explained. "And her husband."

"I'm very sorry for your loss," I said to Mrs. Pembrooke. Up close, I could see she was significantly older than Charles. And I wondered how much she knew about his life in London.

"Thank you," she sniffled, while her husband gave a stiff nod.

"He was a fine man," Mr. Dorian added.

"Allow me to escort you to your seat, Mrs. Harper," the baron said, then looked to Mr. Dorian. "Unless I am intruding . . ."

But Mr. Dorian quickly waved a hand, as if the very idea was absurd. "Not at all. Lead the way."

"I will be right back, Jenny," he said to Mrs. Pembrooke. She nodded while still managing to look absolutely petrified. Then I took the baron's proffered arm, and he led me into the nave, with Mr. Dorian trailing behind.

"This has been a difficult time for her," the baron explained once we were out of earshot.

"I can imagine," I replied as I looked around the church pews. Only the last few rows in the back were open.

"She feels responsible," he continued. "Though I can't understand why."

"He was her younger brother," I said. "It can be hard to let go of a relationship established in childhood."

The baron cast me a surprised look. "How insightful."

I blushed at his praise. "I try."

He stopped at an empty pew only a few rows away from the back. I wondered why he had taken it upon himself to escort me here. We certainly could have found our seats without him. "I suppose it is terribly inappropriate to say given the occasion, but you look very nice," he said. "I like your hat."

I touched the brim. "Thank you. It's new," I added, then

felt like an idiot for even mentioning it. But the baron only smiled.

A throat cleared behind us, and I glanced over at Mr. Dorian. "I think we can manage it from here, Linden," he said blandly.

"Quite right. The service will be starting shortly. Mrs. Harper," he said with a little bow and left.

"That was odd," Mr. Dorian said as we slid into the pew. "I'm afraid you may end up in the gossip pages after all."

"What are you talking about?"

He raised an eyebrow. "I doubt the baron has bothered to usher any other guests to their seats."

"I'm sure he only needed a break from greeting everyone."

"How convenient it happened just when you arrived," Mr. Dorian drawled.

I leaned towards him and lowered my voice, as a few other people had joined our pew. "If I didn't know any better, I'd think you were jealous."

Mr. Dorian looked unamused and I leaned back, satisfied that I had shut him up, at least for the moment. But I couldn't enjoy the feeling for very long as the sound of raised voices drew my attention back towards the vestibule. Mrs. Pembrooke appeared to be arguing with a woman dressed in an extravagant mourning veil. I could only make out a few words: ". . . you have no *right*," before Mr. Pembrooke loudly hushed her.

"Is that her, do you think?" I whispered as I gripped Mr. Dorian's arm. "Mrs. Pearson?"

He glanced down at my hand, and I pulled it away. Then he turned around just as the woman entered the nave. Her entrance appeared to have garnered the attention of the people around us as well, and curious murmurs rippled through the crowd. We must not have been the only ones who heard the rumors about Charles Pearson's mysterious wife. She held her head up high, but did not move to the front of the church, where the family would sit, and instead slid into the pew behind us. She was then joined by a strikingly handsome man with dark hair and olive skin. She glanced towards me, and even through her veil, I could tell she noticed my staring. I immediately turned around.

"Excellent work," Mr. Dorian murmured by my ear. "Very subtle."

I resisted the urge to glare at him and instead kept my gaze forward. Just then the organist switched to another hymn, and the bishop moved to the front. It was time for the service to begin.

Chapter 17

I will admit here, within these pages, that my attention was not terribly focused on the funeral service. Instead, I used the time to look over the crowd and noticed a few familiar faces. Mrs. Braithwaite was seated across the aisle beside a man I assumed was her husband. I also saw Mr. Henshaw seated closer to the front. When he glanced over and noticed me, he immediately turned back. There were also a few people I recognized from the baron's party, but did not know by name. Mrs. Braithwaite displayed far more emotion than anyone else, which seemed odd. This was the funeral of a young man who had been brutally murdered. I had to wonder if most of the people here had simply attended out of curiosity rather than a genuine sense of loss. When the bishop finished the final commendation and we rose, I turned back just in time to see the suspected Mrs. Pearson and her companion disappear through the archway into the vestibule.

I moved to follow them, but Mr. Dorian gripped my arm.

"What are you doing? We must speak to her," I hissed.

"You'll only draw attention to yourself if you follow her,"

he said calmly, still holding my arm. "Besides, I know where she is staying."

"Oh," I replied. "Well, then. Where is it?"

The corner of his mouth lifted as he shot me a chiding look. "If I told you now, you'd only slip away and go there without me."

I let out a huff, though he was entirely correct. There was nothing left to do but wait as the pews slowly emptied out. When it was finally our turn to exit, we shuffled down the aisle and out of the church.

"Are you going to the cemetery?" Mr. Dorian asked as we made our way down the steps. Out front, a long line of carriages had begun to form the funeral procession. Charles Pearson was to be interred in Brompton Cemetery, but I did not plan to attend. I shook my head as I scanned the crowd that had gathered, but there was no sign of Mrs. Pearson. She had disappeared. But someone else caught my eye instead.

"Oh no," I murmured, as Delia stood across the street, watching as Charles Pearson's coffin was loaded into the back of the hearse. Even from a distance, she looked horribly pale and fragile, as if a stiff breeze could knock her clean off her feet.

"What is it?" Mr. Dorian asked, but I was already trying to move through the crowd. My progress was hampered by the number of bodies, but Mr. Dorian must have noticed Delia as well, for after a moment, he was by my side, effectively moving people out of my way. I saw Mrs. Braithwaite, and she too had noticed Delia. Our eyes met, and seeing her guilty expression, I knew she must have been the one who told her about the funeral.

"I didn't think she would come," she said weakly as I moved passed her, but I didn't have time to chastise her.

I hurried across the street with Mr. Dorian close behind. Delia turned to me with a stricken expression. "Oh, Minnie," she gasped as her eyes filled with tears. Then she began to fall into a swoon, but thankfully Mr. Dorian caught her.

"We have to get her out of here," I said to him, though it was too late to avoid the notice of the crowd.

"My carriage is just around the corner," he said, and together we got a barely conscious Delia into his coach.

"You shouldn't be here," I said to her once we were inside.

She blinked at me, her gaze unfocused. "I wanted to say good-bye," she murmured, and my heart clenched despite my worry.

"I know," I said, as I pushed a loose strand of hair back from her face.

As the carriage pulled into traffic, I put my arm around Delia, and she relaxed against me. I let out a sigh of relief and could feel Mr. Dorian's gaze upon me. He hadn't said a word since telling the coachman to drive to Portman Square. But I couldn't look at him just now. I was certain he would see far too much.

Then, just when I thought Delia had fallen asleep, she suddenly straightened. "Something is wrong."

"What?" I asked.

She looked at me as her eyes flashed with fear. "I think . . . I think I'm bleeding."

I had expected Mr. Dorian to leave as soon as he deposited us at our parents' house, but he didn't. Instead, he insisted on carrying Delia inside through the back entrance and, under the direction of the housekeeper, up the servants' staircase and into her bedroom. Mother was out, thank God, and Mrs. Reynolds quickly took charge and sent Mr. Dorian out of the room. But Delia stubbornly refused to let me send for the doctor. "There is nothing he can do anyway," she said tearfully once she was tucked up in bed. Her suspicions had been correct. Her courses had begun once again. "And he'll only tell Mother."

Though she had a point, I was prepared to argue. But Mrs. Reynolds cut in: "My mother was a midwife when I was growing up in our little village. And I have nursed my share of young ladies through this in my time, Mrs. Harper. And given how early it is, I believe there is little risk of infection."

I raised my eyebrow. "How do you know that?"

Delia looked away guiltily, but Mrs. Reynolds remained undaunted. "I know everything that goes on in this house. Including when a young lady has missed her courses."

I stared at her in shock. "Does anyone else know?" If so, that could ruin everything.

But Mrs. Reynolds shook her head. "Absolutely not. Once I had my suspicions, I asked Miss Delia, and together we enacted a plan to put any speculation to rest."

I furrowed my brow. "You mean . . . you *faked* them?"

"Just enough to fool the maids," Mrs. Reynolds said. "It is done in houses like these when one cannot guarantee complete discretion from the staff. Do not be cross with her," she continued. "It was entirely my idea."

"I'm not angry," I insisted. Then I turned to Delia. "I only wish you had told me."

Delia bowed her head. "I'm sorry."

I let out a sigh and sat down on the bed beside her. "I just want to make sure you're well," I relented. Then I looked back at Mrs. Reynolds. "You're certain she doesn't need a doctor?"

"I will keep a close eye on her," she said with a firm nod. "You don't need to worry."

Mrs. Reynolds was terrifyingly competent. I could understand why Delia had confided in her. "Thank you," I said.

"Now, you rest up. I'll come back a bit later with something to eat," Mrs. Reynolds said to Delia, then left the room.

Once we were alone, Delia began to trace her finger on the coverlet's flowered pattern. "I know how difficult it all would have been," she began softly. "But I still feel terribly sad." Then she looked up at me with watery blue eyes. "Is that stupid?"

"Of course, it isn't," I said fiercely as I pulled her into my arms. "You have every right to be upset. Society's arbitrary rules for what counts as acceptable behavior doesn't change what you lost."

I felt her huff a surprised laugh against my shoulder, and she pulled back. "Goodness, Minnie. I had no idea you were such a radical."

I forced a smile. "I think it's called just being a woman."

As she watched me, her gaze filled with understanding. "You've experienced this too, haven't you."

I looked away and nodded, just once. "After Cleo. But I was a bit further along."

After a moment, I felt her hand cover mine, and the warmth of her palm cut through the numbness. "I'm so sorry. That must have been awful."

"It was," I murmured. In truth, I rarely allowed myself to think about that dark stretch of time anymore. Oliver and I dealt with the loss in different ways: I allowed myself to be swallowed up by grief, while he did his best to outrun it at every turn. He began to spend more and more time away on vague work assignments he didn't like to talk about—though I barely noticed and cared even less. Needless to say, this put a terrible strain on my marriage for the better part of a year until I could finally move beyond the fog of grief. Slowly, we began to repair things between us, but they were never quite the same as they had been because I wasn't the same. How could I have been?

And then, after Oliver's death, it had been easier to forget the first great tragedy of my life. But the pain was still there, buried underneath all the rest. I turned to Delia. "Having Tommy helped," I said simply.

"I'm glad," she replied, her eyes full of sympathy.

But it felt wrong that she would be giving me comfort right now. I cleared my throat. "I'll leave you to get some rest."

As Delia held my gaze, I could tell she saw right through my little performance but did not call me on it. "All right."

"I will come back tomorrow," I said as I rose from the bed. "But you can send for me before that."

Now it was her turn to pretend. "I'll be fine. You don't need to worry."

I looked back at her and forced a smile. "I won't."

Hopefully, we could both be more truthful tomorrow.

My mind was so preoccupied, as I stepped into the hall, that it was several moments before I glanced over and noticed Mr. Dorian sitting in a chair opposite the bedroom.

I blinked in shock. "You're still here."

He immediately came to my feet. "Have you sent for the doctor yet?"

"Mrs. Reynolds says there is no need," I explained. "And I trust her judgement."

Mr. Dorian watched me with that inscrutable gaze I had never quite been able to decipher. "Your sister was with child then?"

I glanced away with a nod. "It was very early, but yes. Mrs. Reynolds says she can care for her."

Mr. Dorian was silent for a long moment. "I am sorry. How is she?"

"As well as can be expected under the circumstances."

"And you?"

I turned to him then, surprised. "I'm relieved she is well."

He continued to watch me expectantly, but there was nothing more to say. I raised an eyebrow.

"I just thought . . . you seemed . . ."

"What?" I said sharply. This dithering wasn't like him.

He pursed his lips and gave me a pained look. "You seemed greatly disturbed."

I could only stare back at him. "Well, of course. She is my sister."

He took a step closer to me. "I know," he said gently, lowering his voice. "But it was more than that. The look in your eyes, Minnie." I sucked in a breath as he said my name again. "It was like you were haunted."

I turned away again. "I don't want to talk about it."

"That's fine," he said quickly, and an absurd feeling of disappointment fluttered my chest. "I just wanted to make sure you were all right."

"Yes," I said with a firm nod. "I am. It happened a long time ago," I added before I could think better of it. "And it isn't exactly an uncommon experience."

"That doesn't make it easier to deal with," he said after a moment. There was a note of sorrow in his voice I hadn't noticed before, and I faced him as understanding dawned.

"You've dealt with this before, haven't you?" He gave a stiff nod. "Your wife?"

Mr. Dorian's eyes widened in surprise. "God, no." Then he immediately sobered. "My mother. She began bleeding one afternoon. It couldn't be stopped. Death took them both."

My heart broke for him in that moment. "I'm very sorry. How terrible that must have been for you. And your family."

He gave a halfhearted nod. "My father never recovered."

And you?

But I didn't have the chance to ask the question as we were both distracted by the sound of someone shuffling down the hall towards us.

I looked past Mr. Dorian to see my father in his dressing gown, white hair askew. I had never seen him in such a state.

"Father?" I quickly stepped around Mr. Dorian and approached him.

My father's listless gaze fell on me, and he immediately frowned. "Minnie? What are you doing here?" he asked sharply. "Why aren't you in Corfu?"

Since it was nearly the same thing he had said to me during my first visit, I surmised he was having one of his bouts of confusion. "I came to see Delia," I said gently as I took his arm. "Let's get you back to bed."

But my father shook off my hand. "I told Harper to keep you away," he barked. "It isn't *safe* for you here."

I frowned in concern, due to both his agitated state and his words. "What are you talking about?"

Instead of answering my question, my father took notice of Mr. Dorian then and barreled towards him. "Who the devil are you? Do you work for Mitchem too?"

"Father," I pleaded as I took his arm again, "this is Mr. Dorian. He is a friend."

"Tell that imbecile to get my daughter out of here," my father continued. He was more worked up than I could ever remember. "That was our agreement."

Mr. Dorian, for his part, only nodded. "Understood."

I shot him an irritated look, though perhaps it was better if he played along, as this seemed to calm my father a little.

"Good. Don't let it happen again."

"Who is Mitchem?" I asked.

My father began to respond, but was distracted by the sound of hurrying footsteps.

"Good heavens. There you are!" cried a plump, middle-aged woman in a white nurse's cap and apron. "I'm so sorry. Mr. Everly usually naps at this time, and I must have dozed off as well," she admitted as she rushed over to us.

I arched a brow at her admission. "Just be glad my mother is out."

"It won't happen again," the nurse said with a sheepish nod and took my father. "Come with me, Mr. Everly, and I'll have them send up some pudding."

My father's eyes lit up at this and went with her dutifully, without complaint. He didn't even look back at me. It was as if I had already been forgotten.

I shook my head, bewildered by the entire scene. "What on earth could he have been talking about?" I murmured, mostly to myself.

"I'm not sure," Mr. Dorian replied, his gaze fixed on my father's retreating figure. Then he turned to me. "But George Mitchem was once the head of the Foreign Office."

"My father must have met nearly every man in government at some point," I said with exasperation. "And obviously he is now a very confused old man."

But Mr. Dorian responded with an uncertain hum. "He seemed lucid enough in that moment."

I narrowed my eyes. "What are you suggesting?"

He turned to me, his gaze serious and unyielding. "Nothing. Yet."

I pushed away the uneasy feeling rising in my chest and cleared my throat. "Then may we please remain focused on the current task at hand?" He arched a brow in question, and I rolled my eyes. "Mrs. Pearson. You said you knew where she was staying."

"Ah. Right," he said before his gaze flickered with concern. "Are you sure you want to do that now?"

"Of course," I replied, already moving towards the staircase as, at that very moment, I was quite determined to get out of this house.

Chapter 18

We left through the back entrance, though this halfhearted attempt at discretion would likely have little effect. Mrs. Reynolds may run a tight ship in many ways, but she couldn't entirely stop the servants from gossiping with each other or their neighborhood counterparts. Luckily, I didn't care what people said about me, or so I reminded myself as I climbed into Mr. Dorian's coach. He followed close behind and directed the driver to take us to the Carrington Hotel in Mayfair.

I raised my eyebrows at the exclusive, and expensive, establishment as I settled against the bench seat. "No paltry widow's portion for her, then?"

Mr. Dorian shrugged, taking the seat across from me. "According to Mrs. Langham, she has done well for herself abroad. And that fellow of hers is rumored to be a minor Italian royal."

"Really?" I said, as I recalled the man's dark features and Romanesque nose. "How interesting. He certainly looks like a character out of an Ann Radcliffe novel. I wonder if he is a count?"

Mr. Dorian snorted. "I didn't take you for a title hunter," he grumbled.

I ignored this comment, as it was beneath us both. "I wonder what brought her to London in the first place. The timing does seem rather . . . convenient."

Mr. Dorian nodded. "And while a woman may not have possessed the strength needed to kill Charles Pearson, that fellow you're so fond of certainly does."

"I am not *fond* of him," I protested. "I don't even know the man."

"I only wanted to make sure you are capable of remaining on task while in the presence of such male beauty." As the corner of his mouth curved up, I realized he was teasing me. Well, two could play at that game.

"And yet I've never been distracted by *you*," I shot back, holding his gaze.

To my surprise, this comment seemed to catch him off guard. Mr. Dorian's cheeks turned pink, and he glanced away. The man very well knew he was attractive. Nearly everywhere we went, he drew at least some person's notice—and often used it to his advantage. But now he seemed embarrassed to have it pointed out.

After a moment, he cleared his throat and looked back at me. "Glad to hear it."

As our eyes met, the air felt heavy with anticipation and something more I did not wish to name. Something I had barely allowed myself to feel in many months. I parted my lips, though I had no idea what to say, and Mr. Dorian's gaze shifted to my mouth. His eyes darkened as he leaned forward slowly. But then, just as I felt my own body begin to move as well, the coach rocked to a halt. We had reached the hotel.

Mr. Dorian blinked and sat back, as if he had just woken from a dream. Before either of us could speak, the door was pulled open by an employee of the hotel, and I exited the coach. Once outside, I allowed the strange, heady feeling to dissipate into the air and headed up the steps. Mr. Dorian was by my side within seconds.

"If she is here," I began, keeping my gaze ahead, "how are we going to find her? We don't know for certain what name she is registered under and even if we did, I can't imagine reception would simply give out her room number to a pair of strangers."

"Yes, that is unlikely," he agreed. "But not to worry. We have a number of options to choose from."

I frowned at his casual tone. "Such as?"

"I can distract the concierge while you riffle through the guest book, we can steal waiter's uniforms, then sneak into the kitchens and wait for an order for their room, we can pose as chambermaids . . ." While he prattled on, I pretended to be irritated by his increasingly outrageous suggestions, but secretly I was glad we were back on our usual footing. "Or we can simply say hello and ask if she would like a chat."

I turned to him. "That last one isn't very exciting."

"No," he admitted, as he looked past me towards the lounge. "But it might just work."

I followed his gaze and saw Mrs. Pearson and her companion sitting at a table just past the entrance. He was reading a newspaper, while she idly sipped from a cup of tea, her gaze fixed somewhere off in the distance. She had changed since the church, and while her gown was still black, it was not made of the expected crepe of a widow but something far more expensive, likely silk. A large ivory brooch was pinned to her collar just below her throat. I hadn't noticed it before, but now, without the distraction of the long mourning veil and ostentatious hat, I could see that she was a very elegant woman, and together she and her companion made a handsome couple.

I glanced over at Mr. Dorian, but he kept his gaze fixed on

them as he approached their table. Mrs. Pearson noticed him first and set down her teacup with an expectant look.

"I'm terribly sorry to intrude," he began, looking far more meek than he ever would under normal circumstances. "But I believe I saw you earlier at the church."

Yet this tactic appeared to work, as Mrs. Pearson smiled. "Oh, yes. I thought you looked familiar."

Of course she noticed him, I thought to myself rather unkindly.

"I am Mr. Dorian, and this is Mrs. Harper," he said, gesturing to me where I hovered just behind his shoulder.

She smiled at me in acknowledgment. "Hello. I am Mrs. Murray, and this is Mr. Romano."

So not a count, then.

"And yet, I was told you had a different surname. One you shared with the deceased," Mr. Dorian murmured. As the woman blushed and looked away, Mr. Romano shot him a mighty glower. "I'm not trying to embarrass you, madame," he said quickly, as he held up his hands in supplication.

Her mouth tightened as she bowed her head. "Mrs. Murray is the name I use when I travel," she said quietly.

"Perhaps it would be best if we continued this conversation somewhere in private," Mr. Dorian replied in a gentle tone. "There is much we wish to discuss with you."

"She has nothing to say to you," Mr. Romano stated, in his heavily accented English. "Go somewhere else for gossip, you vulture."

Just as an irate expression began to cross Mr. Dorian's face, I stepped forward. "I'm so sorry, but that isn't at all why we are here. My sister and I had the misfortune of finding Mr. Pearson, and as such, we have become entangled in this case. If we could have just a few minutes of your time, I would be so grateful."

Mrs. Pearson looked up, her dark eyes wide. "Is your sister Delia?"

"Yes," I said with an enthusiastic nod.

Then she turned to Mr. Romano, and they began to have a hushed conversation in rapid Italian. At first, the gentleman shook his head fiercely, but then she said something that looked and sounded like a plea, and he eventually relented with a single nod. She reached across the table and took his hands in her own as she whispered her thanks. All in all, it seemed a very intimate exchange to have right in front of two people they had just met.

Mrs. Pearson then rose. "Let us go to our rooms."

Her companion immediately pushed back his chair and stood, though his full lips were still frozen in a disapproving scowl. The man was taller than I realized, with broad shoulders and well-formed arms. He certainly possessed the physical strength needed to kill Charles Pearson. What remained to be seen was whether he possessed a motive. I exchanged a look with Mr. Dorian, who seemed to share my thoughts, and we followed them out of the lounge to the elevator.

Despite his lover's pleas, Mr. Romano did not appear at all happy with this development and spent the entire ride glowering at both myself and Mr. Dorian. I avoided his gaze as best I could, but it was difficult in the cramped space. Thankfully, it was not long before we reached the top floor. Once we exited the elevator, Mrs. Pearson showed us into a luxurious suite decorated in sumptuous tones of pink and gold.

"Please, sit down," she said, gesturing to a small sitting area by the hearth. Mr. Dorian and I took the sofa, while Mrs. Pearson sank into a wingback chair opposite us. Mr. Romano moved to stand behind his inamorata until she glared up at him. "Dante, I can't think with you hovering like that," she snapped and pointed to the chair parallel to her. "Sit there, and stop glowering at them," she added, giving me an apologetic smile.

I half expected the man to protest, but instead he let out a sulky grunt and took the seat across from me. His manner reminded me of Cleo when she was in a mood about something, and only then did I notice that he was quite young. I estimated that Mrs. Pearson was about my age, but her companion couldn't have been more than twenty-five.

"How is your sister faring?" Mrs. Pearson asked, drawing my attention away from studying his profile.

"It has been a very difficult time for her," I replied, "as I'm sure you can understand."

Mrs. Pearson glanced at her companion. "Yes. But it has been many years since Charles and I were together." Mr. Romano pointedly turned away from her. She rolled her eyes, but did not otherwise comment on this bald display of jealousy. "We were very young and incredibly foolish when we married, you see," she explained. "Neither of us understood what it meant to pledge a lifetime to the other."

I wondered if they had been any younger than Mr. Romano, but kept that to myself. "Is it true that his father didn't approve?" I asked instead.

"Oh yes. He was furious when Charles told him and demanded we get an annulment. But it was too late for that." She paused for a moment, as if sifting through the memories. "And it seemed unthinkable to us at the time. But ever since I heard the news, I can't help but wonder how different everything might have been if we had just ended things then."

I leaned forward. "What do you mean?"

She furrowed her brow. "Charles lied about getting an annulment and insisted that we keep the marriage a secret. But he was constantly worried that his father would learn the truth anyway and disinherit him. It put a terrible strain on us, and eventually I had enough. When the opportunity to perform in Paris came up, I took it. I was happier than I had been in months. Charles was too, though he wouldn't admit it at first. Male pride, you know," she said with a faint smile. "But eventually he came around, and we agreed the marriage would be in name only until his father died."

"But that was several years ago, no?" I asked.

Mrs. Pearson shrugged. "I told him I would sign divorce papers whenever he wished, but he kept putting it off. Though I am certain that was purely due to an aversion to paperwork rather than any lingering affection," she added with a firm look at her companion before turning back to me. "Then he met your sister."

I shifted in my seat. "When was this?"

"He first wrote to me about her last spring. There had been other girls before, of course, but I could tell right away that she was different." A smile flitted across her lips. "By then we had a firm friendship, so all I really wanted was his happiness."

"And you had no reason of your own to ask for a divorce?" Mr. Dorian asked with a not-so-subtle glance at Mr. Romano.

"No, not really," she said with an easy smile. "My illusions about the institution were flimsy to begin with, and my own marriage did nothing to strengthen them. Besides, Dante is terribly religious."

"Is he now?" Mr. Dorian replied dryly, ignoring my warning look.

We couldn't afford to offend her, but Mrs. Pearson seemed unaffected.

"He wants me to convert to Catholicism, but I'm not in a hurry." Then she turned to Mr. Romano with a look so full of love and admiration that I had to resist the urge to turn away. "Being with him is more than enough."

I cleared my throat. "How nice."

She turned back to me, her eyes still full of warmth. "How long have you been married, Mrs. Harper?"

"I'm a widow," I said mildly.

"I'm so sorry," she replied with genuine compassion.

"So what brought you to London after all this time?" Mr. Dorian prompted. "Was it simply a coincidence that you happened to be here when he was killed?"

Mrs. Pearson arched her brow. "Are you suggesting that I had something to do with his death?"

Mr. Romano muttered something in Italian that sounded very much like a warning, and I shot Mr. Dorian a cross look, but he only shrugged. "It's a fair question. And though the marriage may have been in name only, you are still legally his widow."

Mrs. Pearson pursed her lips as she shot him an irritated look. "I came here for several reasons. One of which was to see Charles to discuss our divorce." Then she paused as her eyes filled with regret. "In fact, we were supposed to meet the day after he was killed. It had been ages since we last saw each other, and I was so looking forward to it."

But Mr. Dorian was predictably unmoved. "What do you think prompted this change on his part?"

Mrs. Pearson looked confused. "Well, the proposal, of course." Then she turned to me. "He intended to ask for Delia's hand."

This made me think slightly better of Charles. At least he hadn't intended to ruin Delia completely. But Mr. Dorian let out a scoff. "That's convenient." I shot him another warning look, but Mrs. Pearson shook her head.

"He did," she insisted, then turned to me. "He even spoke to your father about it."

Now that was truly surprising. "What? When?"

"I'm not sure exactly, but he mentioned it in his last letter. Let me find it." She stood and went to a small writing desk and shuffled through a stack of correspondence. "Ah, here it is." Mrs. Pearson scanned the paper. "I received this just days before his death. We were arranging a time to meet, and he mentioned that he had gone to see Mr. Everly and got his blessing."

My mouth dropped open in shock. Absolutely no one else in my family seemed aware of this. Not even Delia herself. "May I see it?"

She nodded and handed it to me. The letter was written in the same casual tone favored by the author and mostly related to deciding a time and place to meet. But there, at the end, was the mention of his visit:

I went to Delia's father last week to get his blessing, as I want everything to be aboveboard this time, which I know you can appreciate. The old man gave me a devil of a time at first, as any good father would, but I wore him down in the end.

I stared up at her. "I don't understand. My father is not a well man, and I'm certain my mother has no knowledge of this."

Would it even be possible for Charles Pearson to visit my father without anyone knowing? I truly wasn't sure.

Mrs. Pearson frowned in concern as she took back the letter. "I don't know what to say. All I know is what is written here."

"What about money?" Mr. Dorian asked, once again completely ignoring the emotional undercurrent of the conversation. "We have reason to suspect that Charles Pearson may have run into some financial difficulties."

Mrs. Pearson let out a disapproving tsk. "Charles was always short of funds. He didn't know how to properly manage money. Men like him never do," she said to me in a confiding tone.

"But, as his widow," Mr. Dorian continued, "don't you stand to inherit everything?"

"I suppose I do, but I'm quite certain anything he does

have is tied up in that collection of his," Mrs. Pearson said evenly. "If anything, Charles owed *me* money. The inheritance from his father, the one he was in such distress over, turned out to not be anywhere near as large as he expected. Of course, by then he had already overextended himself. Luckily, I was doing very well and agreed to help him pay his debts."

"What about his business?" I asked.

"I think he lost more money doing that than he ever made. Poor Charles," she added with a sigh. "Things just never seemed to go his way. That was why I was so happy for him when he mentioned your sister."

But I couldn't share in this as I was growing more and more certain that Charles Pearson had targeted Delia in part because of her dowry. And had possibly gotten her pregnant to make sure she went through with the marriage.

Mr. Romano said something in rapid Italian, and Mrs. Pearson let out a gasp. "Oh, goodness. I nearly forgot." Then she addressed me with an apologetic smile. "I'm so sorry, but we have an engagement this afternoon."

"Not at all," I replied. "Thank you for taking the time to speak with us. It has been very . . . enlightening."

"Of course. And if there is anything more I can do, please don't hesitate to ask."

"That is very kind." I rose from my chair and turned to Mr. Dorian, but his gaze was still firmly fixed on Mrs. Pearson, and I didn't much care for the look in his eye.

"Just one more thing: where were you and Mr. Romano on the night of the murder?"

Mrs. Pearson raised an eyebrow. "As I told the police, we were attending the opera and have a number of alibis to prove it." Then she narrowed her eyes. "I don't suppose you have any relation to Inspector Dorian, do you?"

To my surprise, Mr. Dorian's ears turned pink, and he turned away. "He is my brother," he mumbled.

I met Mrs. Pearson's eyes, and she gave me a satisfied little smile. "How very interesting."

I thanked her again and tugged Mr. Dorian out of the room before he could embarrass himself any further. I could feel both her curious gaze and Mr. Romano's mighty scowl upon us as we fled the suite.

"What on earth possessed you to ask her that?" I hissed, once we were in the hallway.

Mr. Dorian lifted his chin, unrepentant. "I wanted to know if the police had spoken to them, and that seemed like the easiest way."

I pressed the service button for the elevator and whirled back to face him. "You could have just asked them rather than make a veiled accusation of murder."

He flashed me a wicked smile. "Ah, but where would be the fun in that?"

"You are impossible." Then another thought occurred to me. "You haven't spoken to your brother then."

"Not yet," he said in a clipped tone, but I could tell there was far more behind those words.

We both fell quiet for several long moments, and the only sound was the low groaning of the elevator as it made its slow ascent to us.

"She has nerves of steel, that one," he finally replied. "Didn't even blink. An actress through and through."

"Well, of course not, when she had nothing to hide," I said, exasperated by his continued suspicion.

But Mr. Dorian remained unconvinced. "Perhaps not about their whereabouts that evening, but I'm not so certain she was telling the full truth about the rest of it."

I narrowed my eyes. "What are you talking about?"

"Mrs. Langham thought that she and her late husband's connection was not quite as platonic as was suggested, and that her young Italian was terribly jealous," he said. "And I'm inclined to believe her."

I bit my lower lip as I considered this. "It's possible, I suppose."

"Charles was a cad through and through," he began. "But a terribly charming one. Women did not leave his company willingly. Mrs. Langham was under the impression that they still rendezvoused several times a year."

I was unable to school my shock and then immediately felt naïve. Mrs. Pearson had seemed entirely genuine to me, but I should have proceeded with more caution and not so readily accepted the story she gave as the full truth. "How . . . dramatic," I managed to respond.

"Actors," Mr. Dorian said by way of explanation.

I sniffed as I recalled the various gossip columns about him in the company of several different actresses. And that was only the ones that were written about. "Well, you know more about that than I would," I muttered without thinking.

Mr. Dorian shot me a curious look that I blatantly ignored. "In any case," he continued, "it would possibly explain why Mrs. Pearson never sought a divorce herself." Then he frowned, considering something. "Or perhaps she refused to sign the divorce papers unless she got something in return."

I balked. "You think she was extorting him?"

"She had been here for over a week before his murder, yet they were still trying to arrange a meeting. Why would it take that long if it was something they both wanted?"

"But she said he had no money, and she mentioned that she was doing well."

Mr. Dorian shrugged, unconcerned. "Yes, but perhaps not well enough to walk away from a payout, especially if she felt it was owed to her. And I'm sure Charles was perfectly capable of scrounging up some funds, when necessary," he pointed out, then pursed his lips. "But even if that was the case, I'm not sure how that helps us solve this murder."

The elevator finally arrived then, and the attendant pushed

open the gate. Mr. Dorian and I shuffled once more into the cramped space, and I leaned back against the wrought-iron bars, mulling over this scenario.

Then I straightened as something came to me. "Maybe that's it," I said. Mr. Dorian raised an eyebrow in question. "Perhaps he was trying to make a quick sale to pay her off," I continued, now warming to the idea. "Only something went wrong. Or he was swindling someone, and they noticed."

Mr. Dorian nodded slowly. "Yes. I like that idea."

Meanwhile, the attendant looked back and forth at us with blatant curiosity.

"He's a writer," I explained. "We're coming up with ideas. Sometimes inspiration strikes when you least expect it."

Mr. Dorian rolled his eyes, but the attendant immediately perked up. "Really? Have you written anything I would know?"

Just as I was about to say the name of his first book, Mr. Dorian said *no* and shot me a warning look.

The attendant frowned as he considered this. "I don't think I've heard of that, but I've got an idea for you. A story you wouldn't believe."

"Is that right?" Mr. Dorian said flatly, making no attempt to hide his disinterest.

But the young man didn't appear to notice. "It happened to a friend of my uncle's. Or was it his cousin? Anyway, that's not important . . ."

We spent the rest of the ride being subjected to a very long and convoluted story about a man losing his change purse in a pub and then having it returned to him by his long-lost brother, who happened to pass through not an hour after him.

"Now wouldn't that make an excellent story?" the young man said as the elevator bobbed to a stop.

Mr. Dorian eyed the door, which remained closed, and quickly nodded. "I will take it into consideration."

The young man looked thrilled. "Really? I can't wait to tell him!"

"Now, please, open the door," Mr. Dorian said tightly, and I noticed the panicked look in his eyes.

"Oh, right. My apologies, sir," the young man said with a laugh and pushed open the door.

Mr. Dorian practically hurled himself out of the elevator, while I gave the attendant an apologetic smile as I exited.

"I've had that exact nightmare before," Mr. Dorian muttered once I was by his side.

"I didn't know you had an aversion to small spaces," I replied as we made our way back through the lobby.

"I have an aversion to being trapped with a dullard and forced to listen to his inane suggestions," he snapped.

"It wasn't all that bad. Why, I'm sure Arthur Conan Doyle could turn that into an excellent Sherlock Holmes story."

A weaker person may have been cowed by the withering look he cast me then, but I could only smile back. I hadn't had the chance to annoy him like this in a very long time, and I confess, I rather missed it.

Once we were back outside on the pavement, Mr. Dorian turned to me. "What next? Shall we meet tomorrow to prepare for our visit to the auction house?"

I shook my head. "I'm visiting Cleo at her school." I went every Saturday and would continue to do so as long as my daughter welcomed me. "And I'm sure if you will come to my aunt's flat an hour beforehand, we can discuss the details. No need for this to take up more time than necessary."

Something flashed in Mr. Dorian's eyes too quickly for me to name it, but if pressed, I would have been tempted to call it disappointment. "Right. And how is Cleo faring?"

"Good. Wonderful, actually," I amended.

"Glad to hear that," he replied, looking anything but. "Well, I'm happy to take you home—"

"No need. Tommy is at my brother's house in Kensington, and I wouldn't want you to go so far out of your way." I then forced a cheery smile in a desperate attempt to stop the awkward feeling that seemed to stretch between us.

But Mr. Dorian was immune to the gesture. "As you wish," he said with a stiff nod.

I cleared my throat. "Come to my aunt's home at eight. I'm sure it won't take us very long to prepare."

"All right. Until then," he replied, without meeting my gaze before he turned on his heel.

I watched his retreating figure as he stalked over to his waiting carriage, broad shoulders thrown back and head held high. A trio of finely dressed women passed by him on their way into the hotel, and they made no attempt to conceal their interest, but Mr. Dorian either didn't notice or didn't care enough to acknowledge them. It was terribly petty of me, but I couldn't help feeling rather pleased. Then I turned around and headed in the opposite direction to hail a hansom cab, unable to keep from smiling.

Chapter 19

"I'm sorry, but did you just say *Mr. Dorian* went to the Natural History Museum with you?" Cleo looked from her brother to me, her gaze equal parts questioning and accusing.

The three of us were sitting in the large conservatory of her school in Hampstead, along with a number of other people visiting with students, and Tommy had just been catching her up on everything we had done since our last visit.

I bit back a sigh. "Yes. He happened upon us just as we were leaving."

Cleo raised an eyebrow, immediately seeing this for the weak explanation it was. "How convenient."

I turned to Tommy, who was blissfully unaware of the growing tension. "Darling, why don't you go get another biscuit," I suggested and pointed to the long table nearby that offered tea and biscuits for the visiting families. He was out of his seat at once and didn't even look back.

Now that we were alone, I gave my daughter an apologetic smile, which she returned with a skeptical look.

"All right, Mama. Out with it."

Cleo had far more sense than I did at her age, likely because I had not been able to shelter her from the harsher realities of life. I swallowed the guilt that usually accompanied such thoughts.

"We met by chance when I went out for the evening with Aunt Delia," I explained. "And we have seen each other a few times since then."

Her expression lightened, and I knew what she was thinking. "But, that's wonderful."

I shook my head. "It's not like that." I glanced back to make sure Tommy was out of earshot, and sure enough, he was still at the table, piling a plate with far more than one biscuit. I quickly turned away, as I could deal with only so much at once. "Your aunt was in a bit of trouble, and Mr. Dorian was kind enough to help."

But Cleo only narrowed her eyes. "What kind of trouble?"

"She was being courted by a man who was . . . murdered," I said, trying to sound unbothered.

This, unsurprisingly, did not work on my daughter. Cleo leaned forward. "Mama," she hissed quietly, "you were almost killed the last time you tried to investigate a murder. Don't tell me you are doing it *again*."

For one brief moment, I considered lying to her, but knew I could never fool Cleo. That girl could have broken the leader of the Spanish Inquisition. "This isn't like last time—"

"No."

"I'm being careful," I insisted.

But Cleo was unrepentant. She sat back in her chair and crossed her arms. "Then make him do it."

I let out a sigh. "I was trying to protect your aunt. The police were treating her as a suspect, and I was worried that she would be arrested."

Cleo's frown softened slightly. "And now?"

"I think they have determined that only a man could be the murderer."

"So then there's no need for you to continue," she said, with a hopeful look in her eyes that broke my heart.

I shook my head. "No, darling. There's more." I paused to take a sip of tea, and because I was a bit of a coward. Cleo waited patiently while I gathered my nerves. "I've begun to suspect that there may be some connection to your father and the work he was doing in Greece."

She blinked as she absorbed my meaning and finally let out a soft *Oh*. "Do you mean at the embassy?"

I held her hopeful gaze. "I'm not entirely sure yet."

That was technically true, as I had yet to determine if Oliver had used his official position to gain entry into a black-market antiquities ring or if it was merely something he had cultivated outside the office. I grimaced at the thought. But the *how* didn't matter. I was far more concerned with the *why* and whether this had somehow played a role in his death. I could barely bring myself to even conceive of such a thought. To consider that years of pain, both my own and my children's, could have been avoided if Oliver had only behaved differently. But there was also still a sliver of hope. A possibility that this was all a part of some massive misunderstanding and that, even in death, my husband was still the man I had believed him to be. It was that possibility that fueled me now, even in the face of my daughter's entirely understandable concern.

Cleo worried her lip. "Can't you tell someone else to look into it? What about Uncle Jack."

I let out a mirthless laugh. I couldn't trust Jack. He seemed far more concerned with suppressing any possible connection to scandal than uncovering the truth. And I was certain he would destroy any evidence he did manage to find, whether it absolved Oliver or not.

"No. I'm sorry, Cleo. But it has to be me. I *have* to do this," I said with more force than I meant.

Yet it had the desired effect as Cleo reluctantly nodded. "I understand."

"Thank you. And I promise, I will be careful."

"All right," she said, not sounding the least bit convinced.

I longed to give her more reassurance, but nothing short of swearing to stay home every evening darning socks would do. And I simply couldn't promise that.

"Will you at least tell me what you find? Even if . . . even if I might not like it?"

As I took in the apprehension in her eyes, my heart broke. While Tommy barely remembered Oliver, Cleo had idolized him. I suddenly wondered if I was being horribly selfish in pursuing this. For it wasn't only my image of Oliver that was at stake, but the children's as well. I hadn't felt this uncertain since I was trying to decide whether to stay in our home or move closer to the center of Corfu Town after Oliver died. But, in the end, I had decided to honor my late husband and remain in the home we had shared as a family. Now I was choosing to do something that threatened to ruin those last memories.

I cleared my throat and managed a quick nod just as Tommy returned with his pile of biscuits. I halfheartedly told him to share with his sister, which he did with some reluctance. When he then offered me his plate, I shook my head.

"No thank you, darling," I said. For I had lost my appetite.

Visiting hours ended a short while later, and I pulled Cleo into a fierce hug until she tapped my shoulder.

"Mama, I have to go," she said, her voice muffled against my shoulder.

I immediately released her. "Right. Sorry."

"But I will see you next week."

"Yes," I said with a firm nod, hating the uncertainty in her gaze.

The image stayed with me as we left the school grounds and walked to a main road, as I flagged down a hansom cab, and all through the long ride back to Hyde Park Street.

Thankfully, Tommy didn't seem to notice my distraction, as he was preoccupied with a recently published book on dinosaurs that Cleo had lent him from her school's library. One thing I appreciated about her school was that the curriculum was rigorous and well-rounded. The students studied mathematics and science alongside more traditionally feminine pursuits like horticulture and music.

When we finally reached home, I was exhausted, both mentally and physically. I wanted nothing more than to take a long, hot soak in my aunt's exquisite marble bathtub. But as we entered the house, Mrs. Ford greeted me with a knowing smile, and I knew it was not to be.

"You have a visitor, Mrs. Harper. The Baron Linden is in the parlor."

I frowned in surprise just as Tommy shot me an accusing look. "You know a baron?"

"A little, yes," I admitted. "Though I can't imagine why he has come here."

Or how he knew where to find me. Then my stomach sank. He must have gone to Portman Square first. I highly doubted Delia was receiving guests, so the only other person he could have spoken to was my mother. And if that was the case, I would never hear the end of it.

"Thank you, Mrs. Ford. Would you send in a pot of tea?" I asked as I helped Tommy out of his coat.

"Certainly," she said with a nod. Then she turned to Tommy. "Would you like to assist me?"

Tommy's eyes lit up, and I shot her a grateful look. Someday the allure of helping an adult with mundane tasks would lose its thrill for my son, but thankfully that day had not yet arrived.

As I walked down the hall to the parlor, my mind riffled through all the possible reasons for the baron's visit. If it had merely been to pay his respects after the funeral, leaving his card would have sufficed. No. If he had bothered to then come here, it meant there was something specific he wanted to speak to me about. Given how I had been spending my time as of late, I felt wary. Did the baron somehow know that I had undertaken an investigation into Charles Pearson's murder? And if so, how would he react? Would he be angry or intrigued? I didn't know him well enough to even guess.

I pushed open the parlor door and found him standing before the hearth with his back to me. He turned at my entrance, and I was surprised by the uncertainty in his gaze.

"Mrs. Harper, hello." He came to me at once, and I barely had time to greet him myself before he took my hand and brushed his lips across my knuckles.

"Hello. I hope you haven't been waiting long?"

"It's no matter," he demurred as he straightened and gazed at me rather intently.

"I must admit, this is quite a surprise," I said, as I took a seat and gestured for him to do the same.

He ducked his head in a surprising display of contrition as he sat down across from me. "I know. I went to your parents' home first, and your mother was kind enough to give me your aunt's address. I hope I haven't imposed?"

"Not at all," I said with a tight smile. My mother was probably planning our wedding at this very moment. She would be sorely disappointed.

The baron managed a weak smile of his own before his gaze turned serious. "Forgive me for speaking rather plainly, but I've come here on a matter of some urgency."

My stomach turned as I suspected the worst. "Is this

about Delia? I'm so sorry if her presence at the funeral was a distraction—"

But the baron frowned and shook his head. "I didn't even know she was there." I let out a short breath of relief. Then Mr. Dorian and I had acted quickly enough to keep her swoon out of view. "No. This concerns . . . you," he continued.

My eyes widened. Then he *did* know about the investigation. "Oh?" I squeaked.

The baron shifted in his chair and looked rather uncomfortable. "How well do you know Mr. Dorian?"

I blinked for a few moments as I considered how to answer this question. "What do you mean?"

"I understand you met at my party," he began. "And then I saw you together again at the funeral. I know he's a popular author, and that can be a source of fascination for some people."

A laugh burst from me. "Lord Linden, that isn't at all the case here. I assure you."

"Truly?" He looked relieved.

"Yes," I answered with a firm nod and was just about to tell him how I knew Mr. Dorian when the man continued.

"I was worried because he does have a bit of a reputation, you know," he said with subtle disapproval.

Considering that Lord Linden had a reputation of his own, I couldn't help wondering what a man had to do to earn his censure. It was terribly duplicitous of me, but in that moment, my curiosity won out. So I swallowed my admission, and instead I tilted my head. "I'm afraid I don't."

The baron raised an eyebrow. "I'm not one to gossip, of course . . ."

"No, certainly not," I agreed, willing the man to get to the point.

"But I believe he might be pursuing you." Somehow I managed to suppress my snort of disbelief as he went on. "And as you are clearly a woman of unimpeachable character, I feel that it is my duty to tell you that woman he was with at my party—"

"Mrs. Langham," I answered, rather too quickly, and he looked surprised.

"Uh, yes. Mrs. Langham. Well, as I understand it, she is his mistress."

It wasn't anything I hadn't already assumed, and yet hearing it from someone else stung far more than I expected. I sat back in my seat. "Yes. That makes sense," I rasped after a moment. And it *did* make sense. It aligned with everything I had read about Mr. Dorian since leaving Corfu, and he had made no attempt to hide their connection from me. Furthermore, the woman was beautiful and charming. If anything, it would be odder if she wasn't his mistress. I had only myself to blame for not acknowledging it sooner.

He frowned in concern. "Are you all right, Mrs. Harper?"

"Of course," I insisted. "Why wouldn't I be?"

But Lord Linden's wary gaze returned. "I'm sorry if I overstepped."

I immediately straightened. "Not at all. I appreciate your concern, but let me assure you it was not needed," I said firmly.

He held my gaze and seemed satisfied. "Good. Then may I call on you again?"

I gave him a bemused look. "Certainly."

The baron noticed my confusion, and his eyes flashed with amusement. "I confess I did not come here solely out of gentlemanly concern."

Now my confusion deepened. "No?"

Lord Linden smiled. "No. I also wanted to see you. To pay you a call."

Understanding finally dawned, though my confusion did not leave. "*Oh*."

"Yes. *Oh*," he mimicked with a chuckle.

My cheeks heated, but before I could respond, Mrs. Ford entered with the tea tray, followed by Tommy.

"Hello," he said. "We've brought you tea."

She shot me an apologetic look over his head, but I was grateful for the distraction, as I needed a moment to absorb the baron's admission. I had assumed he was the kind of man who flirted the way other men breathed and thus hadn't taken his attentions towards me very seriously. But this was cause for a reconsideration.

Meanwhile, the baron was attempting to converse with my son. "Hello, young man," he said stiffly. "And what is your name?"

"Thomas Harper, my lord," he replied cheerily. "But everyone calls me Tommy."

"Very good." The baron then shot me a slightly panicked look, and I surmised that he was not often in the company of children.

Mr. Dorian may be a cad, but he was wonderful with Tommy. I could not deny that.

"Is it true you're a baron?" Tommy asked bluntly.

Lord Linden looked utterly bemused by the question, and I doubted anyone had ever asked him that before. "Uh, yes. I am."

"Do you have a castle?"

"I do not," he conceded.

Tommy didn't even pretend to hide his disappointment. "What about an abbey? Lord Byron had an abbey, and *he* was a baron."

I attempted to mask my laugh as a cough, while Lord Linden sat up a little straighter. "I have a house here in London and another in the Lake District." Then he looked to me. "It is quite lovely. Excellent views."

I felt myself blushing again as Tommy considered this. "I've never been there. We've come from Corfu and haven't left London yet. Have you been to Greece?"

Lord Linden cleared his throat. "Yes. Many years ago."

While I was very curious to know more about this, I decided that was enough of an introduction. "Thank you, Tommy," I said. "Now why don't you go help Mrs. Ford. I'm sure she can find something for you to do."

"Yes," she said, as she guided him from the room. "Why don't you help me peel potatoes."

"All right. But I want to use the peeler by *myself* this time," he insisted.

"Of course," Mrs. Ford said.

"It's nice to meet you," he called back over his shoulder. "Even if you don't have a castle."

"A charming boy," Lord Linden said rather uncertainly once we were alone.

I managed a smile and began to pour the tea. "Thank you. I also have an older daughter, Cleo," I went on. Best to lay all my cards on the table now and let the man decide if he was still interested.

Lord Linden paused with his teacup in hand and quirked a brow. "Is she here as well?"

I shook my head. "She is attending a school in Hampstead run by Lady D'Arcy. Perhaps you know her?"

"I do. Yes," he replied. "Interesting woman. I've heard great things about that school."

Well, that was a point in his favor. "Cleo seems very happy there," I said.

"And does she plan to follow in your footsteps and go to Girton?"

I was surprised he remembered that about me, and Lord Linden saw it plainly on my face. He cocked his head in amusement. "You truly don't know, do you?"

"Know what?" The words came out more sharply than I intended.

Rather than answer me outright, he took a leisurely sip of

tea while his gaze remained on my face. "You are an attractive woman, Mrs. Harper," he murmured.

I cleared my throat and immediately looked away. Then I silently chastised myself. After all, I was a grown woman who had been married for many years. His pronouncement shouldn't have had such an effect on me. And yet, there was a kind of knowing undercurrent to Lord Linden's words. An assuredness that made it difficult to dismiss this as little more than the shallow flattery I had expected from him.

Oliver had told me I was beautiful before, of course, but I wasn't the same woman he had known. His death had forced me to learn how to rely on myself, and my youthful innocence had been replaced by a clear-eyed strength born out of necessity. If I was being very honest, I wasn't entirely sure that Oliver would have liked this more surefooted version of myself: the Minnie who took odd jobs for even odder men. Who investigated murders and traveled across the Continent. And I certainly couldn't imagine ceding to his wishes as easily or as often as I had when we were married, for I hadn't known myself the way I did now. But then, I hadn't really known Oliver either. At least, not as well as I had once thought. In any case, it was rather gratifying that the baron had both seen this side of me and seemed to appreciate it.

"Thank you," I said after a moment. And when I finally looked back at him, he was giving me an indulgent smile. Dolly's words now echoed through my mind:

I can think of several gentlemen who would happily take on a widow, even one with children. It remained to be seen whether Lord Linden was such a gentleman, but I had to admit I was more than a little curious to learn the answer.

Lord Linden stayed with me for another half hour—far longer than I expected. But even more surprising was how much I enjoyed myself. He may have had a reputation as a scoundrel, but the man was also well-educated and cultured. I discovered that we had a good deal in common, in fact. We even discussed attending a lecture given by the Shakespeare Society later in the week, and he left with a promise to write in a few days' time with the particulars.

I sat alone in the parlor afterwards in something of a daze, mulling over the entire exchange. While I could accept that Lord Linden might find me attractive, he was still one of the most eligible bachelors in England. Men like him married virginal debutants at least ten years my junior.

And they have affairs with experienced widows. Like you.

I nearly dropped my teacup at the thought, but conceded that it certainly made a good deal more sense than him wanting to formally court me. Regardless of the man's intentions, however, I knew what I wanted. And it wasn't to be any man's mistress. If that was his true intent, then Lord Linden would learn that soon enough.

Of course, it was impossible to ruminate on the subject of mistresses without thinking of Mr. Dorian and Mrs. Langham. I swallowed hard before the bitter taste could flood my mouth. It was the height of idiocy for me to feel disappointment, no matter how fleeting. He was nothing more to me than an acquaintance—and a particularly vexing one at that. What did I care how he spent his time and with whom?

I forced myself to think of Lord Linden. Of his delighted smile and the sensation of his lips against my knuckles, until my disagreeableness slowly melted into something softer. Though I could acknowledge that he was a handsome man, I didn't feel that deep tug of attraction. But his attention was a distraction from more inconvenient feelings. And that would have to be enough.

Chapter 20

On the day of the auction, I was on a mission to tire out my son. First, I took Tommy to the British Museum's reading room, so he could read up on the latest paleontological developments. After that, we wandered through the museum's galleries. When he had finally gotten his fill, we took the long way home through Hyde Park. By suppertime, Tommy could barely hide his yawns, and he went to bed shortly afterwards without complaint.

Once I was certain he was asleep, I changed into the dark blue evening gown Delia had deemed not appropriate for the gallery opening, fixed my hair, and went to the parlor to wait.

By the time Mr. Dorian arrived, promptly at eight, I was strung as tightly as a piano wire and nearly shot out of my chair when Mrs. Ford came to announce him.

"Mr. Dorian is here, ma'am," she said with a knowing look. Earlier, I had described him as an old friend from Corfu, but she had immediately assumed there was more between us. And my nervousness was not helping to dispel her misunderstanding.

"Very good," I said in a strangled voice. "Send him in."

Once she left, I wiped my damp palms on my skirt and hurried over to a mirror that hung on the wall. Somehow, I looked even more frazzled than I felt, and I did my best to smooth the curls that had sprung loose from their pins.

"Get a hold of yourself, Minnie," I muttered. "He's only a man, and you don't even *like* him."

But I knew what a horrible lie that was. Speaking it aloud had only made me feel worse—and the truth that much harder to ignore. It had been far easier to bury my feelings while on Corfu, when he was only a slowly fading memory. Seeing him in the flesh, however, was making that task infinitely harder.

"Are you all right?"

I yelped and whirled around to find Mr. Dorian standing in the doorway with an amused expression on his face.

"I'm fine," I snapped, which was not convincing in the least, and forced my arms to my sides.

Mr. Dorian strolled into the room, as calm as ever. His dark gaze quickly skimmed over me, and he gave an approving nod. "You look nice," he said offhandedly, in the way one might compliment their favorite cousin or a hostess's attempt at landscape painting. In other words, it was meaningless.

I would have rather he said nothing at all.

"Thank you. So do you," I replied automatically. He raised an eyebrow, no doubt because I sounded even more awkward than I felt. Then I shook my head and hurried past him. "We should go."

"If you'd like," he said as he followed me out the door. "I had my driver park in the mews, in case you wanted to avoid any prying eyes."

I nodded. "Good idea."

Once I fetched my coat, we exited through the back of the house. Mr. Dorian helped me into his waiting coach and then climbed in after me.

"I mentioned your thought about disguises to Mrs. Langham," he began. I immediately stiffened at the mention of his mistress, but thankfully he didn't seem to notice, as he was busy fiddling with a package on the seat beside him. "While I don't need one, she agreed it would be a good idea to conceal your identity to some extent. So she lent me this." Mr. Dorian then handed me the package, which turned out to be a hat box.

I cast him a curious look and opened it. Inside was a black velvet hat with a short veil. I gingerly took it out. "It's beautiful."

"As I recall, we employed a similar ruse on our journey to Paxos, and that seemed to work well enough."

"Yes. It did," I said. We had also posed as lovers on an illicit getaway, as well as a married couple, over the course of that short trip.

"Then you have no objection to using the same stratagem once again."

I lifted my chin a little. "Not at all." I could handle pretending to be Mr. Dorian's mysterious paramour for the space of a few hours. After Paxos, it would feel like child's play.

He held my gaze with an inscrutable look. "I just wanted to be sure," he murmured.

As my mouth went dry, I turned away, telling myself I needed to try on the hat and not because he unnerved me. "We're only going to be asking questions, anyway," I said, more for myself than him, as I fixed the hat to my head.

I wondered how much he had told Mrs. Langham about our acquaintance. But then, the woman seemed all too happy to help. It was ridiculous to think she was jealous of me. What possible threat could I, a woman on the cusp of middle age with two children, pose to someone like her?

"Yes," he replied after a moment, his voice sounding oddly strangled.

I pulled the lacy black veil over my face. The fabric's design seemed to obscure my features enough to provide a degree of anonymity.

"How do I look?" I asked with a cheeky tilt of my head, hoping to break the tension that had begun to fill the space between us.

But Mr. Dorian remained serious. "Perfect," he said softly. "You look perfect."

I was grateful that the fierce blush I felt heating my cheeks was undetectable under the veil. I cleared my throat before I could manage a reply. "Thank you."

He gave a little nod of acknowledgment before turning to look out the window. I couldn't begin to understand his behavior just now, so instead I sat back in my seat and went over everything I hoped to learn tonight.

We arrived a short time later at the opulent redbrick home of Sir Armstrong-Hughes.

"What do you know about him?" I asked, as I looked out the window.

Mr. Dorian immediately knew who I meant and let out a sigh. "Not much. He spent many years abroad in Egypt with the army. Apparently that was how he earned his knighthood."

I glanced at him. "He must have done something more than that. One doesn't just hand out knighthoods for a job well done."

"You'll have to ask Victoria Regina about the particulars," he drawled.

I rolled my eyes at his insouciant answer. "Mrs. Langham didn't know?" I deeply regretted the question as soon as I asked it.

But Mr. Dorian didn't seem to notice my sarcasm. "No."

Unfortunately, this only emboldened me. "How did they happen to meet?"

"The theater, I suppose. She meets lots of people that

way," he added, entirely unconcerned by the thought of his mistress forming acquaintances with any number of wealthy gentlemen.

Reluctantly, I had to admit it was a point in Mr. Dorian's favor that he didn't seem overly possessive of her. Granted, my understanding of such arrangements was limited, having mostly been gleaned from gossip I heard when I was still married. But as I understood it, protectors usually expected their mistresses to remain cosseted away somewhere and ready to fulfill their duties at any time. Yet Mrs. Langham appeared to enjoy a healthy independence.

"She told him I developed an interest in Italianate glassware when I was abroad and wanted to start collecting pieces of my own."

I raised an eyebrow. "Even though you were in Corfu?"

He smiled. "It was the first thing she could think of. I should have better prepared her. Luckily, Sir Armstrong-Hughes was charmed enough by her tale that he deigned to admit me and a guest."

"Then, who will he think *I* am?" I asked slowly. For surely the man would have assumed a personal connection between Mr. Dorian and Mrs. Langham.

"I'm sure he will make the obvious assumption," Mr. Dorian drawled. "And I trust he is a gentleman and thus will not ask directly."

Fair enough.

By then, the coachman had opened the door, and Mr. Dorian climbed out of the carriage. As he handed me down to the pavement, he pressed his lips close to my ear, and I sucked in a startled breath.

"Just stay close and let me do the talking, all right?"

I bristled a little at this directive, but we didn't have time to argue. Other attendees were already heading inside, and the auction would start soon. "Fine."

Mr. Dorian then held out his arm, and I took it. "Now, remember," he began as we ascended the front steps, "you are supposed to find me irresistible."

"I'll try," I said dryly and pressed a little closer to him.

He glanced at me. "I wish I could see your face clearly right now."

"I'm frowning," I snapped. "An expression you are quite familiar with."

Mr. Dorian chuckled. "I believe I could paint that very image even if I was blindfolded."

My grip on his arm tightened, and I pointedly turned away from him. Something about our exchange made me uncomfortable, which was the exact opposite of the image I needed to project. As we reached the front door, I could still feel Mr. Dorian's eyes lingering on my profile, but I kept my gaze firmly ahead, determined to stay focused on the task at hand.

Mr. Dorian gave his name to the footman manning the door, and we were quickly ushered inside. The entryway reminded me of Lord Linden's home, with its black-and-white marble checkered floor, high ceiling, and walls covered with treasures. I was so distracted by the space that I stopped in my tracks.

"Are you coming, darling?"

That immediately got my attention, and my head snapped to Mr. Dorian. He gave me a beseeching look, and I managed a nod.

Darling.

My stomach had somersaulted at the sound of the pet name, and a wave of shame quickly followed. I should have told him not to call me that, but other guests were close by milling about. Besides, I knew perfectly well he meant nothing by it. My reaction was my own issue.

Another footman directed us towards the ballroom, where the auction was to take place, and as we made our way down the hall, I was stunned by the number of items on display. It seemed like every available surface contained some priceless treasure from every era of civilization.

Even Mr. Dorian was awestruck. "Good lord," he murmured. "Is that a Ming vase?"

We stopped to inspect the vase more closely. I was no expert, but it certainly looked genuine to me. We then glanced at each other with mutual expressions of surprise.

"I was just at the British Museum yesterday," I began. "And this collection is still very impressive."

Mr. Dorian hummed in agreement. "The man may not have the space for Egyptian monuments, but the variety is incredible."

"It must have taken him years to put this all together."

"Try decades," came a deep voice.

I whirled around to find an older man with salt-and-pepper hair, a large black mustache, and spine-straight bearing I guessed came from many years of military service standing just behind us.

"Sorry, I didn't mean to startle you," he said with a faint smile. "But I always make a point to greet new guests."

Mr. Dorian stuck out his hand. "Stephen Dorian. Thank you very much for admitting us, Sir Armstrong-Hughes."

The man shook his hand, but kept his gaze on me. "And who is your companion?"

"Mrs. Collins," I said in a low voice, before Mr. Dorian could answer.

He took my hand and pressed it to his lips. "Lovely to meet you, Mrs. Collins. I've always had a weakness for a woman in a veil. Reminds me of the years I spent in the desert. People always underestimate the romance of the place."

I let out a nervous chuckle, and the man's smile deepened.

Mr. Dorian cleared his throat. "When does the auction begin?"

Sir Armstrong-Hughes tore his gaze away from me. "In

half an hour or so. I like to give people a bit of time to mill around and spread rumors about what will be for sale. I find it makes the bidding more robust," he added with a glint in his eyes.

"Right," Mr. Dorian said in a clipped tone. "Well, I suppose we should continue on. I don't want to take up any more of your time."

"It's no trouble," Sir Armstrong-Hughes replied, though he kept his gaze on me.

I was thankful for the veil, as it made it far easier to deal with the man's forwardness. I gave him a little nod before Mr. Dorian tugged me away.

"You didn't need to be so brusque," I said once we were out of earshot. "What if he decided to make us leave?"

"He was staring at you like you were another item to add to his collection," Mr. Dorian said with surprising force.

"I don't know why," I demurred. "He could barely make out my features."

"As if it would matter," he grumbled as we entered the ballroom.

I narrowed my eyes. "What is that supposed to mean?"

He glanced back, and his expression softened. "I only meant that one doesn't need to see your face to notice your charms."

"Oh," I said dumbly. That wasn't at all what I expected him to say. But Mr. Dorian's attention was already engaged across the ballroom, and then he muttered a curse.

"Dorian!" A portly man with dark hair called out as he approached us. "I thought that was you."

"Hello, Buckley," Mr. Dorian said before gesturing to me. "This is Mrs. Collins."

Mr. Buckley did a poor job of hiding his curiosity as he leaned towards me. "Collins, is it?"

I nodded in response as Mr. Dorian pulled me closer to

him. "I didn't know you were a collector," he remarked, drawing the man's attention away from me.

"Yes," Mr. Buckley said. "I've been coming to this auction for years. Though I don't often buy things, of course. The wife will have my head if I come home with any more Roman coins." He punctuated this with a braying laugh, and Mr. Dorian forced a smile.

"Right. Well, this is my first time. Charles Pearson told me about it, actually," he added after a beat.

Smart man, I thought.

Mr. Buckley immediately looked stricken. "Ah yes. Poor fellow. I didn't realize you knew him. Terrible shame. I heard they still haven't found the culprit."

I must have tensed, because Mr. Dorian pressed his palm against my arm in a soothing gesture. "No," he said. "I heard the same. He came here quite often, didn't he?"

"Yes," Mr. Buckley replied. "He had an excellent eye, Charles did. I would imagine his collection will fetch a pretty price. Do you know what the family intends to do with it all?" he asked, failing to hide his obvious interest.

"I've no idea," Mr. Dorian replied.

The man's face fell. "A pity. It would be a shame if it was all boxed away somewhere. I should write to his sister. Offer to take it off her hands. For a fair price, of course," he said with another hoarse laugh.

"Did you happen to hear about Charles selling anything recently?" Mr. Dorian said.

Mr. Buckley frowned as he considered this. "No, not at all. He was very selective when it came to selling things from his own collection. More often, he found things for other people. Charles was very good at that. He knew everyone and could charm anyone."

"But when he did sell things," Mr. Dorian pressed, "who might have bought from him?"

"Why, I've no idea," Mr. Buckley said, clearly puzzled by the question. "I'd wager it was another collector like myself. Though they would need far deeper pockets than me."

"What about any Grecian artifacts?" I said suddenly.

Both men turned to me, curious. Mr. Buckley shook his head. "I haven't come across anything truly remarkable out of Greece in some time. Not since the government began monitoring the discoveries at archeological sites more closely, anyway. A damned shame, too. If it were up to them, we wouldn't even have the Elgin Marbles." Then he glanced around before leaning in. "There was a rumor that someone at the British embassy was deliberately mislabeling artifacts and exporting them here, but they were discovered around the same time the pieces stopped coming in."

A chill ran down my spine. It was nearly the same accusation Mr. Dorian had made about Oliver. I could feel his heavy gaze upon me, but I couldn't look at him.

"Did Sir Armstrong-Hughes ever auction off any of these pieces?"

Mr. Buckley gave me a coy smile. "He wouldn't knowingly sell anything that didn't have the proper provenance, madame."

I scoffed. "Isn't that the whole point of a private auction?"

But the man only laughed. "One thing I will say about Sir Armstrong-Hughes is that he has a mind like a steel trap. And the records to match. If you get on his good side, he might be willing to share them with you. For a price, of course."

I was just about to ask how much money he thought it would cost, when Mr. Dorian gripped my arm. "Thank you, Buckley." Then he tugged me away.

"In case you forgot," he hissed as soon as we were out of earshot, "we are here to ask about Charles Pearson."

I pulled my arm out of his grip and shot him a glare. "I am aware. I only thought—"

"I know what you're doing, Minnie," he said, his tone gentler now. "But this isn't the time. Nor the place."

"But if I could just look at those records—"

"What?" he demanded with sudden exasperation. "You'll find Oliver's name written in one of the entries? It doesn't work like that."

"How would you know?" I said mulishly. "And maybe it won't be Oliver's name, but it will be someone's name, which is more than I know right now."

He let out a huff, as if this conversation was extremely inconvenient. "We can find out more information at another time."

I bristled at this poor attempt to placate me. "But we're here now. And this might be our only chance," I pointed out. "Who else will have records like that?" He stared at me in silence as a muscle in his jaw ticked. I clenched my hands into tight fists and scanned the room. The auction would start soon, and I worried our absence would be noticed. There wasn't time to wait. I looked back at Mr. Dorian and lifted my chin. "Either help me, or stay out of my way. The decision is entirely yours."

Then I turned on my heel and stalked out of the room. I had a study to find.

Chapter 21

I left the ballroom and headed down a darkened hallway away from the other guests towards the back of the house, trusting that the servants' staircase was somewhere nearby, as was usually the case in great houses like this. After taking a few wrong turns and opening the door of a closet, I finally found what I was looking for. The staircase was even darker than the hall and lit only by a single dim sconce. I pulled back my veil and hesitated, but then Mr. Dorian appeared.

"Having second thoughts?"

I bristled at his smug tone. "No," I said pointedly and began to climb the stairs.

"Try the second floor," he said after a moment, and I glanced back, though his face was mostly hidden in the shadows.

"All right." I suspected this was not merely a guess on his part, but did not question him. When I reached the second floor, I slowly pushed open the door and peered out into the hall. It was empty. I opened it wider and exited the staircase. Mr. Dorian was close behind me, and together we crept through the silent hallway.

"Third door on the right," he murmured by my ear.

"You certainly came prepared," I muttered as I quickly stepped towards it. Then I turned the knob.

Locked.

Before I could even speak, Mr. Dorian had nudged me out of the way and was on his knees.

"Is that a lockpick?" I asked.

"I'm not sure why you sound surprised," he said, while keeping his gaze focused on the task at hand. After a moment, something clunked within the lock, and he looked up at me with a grin. "I did come prepared, after all."

"I didn't realize picking locks was a skill you possessed," I tossed off, since the man looked so ridiculously proud of himself.

Mr. Dorian kept his gaze on mine as he rose. "Oh, I have a number of other skills you haven't even begun to imagine." Then he shouldered open the door with an easy smile.

I will admit this answer shocked me a little, and it was a moment before I followed him into the room. A low fire glowed in the hearth, casting off a dim orange light. It looked like any other wealthy man's study: dark wallpaper, heavy leather furniture, and shelves filled with books and other assorted bric-a-brac. I barely took in the smaller details, as I was here on a mission. Mr. Dorian was already behind a large desk and had turned on the lamp. I reached his side and immediately began pulling open drawers.

He placed a hand on my wrist. "Quietly, now. Try the bottom one. It's larger."

"Fine," I said tightly. I tugged on it, and, unsurprisingly, it was locked. I stepped back and waved a hand at it. Mr. Dorian bent down and got to work. Within moments, he had opened the drawer, which was filled with files, and began riffling through them.

"They're organized by year," he said.

"Try 1889." It was the year before Oliver left the service.

Mr. Dorian glanced up at me, but I avoided his gaze. He pulled out the file and stood, placing it on the desk. I immediately opened it and began scanning the documents. Mr. Buckley had been right. Sir Armstrong-Hughes did keep excellent records.

"This is a monthly inventory of every item auctioned off," Mr. Dorian said. "Look, he even includes the country of origin, the buyer, and the amount paid."

"And the seller," I added, pointing to the column with my finger.

Mr. Dorian let out a low whistle. "I recognize some of these names. This man works for the British Museum. And this one is a famous conservationist." He let out a disbelieving laugh.

But I didn't care about any of that. There was only one name I needed to find. I quickly ran my finger down the column for the country of origin, and while there were a number of entries for Greece, nearly every time I looked to the seller column, only an X was listed. This appeared in a few other columns as well, but most often for Greece.

I let out a cry of exasperation and stepped back. "There's nothing in here. Let's look at another year."

"Minnie," Mr. Dorian said as I bent down, looking for the file for 1888. "What makes you think it will be any different? Clearly Sir Armstrong-Hughes is protecting someone."

"And I need to know who it is," I snapped. I pulled out the file and had just set it on the desk when Mr. Dorian froze.

"Wait," he said and tilted his head, listening for something.

Then I heard it. The faint sound of footsteps down the hall. "Maybe . . . maybe they are going somewhere else," I said in a strangled voice.

"Are you willing to take that chance?" he said. "Because I am not."

Mr. Dorian looked remarkably calm as he quickly organized the file, took the other from my hands, and placed them both back in the drawer. Then he turned the lock and switched off the lamp. The footsteps were louder now. My heart was in my throat.

A cold sweat broke out on my neck, and blood roared in my ears. "What are we going to do?"

He took my hand and pulled me away from the desk over to a chaise in the corner.

I looked around the room wildly, but there wasn't anywhere to hide.

Mr. Dorian placed his hands on my shoulders and forced my gaze to meet his. "If we're caught, they can't know why we are really in here."

I nodded. "Yes. Quite right."

He gave me an imploring look. "Then you understand what we have to do."

I was so tense with nerves that it was a moment before I grasped his meaning. My eyes widened, and Mr. Dorian let out a humorless laugh. "You'll need to look a good deal more enthusiastic than that if we're to convince anyone."

I frowned. This was *not* the time for jokes. The footsteps were very near now, and it was highly likely that this study was the destination. "You as well," I shot back. Then, before Mr. Dorian could make a pithy response in return, I slid my arms around his neck and pulled his head down to mine.

The last thing I saw was a faint look of surprise cross his face before I closed my eyes and pressed my mouth to his.

The only other man I had ever kissed was Oliver, so it had been some time since I found myself in such an intimate position. Luckily, my body seemed to remember the particulars well enough. As soon as Mr. Dorian's lips met mine, I felt something crackle within me. Like a Roman candle flaring to life on a warm summer night. Once Mr. Dorian recovered from his understandable surprise, he slid his arms around my waist and pulled me flush against him. And while our embrace must have looked rather scandalous to the observer, he was a gentleman in every other way. The kiss was surprisingly gentle, which I appreciated. It was only towards the very end, after I became aware that someone was in the room with us and loudly clearing their throat, that the kiss became more insistent, as if Mr. Dorian forgot why we were doing this in the first place. I had to push on his chest more than once before he finally stepped back, a dazed look on his face. I raised an eyebrow, and he blinked, as if coming back to himself. It was a remarkably good performance, I will admit, but rather more than was necessary to convince Sir Armstrong-Hughes, while I was certain that my own weak knees and racing heart were merely due to the heightened excitement of the situation.

Mr. Dorian tore his gaze away from me to address our host. "Hello," he said with a sheepish smile.

However, the man was not in the least bit charmed. "What the hell are you doing in here?"

I turned around then and gave him my most apologetic look. "Please don't blame him, Sir Armstrong-Hughes," I began in a low, silky tone. "This is entirely my fault. I wanted to go somewhere quiet for a moment so Mr. Dorian and I could talk. I took him to the first open room I could find, and then I was simply . . . overcome."

This was a terrible excuse, in my opinion. But I knew that most men were all too willing to believe that women were at the mercy of their emotions.

Sir Armstong-Hughes watched me carefully, and only then did I remember I was no longer wearing my veil. Hopefully, the room was dark enough to afford me some privacy. "Is that true, Dorian?" he asked, still keeping his gaze on me.

"Uh, yes. Yes, it is," Mr. Dorian said quickly. "We would

never have intentionally invaded your privacy. And for that I am very sorry."

Sir Armstrong-Hughes finally looked to him then, his stern gaze full of disapproval. "Fine. But you must leave at once. And don't come back."

"Absolutely," Mr. Dorian said. "Come along, my dear," he said as he led me out of the room. We hurried down the hall as quickly as possible without looking back.

"Do you think he believed us?" I asked once we were downstairs.

"No," Mr. Dorian admitted. "But he won't find any evidence to suggest otherwise."

I let out a breath of relief, and we continued down the hall towards the front door. Mr. Buckley rounded a corner, possibly returning from a trip to the water closet, and caught sight of us. "Leaving already?" he asked, disappointed. "But it's just about to start."

"I'm afraid Mrs. Collins isn't feeling well," Mr. Dorian explained.

"That's a shame. I'm glad I caught you then. I've just remembered something about Pearson that may be useful to you."

Mr. Dorian tilted his head, attempting a look of only mild interest. "Oh?"

"There was a fellow that came with him to the auction sometimes. Not very friendly, though, and kept to himself so we were never properly introduced. But if you can find him, he might know more about who Charles worked with."

"It will be difficult without a name," Mr. Dorian said dryly.

"Sir Armstrong-Hughes might know," Mr. Buckley suggested. But that avenue was quite closed to us.

"What did he look like?" I ventured.

The man paused to think. "Well, he was taller than Charles. And his hair was a similar color, though he always had a hat on."

"I see," Mr. Dorian replied flatly at this rather generic description.

"Oh!" Mr. Buckley suddenly exclaimed. "I did think it looked rather long for a gentleman. Nearly to his shoulders, in fact," he added, sounding slightly scandalized.

My stomach did a little flip. That sounded like a general description of the baron. And it was certainly possible that Lord Linden would have come to this auction with Charles.

"Thank you, Buckley. That is all very helpful," Mr. Dorian replied a tad sardonically, but that was lost on the man.

"Glad to hear it. Now then, I had better get to my seat!" he said before hurrying past us.

"Come on." Mr. Dorian took my arm and led me to the cloakroom, where we quickly retrieved our coats, and then stepped out into the night.

"I think he may have seen the baron," I said once we were a few steps away from the house.

"Do you?" Mr. Dorian then considered this. "I suppose it's possible."

"But why would he be so secretive about coming here?"

Mr. Dorian shrugged. "Sometimes these avid collectors don't want people knowing what they have on hand."

It was reminiscent of Mr. Henshaw's explanation for hiding the identity of the buyer for Delia's painting. "I suppose."

The air had grown quite chilly, and I instinctively hugged my arms close to my chest.

Mr. Dorian then pressed a hand to the small of my back as he guided me towards the waiting carriage. I jolted at the familiarity of his touch, and a rush of heat swept through me from head to foot as I remembered our embrace from only minutes ago.

"Please give Mrs. Langham my regrets," I began, keeping my gaze firmly ahead. "Unless you think it's better not to mention it at all."

It. Goodness, I couldn't even bring myself to say the word *kiss*.

Mr. Dorian stopped in his tracks, and I was forced to look at him. His brow was furrowed in confusion. "What are you talking about?"

"I . . . what we did. In the study," I said haltingly. But as soon as the words were out, I was swamped with regret. It probably hadn't even crossed his mind to mention it in the first place. And now he thought me deranged for even bringing it up. "Never mind," I added. "Forget I said anything." Then I began to hurry away, as if I could outrun my embarrassment.

But Mr. Dorian was beside me in an instant. "Wait," he said as he grabbed my arm to stop me. "I don't understand. What does Mrs. Langham have to do with anything?"

I let out an exasperated huff. Now he was just taunting me. "Because I know she is your mistress. And I certainly wouldn't like it if my paramour kissed another woman. No matter the circumstances."

Mr. Dorian stared at me with a bemused expression. "I told you. We're only friends."

"You never said anything of the sort, actually," I said hotly. "And there is no need for you to hide your relationship. I am not so naïve that I expect a grown man to live like a monk. Do whatever you want. But please don't lie to me."

His eyebrows rose in shock, and I turned away again, but he moved to block my path. "I am *not* lying. I have known Mrs. Langham for years, and she has only ever been a friend to me."

I crossed my arms and looked away. "Fine."

"It's true," he insisted. "I met her through her father."

I glanced back, unable to hide my surprise. "You did?"

The corner of his mouth lifted ever so slightly. "Mr. Rohan Merriweather. A dashedly interesting fellow and the inspiration for the character Rohan Seymour."

"Oh," I said, as I recalled the details. The wryly funny Anglo-Indian solicitor was an excellent foil to the more sober inspector.

"When Merriweather retired from practicing law," Mr. Dorian went on, "he turned his hand to poetry and became a minor sensation. I met him at a reading one evening, along with his very protective daughter, and we all became friends."

"Oh." I cleared my throat primly. "I see."

"Unfortunately, the gentleman passed away a few years ago, but my friendship with Mira has endured."

"Then, Langham is a stage name?" I asked with a casual air in a bid to save face.

The corner of Mr. Dorian's mouth lifted, and he shook his head. "Her late husband was a Langham. He was a director and brought her into the theater world. Quite a bit older, though. Rohan didn't like him much. Mira swore off marriage after he died. Frankly, I can't imagine her being any man's mistress," he added with a chuckle, then quickly sobered. "Even still, I'm sorry if I gave you the impression that we are romantically involved."

I inadvertently sucked in a breath as he stepped closer to me and lifted my chin. "I don't know why you would be," I replied, fighting to remain detached. "But it was Lord Linden who told me anyway." I certainly didn't want him thinking I had even bothered to make such an inference on my own.

That caught him by surprise. "Linden?" Then he shook his head. "That blackguard," he muttered.

"He is nothing of the sort."

Mr. Dorian let out a dark laugh. "You think it was simply a mistake on his part?"

"The baron was only trying to help."

He let out a derisive snort. "He's after something. I've seen the way he has been sniffing around you," he added, his voice dripping with disapproval.

"Right," I said, barely able to contain my outrage. "Because the thought that he would enjoy my company is simply too absurd for you to fathom."

"That is not what I meant—"

"And even if you and Mrs. Langham are just friends, what about the rest of them?"

He narrowed his eyes. "The rest of who?"

"You are written about in the papers nearly every night!" I threw up my arms in frustration. "And always in the company of a different woman. You may not be involved with Mrs. Langham, but you are with someone. Not that I care, of course," I added in a rather pathetic attempt at nonchalance.

Mr. Dorian pinched the bridge of his nose. "It isn't what it looks like." I could only laugh at this clichéd excuse. "You know that I have long been a target for gossip," he insisted. "My activities are often embellished, if not outright invented, simply to sell papers."

I pursed my lips. "Fine. I understand. It doesn't matter anyway," I added softly, more to myself than him.

He held my gaze. "Doesn't it?"

I swallowed and looked away. "I . . . I should go."

It was a cowardly response, but my nerves were already so worn from our evening that I simply lacked the will to endure anything else.

Something like disappointment flashed in Mr. Dorian's eyes. "Take my carriage, then. I'll walk." I began to protest, but he held up a hand. "Please."

There was an unfamiliar weariness in his gaze that caught me off guard. I gave him a stilted nod and then followed him the rest of the way to his waiting carriage. I stood on the pavement as he quickly spoke to the coachman, then he brushed past me and opened the door.

He held out his hand, and I stared at it for a moment before I took it. Once I climbed into the carriage and took my seat, I turned back. Mr. Dorian was leaning in the doorway, waiting for me to look at him.

"Think whatever you like if it makes it easier for you," he began. "But there hasn't been anyone, Minnie. Not since my marriage."

Then he stepped back and shut the door quite soundly in my face.

Unsurprisingly, I did not sleep very well that night. After tossing and turning for hours, I finally gave up and instead set to work recording my latest discoveries. By the time dawn broke, I was bleary-eyed, exhausted, and had little to show for it.

I was nowhere closer to uncovering Charles Pearson's killer nor Oliver's possible role in illegally exporting Greek antiquities, and had quite possibly destroyed my acquaintance with Mr. Dorian in the process. I closed my notebook and stumbled into bed, where sleep finally embraced me. I was awoken later by a soft knock on the door and the housekeeper's concerned voice.

"Mrs. Harper, are you well?"

"Yes, I'm fine," I rasped as I pulled a hand down my face. Then I rolled over and squinted at the small bedside clock. It was nearly 9:30. I threw back the covers and hurried over to open the door.

Mrs. Ford was waiting in the hall, her face pinched with worry. "May I bring you a tray?"

"Thank you, yes. I'm afraid I had trouble sleeping last night," I explained.

Understanding dawned on her face. "You poor thing. I have a tincture that does wonders, if you need."

"I appreciate that and will certainly let you know. How is Tommy?"

"He's perfectly well," she said with a reassuring smile. "Curled up with a stack of books in the study."

"Good." I let out a breath of relief. Between the book Cleo had lent him and the stack we had brought home yesterday, I hoped he could be occupied for the rest of the morning.

"Now you go on back to bed, and I'll be in shortly with some breakfast," Mrs. Ford said.

I nodded at her gentle command and did as I was told. As I nestled under the covers once more, my gaze caught on the desk by the window and the notebook I had pushed aside in frustration mere hours ago. My mind and body were desperate for more sleep, but my thoughts churned with renewed vigor and the need to do something.

By the time Mrs. Ford returned with a poached egg, toast, and tea, I had already dressed for the day.

She raised an eyebrow as she set the tray down. "Going somewhere?"

"I was hoping to visit Delia this morning," I replied, pouring myself a cup of tea.

Mrs. Ford pursed her lips in disapproval. "Might it not be better to let yourself rest?"

I gave her a smile. "Believe me, I have functioned on far less sleep many times," I added with a knowing chuckle that the housekeeper did not return.

"Pardon me, Mrs. Harper," she began. "But I promised your aunt that I would watch out for you, and I must admit that I am not merely speaking of last night. You've been pushing yourself ever since that man's death."

I placed a hand on her shoulder. "I very much appreciate

your concern. Really, I do. But I'm fine. I'll go see my sister and then return for a nap this afternoon."

I watched Mrs. Ford mull over my words and finally give a stiff nod. "All right then."

"Thank you," I said with a gentle squeeze of her shoulder. And it was the truth. I did appreciate having someone looking out for my well-being.

After I finished my breakfast, I went to collect Tommy. He was reluctant to leavc his little pile of books until I mentioned that my parents had a very fine library of their own that he could peruse. Then he was on his feet and barreling down the hall towards the door.

Once we arrived at Portman Square a short time later, I was happy to learn from Morris that Delia was awake and in the parlor. Tommy wanted to escape to the library at once, but I made him come with me to greet his aunt. Upon entering the room, I found Delia curled up on the window seat with a book. She looked so peaceful that I almost hated to interrupt her, but then Tommy charged forward.

"Hello, Aunt Delia! What are you reading? Is it about dinosaurs?"

She broke into a smile and sat up. "Unfortunately, no. It is a book of poems by John Keats."

Tommy immediately frowned, which was to be expected. "I think you would much prefer to read about dinosaurs."

"I agree," she replied before looking at me. "I'm glad you've both come."

Delia wore a plain grey day gown, with an old shawl wrapped around her shoulders. Her face was still paler than normal, but she looked better than the last time I saw her.

I patted Tommy's shoulder. "Why don't you go down the hall to the library. You might even find a book for your aunt."

He looked up at me, his eyes wide with excitement. "All right." Then he bolted from the room.

"No running inside!" I called after him, but it seemed to have little effect.

I turned back to Delia and sat beside her.

"How are you feeling?" I asked, taking her hand in mine.

"Better," she replied. "Physically, at least."

I gave her a sympathetic smile. "And what does Mrs. Reynolds say?"

"She has been an angel. I'm supposed to still rest, of course. But that is just as well. I have no desire to see anyone. Present company excluded," she added.

I squeezed her hand. "I am here for you. Anything you need."

"I know," she said softly, as she squeezed back.

But I knew very well that grief was a road one had to travel largely alone. For after the rites were said and the dead were buried, others moved on much more quickly.

She then inhaled and straightened. "So then. Have you uncovered anything of note?"

I considered telling Delia about our meeting with Mrs. Pearson, but decided it wasn't necessary at the moment. She deserved to mourn the Charles Pearson she had known and loved. And there were other things I could share in the meantime.

"I learned from Mr. Henshaw about a private auction that Charles frequented at the home of Sir Armstrong-Hughes. I thought we might be able to speak with some of the attendants and perhaps discover more about his business."

Delia leaned forward, her interest piqued. "And?"

"Mr. Dorian was able to gain us admission, and we attended last night. I learned that Charles did not often sell his pieces. Rather, he found pieces for other collectors. And apparently was quite good at it."

Delia bit her lip as she considered this. "That makes sense. And could explain his need for a telephone."

"Yes, perhaps." Then I hesitated. Delia rose a brow, compelling me to continue. "I did not only go there to find out about Charles, though. Months ago, while I was still on Corfu, I learned a rumor about Oliver and his work in the government."

Delia frowned in confusion. "A rumor? What kind of rumor?"

I let out a sigh. "Mr. Dorian asked a friend at the Foreign Office to look into Oliver, and they revealed that he was suspected of selling Grecian artifacts on the black market."

Her mouth dropped open in shock. "*What?*"

I hung my head and nodded. "They also suggest that that was the reason Oliver left the embassy and moved us to Corfu."

Delia gripped my wrist. "Do you believe that?"

My nose began to sting as I met her concerned gaze. "I don't know. And I hate that I feel any kind of doubt about him. But I cannot deny that it would explain some things. His sudden retirement, his insistence that we move to Corfu. And . . ." I swallowed hard, past the lump in my throat. "Not long before he died, he made me promise him that I wouldn't come back here. He was quite insistent about it, in fact. And for a long time, I thought it was because he simply wanted the children to have a different kind of childhood than we had. But now I keep thinking that there was more to it. That maybe he was trying to protect us from something. But if that was the case, wouldn't he have told me?"

"Maybe he meant to," Delia said gently.

But death had taken him first.

I wiped the heel of my palm across my eyes, where a few rebellious tears had fallen. "We found some papers in Sir Armstrong-Hughes's study that included a number of items exported from Greece around the time Oliver was still in service. But the name of the procurer was deliberately withheld."

"Good heavens, Minnie," Delia said, looking properly shocked. "And you think it was Oliver?"

"I don't know. But I need to find out who it was. If only to prove it wasn't him."

"How can I help?"

I let out a surprised laugh. "I can't drag you into this."

"Nonsense. After everything you've done for me, let me help you now."

I shook my head. "I wouldn't even know where to begin." But just as I said the words, something came to mind:

Tell that imbecile to get my daughter out of here. That was our agreement.

"Actually," I began. "Father said something the other day that was quite odd. He wasn't in his right mind, I know, but he seemed very agitated to see me here and specifically said it wasn't safe."

Delia furrowed her brow. "He doesn't always have a very good sense of time. It's as if his mind is shuffling through the years."

"Do you think it's possible he worked for the government? Perhaps . . . in secret?"

"You mean as a spy?" She snorted. "He would have been terrible at that."

"But he specifically mentioned someone named Mitchem. And Mr. Dorian said he was once the head of the Foreign Office."

"Well, I can poke around his study, if you like," Delia offered. "Though if he really was up to something clandestine, I highly doubt he would have kept a record of it."

"That's true. But something may turn up. Where is Mother?"

Delia waved a hand. "Out making her usual calls. Honestly, that woman will let nothing keep her from her social schedule. London could crumble all around us, and she would still see Lady Montgomery on Mondays, Mrs. Gilbert on Tuesdays, and Lady Asquith on Wednesdays."

"Oh God," I said with a start. "I completely forgot that I promised to call on Lady Asquith's niece today. She is an old friend from Girton." Then I glanced at the clock on the mantel. "Just about now, in fact."

Delia tilted her head. "Well, go ahead. I can keep an eye on Tommy."

"Are you sure you don't mind?"

"It isn't as though I have anywhere else to be," she said. "And I could use the distraction. Perhaps he can tell me about dinosaurs."

"Do not get him started, or you will never hear the end of it," I warned.

But Delia just flashed me a grin. "I can think of far worse ways to spend a morning. Now shoo. I know you hate being late even by one minute."

It was true. I was already mapping out the route to Cecelia's house in my head. I could take the carriage, but decided it would be faster if I walked and cut through the park.

"Thank you, Delia," I said as I stood. "I won't be gone more than an hour."

She waved me towards the door. "Expect me to be an expert on paleontology when you return."

Chapter 22

Mrs. Cecelia Wentworth lived in a white stucco terrace house on Bayswater Road, which I reached in record time thanks to my very unladylike stride. I barely had time to catch my breath before I was ushered inside to a light-filled entryway tastefully painted in shades of cream, with framed botanical prints artfully displayed on the walls. I faintly recalled that Cecelia had had a particular interest in biology at school.

I handed my card to the butler, who immediately escorted me to the drawing room, where Cecelia was waiting.

"Minnie!" she said with a genuine smile as she hurried over and pulled me into a tight hug. "I'm so glad you came."

I was surprised by this show of affection, as we had last had contact long ago, but it was welcome. "Thank you for inviting me."

She then pulled back and gestured to the sofa. "Please, sit."

Like the entryway, this room was also decorated in calming shades of cream and gold.

"What a beautiful room," I said as I took in the space. The botanical theme continued in here, with drapes in a leaf-printed pattern of green and white, along with furniture in a pale pink floral brocade.

Cecelia beamed. "I decorated it myself."

"You are very talented."

She ducked her head in acknowledgment. "Thank you. I needed something to occupy my time after my marriage. I started drawing botanical prints, and things slowly came together from there."

"Those are yours framed in the entryway? They're marvelous."

"Thank you. It was a bit difficult for me, especially after Girton," she added with a knowing look. "You spend all that time and effort earning an education, and then once you return to the outside world, no one really cares. You're supposed to be perfectly happy managing a household and having children. I love my children, of course. But . . . it wasn't enough," she admitted with a shy glance at me.

I hummed in agreement. "I understand completely."

She relaxed a little and began to pour our tea. "Well, Greece must have been a marvelous adventure. Your mother said you lived in Athens before Corfu. Did you visit the sites there often?"

"Not often, no," I replied. "In truth, most of my days were spent managing the household and mothering." I flashed her a smile. "It's only been in the last year or so that I've begun to focus on myself a little more."

A faint blush stained her cheeks. "Of course. I know how lucky I am to have the time and resources to dabble in my little activities."

"Don't dismiss yourself," I said. "I think it's wonderful what you've done. My path has just been . . . different."

Her eyes softened. "I was so sorry to hear about your husband. My husband, Gerald, was as well. They knew each other at Cambridge."

"Did they? I had no idea."

"Yes." Then she perked up. "He gave me something to show you, actually. Here, let me fetch it."

Cecelia crossed the room to a small writing desk and picked up a leather-bound folder. "It's a photograph from a dig in Greece that they attended one summer with some other fellows from their Hellenic club."

"How lovely." I vaguely remembered Oliver telling me about that. His father refused to pay for his passage, so he talked his way onto a shipping vessel and worked alongside the crew all the way to Greece.

Cecelia sat beside me and handed me the opened folder. The photograph showed a group of young men in various states of dress. Most had shed their coats and ties and had rolled up their shirt-sleeves. They stood outside, some holding shovels and pickaxes as props, all squinting in the sun. I found Oliver immediately, standing front and center with his foot propped on the step of a shovel, his hand resting jauntily on the top of the handle. He smiled broadly at the camera, and I couldn't help smiling back. He looked so young and happy, like there was nowhere else in the entire world he wanted to be at that very moment. A strange sort of gladness filled my chest. His life had been cut so short. But I was grateful that he had been able to accomplish so much with the time he had.

"That's my Gerry there in the back row," Cecelia said, pointing to a tall man with dark hair and round spectacles.

But my eyes were drawn to the gentleman just beside him. I frowned in confusion and drew the picture closer to my face. But no. I had not been mistaken.

"Is something wrong?" Cecelia asked.

"That man beside your husband is Lord Linden," I said slowly. "I'm sure of it."

Cecelia inspected the photograph and nodded. "It certainly does look like him. Though I've only met him in passing."

I turned to her with a frown. "He told me he didn't know Oliver."

"Perhaps he forgot," she offered. "It was an awfully long time ago."

"Yes, but it would be rather odd to forget someone that you were in Greece with for a whole summer, wouldn't it?"

"Then . . . do you think he's lying?" Cecelia's eyes widened, and for a moment, I envied her naïvety.

"I don't know," I said diplomatically, rather than discuss the murder investigation that had been taking up my time these last few weeks.

"I'll ask Gerry when he gets home this evening," she said. "Perhaps he would know something."

"That would be extremely helpful."

"Of course! I'll write to you straightaway and make sure it's sent first thing tomorrow."

I stayed for another ten minutes, but I couldn't tell you what we spoke about. My mind whirled with any possible reason that could explain the baron's actions. But none of them were particularly compelling. The simplest reason was by far the most likely one: Lord Linden had lied to me about knowing Oliver. What remained to be seen was why. And I was determined to find out.

When I returned to Portman Square, I entered the library, still half lost in thought. Then I stopped short and blinked at the scene before me. Tommy was sitting on the sofa with my father, and together they were looking through a book. Delia stood nearby, watching them with a smile on her face. She turned at my entrance and immediately approached me.

"He's having a good day," she murmured, gesturing to our father.

He was giving Tommy the kind of indulgent smile Oliver had often worn when in the presence of our children, but I couldn't remember ever seeing that expression on my father's face before. During my childhood, he had been even more distant than my mother. A mixture of stern and silent that, frankly, made me feel rather nervous when he did deign to spend time with us. At times, he seemed more like a mythical figure than a real person. But as I watched him openly admiring my son, something pinched in my chest, and it was a moment before I realized it was envy. Both for the man my son got to experience and for the father I could never really get to know.

"Let me take Tommy so you can talk with Father," Delia said.

I nodded, as my gaze was still fixed upon the two of them. My son was proudly pointing out all the parts of some kind of animal, as if he was delivering a groundbreaking lecture, while my father reacted with great interest.

Delia swept over to them and held out her hand. "Tommy, darling, why don't you and I go to the kitchen and see what treats Cook has whipped up for us."

Tommy immediately shut the book and placed it beside him before jumping up and grabbing Delia's hand. Then he caught sight of me. "Hello, Mama. May I have a treat?"

"Yes, of course," I said, patting his shoulder. "But just one. Or you'll ruin your appetite."

Delia shot me an encouraging look as she guided Tommy out of the room. I watched as disappointment crossed my father's face while he followed Tommy's retreating form, but then he noticed me. I was relieved to see his mouth curve in a smile, though not quite as wide as the one Tommy conjured. But then I wasn't nearly as charming as my son.

"Hello, Father," I said, taking the now empty seat beside him.

"Delia said you would be back."

She had been right. His gaze seemed sharper than it had either of the other times I had seen him, though admittedly it was still but a shadow of what it had been. As terrifying and distant as he could be, my father had long been considered one of the best financial minds in London. He had likely forgotten more than most people would ever know. How many other people suffered from this same fate? My stomach turned at the thought. The sheer futility of it all.

"I was just calling on an old school friend who lives nearby," I managed. "How was your visit with Tommy?"

My father chuckled. "A delightful boy. So curious and full of energy."

"Yes, that he is," I agreed, smiling back.

"And your daughter? Delia said she is at school here."

I nodded. "Cleo is in Hampstead. And she's doing quite well. I will bring her here for a proper visit over the Christmas holiday."

"Very good. I'm sure it has been difficult for them, losing Oliver. For all of you," he added offhandedly.

"Yes," I rasped.

Then he reached out and patted my hand. "You've always been so strong. But I know what it's like when people come to expect that of you. Sometimes the strongest among us are the ones that need the most comfort."

I was shocked to hear this kind of insight from him. "Father," I began, but my voice broke.

"That was why I thought Oliver would be good for you," he continued, gazing off towards the hearth. "And why I put up with the rest of it."

"What do you mean?"

He shook his head slowly, his gaze turning unfocused. "Taking you so far away. Taking all those risks."

I inhaled and leaned closer to him, trying to draw his eyes to me. "*What* risks?"

"But they weren't worth it in the end," he murmured. "Were they?"

It was as if he was having a one-sided conversation with himself. "Father," I said, gently shaking his shoulder. He finally looked back at me, and I watched the lucidity return, though not as sharp as earlier.

"Sorry, my dear. Sometimes I ramble on."

"You were talking about Oliver. About some risks he took?"

He frowned in confusion and looked away. "Oh. I'm . . . I'm not sure." Then he turned back to me with a sheepish smile. "Your sister says I walk through time. That I don't always remember things correctly."

"Yes," I said sadly, realizing the moment was lost. "She did mention that."

My father sighed a little. "I wish I could help you more. But if you want to know about Oliver, you should talk to the viscount."

I stiffened automatically, as I always did when he was mentioned. "Yes, I'll think about it," I said vaguely. I knew it was better not to push him now, but I couldn't resist trying just one last time. "Father, did a man named Charles Pearson ever come here to see you? To talk about Delia?"

He looked surprised. "Charles . . ."

"Pearson. Yes. Do you remember?" I pressed.

My father frowned, and I could almost see him trying to sift through his memories, searching for it. "I . . . I don't know." He shook his head. "Perhaps?" He gave me a look full of such desperate hope that I felt horribly shameful for even bringing it up.

"Thank you," I said as I patted his arm.

The door swung open then, and Tommy came charging into the room wheeling the tea cart. "We've brought cake!"

My father broke into a delighted smile then, and I could only hope that he would soon forget the discomfort I had caused him. Delia came in a moment later, looking slightly harried, and she immediately sought out my gaze. I gave her a slight shake of the head, and her face fell.

I then began pouring the tea and handing out cake. Once

Father and Tommy were happily occupied, I pulled Delia aside.

"I learned something very odd at Cecelia Wentworth's just now," I began and told her about the photograph and Lord Linden's insistence that he did not know Oliver.

"Perhaps he was mistaken," Delia said, voicing the same possibility as Cecelia, but I shook my head.

"No," I said, even more certain now that the man was being intentionally duplicitous. "There is something else going on here. I'm sure of it.

Delia looked uncertain. "What are you going to do?"

I let out a sigh. "I'm not sure." But that wasn't entirely true, for I would need to tell Mr. Dorian about this. I could only hope he would keep his gloating to a minimum or else I would not be responsible for my actions.

Mother returned not long afterwards and seemed pleasantly surprised to find us all gathered together. After a little while, though, she asked Delia to take Father back to his room, as it was time for his nap. I was grateful to have a moment to speak with her and asked Tommy if he wanted to look at the library one last time before we left. He was out of the door in a moment, leaving Mother and me alone.

"Do you know if Charles Pearson ever came here to call on Father?" I asked, getting right to it. "Perhaps to ask for Delia's hand?"

She sat back in surprise at the blunt question. "Your father doesn't receive visitors anymore."

I let out a huff of exasperation. "I know, but I spoke to Charles Pearson's widow, and—"

"You did *what*?" She looked properly scandalized.

"Mother," I began tersely, "you wanted me to investigate this murder, and that is the sort of thing it requires. We're lucky the woman even agreed to speak to me." I decided not to share the role Mr. Dorian had played in the meeting.

My mother wilted a little at this. "Well, what did she have to say then?"

"She showed me a letter from Charles claiming to have met with Father."

"I suppose he could have," she said slowly. "Depending on when he came."

"And would he have been able to speak to him alone? Without you hearing about it?"

She grimaced. "Possibly. Sometimes he leaves his room while the nurse naps. And he always comes in here. He likes looking at the pictures," she said with a little smile, gesturing to the collection of framed photographs on the sideboard.

Still, I needed to look for holes. "What about Morris or Mrs. Reynolds? Wouldn't they have been about?"

"Not if he happened to come on one of their half days," Mother said. "And Morris was tucked up in bed with a cold for a few days several weeks ago, so the footman would have been alone to man the door. He's new, you see, and I . . . I haven't shared the extent of your father's condition with him yet."

I recalled my own interactions with the footman and how bewildered he seemed when I asked about my father. I suspected it would have been quite easy for a man like Charles Pearson to charm his way inside.

"So then it's possible Charles came to call on Father and actually got to speak with him, alone."

"Yes," my mother said on a sigh. "I suppose it's *possible*. But I don't understand why this is so important. You've seen what he's like. Anyone would have realized he wasn't well right away."

Or he had caught Father in one of his more strident moods. Similar to the one I witnessed with Mr. Dorian. I tilted my head. "Did Father know Lord Mitchem?"

She let out a bemused laugh. "Of course. He knew every man in the cabinet. What is this about, Minnie?"

"It's just . . . something he said to me the other day. It made me wonder if there was another side to him that perhaps we didn't know about. Activities he was engaged in."

I had expected my mother to be shocked by this, but instead she gave me a sympathetic look. "Your father had many secrets, my dear. All men do. And in my experience, it is better to let them keep them. For if you go poking around in their hidden places, you may not like what you find."

Tommy and I left not long afterwards, my mother's warning echoing in my mind all the way back to Hyde Park Street. Perhaps she had been satisfied having such an arrangement with her husband, but I had never knowingly agreed to one myself. And Oliver had left behind far too many loose ends for me to simply ignore them. When we arrived home, Mrs. Ford reminded me of my earlier promise to take a nap, and I admittedly was feeling the effects of my largely sleepless night. So I took her suggestion, without protest, and retreated upstairs. My head had barely touched the pillow before I fell into a deep sleep.

Chapter 23

I ended up sleeping straight through the night. But I must have needed the rest because when I woke very early the next morning, I felt more refreshed than I had since the night of the murder. I got up with a renewed vigor and immediately readied myself for the day. Tommy was still asleep, but I could hear Mrs. Ford downstairs.

"Good morning," I said as I entered the breakfast room, where she was laying out the table.

"Good morning, Mrs. Harper. I trust you slept well?"

"Yes," I replied as I took my seat. "I feel wholly new."

The housekeeper smiled. "I am glad to hear it. What can I bring you? Porridge? Eggs?"

My stomach rumbled at the suggestions, but I was in a hurry this morning. "I think just tea and toast for now."

"Of course," she said with a nod before leaving the room.

As I did not possess Mr. Dorian's home address, I would need to remedy that first. But the only person in London who I was certain would have that information was Mr. Howard, his publisher and the owner of the villa next to my home on Corfu. He was an infrequent visitor to the island, so I didn't know him terribly well, but he was aware of my acquaintance with his star writer, so I felt confident I could procure the information.

Mrs. Ford returned with my breakfast, along with that morning's post. My eyes widened at the envelope addressed to me, and I tore it open before I even touched my tea. It was from Cecelia:

> *Dear Minnie,*
>
> *It was so lovely to see you yesterday, and I hope you will come again. As promised, I asked my husband about the dig and the presence of Lord Linden. As you suspected, he confirmed that his lordship was indeed in attendance that summer. But he also mentioned something else that may be of interest: Apparently Lord Linden and your husband got into a shouting match one evening that nearly came to blows. Unfortunately, Gerry was only a causal observer and did not know all of the particulars, but he suggested it may have had something to do with their opposing views on the ownership of Greek artifacts, which had been a frequent source of conflict between them. Now, I cannot pretend I know much, if anything, about this topic, so it might be best if you speak with Gerry about this directly. You are welcome anytime . . .*

The rest of her words swam before my eyes; my arm fell against my lap, and the letter slipped from my fingers. I was too stunned by what I had learned. Not only had the baron lied about knowing Oliver, but they had had a confrontation that nearly resulted in fisticuffs. My worst suspicions were now all but confirmed. Either Mr. Wentworth was gravely misremembering the events of that summer, or the baron had a great deal of explaining to do.

I pushed back my chair and stood up. "I need to leave immediately."

"Is everything all right, Mrs. Harper?"

I turned to Mrs. Ford, who was watching me with a stricken expression. "I have some very important business I must attend to."

"But you haven't even eaten yet."

I wrapped a piece of toast in a cloth napkin. "Tell Tommy I will be back as soon as possible."

"Yes, of course," Mrs. Ford said with a grudging nod as I left the room. "Do be careful!" she called at my back, to which I merely raised a hand in reply. For I sought answers, and I would do whatever it took to get them.

"I'm terribly sorry, madame. But, as I said, Mr. Howard is very busy this morning. If you leave your card, I will do my best to schedule a meeting tomorrow afternoon."

"I don't need a meeting," I gritted out. "I just need a moment."

I had been arguing with Mr. Howard's secretary for the last few minutes, but the young man was intractable. I could only imagine the desperate writers he had to deal with every day, but the purpose of my visit was very different from what theirs might be.

He let out a short sigh, as if I was very thick, and waved a hand at the bench in the lobby. "You are welcome to wait, but he has absolutely no openings today," he said firmly.

"Fine," I said and flounced over to the empty bench.

The secretary cast a withering look at me before pointedly turning back to his typewriter. I had arrived here a little after nine-thirty, and Mr. Howard was already sequestered in a meeting, but I was certain that, once he saw me, he would immediately beckon me into his office. So I would just have to wait until then. My stomach let out a growl of protest, and I retrieved the piece of toast I had brought with me. I had just taken a bite when the door to the office's lobby opened, and a gentleman breezed inside.

"Good morning, Deveraux," he said. "Staying out of trouble, are you?"

I nearly choked on my toast. It was Mr. Dorian. He turned at the sound of my coughing fit, and his mouth dropped open. "Mrs. Harper?"

I couldn't respond, as I was occupied with trying not to choke, and he hurried over. "Get the lady some water!" he barked at the secretary, who jumped out of his chair and hurried into another room.

"I'm fine," I managed to rasp, even as my eyes were tearing up.

"I beg to differ," Mr. Dorian drawled. In another moment, the secretary had returned with a little mug of water, and Mr. Dorian shoved it at me. I took a long sip, and the cool water really did help. I cleared my throat and wiped my eyes. "Thank you."

Mr. Dorian was still frowning at me in concern. "You are welcome. Now tell me what the devil you are doing here."

"I—"

But before I could explain, the door of Mr. Howard's office opened, and he stormed out. "What is all this ruckus?" he demanded.

"Nothing, Howard," Mr. Dorian replied without taking his gaze off me. "Mrs. Harper has just had a little coughing fit."

The publisher frowned in confusion. "Mrs. Harper from . . . from Corfu?"

"Yes, that's me," I said with a sheepish smile. "I'm so sorry to interrupt."

Mr. Howard rushed over to join us. "I had no idea you were here. Did you come with Dorian?"

"No," we both answered in unison, and the man raised an eyebrow.

"That is," I began again, "I came here to ask you for his address."

"Oh. Well. Lucky for you, he was my nine o'clock meeting," Mr. Howard said with a sharp glance at Mr. Dorian.

"It was for nine-thirty," Mr. Dorian insisted. "I would never agree to a meeting at nine."

"Well, you are still late either way," Mr. Howard huffed.

Meanwhile, I glared at the secretary. "You told me he was busy all while he was sitting alone in his office?"

"Uh . . . I . . ." Mr. Deveraux shot a panicked look between me and his employer.

"I'm very sorry, Mrs. Harper," Mr. Howard said. "Of course, if I had known you were waiting . . ."

"It's fine," I said, irritated. "I only came here because I needed to speak to Mr. Dorian anyway. But go. Have your meeting. I will wait."

Mr. Dorian was eyeing me curiously. "No need. I only came to drop off my manuscript."

Then I noticed the satchel slung over his shoulder. He pulled out a thick manuscript bound in string and handed it to Mr. Howard.

I raised an eyebrow. It was even longer than his last mystery. "Goodness. You have been busy."

The two men exchanged a look I couldn't decipher, and Mr. Dorian held out his arm. "Come. We can talk in my carriage."

I accepted his arm, and he ushered me outside. Mr. Howard's office was located in the Strand, and the street had grown considerably busier while I had been inside. Mr. Dorian expertly steered me through the crowded pavement to where his carriage waited nearby on a quieter corner and handed me up before climbing in after me. Mr. Dorian settled in the seat directly across from me and fixed me with a look.

"Now then. Would you be so kind as to tell me what on earth is going on?"

I cleared my throat and folded my hands on my lap. "You were right."

Mr. Dorian tilted his head in surprise. "Pardon?"

"About Lord Linden. You were right. He is up to something." I then explained what I learned during my visit with Cecelia yesterday, along with the contents of the letter she had sent this morning. Mr. Dorian was silent as he mulled everything over. "Well?" I demanded, unable to contain my anxiety any longer. "What do you make of it?"

"I don't know," he said plainly.

I reared back. "That's all you have to say?"

He let out a short sigh. "A man who didn't get along with your husband lied about knowing him. That isn't exactly a silver bullet."

"Perhaps not," I acknowledged. "But it is odd for the man to then decide to pursue me. You yourself found the idea incredible."

He made a tsk sound. "Not because you aren't attractive," he said in exasperation. "I only meant that you aren't the kind of companion he usually consorts with."

"I'm sure you're right," I replied blandly, as I tried and failed to ignore the flutter in my chest. "Which leaves another explanation altogether for his attentions."

"Such as?" Mr. Dorian prompted.

"I think he means to uncover what I know. Either about Charles Pearson or Oliver, or even both."

He gave me a sympathetic look. "I know how important it is to you to find out what Oliver was doing, but—"

"No," I said stubbornly. "This must all be connected somehow. There are simply too many coincidences for it not to be."

But Mr. Dorian didn't look the least bit convinced. "Then what do you propose we do?"

"I want to speak to your brother. I want to know if he's looked into the baron at all and, if so, what he has learned."

The silence that followed was, in a word, deafening, but I held Mr. Dorian's gaze until finally he looked away. I watched a muscle in his jaw tighten. "Fine. But don't be shocked if he dismisses this little theory of yours outright."

I was unable to hold back my smile. "I welcome his criticism."

He shot me an unamused look as he pulled back the window and gave the coachman an address near St. Paul's Cathedral.

We spent the journey going over everything we knew about the case so far, while I did my best to make the baron fit.

"You can't pin him as the killer just because he lied to you," Mr. Dorian pointed out.

"I know that. But it's awfully convenient, isn't it? He knew Oliver. We know he attended the private auction with Charles—"

"We *suspect*," he corrected me.

"Yes," I amended. "We suspect. And he has an interest in Grecian artifacts."

"Just like dozens of other wealthy men in this city."

I let out a short sigh and stared out the window as that very city passed by. "All right. So I can't explain it all at the moment. But I—"

"I will concede that it is possible he may have some connection to your husband's . . . activities," he began, taking care not to name them. "But as for murdering Charles Pearson, you need a motive. And besides, I'm sure the baron has an alibi. There were dozens of people in his house the night of the murder."

"He could have slipped away and come back without anyone noticing. Or perhaps he had an accomplice." I recalled his large, scary butler, who had been staring daggers at Charles that night.

Mr. Dorian gave a reluctant nod. "I suppose. But Miles will need a hell of a lot more than that for a conviction."

He was entirely right, but I couldn't shake the growing certainty I felt. "I'm sure we can find whatever we will need for that," I said, with a confident nod.

The coach stopped in front of a nondescript brick row house on a quiet road. Mr. Dorian glanced out the window with a wary look.

"If you don't want to go," I began, but he turned to me sharply.

"Nonsense," he said as he pushed open the door. "Let's get this over with."

Mr. Dorian handed me down, and together we approached the house. The wary look had now been replaced with a disapproving frown, which I personally didn't think would be very helpful, but I decided to keep that observation to myself.

When we reached the front door, Mr. Dorian knocked loudly three times, and we waited. "He might not even be here," he said, clearly agitated before knocking once more.

"I know," I replied in a gentle tone.

But just as he raised his fist yet again, there was a shuffling sound from the other side of the door. I could feel Mr. Dorian stiffen beside me as we heard the rattle of a lock being released.

I held my breath as the door was pulled open, then let out a gasp.

It was none other than Mrs. Langham. "Hello there," she said curiously before noticing my companion. "*Oh*. Oh dear."

I turned to Mr. Dorian, but he was slack-jawed with surprise. Then he seemed to catch himself and shook his head in disbelief. "What are you doing here, Mira?" he demanded.

Mrs. Langham blinked in panic. "I—I—"

But before she could formulate an answer, someone inside the house called out to her. "Who is at the door, my love?"

Mrs. Langham flinched and glanced back. "Uh . . . it . . . it is your brother," she replied in an uncertain voice.

An ominous silence followed until Mr. Dorian cleared his throat. "Well. Aren't you going to let us in?" he asked in a dangerously polite tone.

Mrs. Langham's cheeks turned pink, and she stepped back to let us inside. She didn't meet either of our gazes as we entered. Detective Inspector Dorian was in the hall in his shirtsleeves, with his necktie draped around his shoulders. I noticed his hair was damp, and I guessed we had interrupted him in the middle of dressing for the day. But he didn't look at me once. Instead, his eyes were firmly fixed on his older brother.

"Good morning," he said evenly. "To what do I owe the pleasure of this unannounced visit?"

"Don't be an ass, Miles," Mr. Dorian growled. "You know we are here because of the murder."

The inspector twisted his lips in a petulant frown and gestured to a small sitting room to our left. "Fine. But make it quick."

Mr. Dorian immediately stalked into the room, while I followed a few steps behind. "You have a lovely home," I said to the inspector.

"Thank you," he murmured distractedly, his gaze never straying from his brother.

"I'll make us some tea," Mrs. Langham chimed and then hurried down the hall before anyone could reply.

Mr. Dorian stood by the mantel, while I sat on the sofa. The inspector also stood parallel to him, and I had the feeling this was a strange kind of competition between them. "Will you both sit, please?" I said, exasperatedly.

They each looked a little chastened, but said nothing.

Mr. Dorian was the first to move and took the seat beside me, while the inspector occupied a chair. He then crossed his arms.

"I suppose you've come here to plead your sister's innocence?"

"You know she couldn't have done it," I said, but the man merely shrugged.

"I will acknowledge that it is unlikely she possessed the strength needed to wield the murder weapon, but not impossible. And she has the clearest motive by far."

I narrowed my eyes. "Pray tell, Inspector, what is that?"

Then he tilted his head. "She would hardly be the first person to react badly after learning her intended is already married."

"Bad enough to suddenly muster the strength to bash his head in?" Mr. Dorian asked.

The inspector shot his brother a dark look, and I cleared my throat. "Before you decide to charge her, will you at least hear me out?" He inclined his head, and I continued. "It has come to my attention that Lord Linden has been lying to me about knowing my late husband. And I believe that he may be doing so for nefarious reasons."

The inspector raised a skeptical brow. He looked so similar to his brother in that moment that I nearly laughed. "What kind of reasons?"

"I suspect it may be connected to the death of Charles Pearson, though admittedly I have not sorted through all the particulars yet. But I do know that they were well acquainted with one another, and both had an interest in the antiquities trade."

"We've already spoken to his lordship, and he has an alibi for the evening of the murder," he replied. "Over a dozen, in fact."

"But for the exact time?" I pressed. "You don't think it's

possible he could have slipped away, killed Charles, and then returned?"

The inspector let out a huff. "I suppose it's *possible*, Mrs. Harper. But what reason would he have?"

I pressed my lips together. "Admittedly, I am not certain. But I believe something happened that night between him and Charles Pearson." I had been thinking through all the seemingly disparate pieces of information I had learned over the last week, and the one thing that continued to connect them all was Charles. "I want to confront Lord Linden and see if he admits to anything."

Out the corner of my eye, Mr. Dorian turned sharply to me, but the inspector was more measured. "Confront him about what?"

I took a deep breath, well aware that I could not take back my next words. Even if I ended up being proved wrong, it would not erase this betrayal. "That he lied about knowing my husband because they were both involved in some illegal activity in Greece." I had explored every possibility, but this continued to be the explanation that made the most sense. I could feel Mr. Dorian's heavy gaze upon me, but I could not look at him now. "My father also knew this information and may have unwillingly revealed it to Charles Pearson. On the night of the party, or perhaps even before, I suspect Charles Pearson confronted Lord Linden and promised to keep quiet in exchange for money that he desperately needed."

"You mean blackmail," the inspector said.

"Yes," I replied.

Mr. Dorian swore beside me.

"Charles Pearson was indeed in debt," Inspector Dorian said. "But according to my sources, he planned to marry your sister, who has a large dowry."

"That is true," I conceded. "But then you must also know that he was still legally married to someone else. And I don't think she intended to go quietly without getting something for her trouble."

"So the money was for her, then," the inspector said.

"That is my theory."

He narrowed his eyes as he mulled this over, then turned to Mr. Dorian. "What do you think?"

"It's worth a try," he said. "Unless you have a better idea, of course."

The inspector barked a laugh. "Unfortunately, we do not. Which is the only reason I'm even considering this," he said, shooting me a severe look. "What do you have in mind?"

"Well, Lord Linden and I are supposed to attend a lecture tomorrow evening," I began, and noted Mr. Dorian stiffen. "I thought that perhaps I could confront him there while you waited in a concealed location."

"That sounds like a plot out of one of his books," the inspector said dismissively.

"It is not the most elegant plan," I admitted. "But I do think that if I confront Lord Linden, he will admit to . . . something."

The inspector looked unimpressed. "And why is that?"

I narrowed my eyes. "Because men like him do not respond well to being challenged. And I think he is just arrogant enough to believe that he will get away with this."

"I don't like it," Mr. Dorian suddenly grumbled. "It puts you in a vulnerable position. And if we really think this man is capable of murder, then what will stop him from trying to harm you?"

"That is why the inspector will be on the scene," I said.

"Anything could happen in the space of a moment, Minnie," Mr. Dorian murmured.

I could feel the inspector's curious gaze flicking between us, but I remained undaunted.

"I plan to do this with or without you," I pronounced. "So it is entirely your choice whether or not you attend."

Mr. Dorian let out an exasperated huff. "Don't be absurd—"

"Now, now," the inspector said as he raised a hand. "I don't think it needs to come to that. I will attend, if only to hear what the man has to say for himself. But if you don't get the answers you are seeking, Mrs. Harper, then you must promise not to involve yourself any further."

"Fine," I said, crossing my arms.

We then arranged for Inspector Dorian to arrive at my house by seven o'clock. He and another officer would hide in the dining room, which was connected to the sitting room by a door. His lordship would then arrive by seven-thirty, and hopefully he would be arrested by eight.

Once we had squared away those details, Inspector Dorian rose. "I'm afraid I must be going. But do let me know once you have confirmed everything with Lord Linden." Then he turned to his brother. "Stephen," he said with a quick nod and then left the room.

Once we were alone, Mr. Dorian let out a long breath. "I don't like this."

"Yes, you've made that abundantly clear."

He leaned towards me. "What about Tommy?"

"I already arranged for him to spend the evening with his cousins," I said with a wave.

Mr. Dorian watched me closely, but said nothing. Then the door swung open, and Mrs. Langham entered empty-handed. "Sorry, my doves. It appears we used the last of the tea this morning," she said with a chuckle.

Mr. Dorian glowered. "Explain yourself, Mira."

She sat down in the chair the inspector had occupied and let out a mournful little sigh. "Must I?" Mr. Dorian's only response was a stony look, which seemed to do the trick. "He came around to mine one day looking for you."

That seemed to catch Mr. Dorian entirely off guard, and he leaned forward. "Why would he do that?"

She gave a little shrug. "He thought we were together. A mistake which I quickly corrected," she said to me. "But then, we got to talking and . . . well . . . you know."

Mr. Dorian glowered. "Out of all the bloody men in London, *this* is who you've finally chosen? It cannot go on. You must know that."

"That is not your decision to make," she said with surprising firmness. I was quite impressed with the way she took him to task. "And furthermore, he doesn't like you treating him like a child."

Mr. Dorian reared back in surprise. "I'm doing no such thing," he blustered, but his protest was weak.

"Well, according to Miles, you have done it quite a lot. And now might be a good time to show that you trust his judgement."

Mr. Dorian gaped at her, and I couldn't help smiling a little.

"Very well," he said in a clipped tone as he got to his feet. "If you are both so certain of your feelings, I won't stand in your way."

"Thank you," Mira said with a graceful nod before turning to me. "It was very nice to see you again, Mrs. Harper. I hope we can all meet again soon," she added, shooting Mr. Dorian a significant glance.

"I'd like that," I replied with a warm smile.

Mr. Dorian pursed his lips, but kept quiet as we exited the house.

"I won't pretend to know how you feel," I began, but Mr. Dorian gave me a sharp look.

"The word 'betrayal' comes to mind," he drawled.

"Surely it is not so bad as that."

He turned away with a sulky shrug. "She should have told me."

"That is understandable. However, don't you think it's interesting that your brother was inquiring after you?"

"Then he should have tried my home," Mr. Dorian said.

"Maybe he did. Or maybe he was trying to look out for you." Mr. Dorian merely grunted in reply. "In any case," I continued, "it seems clear that he is trying to reach out to you in some way."

Mr. Dorian met my gaze. "A pity then that he fell into bed with Mira and got rather distracted." I looked away and felt my cheeks heat. "I'm sorry," he said. "That was a crude way to put it."

"Yes, it was," I said, forcing myself to look back at him. "And I think it does a disservice to them both." For if Mira Langham felt comfortable enough to answer the door and discuss Miles Dorian's issues with his brother, it seemed reasonable to assume that something serious was developing between them.

"A fair point." The corner of his mouth curved up for a moment before he turned serious once again. "I want to be there," he murmured.

I cocked my head. "What?"

"At your house. When you meet with Linden."

"But if he sees you, he might not—"

Mr. Dorian held up a hand. "I'll hide in the damned closet, then," he said sharply. "You can't expect me to sit at home twiddling my thumbs while you confront this man."

"Very well," I conceded. "Come at the same time as your brother, then."

"I will," Mr. Dorian said, looking slightly more at ease now. But despite my acquiescence, the tension lingered between us, and we were both too lost in our own thoughts to exchange more than a handful of words during the long journey back to Hyde Park Street.

"Until tomorrow night," Mr. Dorian said in parting.

"Yes. Until then," I replied.

"I hope you are right about this," he called to me just as I made to exit the carriage. "Because if not, the baron may prove to be a nasty enemy."

I paused with my hand on the door handle and turned to face him. "That is a chance I am more than willing to take for the answers I seek."

Mr. Dorian watched me intently for a long moment. "I can't decide if your bravery is one of your most admirable traits," he began. "Or most infuriating."

I smiled. "Why not both?" Then, before he could answer, I pushed open the door and stepped down onto the pavement.

Chapter 24

The next day passed more quickly than usual, likely on account of my nerves. It had been merely a stroke of luck that my plans coincided with Mrs. Ford's half day, but I was exceedingly grateful for it, as I highly doubted I could have found a way to convince the woman to leave otherwise. As usual, she left me a cold supper in the icebox and was out of the house by one.

When I first made my plans with Lord Linden, I had arranged for Tommy to spend the evening with his cousins, and this proceeded accordingly. However, I had failed to account for Dolly's litany of questions when I dropped Tommy off in the late afternoon. I did my best to pretend to be excited at the prospect of spending the evening with a handsome and eligible bachelor, but quickly grew tired of fielding Dolly's veiled insinuations that wedding bells would shortly follow and made my excuses. Luckily, she was all too understanding when I claimed I needed ample time to prepare myself, and shooed me out the door.

When I finally returned to my aunt's empty home, it was

close to five o'clock. For one very brief moment, I wished I had told Mr. Dorian to come earlier, but then quickly dismissed the thought and set about readying myself for a presumed evening on the town. I took more care with my toilet than usual, because the occasion seemed to call for it and I didn't want to do anything that might cause the baron to be suspicious.

As I sat at my aunt's grand vanity applying a touch of kohl to my eyes, I was reminded of the evening last spring when Cleo had insisted on helping me prepare for a small party welcoming Mr. Dorian to the neighborhood. That was also the first night we were properly introduced, though we had seen each other briefly from a distance a few days earlier. Unfortunately, just after I arrived at my neighbor's home, I overheard Mr. Dorian make a rather unkind remark about my appearance to the host. While he later apologized, it struck me now that a part of me had never really let go of that disastrous encounter. And I was still letting it color all of our interactions. I sat back in the chair and admired my reflection in the three-paned mirror. Perhaps, then, it was time for us to have a proper fresh start. I donned my sapphire gown and checked my hair one last time before I headed downstairs.

My stomach still jangled with nerves as I waited in the parlor, and I picked up a bit of embroidery just to keep my hands occupied. I was strongly considering pouring a drink from my aunt's well-stocked bar cart when there was a knock at the front door. The clock on the mantel showed that it was exactly seven o'clock. I rose from my chair and rushed over to open the door. Mr. Dorian was on the front step, looking nearly as anxious as I felt. Given that the man was usually cavalier to a fault, this was not particularly comforting.

"Is my brother here?" he asked sharply as he entered.

"No, not yet," I replied and showed him into the parlor.

Mr. Dorian let out an aggravated sigh, then turned to me. His dark gaze skimmed over my figure.

"You look lovely," he murmured.

"Just trying to look the part," I said, as I felt a blush coming on. Then I returned to my chair and gestured to the sofa across from me, but Mr. Dorian shook his head.

"I can't sit," he said, as he began to pace the room. Then he stopped before the hearth and braced a hand on the mantel, staring down into the fire. I allowed my gaze to linger on his profile, which was illuminated by the flickering flames to great effect. Then, suddenly, he turned to me, and our eyes met. Something bolted through me, and I came to my feet.

"Would you care for something to drink?" I asked in an attempt to distract him, but he shook his head.

"I need to be clearheaded for this."

"You're starting to make me even more nervous," I grumbled.

Mr. Dorian stopped in his tracks and shot me a look. "Then we should call this off. Just say the word. You don't need to do this."

"No." I shook my head. "Everything has already been arranged, and we may not get another chance."

Mr. Dorian frowned and approached me. "Perhaps now isn't the best time, but I did want to mention that I know this must be very difficult for you. And for what it is worth, I hope I am wrong about Oliver."

I stared at him for a moment as my mouth went dry. "Thank you," I rasped. "I appreciate that."

He took another step. Then another. "And I am sorry about the way things ended on Corfu. I . . . I shouldn't have left the way I did."

I swallowed my surprise. "I understand. But I wasn't very kind to you, either. I said some things I regret."

He nodded, keeping his gaze on me. "Is that why you came to the villa the next morning?"

My eyes widened. "How did you know that?"

His mouth curved in the slightest hint of a smile. "When Mr. Howard visited Corfu over the summer, Mrs. Nasso couldn't wait to tell him all about the two of us."

I felt a little prickle of betrayal that the housekeeper would have told anyone about my mad dash to speak to Mr. Dorian, and the crushing disappointment I had felt when I learned he had already left.

"Oh. Well. I can't imagine why," I insisted with false bravado.

Mr. Dorian wasn't the least bit fooled. He watched me in silence for a few moments. "Can't you?" he murmured as he moved even closer. The tips of his freshly polished shoes kissed the hem of my gown, and I fought against the instinct to step back. The blood roared in my ears, but it still wasn't loud enough to drown out my thundering heartbeat.

"Then, the dedication in your book . . ." I couldn't make myself finish the sentence.

His smile grew a little more. "In my defense, I never expected you to read it."

I let out a laugh. "I didn't. Cleo showed it to me."

"Ah. I see," he said with a self-effacing grin.

"Well, I *had* already read it more than once," I pointed out, unable to keep from smiling back.

"Fair enough. No need to torture yourself any more," he quipped.

My smile faded. "You know how talented you are."

He ducked his head and swallowed. Then he looked back at me, his expression now serious. "I don't think you understand the inadequacy I feel when I am in your presence."

I frowned and slowly shook my head. "Whyever would you?"

"Because," he began. "Minnie, I—"

But before Mr. Dorian could continue, there was a loud knock at the front door that startled us both. "That must be your brother," I said as I stepped away, pressing a hand to my heated cheek.

Mr. Dorian was still watching me with that sharp gaze of his, but he seemed to acknowledge that the moment was over. At least for now. "It's about damn time," he grumbled.

"I'll get it."

"Wait." Mr. Dorian grabbed my arm just as I moved by him. He then crept over to the picture window and gently pulled aside the velvet drape. He let out a muttered curse. "It's Linden."

"But he's early," I insisted, as if that would change anything.

Mr. Dorian raised an eyebrow. "Only by a little bit. And if my blasted brother wasn't late, it wouldn't matter."

I began to wring my hands, unable to mask my nerves any longer. "What should we do?"

Mr. Dorian grimaced. "We stick to the plan for now and hope Miles shows up very soon. Do you think you can stall him?"

"I can try," I said, sounding uncertain.

"I'll make myself scarce and keep an ear out for my brother," Mr. Dorian said as he headed towards the door that connected to the dining room. Then he paused and turned back to me. "If you can't, there's no harm in letting this go. Tell him you have a headache."

I gritted my jaw. I had no intention of letting the baron leave without answering at least some questions, but I simply nodded. "All right."

Mr. Dorian held my gaze. "Just . . . be careful." Then he turned and left the room. I took a deep breath and headed for the door. It was time for the performance to begin.

Lord Linden had been understandably surprised when I answered the door, but did his best to hide it as I showed him into the parlor.

"Would you like a drink?" I asked, attempting to sound blasé and failing miserably.

His mouth curved in amusement. "A whisky, if you have it."

"Of course." Then I made my way over to the bar, relieved that I had something to do. I measured and poured the drink, then handed it to the baron. As he took it, his fingers grazed mine.

"You're shaking, Mrs. Harper," he said with a smile.

I certainly was, but not for the reason he was thinking. It made for a good cover, though, so I decided to lean into his impression. I bowed my head shyly and moved to sit on the sofa, which provided a clear view of the door, behind which Mr. Dorian was currently standing. Just the thought of him calmed me a bit. I gestured to the chair in front of me and turned to the baron.

"Please, sit."

He obeyed and crossed his long legs. "You are all alone here, then?"

The question, along with the look he gave me, took me by surprise. "Uh, yes. I am. My aunt doesn't keep a large staff since she travels so much, and tonight is the housekeeper's half day," I explained.

"And your son?"

"He is spending the night at my brother's house."

Lord Linden smiled again, but there was a gleam in his eye that rather reminded me of a lion. "I don't know very many women who could survive an evening without their lady's maid at their beck and call, let alone a full staff. Yet here you are."

I managed a chuckle despite my nerves. "Well, I've never had a lady's maid, my lord. The closest I came to that was when I still lived at home and my mother deigned to let her maid fix my hair." And even that had been more trouble than it was worth. "Perhaps you need to expand your circle."

Lord Linden let out a chuckle. "I am *always* looking for ways to expand my circle, I assure you."

I cast a glance at the door, but it remained closed. I didn't much like the idea of flirting with this man, but I didn't know how else to stall for time. I leaned towards him a little in my chair. "Yes, I have heard such things about you," I said, attempting a coquettish smile.

It must have worked because he too leaned forward. "I'm sure I don't need to tell you that you shouldn't listen to everything you hear."

Though I knew it was only meaningless banter, it still struck a nerve, given that he had freely spread gossip about Mr. Dorian. It also provided a nice opening to ask about the photograph, and I didn't want to waste it. I could only hope that Miles had already arrived, or would very shortly. "Yes, about that," I began. "There was something I learned about you recently that I wanted to discuss."

The baron tilted his head in interest. "Oh?"

"I recently visited an old school friend, Cecelia Morton, though she has now become Cecelia Wentworth. I believe you knew her husband, Gerald, at Cambridge."

Lord Linden took a sip and considered this. "The name sounds familiar," he said vaguely.

"She said you were both members of a Hellenic club that participated in a dig one summer in Greece."

"Oh. Yes. I do remember that."

"I thought you might," I said with a strained smile. "I bring it up because she happened to have a photograph of the members and wished to show it to me because my husband, Oliver, was also a participant."

I held my breath as Lord Linden watched me, then his face fell, and he looked down. "Ah. I see." Then he let out a sigh and met my gaze, a distinct look of remorse in his eyes. "You must have some questions then."

I was so taken aback by his reaction that it was a moment before I managed to respond. "Yes, I do."

"You must understand," he began, "that I was taken completely by surprise the night we met. I hadn't thought about Oliver in years."

"All right," I said slowly, beckoning him to say more.

Lord Linden dragged a hand through his hair. "And then I didn't exactly want to admit to his widow that the two of us had once been adversaries," he said with a sheepish look. "But still, it was wrong of me to lie."

"You must have known that I would learn the truth eventually," I pointed out.

"I wasn't thinking very clearly," he admitted. Then he suddenly moved from his chair to my side and grabbed my hands. "I'm so sorry. I hope this doesn't change things between us."

I tugged on my hands a little, but he only tightened his hold. "My lord, we barely know each other."

"Yes, but I know what I feel. And I know you feel it too," he continued.

I cast a glance at the door, well aware that his little declaration had an audience. "I am sorry if I gave you that impression, but—"

He chuckled again. "You invited me here and arranged for us to be alone. Forgive me, darling, but what else was I supposed to think?"

I turned back to him, now quite shocked. "Well, certainly not that!"

"There is no need for you to worry," he began as he drew me against him. "I assure you that I am the very picture of discretion."

"That is not at *all* what I am worried about," I said as I shoved him back.

This caught him by surprise, and I scrambled out of his reach. Lord Linden shot me a confused frown as he stood.

"Now see here. I don't know how these things are done on Corfu, but in London if a lady invites a man to her home under such circumstances, one expects certain things."

A surprised laugh erupted from me, but before I could speak, the connecting door slammed open, and Mr. Dorian stormed into the room.

"You have got a hell of a lot of nerve, Linden," he growled as he came to my side. I tried to meet his gaze, but it was firmly fixed on the baron. There was also no sign of Miles anywhere. This entire operation was a disaster.

Meanwhile, the baron stared at Mr. Dorian in shock. "Were you listening to us?" he asked, incredulous.

"I was listening to you try to cajole a woman into giving you favors, yes," Mr. Dorian spat.

I then grabbed his arm and tugged on it. "That is quite enough, Stephen." Only when I said his name did he finally look at me. "Obviously, this has been a gigantic misunderstanding," I said through gritted teeth as he turned back to the baron.

"I'm not so sure of that," he said dryly.

Then I heard the distinct click of a gun. My fingers tightened on Mr. Dorian's arm, and he covered them with his warm palm. I whipped my head back to the baron and found him staring at the two of us with a bored expression, all of his earlier outrage completely gone. "You know, I really did come here tonight intending to take you to that lecture. A pity things have taken such an ugly turn."

"Then why bring a gun with you?" I marveled.

"One can never be too careful," he replied easily.

Mr. Dorian snorted. "Yes. Especially when one is trying to cover up a murder."

The baron chucked. "Something like that."

"Then it *was* you," I said. "You killed Charles."

The baron let out a sigh, as if he was being terribly inconvenienced by this discussion. "The idiot left me no choice."

"Then he was blackmailing you?" I asked. Admittedly, I wasn't very keen on hearing the particulars at the moment, but given that we had a gun trained on us, the only thing I could think to do was keep the man talking for as long as possible.

"He *tried* to blackmail me," Lord Linden corrected. "It never got that far. But Charles was rather desperate for money, and desperate people make mistakes."

"Do you know what he needed the money for?" Mr. Dorian asked, catching on to my plan to keep the man talking.

"Some business about that inconvenient wife of his," the baron said, flicking his fingers. "She wanted money in exchange for finally giving him a divorce, and Charles couldn't come up with the funds fast enough."

"And you couldn't simply lend them to him?" I asked.

The baron looked affronted. "My dear, I am not a bank. And everyone knew that Charles Pearson went through money faster than quicksand. I never would have gotten it back."

"But what about his collection?" I insisted. "Surely he could have sold you some pieces—"

Lord Linden shook his head. "It may have been a decent collection for a man like him, but there was nothing to tempt me. For what it's worth, I do think he truly cared for your sister," he added in a solemn tone that only enraged me.

"And yet you were willing to stand back and let the murder be pinned on her!"

"It was a possibility, of course," he acknowledged. "And I did try to make it look like a burglary, but I was interrupted when she turned up at the flat that night. Naughty girl." The baron narrowed his eyes. "And then you took quite an interest in the murder. My butler was certain you were just a silly little woman who wouldn't give us any trouble. But I knew better. There is no one more meddlesome than a lonely old bluestocking," he said with a sneer.

I could feel Mr. Dorian tense beside me, but now was not the time for him to lose his temper. "It's all right," I murmured, then addressed the baron. "A fair point. Is he your accomplice, then?"

"I don't need an accomplice," he insisted. "Only an imbecile would allow themselves to be pinned for murder. No, he is my loyal servant and does whatever I ask."

"Including, perhaps, following people?" I suggested.

"Oh yes. He is quite good at that," Lord Linden said, his eyes glinting. "Was in the army for many years, you know. Under the command of someone we both happen to be acquainted with."

Sir Armstrong-Hughes.

My jaw tightened. "You knew we went to the auction."

"I knew Dorian went there," he corrected. "And was caught embracing some mysterious woman that may have been you. I will admit that some of my actions tonight were in part designed to determine exactly what kind of relationship you have. But Dorian here has made that very clear."

I turned away, unable to hold the odious man's gaze.

"So what did Charles have on you, then?" Mr. Dorian prompted.

"Haven't you figured that out yet?"

I glanced up to find him giving me a hard look. "My father told him something about your activities in Greece."

Lord Linden's eyes flashed with surprise. "That's all you know?" Then he let out a laugh. "My God, I was sure you knew the whole of it. Your husband never told you?" I sucked in a breath at the disbelief in his gaze. Then he shook his head. "Oliver always acted like he was some great champion of the Greeks. He would go on and on about how important it was for the country to keep their heritage. Never mind that there was an entire economy thriving around the export of artifacts. But then, in the end, he succumbed to greed, just like the rest of us."

I closed my eyes for a moment as his words hit me like a blow. "He was your contact at the embassy," I said softly.

"Actually, I didn't know it was him until Charles told me," Lord Linden said with a dry laugh. "There was growing pressure from the government at the time to tighten the existing antiquities law and a lot of grumbling about diplomatic ties, so I wasn't entirely surprised when our contact seemed to vanish out of thin air. It was a terrible shame, really, and a great deal of money was lost. And then, years later, Charles comes round boasting about some big secret he's learned from some addled old man. That I was named as the leader of an illegal antiques ring uncovered by none other than my old *friend* Oliver Harper. Then he brought you to my home to taunt me, and I knew I couldn't let this continue."

"So you went and killed him?" Mr. Dorian supplied. "Why not just pay him the money?"

"Because that is not how blackmailers operate," he said slowly, as if we were both very thick. "The extortion never truly ends, as he would have just kept digging for more information. And while being exposed as the leader of a now disbanded black market antiquities ring would have been an inconvenience, I have far more interesting skeletons in my closet that I need to keep hidden."

I tried to swallow, but my throat had gone bone-dry. "Then you did it for insurance."

Lord Linden considered this. "Yes, I suppose that is one way to put it. And everything would have worked out beautifully if you hadn't gone poking around into things you shouldn't have," he said, giving me an arch look.

"That was why you pretended to take an interest in me."

"I wanted to see what you knew, and who you might have told," he explained. "And then decide what to do. Unfortunately, I fear now that decision has been made for me. But rather than simply kill you both and give the police more to investigate, I'll have to make this look like a murder-suicide."

"No one will believe that," I spat out.

But the baron merely raised an eyebrow. "Are you sure? I've heard enough rumors about the two of you to make the idea plausible." Then he gave me an assessing look. "What do you think, Dorian? You're the writer. Is it too far-fetched to think anyone would kill for a woman like her?"

"Go to hell," he growled.

The baron laughed. "Settle down, old man. Now that delectable former wife of yours I could understand, but—"

Something in Mr. Dorian seemed to snap then, and he barreled towards Lord Linden. I immediately thrust myself in front of him in an attempt to block his way, just as the baron raised his gun at us and aimed. Mr. Dorian wrapped me in his arms, and I felt both of us brace against the shot as a loud bang filled the room. I let out a little whimper against his chest and then . . . nothing.

I looked up to find the baron standing stock-still before us with a dazed expression. Then he slowly looked down at his chest, where a spot of scarlet had begun to bloom just below his collar.

He touched the wet spot and stared at his blood-smeared fingertips, then turned to us in shock. "I've been shot." Then he fainted dead away, revealing Miles standing in the doorway behind him, still holding a smoking gun.

"About time you showed up!" Mr. Dorian bellowed.

"That's a funny way of saying thank you for saving my life," the inspector quipped as he moved into the room, accompanied by two officers in uniform. "We were delayed by an upturned omnibus in Picadilly. Then I needed to hear him confess to something," he explained. "The man did go on, rather."

I rushed over to Lord Linden's side as the two officers approached him, but he didn't move. "Is he dead?" I asked.

"Better for him if he is," the inspector said. "Otherwise, it will be a trip to the gallows."

"Come," Mr. Dorian said, gripping my arm and pulling me away. "You don't need to see this."

I regret to say that my recollection of the next hour or so was rather disjointed. Mr. Dorian mentioned that I was in shock, and I am inclined to agree. I had a vague memory of watching him argue with his brother, because he wanted to discuss the situation with us in detail, and then being told that I could not stay the night, as the house was now a crime scene. At some point, Mr. Dorian bundled me into his carriage, and the next thing I knew, Morris was ushering us into the drawing room of my parents' house, where my mother, Delia, and, unfortunately, Jack were all gathered. While Mr. Dorian explained what happened to my increasingly irate brother, my mother guided me over to the sofa and draped a blanket over my shoulders, while Delia brought me tea, port, and a nerve tonic, in that order. But I waved it all away. I looked around the room, but Mr. Dorian and Jack had disappeared.

"Where . . . where is Mr. Dorian?" I asked, craning my neck trying to look past my mother.

"He went to speak with Jack privately," Delia explained, taking the seat beside me. "Here. You should take this." She pressed a sherry glass into my hand. I took a sip, if only to keep them from offering me things, barely noticing the bitter taste as I swallowed. That must have been Mother's nerve tonic. I settled back against the sofa, and Delia nestled beside me, taking my arm in hers, while Mother took a chair. As I stared at the crackling fire in the hearth, a warm sense of calm slowly lapped over me. The nerve tonic worked rather quickly.

"Don't let him leave without speaking to me," I murmured after a while.

"Of course, darling," Delia said.

I meant to say something more in response, but I'm not sure I managed the words, as in another instant my eyes closed, and I drifted off to sleep.

Chapter 25

I woke gradually the next morning, feeling uncommonly sluggish. It was as if a heavy fog had descended upon my brain, and it was a moment before I recalled where I was and what exactly had happened last night. Then I opened my eyes to find my great-grandfather staring down at me in cold disapproval. I sat up with a start and realized I was still in the drawing room, on the sofa, which offered an excellent view of Lord Percival Everly's oil portrait. Someone had made up a little bed for me on the sofa, and I had to push aside the blanket in order to put my feet on the floor. Then I dragged a hand down my face and shook my head, but the foggy feeling barely dissipated.

"Still feeling the effects of Mother's nerve tonic?" a voice asked to my left.

I glanced over and found Jack seated in an armchair reading a newspaper. "Yes," I rasped. "How on earth is that allowed to be sold as a tonic?"

"Damned if I know," Jack said as he set aside the paper. "Shall I ring for a tray?"

"Please. But may I have a glass of water?" My mouth felt as dry as sand.

"Certainly," my brother said as he rose. I watched him cross the room to tug on the bellpull and then pour me a glass of water from the drinks cart.

"Here you are," he said, handing me the glass.

I drank it deeply in one long gulp. "Thank you," I gasped as I gave the now-empty glass back to him.

He raised an eyebrow, but said nothing as he returned the glass back to the cart.

"Where is Mr. Dorian?" I asked, once he took the seat closer to me.

Jack hesitated, and my stomach sank. I knew I would not like what he had to say. "We both agreed that it would be best if he kept his distance from you."

"*What?*" Despite my weakened state, I still managed to be properly outraged.

But Jack was unrepentant. "Not only did he put you in danger—"

"He did no such thing," I insisted. "Last night was my idea."

That seemed to catch Jack off guard for a moment. "Nevertheless," he continued, "I understand that it is far from the first time you have gotten yourself mixed up with him."

"I'm not *mixed up* with him. We are . . . friends."

My brother, rightly, gave me a skeptical look. "Well, he isn't the kind of man you should be friends with."

"That is not your decision to make," I said through gritted teeth.

He opened his mouth to say more, but the maid came in then. We both waited in strained silence while she set down a tray laden with tea, muffins, and a dish of eggs. "That will be all," Jack said sternly, and the poor girl fled from the room without a backwards glance.

He let out a sigh and pinched the bridge of his nose. "When I had my solicitor look into Inspector Dorian, he found nothing of consequence. But his brother was another matter entirely."

"I am aware of his past," I said, as I poured myself a cup of tea. "And he explained the particulars himself while we were on Corfu." Mostly, anyhow.

She demanded an annulment within a month, in fact, but I refused. Still had a scrap of pride left.

But my brother looked unconvinced. "Do you know how a woman obtains a divorce in this country, Minnie?" Jack asked as his dark eyes narrowed. "Not only must she accuse him of adultery but also a secondary offense. In this case, she chose desertion."

I took a measured breath. "As I understand it, the law is quite limited on the grounds for divorce and doesn't allow for reasons besides adultery. So she had to make that accusation in order to end the marriage, but that doesn't make it true—"

"He *abandoned* her on their wedding night," Jack cut in. I closed my mouth. Well, that certainly didn't sound good. "And since his divorce, he's been connected to every lightskirt in London."

Now it was my turn to sigh. "Yes, but Mr. Dorian said it's only gossip to sell papers."

Jack crossed his arms. "And you are willing to risk your own reputation, as well as the children's, on his word? Even he doesn't want you to do that."

I don't think you understand the inadequacy I feel when I am in your presence.

If that was truly how Mr. Dorian felt, how easy it must have been for my brother to convince him to keep his distance. My throat tightened, and I swallowed past the lump that had gathered. "Fine," I said with more resolve than I felt. "But he will need to say that to *me*. And while I appreciate your intentions, I do not need my brother to handle my private affairs. How would you react if I tried to manage your relationship with Dolly without your knowledge? You overstepped."

Jack stared at me for a long moment, and I watched a muscle in his jaw tighten as understanding dawned. "Perhaps . . . perhaps I did," he finally said. Then he frowned. "You don't need to look so shocked. I can admit when I've erred." I raised an eyebrow, and he sat back with a chastened expression. "All right. Fine. I don't like being wrong."

"No one does, Jack," I said. "But none of us are infallible. Not even you."

The corner of his mouth lifted. "I suppose." Then he grew serious once more. "Just promise me you'll take care."

"I will," I said with a nod.

Then his expression turned sheepish. "There is something else."

"Goodness. It can't be worse than leaving a dead baron in Aunt Agatha's parlor, can it?"

"Well, last I heard, he wasn't dead, but unconscious. And no, this isn't worse than that. But it does involve the viscount. He has learned of your presence in London. Though I swear he didn't learn it from me."

"Ah." I set down my teacup. "And I suppose I am being summoned?"

Jack nodded. "He would like you to visit him at Mandeville House this afternoon. And don't worry about Tommy. He can stay with us as long as you need."

"Thank you. I appreciate that."

"Then . . . you'll go?" Jack said in surprise.

I very much did not want to give the impression that I would be at that man's beck and call, but the fact remained that he was the only person who could tell me the truth about Oliver. And there were a number of unpleasant circumstances I was willing to endure for that information. "Yes. I think it's high time we put some things to rest."

Jack looked uncertain. "You aren't going to quarrel with him, are you?"

"Only if he forces me to," I said archly, as I picked up a muffin. I would need sustenance for the battle ahead.

"God help him, then," my brother muttered.

Chapter 26

By the time I left Portman Square for Mandeville House several hours later, the effects of my mother's nerve tonic had finally faded. Thus, the butterflies swirling around my stomach could only be on account of my destination. The feeling increased as I ascended the front steps of the imposing red-and-white brick mansion in Mayfair.

I had never met any of Oliver's family members. His mother had died when he was away at Eton, and his father a few years before we married. Then, when his brother was made viscount, they had some kind of disagreement about money, but Oliver never divulged the particulars, and I never asked. He had a younger brother as well, Archie, but he was something of a libertine and, from what I knew, didn't show much interest in his family. I had never even communicated with him, aside from a short note of condolence after Oliver's death.

Harold was another matter. He had no sons of his own, so after Oliver died, he encouraged me to send Tommy to Eton, claiming that it was necessary for his heir. When I politely but firmly declined, he then tried to claim guardianship. It was an ugly business, conducted at the worst possible time. If we had been in England, he might have been able to use his position to force my hand, but it was much harder to do so from across a sea. Eventually, he relented, and I agreed to allow him to have written contact with Tommy. But privately, I still held out hope that Harold would have a son of his own so he would stop focusing on mine. Though at this point a grandson was more likely.

An ancient butler ushered me inside to an imposing drawing room: high ceilings, pale green walls decorated with Adam-style plasterwork, a gold-and-crystal chandelier, massive marble fireplace, and Louis XIV–style furniture in gold and pale green silk coverings. I was so taken by the space that I did not notice the man in the far corner of the room, standing before a large window with his back to me.

"Mrs. Harper to see you, sir," the butler rasped.

"That will be all, Bodwin," the viscount said in a deep voice that easily carried across the space.

I felt a little shiver of foreboding as the door clicked shut behind me, the sound echoing throughout the room and leaving us alone. I moved with slow, cautious steps, my gaze fixed on the man's back. He was tall, about as tall as Oliver, and his hair was the same shade of blond, it was shot through with silver.

He turned around then, all at once, and his blue eyes met mine. Perhaps I should have prepared myself for the likely family resemblance, but it was still a shock. The viscount was the near picture of my late husband and I inhaled sharply, stumbling over the edge of the carpet. The viscount was beside me in an instant, his firm hand on my arm, steadying me.

"Thank you," I said, my voice trembling.

"Of course," he replied as he led me to the sofa.

I was grateful that at least he didn't sound like my husband. His voice was deeper and far colder than Oliver's had ever been. I doubted he could have sounded that stern if he had tried. The thought brought me some comfort, and I held on to it as the viscount took the straight-back chair across from me.

Now that he was closer, I could see that the resemblance wasn't quite as identical as I had first thought. For one, the viscount was older than my husband would ever be, with deep furrows across his brow and the beginning of jowls on his still admittedly strong jaw. But most notably, he lacked Oliver's spark, the infectious zest for life that had immediately drawn me to him. Rather, the viscount exuded a sober air that perhaps was expected of a man in his position and with his responsibilities.

He cleared his throat, and only then did I realize I had been staring at him rather rudely. "Thank you for agreeing to meet me on such short notice," he said. "I understand you had an . . . eventful evening."

"You know about that?" I had assumed this summons was to do with Tommy and had not even considered the timing. Perhaps Mother's nerve tonic had addled my mind more than I thought.

"When a peer of the realm is shot, word does get around rather quickly," he said dryly. "I was at my club last night when I first heard the news and was further shocked to learn that *you* were involved."

I lifted my chin at the disapproval in his gaze. "It was regrettable that someone was injured, but his lordship was pointing a gun at me at the time."

"So I heard," he said, arching a brow. "You and Mr. Dorian, the writer."

His words practically dripped with disapproval, but I simply held his gaze. When it became clear I had no intention of elaborating any further, the viscount huffed. "I did not ask you here to remonstrate with you, Mrs. Harper. I am only trying to understand how on earth the mother of my heir found herself in such a frankly scandalous scenario."

Though I saw no need to explain nor defend myself to this man, I didn't like what he was implying. "I was investigating the murder of Charles Pearson. Surely you must have heard about that?"

He frowned. "Of course. But why were you involved at all?"

"Because my sister was the one who found him, and I was worried that she would be falsely implicated in his murder. Mr. Dorian is an acquaintance of mine and agreed to help. Eventually, I began to suspect that Lord Linden was involved, and last night I confronted him."

The viscount's frown deepened. "Surely, you did not."

"I most certainly did. He confessed to everything and then attempted to shoot Mr. Dorian. Luckily, the police had arrived by then, and the inspector stopped him with a bullet."

The viscount stared at me in bewilderment. "Good lord. But you could have been *killed,*" he said in outrage, as if that had somehow escaped my notice.

"Yes, I know. Luckily, it did not come to that." The viscount continued to stare at me in shock, so I pressed on. "You should also know that while I was investigating the murder, I learned some things about Oliver that I had hoped you would be able to shed some light on."

He immediately shifted in his chair, and his face went blank. "Oh?"

But I wasn't at all fooled by his bored tone and scoffed, which seemed to catch him by surprise. I gathered he was used to people always deferring to him. I leaned forward and held his gaze. The butterflies were entirely gone now. This man had answers. And I would not leave this room without them. "I know he was illegally exporting artifacts while he worked at the embassy in Athens. The baron confirmed it last night. That was why he retired so suddenly and why we moved to Corfu." The betrayal I had felt when I first put the pieces together was not as sharp and piercing as it had initially been. Now it was more like a dull edge of disappointment. "Because it wasn't safe for us to return here," I continued. "He had made too many enemies. And you used your position to help cover it up."

The viscount gave me a hard look. "You're wrong."

"He was your brother," I said. "I understand that you were protecting him—"

"No," the viscount barked. "That is not at *all* what happened. Frankly, I expected you, of all people, to know the kind of man you married."

I sat back in my seat. That accusation stung. "I certainly thought I did, but what else am I to think?"

The viscount took a breath. "I apologize. I shouldn't have said that. And I know that it must have been a difficult thing to learn. I told Oliver many times that he should have been more honest with you—"

"Honest with me about *what*?" I could not control the surge of anger flooding my veins. I was so tired of being kept in the dark by men who thought they knew better.

"Oliver was a spy, for lack of a better word," the viscount said plainly. "He worked for the embassy, that was true. But he also took on other projects for the Foreign Office as needed. He wasn't illegally exporting artifacts. He was infiltrating a black-market ring of powerful collectors across Europe who were exploiting loopholes in the existing laws regarding the export of antiques."

It felt as if someone had struck me on the head. "Oh," I breathed. "I . . . I had no idea."

The viscount gave me a grim smile. "Yes, I know. Oliver was recruited when he was first hired by the Foreign Office. I told him he shouldn't have married you because of his work, but he said it couldn't be helped." I glanced away at the knowing look in his eye. "Your father found out later and was livid, naturally. But somehow Oliver convinced him it would be all right. And perhaps it would have been, if he hadn't died," the viscount added softly.

When I looked back at him, he was staring past me, lost in thought. "What happened then? He was discovered?"

The viscount shook his head. "Oliver uncovered the identities of the British participants, and the powers that be decided it would be far worse if their identities were unveiled. For diplomatic relations and public morale," he said in a mocking tone.

"You mean because one was a baron and the other a knight?"

Lord Linden and Sir Armstrong-Hughes.

"Among other illustrious fellows, yes. Anyway, Oliver didn't much care for that decision and was determined to expose them. Eventually, your father and I managed to dissuade him, and it was politely suggested that he retire instead." The viscount let out a long sigh. "Oliver never really forgave me for that, I'm afraid. Not that we were on the best of terms anyway. But he genuinely wanted to do good in the world and hadn't realized he was only a pawn in a much larger game."

"He could be idealistic to a fault sometimes," I said after a moment. After all, he had married a young woman he barely knew and bought a house sight unseen. And those were just the things I knew about. "He always expected things would turn out right in the end, if only because he willed it to be so."

The viscount's brow rose in surprise. "I didn't realize you were such a cynic."

"I try not to be," I said with a grim smile of my own. "But life has a way of wearing one down."

"I'm sure these last years have been incredibly difficult. And I know I did not help," he added, looking slightly grieved.

I narrowed my eyes. "No, you did not."

"I apologize," he said stiffly, and I wondered if he had ever spoken those words before. "I suppose my own grief got the better of me."

"Thank you. I appreciate that."

"How is Thomas?" he asked.

"He is well. Very curious about the world, like his father."

"I'm glad to hear it. I do enjoy his letters." The viscount smiled a little then, and for the first time, I noticed that his stern, stiff bearing was hiding something: he was sad. Maybe a little lonely as well. And I found I felt rather sorry for him.

"Perhaps we can return for a visit," I said.

The viscount's eyes lit up then, and he looked so much like Oliver in that moment that my heart hurt. "That would be greatly appreciated," he said, attempting a sober tone that couldn't quite mask his excitement.

"I think he would like it too," I admitted.

We spent the next half hour sharing memories of Oliver, and when I recalled his disastrous attempt to rid our house of an infestation of bugs, the viscount laughed so hard he had tears in his eyes. Then, just as I was preparing to leave, the viscount turned apprehensive.

"Forgive me for prying into your personal affairs—"

I gave him a look. "More than you already have?"

He bowed his head sheepishly. "Fair point. But I must ask what the nature of your relationship with Mr. Dorian is."

"Must you?" I said tightly.

"I only come from a place of familial concern. I trust you know the rumors that surround him."

"Yes. Quite well, in fact. And I know most of them are baseless," I insisted with more confidence than I actually felt at the moment.

The viscount didn't look convinced. "Then, you can

understand my apprehension regarding a . . . a relationship between you."

Though a part of me longed to put him firmly in his place, I settled instead for the truth. "I told you before, we are only acquaintances."

He watched me for a moment. "And will you remain only acquaintances?"

I pursed my lips. "Forgive me, but I can't even begin to know how to answer that."

"I think you already have," he said a little sadly. "I don't expect you to stay a widow forever, you know. And I don't think Oliver would want that either."

I stiffened. "That is not your place to say, sir."

He smiled again and took my hand. "Yes. I know. Hazard of being a spoiled viscount, I suppose. I hope you aren't too angry with me, but I had to ask."

"I'm not sure I agree with that, actually," I grumbled as he gave me an admittedly charming bow.

"Take care, Minerva," the viscount said with genuine concern. "And please, do come again soon."

One Week Later

"Remind me why I agreed to attend this?" I asked as I shrank against an inconvenient gust of icy November wind.

"Because I decided it was time for me to leave the house and you wanted to support my endeavor," Delia replied as she pulled me closer to her side.

"Oh yes. Right."

We were on our way to a literary club meeting just a short walk away from my aunt's home. Delia claimed to be good friends with the organizer, but hadn't bothered to find out the topic of tonight's event. As someone who never failed to complete an assignment, I found this oversight rather distressing.

"And because I thought you needed a little cheering up," Delia added gently.

I grimaced, but I couldn't exactly deny it. Since the viscount had revealed the truth about Oliver, I had wavered between guilt for ever suspecting him of committing such dastardly acts in the first place and anger that he had left me in the dark for our entire marriage. Adding to my confusion was Mr. Dorian. While I was willing to understand why he had left my parents' house that night without speaking to me, his continued silence was growing more deafening by the day. But I couldn't go to him. Not this time. I did have *some* pride left.

"Thank you," I said as we approached our destination: an elegant brick town house on a quiet garden square. "I appreciate that."

Delia squeezed my arm, and together we were escorted into the home of Lady Burton, who was waiting by the entryway greeting guests. She looked about my age but was rather eccentrically dressed in what I can only describe as a caftan with matching turban and lots of large gold jewelry.

"Delia, darling!" She let out a squeal of delight when she spied my sister. "I'm so glad you were able to come," she said before turning her infectious smile to me. "And who have you brought?"

"My sister, Mrs. Minnie Harper. She's terribly clever. Went to Girton, you know."

"Heavens! Welcome, Mrs. Harper. We are very glad to have you."

"Thank you, Lady Burton," I said, but before I could ask the subject of tonight's discussion, we were waved into the large drawing room.

"Come in, come in," our hostess said. "Take a seat. The program is just about to begin."

My eyebrows shot up as we entered the room. Rows of chairs had been arranged before an empty lectern, and nearly all were filled. This was no small gathering, but a proper event.

"Goodness," I said to Delia. "Who on earth is speaking tonight?"

My sister did not meet my eyes as she led me over to two empty chairs in the very last row. "Here we are," she said.

The back of my neck prickled with suspicion. "What's going on?" I asked as I slid into my seat.

"Nothing," Delia replied much too quickly.

I frowned and looked to my right, where a young lady was clutching a book to her chest and staring eagerly at the front of the room. She turned to me with wide eyes. "Isn't this exciting? Do you think he'll be signing books afterwards? Oh, I do hope so." She said this all in a great rush, and I didn't have the chance to respond before a ripple went through the crowd as a side door opened. "It's beginning!" she said in a thrilled whisper as she moved to the edge of her seat.

I shot Delia a look, but she was still avoiding my gaze. Then I turned to the front, where a man walked to the lectern and addressed the room.

"Good evening and thank you all for being here." My eyes widened. It was Mr. Howard. "And thank you to Lady Burton for the invitation. I am Arthur Howard, owner of Howard Publishing, and I am delighted to introduce tonight's speaker. Now, I know many of you are great fans of his mysteries, but tonight he has something different prepared. It is a selection from his forthcoming book on his recent trip to Corfu. Now, without further delay, Mr. Stephen Dorian!"

The room absolutely erupted into thunderous applause, and I watched in shock as the man himself strolled in, shook hands with Mr. Howard, and moved behind the lectern.

"Jack isn't the only sibling who can do a little meddling," Delia murmured by my ear.

I turned sharply to her, and she gave me that devious little smile I hadn't seen in weeks. "You knew this whole time?" I hissed, but she merely shrugged, unrepentant.

"You don't have to speak to him if you don't want to," she said. "But I wanted to give you the opportunity."

I opened my mouth to respond, but the girl beside me loudly shushed us, so I shut my mouth and faced forward. There was nothing I could do but sit there and listen.

Mr. Dorian was shuffling through his pages and then came to a stop. He cleared his throat and began to speak:

" 'Corfu is often described as an earthly paradise without equal. But I confess that, when I first arrived, it felt like hell on earth.' "

A little gasp rippled through the crowd, to which he glanced up with that all-too-familiar gleam in his eye before continuing: " 'In time, though, I came to appreciate the unique beauty of the island and the hospitality of its inhabitants . . .' "

He went on to describe our little corner of Corfu in such lyrical detail that I could almost smell the early-spring flowers and feel the salty sea breeze ruffling my hair. My heart swelled with a longing so fierce it nearly stole my breath. Mr. Dorian did not mention the murder, which I was grateful for, but he did include little sketches of people he had met, including myself and Tommy, though he did not use our real names. My son was described as a relentlessly curious boy with a penchant for insects, the more horrifying the better, while I was his endlessly patient mother who indulged his curiosity while also keeping firm boundaries as to what was allowed inside the house. He presented us in such a charming manner that I couldn't help smiling while the crowd chuckled along accordingly. I glanced at Delia to find her beaming at me. He spoke for about fifteen minutes, and when he stopped, the crowd cheered loudly, eager for more.

Mr. Dorian looked relieved at the reaction and ducked his

head with a bashful smile as Mr. Howard came over to shake his hand once more.

"Wasn't that wonderful?" he said, once the clapping had subsided. "You can read the rest in his forthcoming book, *A Spring on Corfu*, which we are publishing in serial beginning next month. Mr. Dorian will also be leaving in a few days to tour America for the first time—"

"*No.*"

The word shot out of me like a cannon and was so loud that even people in the front row looked back. I sank low in my chair as I blushed to my hairline and prayed that no one could tell it was me.

"Not to worry," Mr. Howard said with a chuckle. "He will return, of course. But we are both very hopeful that this will bring him new readership in the States."

Mr. Dorian had also been looking towards the back. Then he blinked and nodded. "Yes," he said, distracted. "Yes. Thank you."

Lady Burton came to the lectern then to announce that refreshments would be served in the next room, and everyone began to stand.

"I need to leave," I muttered to Delia.

"Now?"

"Yes, *now*." I did my best to stand up, while also keeping a low profile. Mr. Dorian was still at the front of the room, speaking with Lady Burton and Mr. Howard, but he kept casting furtive glances in my general direction. I had to get out of the room before he spotted me.

"But you haven't even spoken to him yet," Delia said.

"Some other time." Then I urged her out of her seat and pulled her from the room.

I had just retrieved our coats and was throwing mine on when someone called out to us from down the hall.

"Wait."

I pretended not to hear as I threaded my arm through Delia's and made for the exit.

But she dug in her heels. "What are you doing?" she hissed and came to a stop.

"Traitor," I whispered before I slowly turned around.

Mr. Dorian approached us, looking apprehensive. "Mrs. Harper."

"Oh. Hello there," I said, as if we had just crossed paths in the park and not at the man's own literary event.

He raised an eyebrow, and Delia slipped out of my grasp. "I'll just go talk to Lady Burton for a moment." Then she hurried away before I could stop her.

He cleared his throat. "How . . . how have you been?"

I let out a sharp laugh at his overly formal tone. "Oh, very well," I said dryly.

Mr. Dorian must have been quite out of sorts because he did not pick up on my sarcasm, which was unlike him. "Truly?"

This only irritated me further. "In fact," I continued, narrowing my eyes, "just the other day I found out my husband had been a spy for our entire marriage."

Mr. Dorian finally caught on and looked ashen. "My God. Who told you this?"

I glanced away. "I met with the viscount, and he confirmed everything. Apparently, instead of colluding with Lord Linden, Oliver was actually working to bring the entire black-market ring down until the powers that be decided there was too much at stake and suggested he retire instead."

Mr. Dorian let out a low whistle. "But that's good news, no?"

I met his uncertain gaze. "It's better than the alternative, yes. But I still wish he had been more honest with me. About any of it."

"That is entirely understandable," he said, as his eyes filled with sympathy, but just as he began to say more, there was the sound of multiple footsteps behind us and someone loudly whispered, "I think he went this way." It sounded very much like the young lady I had been seated next to.

Mr. Dorian subtly rolled his eyes and took my hand. "Come with me," he said, as he led me through the nearest door into a receiving room and then through another door. This appeared to be a small sitting room, and a fire crackled happily in the hearth. Mr. Dorian firmly shut the door behind him and let out a breath. Then he fixed his dark gaze upon me and let out a breath. It was only then that I noticed just how out of sorts he seemed.

"I didn't expect you to be here," he murmured after a moment.

"Neither did I," I admitted. "That is . . . Delia didn't tell me you were speaking tonight."

Disappointment flashed in his eyes. "Ah."

"I liked it, though," I said quickly. "Very much."

"I'm glad," he said, looking relieved. "I wanted to see you before I left."

I arched a brow. "You mean you didn't intend to leave the country again without speaking to me first?"

He grimaced. "I deserved that."

"Yes, you did," I snapped, as all the confusion of the past week suddenly burst through me. "I woke up the next morning to Jack saying some rubbish about you agreeing to stay away from me."

"It isn't rubbish, Minnie," he murmured and looked at me with such remorse that my anger was nearly snuffed out.

I crossed my arms in an attempt to at least look cross. "What are you talking about?"

He stepped towards me. "Your brother suggested that my reputation could negatively affect you—"

"Well, that's ridiculous," I insisted.

"—and I happen to agree with him."

"Oh." My arms fell by my sides. "But . . . you said yourself it's only gossip to sell papers."

"Yes. And it's true." He came to a stop just before me, as close as he had been the other night, and once again my heart thundered in my ears, though it wasn't loud enough to drown out what he said next: "But that doesn't change the fact that right now I am something of a target for tawdriness. I don't want to bring you into that. Nor your children. You've all been through quite enough."

My chest pinched at the clear regret in his eyes, and I looked down. "I see."

Then I felt his warm fingers slide under my chin as he tilted my face up. "I'm trying to be better. I'm trying to deserve you. That's what this book and this tour is about. I need to change who I am and what people associate with me."

I blinked rapidly as I tried to understand his reasoning. "And to do that, you need to leave me?"

His dark gaze bore into mine as he slowly nodded. "I wish there was a better way—"

"There is," I insisted. "Ignore them."

The corner of his mouth lifted for a moment, and his eyes flickered to my lips. "It isn't that simple."

"All I care about is that you are honest with me. Not what some bloody newspapers say."

He raised his eyebrows in surprise at my curse, then shook his head again, more firmly this time. "I'm sorry, but I would regret it if I didn't at least even try." Then he slowly dragged his fingertips along my jaw and cupped my face. "For nearly two years, my life was mired in nothing but darkness. And rather than fight for myself, I chose to wallow. To be dragged down into the muck. Because I didn't have a reason to care. Then I met you. And it was the best thing that had happened to me in a very long time."

My heart began to swell in my chest, and I glanced away from the emotion in his gaze. "Well, maybe not so much the meeting part," I quipped.

He chuckled. "As I've told you, I was an ass that night. But you were wonderful. You've always been wonderful. And that gave me something to wish for. That one day I might be worthy of you. Be the kind of man you deserve. So, will you let me do that?"

I let out a huff as I leaned into his touch. "How on earth am I supposed to say no."

"It's only two months," he murmured as he nuzzled my neck. "And if Howard's right, I will come back a sensation. And no one will say a word about my blasted divorce ever again." I shivered as he tilted my head back and leaned in. "Will you wait for me?" he asked, his breath fanning out against my lips.

"Of course," I rasped. "Of course I will, Stephen."

He suddenly pressed his mouth to mine in a desperate, heated kiss. My hands snaked around his strong shoulders, and I slid my fingers into his thick hair, tugging him even closer to me. His warm hands circled my waist, and he bent me back, deepening the kiss further. It felt like someone was shooting electricity through my veins. I couldn't exactly say how long this went on for, only that, at some point, when he finally pulled back, we were both breathing hard, and his dark eyes were filled with a mixture of heat and wonder that was, frankly, very gratifying.

"Two months," he said.

"Two months," I repeated breathlessly. "And then . . ."

He gave me a wicked smile as he leaned in close again. "Everything, Minnie Harper," he murmured against my lips. "*Everything*."